DANGEROUS JOURNEYS

A Teaching Story
by
Serge Kahili King

Aloha!

First Edition 2002
ISBN #1-890850-17-9

Published by
Hunaworks
P.O. Box 223009
Princeville HI 96722 USA

Author's Note

This is a work of fiction, but it is not just a novel. I call it a "teaching story" because it is full of practical ideas and techniques that you can use to make your life easier and the world a little better. The locations are real and the ideas are valid, and any resemblance between the characters and persons living or dead is purely coincidental, except for a few incidents where excerpts from my personal experience creep in. As an example of "Urban Shamanism" in action, the story is sometimes ugly and violent, sometimes tender and loving, and most of the time, I sincerely hope, it is also interesting.

Regarding non-English words, I have italicized them whenever they are not commonly used in English. For the Hawaiian language in particular, to simplify typesetting, I have used an apostrophe to represent the glottal stop, and I have omitted the macron. Words in Hawaiian and other languages that are commonly used in English have been spelled as they are used.

Acknowledgments

Thanks first of all to my father, my mother, and my maternal grandmother, who were the first ones to teach me shamanic techniques. Deeply felt thanks to Joseph Kahili, my Hawaiian grandfather, for adopting me and settling me into the *kupua* path; to my Aunty Laka for her wise guidance in regard to human relationships; and to Uncle William who taught me most of the things that come out of the grandfather character's mouth.

Special thanks to my wife, Gloria, for her unwavering support; to Susan Pa'iniu Floyd, for her unwavering encouragement; and to Peggy Kemp for proofreading the final version and enjoying it. *Mahalo a nui loa* to the *kupuna* who keep the old wisdom alive for future generations. Oh, I almost forgot. Many, many thanks to my faithful and devoted computer, Silverado.

Contents

One

The Decision

Keke'e ka mai'a o ka 'e'a, wili ka 'oka'i
(Even a twisted banana tree in the mountains can bear fruit)

Her name was Nazra, and she had no other. As far back as she could remember she had lived on the streets, scrabbling among other homeless children for scraps of food, and clothing, and shelter. There were no warm, emotional memories of being held and comforted by a loving mother, or of playing children's games with siblings and friends; nor even memories of physical warmth by a blazing hearth, or in a cozy bed. No memories of parents, or brothers, sisters, uncles, aunts, cousins, or any family at all except a vague recollection of a grandmother that carried a very slight tinge of what might almost be called pleasure. All her memories, when she bothered to think of them, were of survival, even after she had been taken off the streets.

Looking into the cracked mirror now, streaked with soot where a falling beam had brushed against it, her nose wrinkled at the smell of burnt wood and smouldering horsehair that filled the cold air. Around her, the place she had known as home for over ten years lay in total ruin. Although the concrete walls still stood, parts of the ceiling had collapsed, broken windows let in the icy Arctic wind, and the old pine furniture that had defined her space was mostly reduced to ashes. The horsehair stuffing used in the chairs and the beds, always uncomfortable, was smoking and glowing, and oil paintings had curled and cracked out of what remained of their frames. She pulled her gray, wolfskin coat more tightly around her body. It was time to leave. She knew that she had to leave or die, but it was hard to take that

1

step, hard to leave even this burnt-out shell of blackened concrete to face the deep, seemingly endless forest that surrounded her on all sides. So she lingered in front of the mirror, thinking, and gazing at the reflection of her eyes.

With unusual clarity she brought to mind the night, so long ago, when the Fates conspired to change her destiny. She felt again against her skin the dirty, ragged scraps of abandoned and stolen clothing, layers and layers of them, that failed to protect her twelve-year-old body from the bitter cold of a Spring night in the city of Minsk. She saw the patches of stained and gritty snow in the narrow alley behind the commissary of the government secretarial school, heard the crunch of the brittle ice beneath her rag-bound feet as she shuffled from one pile of garbage to the next, inhaled the reek of spoiled meat and vegetables, kept as long as possible in hidden corners by the kitchen staff before they were forced to get rid of them. She could even taste the mushy sourness of whatever frozen mess it was that she stuffed into her mouth as it melted between her teeth. It wasn't with the disgust of her present refined appetite that she remembered this; it was with the original sense of pleasure and strengthening that had been sharpened by days without nourishment of any kind.

Just as she had begun to bless her luck at finding some edible garbage in that alley, the older Nazra remembered, the sound of crunching ice from other feet had made her whirl around and crouch, searching for a way to escape or attack. Too late! A heavy mass of burlap was thrown over her, strong hands grabbed her, ropes bound her, arms lifted her, and she was dropped onto something hard. A survivor even then, she had immediately stopped struggling or wondering or worrying and concentrated her whole attention on breathing through the thick, rough jute that covered her head. She was barely aware of the sound of an engine and the movement of a car or truck.

Such a long time passed that she had fallen asleep, to be awakened with startling suddenness when she was lifted again, apparently carried for a short distance, and once more tossed onto a hard surface. She was stiff ahd sore and her wrists bound in front of her were hurting, but breathing was still the most essential thing to focus on. After awhile there was a different

2

kind of movement and a different kind of sound, a sort of swaying to a clicking rhythm, a train for certain. She had almost fallen asleep again when she was pulled to a sitting position and shoved against what seemed to be a wall. The burlap was pulled off her head, but her hands and feet remained tied. The first thing she saw was an old man, in her eyes, in a soldier's uniform, holding a bowl of something that steamed and smelled like turnips. She immediately salivated and licked her lips and he held it up and tipped it carefully so that she could drink. It was very thin, almost a broth, but at that moment it was an incredible luxury. As she sipped from the wooden bowl she noticed two more soldiers, much younger, sitting a little further back on either side of the one who was feeding her. And beyond them, a huddled group of children heavily bundled against the cold and all sipping from their own wooden bowls.

In the present, still gazing in the smoky mirror, she smiled grimly and clearly recalled how that twelve-year-old girl had wondered for a full second why the other children were free to hold their own bowls and she was not, before she was dragged forward and forced to lie flat. The soldiers had had their way with her six times before they reached their destination, but Nazra didn't bother to remember who had done what because it was no longer interesting. Even then, she had not felt any resentment. Resentment took energy, and energy was needed for survival. That was something she had learned thoroughly in her first twelve years. Besides, she had eaten better on that train ride than she had for the previous six months.

The destination turned out to be a large concrete building of three floors and many rooms, with several wooden buildings around it, all set deep in a vast pine forest. Only years later would she learn where it was in relation to the rest of the world. And only after she had learned how to read would she know that it was called the Narovskaya Institute for Abnormal Brain Research. However, she learned immediately that survival skills were a prime requisite for existence in this mountain wilderness. As soon as they had arrived she was dumped, untied, into a bunkhouse with twenty other girls the same age as she. She had had to defeat three other girls in a no-rules brawl before earning the right to a bed of her own. Some girls had to sleep on the floor

3

the whole time they were there. There were plenty of beds, but the strongest girls "owned" as many as three, which they reserved for their "little friends."

Over the following weeks and months she discovered that she was one of hundreds of orphaned boys and girls who had been snatched off the streets of Soviet cities and brought to the Institute for reasons that were hard to understand. Day after day they were forced to do odd things involving tests of physical coordination and strength, emotional stability, intelligence, and intuitive skills. Some of the tests were fun in a way. Others were unpleasant, disgusting, and dangerous. Then there were the drugs, which drove some children mad and some to death. The worst part, for her, was the loneliness. She had been lonely all her life, and to be thrust in among so many other children gave hope that she might find friendship at last, but socialization and friendship were radically discouraged at the Institute, and spying and reporting on "suspicious" activities were part of the curriculum. Gradually, the number of children at the Institute diminished and she never knew what happened to them. As years went by she was part of a group of a hundred, then of twenty, then of five. By that time she was sixteen and ready to graduate.

On "Graduation Day" she and the four other teenagers, three boys and a girl, were taken by truck to an area of the forest that had been sealed off with a three-meter fence topped with barbed wire. The five teenagers were told that only one of them would be allowed to exit the forest alive, and that they themselves would have to decide who that would be. Each child was dropped off at a different point on the perimeter without food, water or tools, and ordered to make their way to the main gate, wherever that was. As this was an extremely unpleasant memory, Nazra did not dwell on it. She felt neither guilt, nor pride, nor any desire to relive it. Three days after going in she had stood at the gate, waiting to be let out.

Standing now at the mirror and willing warmth into the surface areas of her skin, she was still reluctant to leave. There was no valid reason to stay because her life had been destroyed and all purpose taken with it, yet she stayed because she didn't know what else to do. In her reflection she noted how her bright blue eyes, high cheekbones and fair skin of her Slavic heritage went

4

well with her straight black hair, probably the result of some ancestor's dalliance with an Oriental lover. Yes, she might even have had a future as a model or an actress or a call girl or a secret agent. Except for her other eyes. Her real ones. The strange ones.

Soviet researchers at the highly secret Institute had determined that energetic stimulation of the pineal gland not only increased the production of melatonin, which enhanced physical functioning in many ways, but it also increased the production of harmaline, a psychedelic alkaloid produced naturally by the pineal gland and found in many plants in very small amounts. Only two plant sources containing harmala alkaloids were known to be used as psychedelics: a beverage called yage, made from scrapings of the bark of a particular species of Banisteriopsis vine, also known as ayahuasca; and the seeds of a Near Eastern desert shrub known as Syrian rue. However,the researchers were looking for a kind of stimulation that would be easily available under most conditions, able to take place automatically as well as being adjustable, be non-threatening to health, and be effective for their intended purpose. Ideally, once that was achieved, a properly trained subject should be able to induce a psychedelic state at will and control the various abilities associated with it, such as enhanced visual, telepathic, sexual, artistic and therapeutic potentials. They found that the stimulation of the pineal gland could be done equally effectively by means of organic and synthetic chemicals, emotions, electricity, magnetism and light, but it took a long time for them to arrive at what they considered to be the ideal solution.

So, she was a freak. A beautiful, talented, freak. She was warm, now, but she shivered anyway and turned away from the mirror, only to see a rainbow sparkle of sunlight shining in the crystal shard of a broken chandelier. A reminder of her eyes.

While some researchers at the Institute worked on protocols for inducing abnormal brain function, the harmaline team had found a solution to their problem, thanks to Pyotr Lernov, a brilliant Russian eye surgeon. Lernov's contribution was a radical, highly unethical, reformation of the lens of the human eye in order to concentrate light energy along non-visual neural pathways leading to the pineal gland, thus raising the levels of both melatonin and harmaline, also known as telepathine, whenever a light source was gazed at wih concentrated attention. Side effects of the surgical and chemical procedures used, well within research guideline tolerances, were that the eyes appeared to be faceted and their pigmentation was multi-colored. So she was a freak, with eyes that looked like opals.

On the other hand, she had never been expected to leave the KGB-sponsored institute tucked far away in the Siberian forest. She had been designed—yes, that was the word—designed to administer one of the most bizarre projects ever conceived by power-mad politicians: the economic control of the West by a vast network of scientifically-trained psychic assassins. She herself had been prepared to train and direct the network from the Institute, so as far as the KGB was concerned it didn't matter what she looked like.

Nazra took a deep breath and allowed her mind to dwell on those who had prepared her for such a role. The first one to appear in her memory was, of course, Feodor Krazensky, director of the project and a colonel in the KGB. He was the one who had the greatest effect on the development of her psychic abilities, although not as a teacher. In fact, she never even had a live teacher for her more esoteric skills like remote viewing, divination, psychokinesis and others. Instead, Feodor inundated her with hundreds of books, videos, audio tapes and reports on those who had demonstrated these abilities, both in the laboratory and in the field. Out of all of that he wanted her to sift for the essence, unencumbered by loyalty, tradition or intimidation. Then he himself would test her and prod her unceasingly, and some of their encounters were very strange.

"Move that object with your mind," he would say, pointing to a yellow pencil on a glass-topped table. His shaggy hair and bulky build made some of the staff refer to him as a bear, but to Nazra he was more like a werewolf.

"I don't know how," she would answer, always squeezing her fists in irritation when he pushed at her.

"Move it anyway."

"I can't!

"Try!"

She never did move that pencil, but she did learn more about psychokinesis, the talent of moving matter with the mind, and

6

how to apply it. Under Krazensky's prodding she also learned how to use Tarot cards and more than a dozen other divination systems, how to see and manipulate energy fields, called auras in some books, and how to perform many of the practices attributed to shamans around the world. In some cases she had developed techniques on her own that went beyond anything that she read, or viewed or heard. She had almost developed an affection for the crusty old man who had pushed her past her limits, until he had abandoned and betrayed her.

Letting Krazenky fade away in her mind, she recalled one of her real teachers, Gregori Balenkov, a behavioral scientist who taught her in very specific, graphic, mental and physical ways how to seduce both men and women, and how to intimidate and exploit anyone with less than a rock-solid ego. Gregori was tall, blond, arrogant, and totally in love with himself. Naturally, she had to be subjected to intimidation, exploitation, humiliation, abuse and helplessness herself as part of her training. It was years before she was able to use any of his methods against him, and when that happened the lessons stopped abruptly.

Then there was Boris Orlov, dark-haired, squat and ugly, the psychiatrist and drug expert whom she hated with a passionate intensity. He had insisted that she learn by doing, and he took great pleasure in using her while she was experiencing the nightmarish effects of some of his concoctions. After him came Dimitri Treffsky, the only man she truly admired, in spite of his cold-heartedness. Dimitri was youngish, with sandy hair, and attractive rather than handsome. The admiration, however, was not for him as a person, but for his skill in a wide variety of martial arts. It was he more than anyone who had helped her to strengthen her mind and body, teaching her the secrets of poise, grace, charisma and chess along with the art of killing in numerous ways. If it hadn't been for the pleasure he took in watching her do embarrassing things with other people, he might have been the only one she didn't hate. Finally, there was Ivan Mikalov, who had taught her how to heal her own body and make it do things that were not considered normal. Yet he, too, had ...exotic...tastes that she was required to satisfy. There were also other teachers who taught her about weapons, spycraft, and more mundane subjects like geography, science, English and more, but none of them were there long enough to affect her very much.

Nazra took another deep breath, let it out slowly, and allowed the memory of one more man to surface, a man whose mere name caused such fear and loathing to rise up in her throat that she had to suppress the urge to vomit—Pyotr Lernov, the surgeon who had desecrated her eyes. It wasn't just that which provoked her reaction, though, it was something else. She could accept and deal with verbal, emotional, mental and physical abuse. Sometimes it was hard, but she could get through it without losing her self respect. What Dr. Lernov had engaged in, however, was more akin to spiritual abuse, although she disliked using that word. From the first days of the experiment and during untold numbers of check-ups, she was "the thing." "Get the thing on the table," he'd say with practiced disdain. "Tell the thing to take off its clothes." "The thing's nerves are responding well, but we shall have to reshape the lens." Never once did he address her directly, never once give any indication that she was a human being. She believed sincerely that he treated his rats better than her. Nazra spit to the side as if to expel his memory from her body, and remembered what had occured after she had become their perfect tool.

Once her skills and knowledge and special talents had been honed sufficiently, she had trained the only four agents they had in the field as yet and worked on plans for hundreds more. Throughout the whole experience she had made only one demand, based on the need to maintain an effective emotional and psychic rapport with her trainees: that she be provided with colored contact lenses for her eyes.

Unfortunately for the project, the mighty Soviet Union fell victim to one of the tenets of chaos theory: that overcontrol leads to dissolution. In an incredibly short period of time the giant Humpty Dumpty was in pieces that could never be put together again. With the change in politics came a stoppage of the secret funding, of course, and for several months the Institute was in a state of confusion. Key personnel began leaving, expensive equipment was packed up and delivered to government warehouses, or stolen and sold on the black market, and food supplies dwindled. The future of the project was no longer in doubt. It was over. Everything she had been trained for had turned to vapor. When the last technician had left, when even the janitorial staff had packed up its supplies and gone home, she sat alone in her private library, pondering her fate and organizing her last week's worth of rations. It was early June and she had still not decided what to do when circumstances forced her to make a choice.

While carrying a tray of green tea, black bread and lingonberry jam to a table, her mouth already salivating from the sweet aroma of long-denied food, a flash of vision had jolted her to a stop in mid-stride. The tray fell from her uncaring hands and crashed noisily to the floor, spilling tea, jam, and bread together at her feet. Unaware of the fallen tray and wasted meal, she was fully focused on an image of three black limousines pulling into the long drive through the woods that led to the Institute. She had willed her vision into a close-up of the first vehicle and recognized a KGB official in the back seat, one who had voiced considerable skepticism of the project on a visit less than a year ago. The driver and the other passengers had the look of KGB thugs. A quick scan of the other two cars showed more killers, all with skulls instead of normal faces. She still marveled at how unbidden visions could present such appropriate distortions in spite of intensive training for objective accuracy. Willing herself back to her immediate surroundings she had ignored the mess on the floor and concentrated instead on what she could do in the few remaining minutes before the killers burst through the doors to end her life, because there was no doubt that they had come to destroy all remaining traces of the illegal Institute.

In her cold weather gear, presently stepping over jagged piles of plaster and still-burning embers, she almost smiled at the memory. She moved slowly toward the main entrance, now an empty hole, as memory and inspiration mingled in her mind.

When the KGB team had finally entered the library of the Institute only yesterday, after searching all the other rooms, they had found books strewn everywhere and saw her body hanging by a knotted electrical cord from an overhead beam. Her eyes were closed and sunken; her tongue, swollen and black, protruded from colorless lips; her hair hung in greasy strands; her skin was pale and translucent; and the stench of her rotting flesh was overpowering. Handkerchiefs were whipped out and one man gagged and left the room.

"What shall we do with her?" asked an agent, his voice muffled by white cloth.

"Leave her," said the chief, turning to exit the library. "Krazensky wants the whole place burnt to the ground, with her in it. This just saves us some time," he said on his way out the door.

After the institute had been set ablaze and the KGB men were gone, Nazra had used every bit of remaining awareness and will to reach behind her head and pull a slip-knot that released the cord and let her fall to the floor. Still lying down, she first began breathing slowly and deeply to re-oxygenate her system, suppressing each pain response as it occured. As soon as she could think clearly she had used her mind to expand the net-like surface of her blood vessels while she willed the blood back into them. When her color and warmth returned she sent messages to her muscles to relax and allow her body to normalize itself. The soreness of her neck muscles, held rigid for so long to protect her from the cord, faded quickly away as freshly-oxygenated blood reached the cells and carried stress toxins away. Lastly, she applied a variation on the yogic technique she had used to exude the rotting smell from her skin and replaced it with a pleasant scent of flowers. In five minutes she had been transformed into an ordinary freak again.

She had had plenty of time to gather the last of the food and all her warm clothes and go to the separate toilet and shower facilities built for the non-scientific staff of the institute before the fire destroyed her past and any knowledge of her existence. A small wood stove in a maid's room had kept her warm during the night and in the morning she had surveyed the damage, trying to make a decision. Now she was no longer in doubt. On reaching the former entrance to the Institute a wayward shaft of weak northern sun touched her face and seemed to reach deep inside, perhaps along the pathways of her eyes, to a place where doubt could not exist. The first task, of course, was survival. She had no doubts about her ability to do that. The next task was revenge. She had absolutely no doubts about her ability to do that, either. Those who had destroyed her life must have theirs destroyed as well. She knew that this was not a logical progression of thought, and that she had multiple other options as well, like starting a new life in a new land with all of this put behind her. But she had grown up with lack and she hated waste. In a way that had nothing to do with logic it felt appropriate that those who had, in a sense, created her, should know the consequences of their creation. Revenge would give her purpose, and she herself would be the weapon.

Stepping onto the road that led away from the only home she had ever known, she glanced back and noticed that the Institute's sign had been knocked down and all but its proper name had been burned off. For the first time in months she actually smiled. Nazra Narovskaya turned and walked into the woods.

Two

A Hawaiian Custom

He 'ike 'ana ia i ka pono
(The right thing to do is known)

Uncle Willy put down his ukulele, wiped his forehead with a can of Bud, and took another sip of the icy beer. He was wearing flip-flops, jeans and an extra-large T-shirt with "Hawaiian Style" printed in large, golden letters across the front. The big rattan chair with flower-patterned cushions that he was sitting in creaked as he shifted his weight on the wide front *lanai*, or porch, of his sister's clapboard house. It was a hot day on the western slopes of *Hualalai* Volcano on the Big Island of Hawaii, and heat waves shimmered as he looked out over a mile-long expanse of descending land studded with trees, flowering bushes, and other homes toward the touristy town of Kailua-Kona, sitting right on the edge of the calm Pacific Ocean. From here, if you wanted to, and Uncle Willy didn't want to and saw no reason to, you could sail or fly in any direction for twenty-five hundred miles or more without meeting another significant piece of land. Directly to the south was Antarctica, to the east was Mexico, to the north was Alaska, and to12 the west, from this point on the Big Island, were the Phillipines, all the way in Asia. It was the most isolated land mass on Earth. And the most beautiful, thought Willy.

Uncle Willy was an imposing Hawaiian man, large but not fat, and the instrument he held was a concert-sized, hand-made Kamaka ukulele of polished *koa* wood. It looked tiny in his hands, and his fingers looked too large for the strings, but the music he produced was soft, and sweet and comforting. Willy had come all the way from Honolulu for this meeting.

12

Cousin Hank, in a plain blue T-shirt, jeans and bare feet, was sitting on the other side of the *lanai* in an old rocker bleached white from the sun, keeping up a nameless slack key tune on his battered old guitar as a kind of background to the family noise of laughing, talking and eating. The melody resembled Gabby Pahiniu's rendition of "Ulili E," except that the tuning was different and so was the rhythm. Hank, also Hawaiian like most of the family, was in his thirties and played at the bar of the Keahou Beach Hotel three nights a week. During the day he worked on cars at a garage in the village of Captain Cook, just a few miles south on Mamalahoa Highway, so he didn't have a long way to travel.

Inside the house, Keoki McCoy sat at an old oak table, supposedly brought to the islands by a whaling captain more than a century ago, and turned down another serving of fish and poi that his mom was trying to push at him. Lily, his mom, was wearing a blue Hawaiian dress with yellow plumerias printed on it that she had bought from Hilo Hattie's. She was small and always moving, like a bird, from one thing to another. Keoki, a young man in his twenties who worked as graphic artist in Honolulu, smiled at his mother as she checked the regrigerator for the third time, making sure there would be enough lemonade, sodas and beer for everyone. Keoki was of medium height and well-built in a rather slender way, wearing white shorts and a pale blue pullover Hawaiian shirt with petroglyph figures all over it. His hair was dark brown and so were his eyes, and most girls thought of him as good-looking, rather than cute. Like everyone else inside the house, his feet were bare.

His Aunty Nani, wiping perspiration off her face with a napkin, looked bigger than she was because she wore frilly clothes and she bustled around so much she seemed to be everywhere at once. She was Hank's mother and Lily's sister and lived just down the road. Her husband had died in a boating accident a few years before and she spent a lot of time at her sister's house, caring for the grandchildren who always seemed to be underfoot. Just now she was back in the living room arranging folding chairs, borrowed from their local church, into a circle, more or less, in preparation for the meeting.

Keoki's sister, Keani, stopped dancing her hula when Uncle

13

Willy put down his uke, and began to help Aunty Nani to arrange the chairs. Keani was one of the `olapa`, dancers, of a local hula troupe that specialized in the *kahiko*, or traditional-style hula, even though they did well with auwana, the modern style. A lovely girl, dressed in jeans and a black tee, with an excellent figure and the long, dark hair so favored by dancers in modern times, Keani intended to make a career out of Hawaiian dancing.

Betty, Hank's blonde *haole*, Caucasian, wife, put away things in the kitchen. "Bright-eyed Betty," as the family sometimes called her, had come from California on vacation, fallen in love with Hawaii, and then had fallen in love with Hank. The night she met him she had torn up her return ticket. She had on tan shorts and a loose, tan blouse.

Grandpa Lani, who had been eating standing up while watching Keani, put his plate down on the kitchen table, licked his fingers, and sat in one of the rough circle of chairs. He was sixty-two, with peppery gray hair, wearing jeans and an old, faded T-shirt that advertised Hofbrau beer, but he was strong and healthy and normally moved with a certain assured grace. Today, however, he looked just a bit stooped and his movements were ever so slightly uncertain.

Reverend Isaac Kapuolani, in black trousers and a loose, white, Portuguese-style shirt, came out of the *lua*, the bathroom, and sat down next to Lani, on his left. That was the signal for everyone to take a place in the circle. Uncle Willy left his flip-flops on the lanai and sat on the other side of Reverend Isaac. Lily and Nani sat next to him. Keani, Betty, Hank and Keoki filled up the rest of the chairs.

The room they sat in was spacious and clean, obviously designed for a large family. It faced west, toward the Pacific, which could be seen through a large window that didn't have any curtains because there was no one other than family to look in. Under the window was a row of wooden louvres, open now to catch whatever breeze there was. The regular furniture, an odd assortment of unmatched chairs from various times and places, was pushed up against the off-white painted walls. There were low sideboards against the walls for storage and for putting food on, but no TV. Lily wanted the living room "to be a

14

place where people live, not where they go into trance." So this space was for visiting and talking, and the TVs were in the bedrooms and the family room. Above the sideboards the walls were filled with family photos, some so old that no one but Gramps could remember who they were. It was, indeed, a place for living, and singing, and healing.

When the shuffling was over and cold beverages had been sipped, they all looked expectantly at Reverend Isaac. He was a lean man, a Congregationalist minister in the same tradition as the early Christian missionaries from Boston who tried so hard to suppress the culture of the islands, except that he also had Hawaiian blood and a healthy respect for what he considered the best aspects of his own father's heritage. Because of the heat the Reverend pulled the front of his shirt out and shook it to let some air in. Then, when all was quiet, he recited the Lord's Prayer and asked for God's blessing on what they were about to do. The Reverend's voice, when he spoke, was smooth and gentle, English words with a Hawaiian lilt. After the prayer he stretched out his long legs and steepled his hands.

"You called me here to do a *ho'oponopono* for you, because there's a conflict in the family and you want to find harmony again. Is that right?" Everyone nodded in agreement; Lily and Nani said "*Ae*," meaning yes. Keoki felt like saying 'Amen.' Reverend Isaac rubbed his largish nose like he did in church just before saying something he thought was important. "And this conflict has to do with the fact that Anton here," he put his hand on Lani's' shoulder, "wants to go to Europe. Is that right, too?" He knew it was, of course, but he had to make sure that everyone else knew it, too. More nods all around. "Okay," he continued, "these are the rules." And so the ritual began.

Before Captain James Cook of the British Navy stumbled across what he arrogantly named the Sandwich Islands in 1778, Hawaii had a stone-age technology, a feudal society, and a highly advanced system of psychology. Part of that system was called *ho'oponopono*, or "a straightening out," and it was basically a process of conflict resolution that had been developed long ages ago. It was derived from the highest value of Hawaiian society, that of harmony between people, between people and nature, and between people and the world of spirit. The goal of *ho'oponopono* was not to negotiate a settlement, it was to modify behavior.

Reverend Isaac, as a respected *kahuna pule*, minister, from outside the family, was called in to preside over the process. First he established the rule that only one person would speak at a time, and that person would speak directly to him and to no one else. Keoki had attended another *ho'oponopono* where the leader had given a stone to the person speaking to confirm his right to have the floor, so to speak, but that would probably have seemed too heathenish to Reverend Isaac. The minister also ruled that no interruptions would be allowed, and that once the problem was resolved it would never be brought up again. He made a few more comments about the virtues of family harmony and then the family got down to work.

Grandpa Lani was the first to give his side of the issue, and he cleared his throat before he spoke. With his grey hair, light brown skin, solemn expression, and dignified bearing, Anton *Ke`alapuniaokahiwalani* Müller, called Lani, or Gramps, by most people, was the perfect picture of a typical Hawaiian chief from the old days. A Hawaiian chief with blue-gray eyes, that is. He had been born and raised in Kohala on *Moku Nui*, the Big Island. His father had been a German employed by The Ranch and his mother had been a Hawaiian who claimed some sort of relationship with the royal family of Kamehameha. "Officially" Lani had 50% Hawaiian blood ("Don't you believe it," he liked to say. "There's some Menehune in there, too.") and therefore had a right to some Hawaiian Homelands, but of course the government never got around to giving him any. Lani had also worked for The Ranch as a *paniolo*, a cowboy, for a while, but his father used some pull no one knew he had and got young Lani shipped off to the University of Munich to study tropical agriculture. Between study in Europe and field work in Hawaii he managed to pick up a couple of degrees and eventually established a nice little career as an ethnobotanist. That was his normal side.

Lani also had a reputation as a *kupua*, a sort of magician or shaman, although that reputation was known to very few. In the old days he would probably have been called a *kahuna kupua*, or master shaman, but Lani was of the opinion that the once-honorable title of *kahuna* had been so abused that not many Hawaiians even knew how to use it properly any more. *Haoles*, whites, of course, just thought that "kahuna" meant a big chief or a good surfer, or some kind of healer.

So Lani had his say in the circle. He stretched his neck to one side as if to relieve some stiffness, and said he really didn't understand why the family was making such a fuss. He had received an invitation from the Pan-European Research Institute to attend a conference in Copenhagen. They had even sent him a ticket and promised to pay for his meals and lodging. Why didn't the family want him to go? He was healthy and fit, considering his age and all. His arthritis hardly bothered him, except in the morning, and as long as he took his medicine regularly his heart shouldn't give him any more trouble.

That's what gave Keoki, sitting almost across from his grandfather, his first indication that something slick was up. Gramps hadn't seemed to have any physical problems at all the week before when he had easily beaten Keoki and three of his friends in a surfing contest.

Keani spoke next. A quietly happy girl of eighteen, engaged to a hard-working Filipino boy, she expressed her concern that Gramps would get too worn out by the trip. After all, she reminded everyone, he hadn't been on such a long journey for twenty years.

Betty, given full family privileges and responsibilities because of her marriage to Hank, only said that she thought it was really great that the family cared so much about each other to have a meeting like this. In typical Hawaiian fashion no one paid any attention to her blonde, fresh-faced, "California-girl" looks. It wasn't that they tolerated them. They just didn't notice.

Hank started to tell Lani he should stay home and let the Europeans take care of themselves, but Reverend Isaac made him stop and speak through him as the leader. The rule sounds awkward, but it kept emotions from taking over and disrupting the purpose of the gathering.

Keoki wasn't sure what to say. His grandfather could be very tricky at times and Keoki had a strong feeling that the old man was using this meeting for something. Keoki's name was a Hawaiianized form of George, just as Keani was a form of Jean.

Keoki's full name was George *'Okamea'ekanoa* McCoy. His father had been a sailor from Kansas who claimed a bit of Cheyenne blood. He had died in a submarine accident when Keoki was eight, so Gramps had had a big hand in raising him. Keoki's mother said she got his Hawaiian name in a dream the night before he was born. Actually, some misty figure in her dream said those words and she used them for his name. A very rough translation might be "The weird one, the free one," so it got shortened to Kanoa, but now his mother and Gramps were the only ones who used that name. Keoki liked to identify with his Hawaiian side to some extent. It had the double benefit of giving him a touch of uniqueness among his working peers, and giving him a sense of belonging to something old and deep and good at the same time. As sometimes happens, however, the genes play tricks, so while his sister, Keani, looked like a full-blooded Hawaiian, away from Hawaiians Keoki looked more like a *haole* and among Hawaiians you could see just a bit more than a hint of his Polynesian legacy. For now, he decided to remain neutral and stated that he needed to hear more before he could say anything useful.

Aunty Nani and Keoki's mother, Lily, both daughters of Lani, really jumped into the problem. It had been so hard for them to keep still while waiting for their turn that they were practically jumping up and down before they got to speak. What it boiled down to for both of them was their worry over Lani's health. How could he even think of going on such a long trip with his arthritis as bad as it was and his heart ready to give out at any moment? Lani absently rubbed his knee as if to ease the pain while Lily was talking and Keoki thought that was overdoing it somewhat.

Uncle Willy, Lani's only son, came up with the solution, although it took a lot more talking to make it official. Good ol' Willy, who played ukulele like a professional beach boy and represented Hawaiians in court as a professional attorney, hid a mind as sharp as sharks' teeth until he was ready to bite behind his homeboy Hawaiian looks and drawling speech. He spoke flawless pidgin to his clients and perfect American English to his peers, and he was so good he fooled most of the family most of the time. In the sort of half-pidgin the family used he casually

18

suggested that maybe someone could go with Gramps on the trip to take care of him.

There it was. The Plan had been revealed. Everyone looked at Keoki.

Three

Rocks On The Beach

Ka i'a huli wale i ka pohaku
(The fish who discovers what is hidden beneath the stone)

It had been a long time since Keoki had been in Waikiki. Unless you had specific business there, Kalakaua Avenue from the Alawai Canal to the edge of Kapiolani Park was not a usual haunt for native Hawaiians. One local name for Waikiki was "Haolewood," a play on the word, *haole*, meaning "white." But on now in the early nineties it resembled downtown Tokyo, only with fewer people, less traffic, no smog, and more palm trees.

Walking along the busy street with his grandfather, Keoki noticed a number of changes since his last visit about five years before. Sizzler's was still there, going strong, but the fifties-style "Tiki-Deco" restaurant nearby had been closed. Quite a few of the smaller shops had been closed, in fact, and T-shirt vendors and time-share shills were taking up most of the sidewalk space. Tony Roma's was hanging in there, but from the street the venerable International Marketplace, created in the fifties as an ersatz Polynesian village by the original Don The Beachcomber, now looked more like a village of Korean street merchants.

On the *makai*, seaward, side of the street, the parklike area of Fort De Russy, an R&R center for the US military left over from World War II and never given up, looked pretty much the same, and the fairly new and massive Hawaiian Village shopping center was crowded with tourists. Keoki couldn't help noticing that there were a lot more high-rises, both condominiums and hotels, than he had seen before. He remembered a visit when he was very young, in the seventies, and at that time behind the stores on the *mauka*, inland, side of Kalakaua there were still plenty of small, two-story apartment buildings. Looking up at the tall, new skyscrapers he wondered if Waikiki would ever look like New York. The *kanaka maoli*, the Hawaiian People and their culture were getting stronger everywhere else in the islands, and this place, the big Tropical Paradise symbol, was dying, in Keoki's opinion, because the roots had been pulled out. The Brothers had left and Willy Kekuni, a musician friend with his own small band, told Keoki that to keep their gig at the hotel they had to play mainland soft rock and movie tunes.

Keoki wondered what he was doing here shuffling along with Gramps in "Visitorville," another local name for Waikiki, when he should be working. He had a job as a freelance graphic artist, and he was good enough to have a pretty steady list of clients. Until a year ago he used traditional media, but then his girlfriend at the time turned him on to computers, after just turning him on. He found it so exciting — the computers — that digital graphics soon became his specialty. Recently he had begun to work with media presentations and 3-D rendering for games. Some artists made as much as $10,000 a month and he wanted to get that good.

"Hey, Gramps," he said, "why don't we walk along the beach? At least the ocean still has a nice view." In spite of everything, Waikiki Beach was still one of the most beautiful in the world, and still one of the best for surfing.

Lani kept walking and didn't even look at him. "Because I want you to look around and learn something."

Oh boy, thought Keoki. The old man was already on his usual trip.

According to family legend, when Lani was young he had shown some paranormal abilities, so he had been taken in hand by his maternal grandfather to be a *haumana kupua*, a shaman's apprentice. Keoki knew that story, but so what? Let everybody do their own thing, right? Unfortunately, so it seemed to him, Keoki had also shown some paranormal tendencies as a young-ster, so he had become Lani's apprentice. It was kind of fun when he was a kid, pretending to talk to plants and animals and rocks. In school, however, he quickly found that this was *kapu* stuff, taboo, especially if you wanted to play sports and go out with girls. And some of the stuff wasn't fun at all, it was creepy-scary. Like the time he found himself without a body at his cousin's house; or the time he suddenly noticed that he was surfing as a dolphin and not as a human being. Not like a dolphin, *as a dolphin*.

By the time he was old enough to realize that Gramps' way of thinking was definitely not the norm he tried to pull away, but he couldn't, at least not entirely. Gramps was not just weird, he was also wise. Apart from the "spooky stuffs" he had a rich knowledge of nature and human psychology, even though his point of view was often quirky. Some of Keoki's best memories and most useful insights came from the hours and days they spent together hunting, fishing, hiking and sitting as far from the rest of the world as they could get. And now they were in downtown Waikiki.

"Look," Keoki said, brushing aside a bearded young man who wanted him to buy a T-shirt with a picture of Buddha on it, "I promised I'd go with you on this trip to Europe, even though you suckered me into it. So what are we doing here?"

"We're going to talk to some rocks."

Great. Just great, thought Keoki. *I thought that was all behind me when I left home to attend the University of Hawaii here on Oahu*. Part of him, *maybe the German part*, he thought, was irritated at the absurdity of talking to rocks. Another part of him, Hawaiian or Menehune, who knew which, started wondering in spite of himself what the rocks had to say. He shook his head to bring his thoughts back to what he considered normal thinking, which included communication at totally rockless levels. "Let's stop for a drink, at least." Keoki made a show of wiping sweat from his brow and stopped walking.

Lani paused, looked over and gave him a twinkling glance. "There's water in the air."

Keoki couldn't help smiling and looking upward at the coconut palms lining Kalakaua Avenue, waving their fronds in greeting at the birds in the blue, blue sky. Oh yes, the palm trees. He remembered walking with Gramps on lonely, palm-fringed beaches under the burning sun and complaining about being thirsty. Gramps would always say, "There's water in the air," and Keoki would go on being thirsty and complaining until they got to a place that had a well or a spigot. Then one day, hiking alone on one of those beaches, a coconut dropped onto the sand just as he was building up a thirst. Without thinking he picked it up and found a rock to help tear away the husk and break open the nut. It wasn't until he had raised it to his lips to drink and his eyes were lifted to the tops of the palms that he realized with a shock where the water had come from. Waves of emotion had flooded though him. Anger first, at Gramps' game; shame for his own denseness; and finally a joyful pride of understanding. Next time they were doing a beach hike and Gramps put out the same line he quickly scrambled up the nearest palm and brought down a nut for Gramps to open with his machete. Keoki could still remember the warmth of his grandfather's rare and sun-shiny grin. But that was then and this was now.

"And there's beer right next to us," Keoki said. "Less risk of arrest." Lani grunted and they went into the Pacific Grille, beckoning like a shady cave just a few steps from the International Marketplace.

Local microbrews cooled them down as they took a rest. "What rocks are we going to talk to?" Keoki asked, trying to keep the tinge of sarcasm just below the level of disrespect. He sipped a glass of Firerock Ale from the Big Island, enjoying its strong taste.

Lani didn't notice, or didn't act like he did. "Just some old friends at Kuhio Beach," he said, contentedly sipping the same tasty ale.

Keoki rolled his eyes. "Couldn't we have parked at the Zoo? Would've been a lot closer."

"Then you wouldn't have had a chance to learn as much as you're going to, Kanoa."

He winced a little. 'Kanoa,' his nickname that only Gramps and his mom used, reminded him too much of the apprentice years. He made a wide gesture, one hand brushing the mini-skirt of a passing waitress. Both he and the waitress studiously ignored it, but the memory of strong thighs lingered in his fingers. "What's to learn here? Commerce, architecture, exploitation, pollution. Those are not my fields."

"`A`ohe pau ka ike i ka halau ho`okahi," Lani said. He rarely spoke Hawaiian to Keoki, mainly because the young man hardly knew any. Only recently was it becoming the in thing for *kanaka*

23

maoli, the Native Hawaiians, to speak their own language. Keoki was beginning to study it, but fluent he was not. The phrase Lani just spoke, however, was one Keoki knew because his grandfather had used it so often and it was one he liked. It was a proverb: "All knowledge is not taught in one school". Gramps was reminding him not so subtly of other ways to look at the world. "What were we talking about last time we camped out?" Lani asked, pouring some more ale into his glass.

That was three years ago. Keoki tried to remember. Then he recalled a memory technique Gramps had taught him. He relaxed and recalled the tent, the fire, the stars, the hot chocolate, Gramps talking. No words came, though. He took a slow, deep breath, held those images, and sort of scanned his body with his mind, letting his attention rove over every inch of skin from the crown of his head downward while keeping his intent to recall the conversation. *Ta-da!* On reaching his left forearm the conversation recreated itself. It was such a neat trick that he had used it often while taking tests. It was not a welcome topic in his psychology and physiology classes, however. "We were talking about how lost urban people are in jungle settings."

"And?"

"How lost jungle people are in urban settings."

"Because?"

"Each are skilled in their own environment and helpless elsewhere until they adopt a new environment as their own." He felt a little pride at being able to recall all of that. The feeling didn't last long.

"Ah."

There it was, that damned expectant interjection. Now, Keoki knew from painful experience, he was supposed to apply that three-year-old conversation to his current experience in such a way that he could learn something new. It was just a game. His current profession being what it was, however, he could hardly say he was too old for games, so he played.

Keoki looked out at Kalakaua Avenue and its denizens differently, as if this were as natural an environment to humans as a reef is to a fish. He looked at the restaurants, the hotels, and the shops as places to seek food, shelter, clothing, medicine; as places for trading, sharing, teaching, learning, loving, laughing. The street itself was like a river; the cars and buses like boats, loading and unloading passengers and cargo at the designated loading docks where the palms provided some degree of shade.

He looked more closely at the people themselves, at their behavior in relation to this environment. The Japanese were ubiquitous, but not overwhelming. They were so noticeable mainly because they tended to herd together for security. This was unfamiliar territory, potentially dangerous. They paused longer than necessary on the corners because the cars were traveling on the wrong side of the street for them. They usually had guides, usually went into the high end shops like Gucci that had sprung up all over this tourist trap and which sold leather goods (*leather goods in Hawaii!*), and they usually never looked where the guide didn't point. Not all of them had cameras, but they did take a lot of pictures, because this was an exotic land, a great adventure. Small wonder they were always more than willing to have a *haole* American in the picture with them. *See, dear, this is what the natives look like.*

Those other haoles pausing at the corners, but talking and laughing loudly, were probably Australians. They didn't herd, but they did tend to form family or clan groups. The white backpackers, sitting wherever they could, singly or in small groups of two or three, and looking hungry and ready for a bushwalk — most likely Europeans and especially Germans who loved to trek everywhere. The rich Europeans would be at the big resorts, not here, and American backpackers as a rule dressed more sloppily and headed straight for the outer islands. How about the badly sunburned strollers? Mostly from the Eastern States, no doubt: honeymooners, secretaries and teachers, illicit lovers. Any locals? Meaning local residents, not just Hawaiians. There they were. Not wandering, not sightseeing, not shopping. Moving slowly or quickly, they had more purpose and sureness to their movements, and their eyes were either inward or on people and nothing else.

And here were he and Gramps. The medicine men. So he could look at things differently, so he could observe. So what? What did this have to do with their excursion this day? With the upcoming trip ...

Keoki's head rose sharply as it hit him. There was a lot more

25

to this trip than just babysitting his grandfather. Lani gave him a fleeting smile over his glass. "How's your German, by the way?"

Keoki sighed and took a big gulp of ale. "A lot better than my Hawaiian. But I thought we were going to Denmark."

Lani finished his drink, winked at Keoki, and got up without replying, making his way between the tables and back out to the street, letting Keoki pick up the tab. Keoki caught up with him on the *makai*, seaward, side of the street and they walked on toward Kuhio Beach in silence, refusing T-shirt vendors and avoiding time-share sellers as best they could.

Past the last hotel, and just beyond the tiny, concrete Waikiki Police Station, was the beginning of Kuhio Beach, marked by a sidewalk heading for the water on this side and a breakwater on the other. Beyond the breakwater was Kapiolani Beach, *makai*, seaward, of Kapiolani Park and the Zoo. To the right of the beach walk where they stood now, facing the water, was the famous Waikiki Beach fronting the luxury hotels, still beautiful and with great surf in spite of everything. Prince Kuhio Beach, named for an heir to the throne who became a politician after the overthrow of the monarchy in 1893, was right in front of them, a sort of poor man's Waikiki Beach, mainly frequented by locals, especially families, and tourists on a budget. It was at the quiet end of Waikiki, away from the intense shopping areas and the beachboy outrigger and kayak stations.

At the time of this visit, right at the corner where the two sidewalks met amidst a sparse group of ironwood trees, were four small lava boulders, or four largish, irregular rocks, depending on your point of view. To Keoki they looked very ordinary, and the only thing that made them a group was that they were fairly close together. As Lani nudged him closer Keoki noticed that the one nearest the street had a bronze plaque embedded in it which stated as a fact that into these stones, in ancient times, four healers from Kahiki had poured their mana, spiritual power, before leaving for home. The plaque gave their names as *Kapaemahu*, *Kahaloa*, *Kapuni*, and *Kinohi*. Keoki was astonished that he had never even noticed these rocks before.

"Touch them," urged Lani. Dutifully, Keoki laid his hand flat on the stone with the plaque. "That's *Kapaemahu*," Lani said. And as Keoki touched the others Gramps named, them, too, identifying each stone with the healer who supposedly left his power there. To tell the truth Keoki didn't feel anything special. Well, maybe the tiniest bit of tingling in his fingertips, but that had to be his imagination, didn't it?.

So as not to bother the homeless lady sleeping with her back on the stone nearest the ocean, they moved off onto the sand in the shade of another ironwood. Lani sat down and Keoki joined him, facing the stones. To their left the famous Waikiki surf made its regular, dignified, frothy way into shore, each wave seemingly aware of the reputation it had to maintain. Only a few surfers were out and they looked almost bored on these perfect breakers. On the right of Lani and Keoki a few strollers kept walking toward Kapiolani Park and traffic roared by at a decent, irregular pace.

The two men sat for awhile until Keoki realized they were in question-and-answer mode, meaning that if he wanted to gain anything more from Gramps about this experience he would have to prime his pump with questions. Lani had this quaint idea that true learning came from the head and the hands working together. Hand Learning was sensory, experiential, no matter what part of the body was involved. Head Learning was analytical and synthesizing. The Hand learned by touching, feeling and moving; the Head learned by asking questions based on observation and reflection. You needed the Hand to be able to do things, and you needed the Head to be able to change things. Anyway, Keoki had felt the rocks, and now it was time to ask questions about them. He thought hard to do it right. "What's the rest of the legend?" he asked, finally.

Lani nodded as if Keoki was on the right track and the young man felt a rush of pleasure that took him by surprise. Lani picked up a handful of sand and let it trickle slowly through his fingers. "Seems that a long time ago these islands were in a great deal of trouble, much worse than anything you've ever heard about. So all the people prayed for help and from *Kahiki* came four *kupua*, shaman healers of great power. After some hard times they healed the trouble, and before they returned each one of them put their special power into a rock, into these rocks, in case they should ever be needed again."

"Which *Kahiki* did they come from?" Keoki asked, a little

proud that he knew enough to ask the question. For most people familiar with Hawaiian, *Kahiki* is just a Hawaiian way of referring to Tahiti, the island down south, but it really means any place out of sight, from a distant place over the horizon, to outer space, to the spirit world. The sky is divided into five kahikis, from the horizon to the zenith, depending on which direction something appears from. So Keoki thought his question was cool. It wasn't. Lani just shrugged. The question was irrelevant.

A girl walking by in a skimpy bikini caught his attention for a moment before he tried again. "What were the powers that they left in the stones?"

Lani leaned back on his elbows and crossed his legs, without taking his eyes off the stones. "There's disagreement about that." By whom? Keoki wondered. "The legends don't say exactly what the powers were, but some people think the clues are in the names of the *kupua*. You know how difficult it is to translate Hawaiian without knowing the original intent."

Keoki knew that, all right, from his Hawaiian Studies class at the University. The professor liked to tell the story of two Hawaiians fishing from a canoe late in the day. As the nearly full moon appeared over a hill one man said, "*Kau ka mahina*, The Moon is shining," whereupon the second man, who had lost most of his hair, promptly smacked his partner with a paddle. The phrase also means, "Hey, look at baldy!" Keoki returned his thoughts to the stones. "So what do you think about it, Gramps?"

"I think the powers are in the names."

"And do you think you've translated them correctly?"

"Yep."

Gramps could be so exasperating. Sometimes he acted like a reluctant witness in court. "Well, would you share them with me, please?"

"Okay." Lani sat up in the sand. "*Kapaemahu* can be translated as 'The Peaceful Level.' I could be wrong, of course, but because of some obscure root meanings I think it's the power to become invisible. *Kahaloa* could be 'The Far-Reaching,' and I think it's *kahoaka*, the power to project your spirit out of your body, what some people call astral travel. *Kapuni* is 'The Controlling,' probably the power of psychokinesis or mind over matter. And *Kinohi*, 'Origin,' is most likely clairvoyant ability.

That's what I think."

Keoki was thinking, too. Intensely. Why did Gramps bring him here? But that wasn't the right question. "Those sound like things you tried to teach me as a kid. What makes the power in these stones so special?"

"Think of it as the difference between doing graphics by hand and on your computer."

Keoki was impressed. "Do those powers actually exist in these stones?"

"Let's say I think there's a way to find out."

He was being deliberately coy. The answer always reflects the question, he would say. Keoki decided to be more direct. "Gramps, do you know how to get those powers out of the stones?" He felt a coldness in his chest even as he spoke the words.

"My *kahu* taught me how to do it." Lani always referred to his own grandfather as his *kahu*, a term that implies something less than a guru and more than a mentor. He idly let some more sand drift through his fingers.

Suddenly Keoki began to tremble. *Oh shit, he has really set me up. I'm on the edge of a cliff. One more question and I'll fall over the edge, leaving my nice, tidy life behind. There's nobody pushing me; I could still step back into safety. I could keep my mouth shut, get up and walk away to my nice job, my nice apartment and my nice girlfriend. My relationship with Gramps would change, probably permanently. I know he would still love me, but it would be different. On the other hand, if I take another step forward I'll tumble into a sea of magic and mystery and adventure that could change all of my relationships forever. It's a crisis point, a dangerous opportunity as my Chinese friends might say; a cusp of transition as my new age friends might say; pupule, craziness, as my Hawaiian friends and family might say.*

While his soul was wrestling with the decision his spirit got fed up and took over. "Will you teach me?" he heard himself asking, stunned.

"Sure," Lani said, flashing his sunny grin. "But not today. You aren't ready and the powers aren't needed yet." Lani got up, brushed off the sand, and began the long walk back to the car with a confused Keoki trailing behind.

Four

Spooky Stuff

'Au i ke kai me ka manu ala
(He crosses the sea like a bird)

It wasn't easy, deciding what to pack. Keoki's blue, soft-sided Kevlar bag was open on the bed of his apartment in Mo'ili'ili, a suburb between Waikiki and Manoa Valley. Gramps, standing and watching by the door, had said that Copenhagen could be pretty chilly at the end of April, but then again it could be warm. That was so typical of his advice. On top of all his socks and all his briefs, an extra pair of jeans and half a dozen short-sleeved shirts, Keoki threw in a ski jacket he had used once for a trip to Utah with a former girlfriend, and a couple of borrowed sweaters. Then he added his electric razor and toilet kit and figured that was enough. He was set to be happy with jeans and pullovers and a light windbreaker for the rest of it. Gramps, however, had different ideas.

"I think you need a few more things," he said, mildly.

"Like what?" asked Keoki, honestly puzzled.

Lani lifted a hand and touched different fingers as he spoke. "Oh, like a suit, and a tie, and some dress shoes, and some undershirts, and some long-sleeved shirts..."

Keoki protested loudly, but Gramps finally got him into his car and drove him all the way across Honolulu, past Pearl City and Ewa, to the factory outlet stores in Waikele. Keoki sulked most of the way, reluctantly entering the store and letting Gramps choose some white shirts for him and allowing himself to try on a dark blue suit. But when Gramps picked out a tie for him, "that incredibly stupid sign of social correctness", Keoki rebelled.

"Gramps," he said, "I feel like I'm wearing a costume for a

30

masquerade party."

"That's exactly what it is," Lani agreed as he added the tie and several pairs of black socks to Keoki's pile.

"But why should we dress up in costumes? It's not real." Keoki held the tie and looked at it with distaste.

Lani grinned slyly. "I suppose," he said, dragging Keoki over to the shoe department, "that we could go in native dress. You'd look good in a *malo*, a breechclout, and I'd look very dignified in a *kihei*, a cloak."

"That's not what I mean and you know it. I just don't see why we can't be ourselves." Keoki sat down reluctantly.

"Ah," Lani said, after telling the sales clerk exactly what kind of shoes to bring over for trying on. "You have just opened up a bowl of *he'e*, octopus, about who you think you are that I'm not going to touch right now. So think of it this way: all forms of dress are really costumes. Anything you add to clothing beyond the need for warmth and protection becomes a political, social or economic statement. Our island ancestors used colored dyes for political affiliation, feathers and cloaks for social status, and masses of *kapa*, barkcloth, to demonstrate their economic level. Our European ancestors did similar things, and their influence still dominates the world." Lani took a moment out to reject three pairs of shoes and to make Keoki try on two others. "Didn't you ever read about the first missionaries? How they used to put on their woolen underwear when winter came in spite of the heat and humidity? It's one thing," he went on, "to enjoy comfortable clothes like you're wearing now, and another to make them a symbol of your identity." He made Keoki walk around in a pair of smooth, black slip-ons and shrugged when Keoki complained that they felt too tight. "They'll stretch, and you won't have to wear them too often," said Lani.

"I still don't know why I have to wear them at all. Who cares what kind of shoes I wear?" He slipped the new shoes off and stuck them back in their box.

"You seem to," Lani pointed out. He paid for the purchases and they headed back to the car. "What it comes down to is that, besides protection, the three most fundamental reasons why people wear clothing are to blend with a group, to assert their independence or to attract attention. Really clever people can do

31

all three at the same time." He was quiet until they were heading toward Diamond Head. Then he took it up again. "The quickest way to make friends with someone is to talk like they do, dress and behave in a way that makes them feel comfortable, and stay different enough to be interesting. You've seen pictures of our kings and queens in all that Victorian royal finery. You really think they enjoyed that? Well, maybe Kalakaua did. But the main reason was because they desperately needed friends to avoid being gobbled up and torn apart. They were able to stay independent for over a hundred years, which was pretty good back then for a country with no power and few resources. Anyway, we're going to need to make a lot of friends in Europe, and the costumes will come in handy."

His grandfather still hadn't told Keoki the reason for the trip, other than that someone needed his help. After all that talking Lani went into his quiet mode, so Keoki was left with his own thoughts on the drive back. If Gramps was right about making friends by dressing and acting the way they did, then maybe that had been part of the problem with his and Dyanna's relationship.

Dyanna was Keoki's most recent former significant other; she had actually been his girlfriend until last night. They had met at a party in Manoa six months ago and had felt instant hots for each other. Along with a great body she also had a great mind and a great heart. She worked at one of those eyeglasses-in-an-hour places at Pearlridge while studying to be an opthamologist, and every time Keoki picked her up after work she had a gift for him. Sunglasses at first, and then, as she got to know him, little things related to his work and his hobbies that she thought he would like. Keoki tried to respond in kind, but his gifts were either too expensive or otherwise inappropriate. Like the dangling earrings he got her after spending enough time with her to have noticed that she never wore them. But he didn't notice that and he didn't notice a lot of things until it was too late. One of the important things he didn't notice was how desperately she needed acceptance, and how afraid she was of anything that might threaten it.

Like most human beings, Keoki wanted to belong, and so most of the time he went out of his way to conform to the prevailing fads and fashions of his peer group, changing his hair or his clothes or his speech according to what was current. At the same time, he liked being just different enough to be noticed. He knew enough psychology from his undergrad classes to realize that this was just another way to seek acceptance, but understanding didn't change the impulse. He wasn't satisfied with being accepted; he wanted to be accepted as someone special. The problem was that Dyanna didn't want to stand out, and didn't want him to stand out because it might threaten her acceptance. She liked him enought to try and tolerate his little eccentricities, like his refusal to wear a tie, even at the stuffy cocktail parties she was always taking him to. Thinking to meet her halfway he had offered to wear a bolo, but she almost got hysterical at that and he didn't know why. She also got angry at him for wearing his Aloha shirt hanging out, Hawaiian style, when all of her male friends and colleagues tucked theirs into belted trousers. It had seemed like nonsense to him at the time, because at least he had worn dress pants instead of his more usual jeans. Now he remembered how much time she had spent on the phone with his sister before each of his family's gatherings he had invited her to, making sure that what she would wear would be appropriate. He had laughed at her then, but now he thought he understood. Still, in spite of how they felt about each other, Keoki could never meet her ideal of a safe, secure, comfortable conformist. When he had told her last night about the trip - "No one goes to Europe with his grandfather!" - he had blown up, she had blown up, and now she was his former significant other.

On the other hand, he couldn't imagine visiting his mom wearing a tie, or going to one of his cousins' homes with his shirt tucked into a belt. Rather, he could imagine it, but along with the image came a strong expectation of uncomfortable laughter and teasing. He smiled ruefully to himself. Actually, the shorts he'd worn to the family meeting had put him right on the edge, causing raised eyebrows and smirks even in his own family. Suddenly he had an insight. The problem wasn't with what he did or didn't do, it was with other people's reactions in relation to the effect you wanted to create. If being different would serve your purpose, whatever it might be, then it would make sense to be different enough to get that purpose served. If, however, not being different would serve your purpose better, then conformity would be the way to go. Obviously, Gramps wanted to create some kind of effect on the Europeans.

"I think I've got it," Keoki said aloud. Gramps glanced at him, inviting him to say what it was, and Keoki did.

Lani frowned, sighed, and looked back at Keoki like he was an idiot. "*Moʻopuna*, grandchild, you fished for *mahimahi* and you caught an old sandal. The fish are still in the water."

Meaning he didn't get it yet, so try again. Keoki hated it when Gramps made him think harder.

That night they took a late overnight flight to Chicago, both of them dressed in casual comfort for the trip. Lani made his grandson keep a jacket handy in case it was cold when they arrived in Denmark, because their luggage would be going all the way through. To Keoki's great astonishment they had seats in the first class section, where a flight attendant immediately took their coats and hung them up. His grandfather said someone else was paying, so not to worry. Keoki was totally unused to such luxury on an airplane. He had never dreamed of sitting anywhere but coach. First class was so far out of his thinking that it barely seemed real. It was like staying at the Royal Hawaiian Hotel. You knew that people did it, but it never entered your mind to do it yourself. At his age he believed he was supposed to act cool, but he was excited and delighted by everything that happened next. They had hardly seated themselves when an unusually friendly flight attendant offered them champagne or juice. *Hey, what the hell*, thought Keoki. He took the champagne, of course, and had two more glasses before they even started moving.

Shortly after take-off they were served warm mixed nuts without peanuts in a little ceramic cup and anything they wanted to drink for free. Keoki had a glass of Kendall Jackson Chardonnay and stretched out in the huge, comfortable seat complete with a footrest. He had never had a chair this comfortable before, even on the ground. They were given free headsets and a delicious meal served on real china with real silverware. This was the way to travel, he thought. When he asked, his grandfather said the roundtrip ticket to Copenhagen was worth about ten thousand dollars each, so Keoki had some more wine, two desserts and some cognac, never even questioning why someone would pay out all that money just so he could accompany his grandfather. He was full to hurting and getting a good buzz on, but he didn't expect to have this kind of opportunity very often in the future. The movie was some romantic thing he'd seen on a date the week before, so he spent the time thinking about his work, guessing what would happen in Copenhagen, and checking his watch and wondering what the family was doing right then. And he listened to music and dozed. Breakfast was another experience of luxury—all that white linen!—and then the sun was up and they were landing in Chicago.

The airport terminal had an ultramodern look, all bright steel or aluminum framing with huge amounts of glass overhead, allowing the place to be filled with natural light. On their way from the gate they had to take an underground walkway with a choice of moving sidewlks or unmoving floor tile. Neon tubes crossed over the low ceiling and rainbow lights rippled overhead, accompanied by a weird voice saying something incomprehensible. It looked like an unimaginative architect's vision of what a futuristic spaceport should look like.

They had a twelve-hour layover and Keoki would like to have seen the Windy City, but he was so wiped out they got a day-room at the connecting airport hotel and Keoki slept eight hours while Lani did some some sort of meditation. When it was time to get up and go to the gate for their next flight Keoki felt awful and Lani looked great. "Okay, Gramps, what's the secret to not getting jet lag?" Keoki asked after they had dressed and showered. "Cut down on the food and cut down on the booze, maybe?"

Lani chuckled. "That would probably help."

Keoki took a good look at his grandfather as they walked toward the security checkpoint. Grey-haired, but not stooped. Springy step. Twinkly eyes. My God, he looked happy! "I'm serious, Gramps. What're you on? There's no way you could look that good this soon with such a time difference unless you were taking something."

"You've got it all figured out. Why ask me?" He said it so gently Keoki knew he had made another wrong assumption.

Keoki's stuff went through the x-ray without a hitch, but Lani had to open his carry-on and show the supervisor a small bag of lava rocks, each about the size of a marble shooter, even though it had gone through security at Honolulu International with no problem. When asked what they were, Lani just said "They're my lucky stones." The supervisor shrugged like he'd heard crazier things and waved them away. Keoki wasn't sure he wanted to know what the stones were really for, but at the same time he knew he would probably learn anyway.

As they headed for the gate Keoki said, "Gramps, if there's a way to avoid jet lag I'd like to know. Really."

"Okay," said Lani, stepping around a lady who had stopped in the middle of the passage to look at her ticket. "First, assume there's no such thing as jet lag. That's just somebody's theory."

"But ..."

"Sure, there are symptoms associated with extended air travel, like tiredness, achiness, headaches maybe, grogginess, disorientation and so on. but don't assume they come from time differences that you can't do anything about. Let's assume they come from things you can do something about."

"Like what?" Keoki asked groggily, struggling to keep up with his grandfather's brisk walk.

"Start with sleep," he said. "If your sleep is interrupted at home, you're likely to feel groggy the next day. Sleeping on a plane is worse. You are trying to sleep in a chair, in your clothes, you get a lot of interruptions, it's noisy, and there are a lot of people around that you have to worry about annoying. Some of them annoy you, too. And then rich food, lots of sweets and sugared drinks, alcohol and coffee. All these can interfere with a good sleep." They showed their passports and boarding passes at the gate and took seats in the lounge. "Then there's the positive ions..."

This was the side of Gramps that always threw Keoki. Here was this old Hawaiian guy who loved to fish, danced a mean hula, spouted proverbs, and was full of ancient wisdom. And he was also a scientist with a graduate degree who had traveled all over the world. Keoki knew he shouldn't think those things were incompatible, but he couldn't help it. He'd been taught the stereotypes too well. And if he thought that way, what about others? That must be hard on Gramps, he mused, ... unless he changes costumes a lot. Hey, here's a new idea. Maybe Gramps can change

36

costumes without even changing clothes. Keoki tuned back in.

"...ions can be too stimulating. Negative ions can, too, of course, under the right conditions, but the positive ion effect is more common. So when you spend hours in a plane with central air conditioning and so many static electric fields it's not surprising that you get a lot of stress build-up. And the ions, plus too much alcohol and coffee, can cause dehydration and all of its symptoms. Finally, time does matter, at least mental time does. I noticed you checking your watch a lot. What were you doing?"

Keoki shifted his position in the black sling seat of the lounge. "I was mostly thinking about home, and what people were doing."

"Were you thinking about things you hadn't finished doing?" The tone of Lani's voice indicated that he knew the answer already.

"Yeah, and about how weird it would be doing things eleven hours off in Copenhagen."

Lani deliberately began to adjust his watch. "Right now I'm setting my watch for Copenhagen time. As of this moment I'll be thinking and feeling and acting as if I'm already on Copenhagen time. And as of this moment I will definitely not think of anything that might be happening at home, at least in terms of Hawaiian Standard Time. Except for spontaneous thoughts or deliberate imaginings my attention will be on the here and now, which may include a movie or a magazine if I feel like it. When the mind and body are too far out of synch, timewise, it causes physical stress. On the plane I'll eat fairly light, limit my alcohol and coffee, and drink a lot of water. I'll rinse my hands frequently to discharge static build-up, breathe deeply, stretch my muscles, and use self-hypnosis for resting. And I expect to arrive fresh and sassy and ready for whatever's waiting. Come on, they're calling for first class." They picked up their carry-ons and gave their tickets to the agent, taking the stubs and making their way to the first class section where they turned their coats over to an attendant, stowed their bags, and stretched out in the comfortable seats.

It was a very, very long flight, the longest Keoki had ever taken. He set his watch to Copenhagen time as soon as they got seated, drank only water until the meal service started, read magazines, listened to music, watched movies and short subjects, dozed on and off, and got so bored he began designing characters for a new game on napkins. It really was a long flight.

There were scattered clouds over the capital of Denmark when the plane made its approach to the airport on the morning of the next day. Lani looked out the window with pleasure. *Aloha welina*, Copenhagen, old friend. I extend my *la'a kea*, my sacred light, to bless our shared memories and smooth our way through the formalities.

Thanks to Lani's advice Keoki was feeling a lot better when they landed, although it had been hard for him to cut down on all the free drinks. The Copenhagen airport was clean, efficient, and very busy. This was Keoki's first time in a foreign country and his first time through an immigration and customs check. Everybody was courteous, but it was still intimidating. When he handed in his passport the woman officer put it on a scanner and checked a computer screen, and Keoki wondered what kind of information they had on him. He wondered if something would come up that would make them refuse him entry. Not this time, anyway. The officer said "Welcome to Denmark" in a perfunctory way, handed his passport back with no questions and no smile, and looked toward the person behind him before he had even left the counter. It took Keoki a moment to realize that it was okay for him to go on through. Gramps was waiting for him with a luggage cart, which Keoki was surprised to find out was provided free. In about fifteen minutes they had their bags, thanks in part to the first class tags on them, so he loaded them on the cart and pushed it toward the customs area. There he imagined their bags being ripped apart to look for contraband—drugs, diamonds, priceless jade figurines, whatever—but the customs guys just ignored them as they rolled past and through the automatic doors from quiet into chaos.

About six feet beyond the doors was a metal bar with a great mass of noisy people crowded behind it. For a brief, thrilling instant Keoki thought they were waiting for Gramps and him, but that thought didn't take long to die. Because of the bar they had to go right or left and Lani chose right. They walked a short way past the customs exit and Lani told Keoki to wait while he went and changed some money.

Keoki did the usual scan for pretty girls and then focused inward. This was one thing Gramps taught him that had become a habit because it was so useful. He would look at something, maybe an image on a computer screen or even a tree, and then check his internal responses. Based on those, he would look again and almost always see more than he had the first time. His feelings now were a mixture of confusion and peace. Part of him was disoriented by the strange words being spoken around him, the incomprehensible signs, and the plain fact of being in a place he'd never been to before. Underneath that, however, was something else, a kind of familiarity. That didn't make any logical sense, but Gramps had taught him once that if he would just hang out for awhile with a thought or a feeling it would lead him to its relatives and ancestors and eventually to whatever he wanted to know. Gramps called it "following the *aka* threads." So Keoki stayed with the familiarity feeling, not pushing or pulling, just following where it led. Suddenly a memory jumped into his mind, of when he was twelve and camping with Gramps in the *Haleakala* crater on Maui and Gramps was introducing him to the spirits of the area. "Every place has a spirit," Gramps had said, "and every spirit is part of a larger spirit. Like a tree that's part of a forest that's part of a mountain that's part of an island that's part of a planet. Each spirit is unique, yet it isn't separate from any of the others. Still, when you visit a place it's good to make friends with the spirit of that place because it can be a great helper and teacher. And sometimes you meet spirits who are old friends that you've forgotten."

That memory faded and a new thought leaped up in Keoki's mind. I knew this place, or at least the spirit of this place. Not the airport, but the land. I knew this land. But what did that mean?

Lani came back to see his grandson almost in a trance, and he smiled. *I see my grandson knows you, too,* he thought. *Now let me seek out the essence of our guide in the Spirit Web. Ah, there she is. This way, lovely spirit. Look this way.*

Keoki was snapped back to the outer world by a flash of yellow, a waving arm, and an accented voice calling out, "Dr. Müller, Dr. Müller, Here! Over here!" Bustling toward them was an attractive woman, maybe in her forties, wearing a yellow cloth coat that flapped around her like plumage. She fit Keoki's image of a Scandanavian type because she reminded him a bit of Anita Ekberg, whom he had seen in an art film course. Ekberg as a smothering mother, however.

"Oh, Dr. Müller, I'm so glad you could come," she said, shaking Lani's hand. "I am Helle Andersen, the conference co-ordinator. You'll be staying at the Skovshoved Hotel, where the conference is. How was your trip? Oh, it must have been good. This is your grandson? Welcome to Denmark. Let's go. You have your bags? This way." She led them out of the terminal, across a street to the parking lot, and into a Ford Escort. The little trunk couldn't hold all their bags, and more than half of the back seat beside Keoki was taken up with the rest. The air was chilly and he was very glad that Gramps had made him carry his jacket.

During the ride through the center of town and on to the boulevard leading north where the hotel was, Lani extended his spirit out over the city, just to make contact in a friendly way. At one point, though, the contact did not feel all that friendly. *Aue! Did I sense something in Christianaville? Something dark, but so fleeting. Maybe not, no trace of it now. Just a flare of anger, perhaps.* Lani searched again, found nothing, and turned his attention elsewhere.

Keoki's memory of the ride was rather blurry, partly because it was all so new and partly because Madame Andersen kept up a running commentary all the way, stuffing them with names and dates and events till Keoki just had to tune most of it out. One impression stood out, though. Helle took them on a side jaunt for a glance at the bronze statue of the famous Little Mermaid of Hans Christian Andersen's story (*a relative of Helle's?* Keoki wondered) and the Disney movie. Keoki remembered it particularly for two reasons. First, he had expected to see it out in the harbor, but it was only a few feet from shore, near a small park. And second, he was reminded of how much sickness there was in the world by Helle's story of how the mermaid's head had been sliced off by an unknown person for unknown reasons and a new one had had to be cast and attached. Keoki reminded himself that she had been healed, and that was a good sign at least.

Outside of the city proper they drove through shopping areas of brick buildings that looked like what Keoki thought European buildings should look like, past areas where they could see the gray waters of the Baltic Sea on the right and green woods on the left, past more buildings of a residential type, until finally they came to a stop on a side street in front of the hotel. *Aloha welina, Skovshoved,* thought Lani as they got out of the car and began unloading the luggage. *Do you remember the boatride with Greta, and her brothers and uncles waiting to punish me, and how we all ended up drinking together till the police chased us home?*

Skovshoved Hotel (Keoki soon discovered that, like most Danish words, it didn't sound anything like it was spelled) was a pleasant little three-story, white-painted place well north of City Center on a quiet side street just inland of the coast highway. It was named after a tiny harbor a couple of blocks away. Once inside the foyer they had a choice of taking stairs upward along the left wall, heading straight back through a short hall to a reception desk and employee world, or turning right into a small bar area and beyond to the garden restaurant. Helle led them first to the reception desk where Lani signed them in, and then upstairs and to the left. Helle bustled them into their room, informed them that they could rest for the remainder of the day, that the conference would begin at ten the next morning, that she would pick them up at eight that night to go out to dinner, and then she bustled her way out. The silence when she left was wonderful.

Their room was clean, but pretty basic, with a view out back onto greening trees and another building. Fortunately, it had its own simple bathroom with a shower. Lani told Keoki that it was still common in Europe for less expensive hotels or less expensive rooms to use common bathroom facilities for the guests, and not necessarily on the same floor as the room. Skovshoved was the kind of hotel you'd expect to find in a small town in the States, and expect to pay about $45 a night for. Here, Keoki found out, it was considered high class and their room was the equivalent of $250 a night.

After they put their stuff away and freshened up, Lani suggested they get something to eat and take a walk before getting some rest. They went downstairs and got some snackables—chips that were different from anything Keoki had ever seen, and familiar Cokes—from a little store next to the hotel. That would have been ordinary except for the pornographic magazines so casually displayed next to the food. This was not soft porn like Playboy, but real hardcore action. Keoki had heard that the Danes were more open-minded about sex, but this shocked even his freedom-loving soul. He looked around. Nobody in the store seemed depraved, and a couple of kids who walked in didn't even pay attention to the magazine rack. If it didn't bother them, Keoki thought, he wouldn't let it bother him. He was too embarrassed to buy one, though.

Lani paid for the snacks and led Keoki to the harbor, a few blocks away. It was a small boat harbor protected from the sea by two breakwaters made of mortared granite stones that encircled it like loving arms, leaving a space for entry and exit in the center. The sun was shining, but the Baltic wind was blowing and both of the men were glad they had worn their jackets. They walked left all the way past the racing boats and closed kiosks to the end of the northern breakwater and sat on a wooden bench facing the sea. They munched the chips and sipped the Cokes and watched the sailboats struggling with the wind and waves. It was a while before Lani said anything, and when he did it created another shock for his grandson.

"Kanoa," he said, using the nickname for his grandson that he preferred, "I'm going to tell you why we're here. I didn't tell you before because you would have found an excuse not to come, and I'm really going to need your help. You can still refuse, I can't force you to help me—no, let me talk for awhile—but tomorrow you will meet people who will back up what I say, and I hope you won't make a final decision before you listen to them also."

Lani got into his favorite 'start-to-talk-story-posture', leaning back, hands laced in his lap, legs stretched out and ankles crossed. He paused for a long time, like he was figuring out the best way to say what he had to say. He took a sip of Coke and put the can down on the bench. "I've taught you a lot of things about the traditions of my lineage, and about our special ways of looking at the world. I know you use some of it, and some of it you discard as too far out. Well, it's far out time, *mo'opuna*, grandson. Tomorrow you'll find out just how far out it can be,

42

so I'm trying to prepare you now."

Keoki was quickly getting uncomfortable. It was one thing to use a few mind-tricks to make life easier, but Gramps' world included a lot of wilderness that scared the hell out of him. He didn't really know why he was so afraid of it; probably because it was so different from the world he had grown used to. And probably because he didn't know how to deal with it. What was it that Gramps had said to him once? "Fear of the unknown is just the fear of not knowing." Keoki waited nervously for his grandfather to go on.

Lani shifted a little on the bench and said, "When something happens in the normal world, when a problem occurs, the most natural thing to do is to look for normal solutions, and most of the time this works pretty well. But sometimes abnormal things happen in the normal world, and normal solutions don't work anymore so you have to use abnormal solutions."

Keoki threw one of his grandfather's sayings back at him. "Gramps, you're going to Maui by way of Kauai. Just get to it."

Lani grinned wryly and leaned forward. "Among other things I do I'm part of a group that's like a think tank."

"Like the Rand Corporation?"

"In a way. But the problems we deal with are different and so are the solutions." Lani paused a moment. "What I've been told so far is that someone has apparently been using paranormal abilities to hurt people in Germany."

Keoki felt the hairs on his neck stand up. "Uh, by 'paranormal' you mean psychic stuff, right?," he asked.

"Right, but it's not like this person is doing it with his or her mind alone. He or she seems to be using the mind as part of the process."

Keoki was feeling very uncomfortable. "'Part of the process' sounds like professor talk. Give it to me straight, Gramps."

"Okay." Lani looked into Keoki's eyes. "There seems to be an assassin on the loose with very unusual abilities, and I've been asked to help track the person."

The younger man stood and took a deep breath, feeling shivers up and down his spine. "I don't suppose your're talking about tracking in the usual sense, are you?" Gramps slowly shook his head. "Jeez, Gramps, you're talking about the spooky stuff you know I can't stand. And you're talking about using it to find a killer. Jeez!" Keoki waved his arms wildly.

"You're good at the spooky stuff," Gramps said with great calm. The older man finished his Coke and put the empty can back in the bag.

Keoki stared at Gramps like he was out of his mind. "Jeez!" Keoki stomped off and paced around the end of the breakwater for a few minutes. Memories boiled up and he reluctantly peeked at them. He was eight, traveling out of his body, exulting in the freedom and the wondrous colors, laughing soundlessly as he floated through the clouds above the earth. He was fourteen, free-diving off a reef, warily but respectfully greeting a large shark as an ancestor, and feeling the greeting returned deep inside him just before the monster swirled away into the gloom. He was twelve, intimately experiencing the wild, rushing life of the breadfruit tree standing in his yard, then the carefully controlled life of the shama bird flying off from its branches, then the intensely self-centered life of the cat wistfully following the bird with its eyes. He was ... remembering being other things, doing other things, all in a quick jumble before he shook his head and unlocked his cramping hands from the railing. He looked back and Gramps was just sitting there, calm as ever. Jeez!

Lani gazed compassionately at his grandson. Kanoa is troubled because his mind, so clogged with *ike papakahi*, first level ideas, is afraid, and at the same time his spirit is so excited by the promise of adventure. He knows without knowing that this journey, dangerous as it is, gives him an excuse to plunge into my world again. *E Kanoa, i ku a hele mai i ka 'aina, he hale, he 'ai, he i'a nou, nou ka 'aina. Should you wish to come to my land, there is a house, poi, fish for you, the land is for you.* Lani waited until his grandson had calmed down a bit before stuffing their trash into the little shopping bag and quietly leading Keoki back to the hotel.

Five

A Bowl of Numbers

Alahula Pu'uloa, he alahele na Ka'ahupahau
(One who goes looking everywhere)

There was a tremor in the Force. Nazra laughed at herself, silently and without mirth, as she let the man's hands do what they wanted with her body. She remembered seeing the old Lucas film during her research, identifying with the tragic Jedi, twisted into a monster by an evil emperor, and she adopted the Force as an apt metaphor to describe her sensory interactions with the energies around her. Giving it all one name increased her efficiency while still letting her deal effectively with all the variations. It was like working with the weather, which really meant working with wind and rain and clouds and lightning and thunder and air pressure and heat and cold and on and on.

So there was a tremor in the Force. Which meant that she felt a strong presence in Copenhagen sweeping over the city like radar looking for an unusual pattern. Ignoring the growing excitement of the man beside her, she automatically evoked a specific symbol in her mind which triggered biochemical changes that had the effect of adjusting her personal energy field to blend with her surroundings. It would make her invisible to psychic prying as long as she stayed psychically passive. While it wouldn't make her invisible to physical eyes, she would be barely noticed in a room with other people. Now she was virtually alone, however, in a reasonably comfortable apartment in the center of Christianaville, Copenhagen's radical city within a city where people ruled themselves in the closest thing to a viable anarchy existing in the world. She was currently living with the unofficial leader of the Free People's Council, who was currently taking great pleasure in using her body. That was not a problem. She let him have his way and made the appropriate sounds and movements while she delicately explored the Force to find out who was using psychic abilities to locate her. The man she was with grunted a few times, but she hardly even noticed.

There was no repeat of the sweep, so perhaps the person who did it was thrown off by the brevity of the contact. She would have to be subtle, careful enough to catch without being caught. Like a paparazzi stalking a celebrity who succeeds in taking scandalous pictures without the subject's knowledge. She took her time, making little probes here and there until her bedmate was exhausted and sleeping.

Then she did a quick sweep of her own over the city, checking only for points of power, where the Force was strong enough in a human field to be a cause for concern. There were twenty-five of those, but eight were clustered in one place north of the city and the rest were widely scattered. She concentrated on the cluster, a happening unusual enough to merit close attention. What could produce a cluster signature like that? A secret meeting of political leaders? A convention of business entrepreneurs? She tuned in obliquely, using frequencies associated with meetings and organizations, seeking location more than anything else. A name flashed into her mind. *Skovshoved.*

She gently pushed the sleeping man aside and slipped out of the bed to use the phone, speaking in unaccented Danish. *Yes, there is a hotel in Skoveshoved. Would she like the number? ... Yes, this is Skoveshoved Hotel. Yes, we have conference rooms. Yes, there is a conference starting tomorrow. Let's see, it's called Healers International: Paradigm for a New Age. You're welcome.*

She hung up the phone and crossed her bare legs, almost satisfied. So, it was most likely just one of the healers looking for clients or competition. The Force would be strong in good ones. She was about to dismiss the whole thing when her trained caution urged her to make one more check. She used the phone again. "Harald," she said as soon as the call was picked up on the other end, "I want you to go to the Skovshoved Hotel tomorrow, north of the city. There's a healers' conference and I want you to attend and check out the participants. Don't give me that.

You can do your fun and games later. That's an order." It was probably nothing, but there was no point in being careless. She put the phone down, glanced around at the stuffy room with unopened boxes of stolen electronics piled in a corner, and made her way to the bathroom to shower and dress. When she was finished she left the apartment and took some narrow stairs to the roof, where she sat in a comfotable lounge chair under an awning, facing the sea.

It was quiet on the roof and she felt like sleeping, but that could be done later. Meanwhile, there was other work to do. Feodor Krazensky was here in town and she must find him. A brief image of the KGB chief who had ordered her execution flashed in her mind and, with a brief smile, she made it explode into uncounted fragments. Soon, Krazensky. Soon it will be your turn. You're not at the Russian embassy and not at the flat of your latest whore. Where are you? Methodically, she formed a grid in her mind and set it over the city, then slowly began to probe each section of the grid. She had programmed the muscles of the little finger on her left hand to respond to Krazensky's vibration. As she probed with her mind she waited expectantly for the telltale quiver that would tell her she had found him, but it didn't move.

The next day Harald made his way to Skovshoved and was sorry he had. Tall, with aristocratic features and posture, impeccably dressed in a light gray suit with a white shirt and darker gray tie dotted with tiny bits of red, he was bored. Bored with this insignificant hotel. Bored with the process of registering for this stupid conference as if he were a schoolboy again. Bored with the oh-so-polite people who wanted to help him sign up for the right lectures and workshops for his "personal lifepath." Bored with having to wear a name tag, for God's sake. And penultimately bored with the wannabe amateurs trying to pass themselves off as healers and psychics. Bored from his Italian leather shod feet to his immaculately coiffed, whitish blond hair.

Today he should have been playing with the children. The pretty twelve-year-old he had picked up yesterday had a beautiful scream, an ideal counterpoint to those of the eight- and six-year-olds. Today he would have blended them into his new composition. But no, it was not to be. Nazra—that bitch—insisted

47

that he bore himself to death instead. Sometimes he was sorry he had ever met her. But then he remembered how she had helped him to develop his gift, and how she had set him up with a source of income that left him time to pursue his artistic interests. Not that he felt any obligation toward her for that, of course. It was only right that he be supported in his work. But in addition to that she was able to cause such pain that he found it smarter to be at her beck and call than not to.

"Good morning, sir. Are you here to attend Dr. Delphini's lecture?"

From his bored six-foot three-inch height, Harald looked down on a nonenity, a plain woman with plain hair in a plain dress and a big smile. The only unplain thing about her was an over-large, golden dolphin with a green-jeweled eye that hung from an over-large golden chain around her over-large neck. Harald glanced into a room filling up with boring people. The choice was simple. Should he be bored walking around or bored sitting down? He chose to sit down. Taking a boring flyer from the boring woman, he entered the boring room and took a seat as near to the door as he could get.

Harald's "gift" was an acute sensitivity to sensory input. For him, sight, sound, touch, taste and smell were extraordinarily broad experiences compared to the human norm. This, of course, led to unbearable complications. His parents thought him mentally deformed, his schoolmates—while he still attended school—thought him frighteningly weird, and his doctors thought him excitingly grant-attracting. Everyday experience was bad enough, but their tests had sent him over the edge of sanity.

Nazra's agents had rescued him (the news reports said kidnapped) from an institution and she had helped him to control and refine his talent. She hadn't cured his insanity, but had guided it and modified it so that he could pass for a "normal" if he wished. When he wasn't creating his bizarre works of acoustic art he worked as a "nose" for a perfumery, creating exotic scents of such complexity that few people would be able to think of them as any more than "heavy" or "light." The price for Nazra's care and consideration was boring assignments like this one.

The lecture, given by a hyper-energetic fat man who jumped around the stage and waved his arms a lot, was a tiresome monologue about how wonderfully cuddly, cute, wise, prophetic, psychic and morally superior dolphins were supposed to be. All over the curtains and the walls were posters of cuddly, cute, wise, prophetic, psychic and morally superior cetaceans both under the water and above it. Harald perked up once during a short recording of dolphin sounds and he wondered briefly how much pain they could endure and in what ways that might modify their voices, but he quickly calculated that the cost of acquisition and care of stray children would be far less and he lost interest. Apart from that he spent the time classifying the audience by body odor, with sub-categories by brand name for cheap colognes and after-shave lotions. At another level, his brain remained actively open to unusual or familiar sights and sounds around him.

Toward the end of the lecture, while Dr. Delphini was trying to look cetaceous and promising the audience that they would be able to learn an ancient Atlantean healing technique held in trust by generations of dolphins if they took his afternoon workshop, Harald heard a familiar name spoken in the hall outside the lecture room. Krazensky. A name in which Nazra was intensely interested. Harald extended and focused his hearing. He picked up the words "...time for your presentation..." through the closed door before the speaker moved too far into the babble of a crowd for him to get more.

Dr. Delphini was just getting warmed up for his promotion of a $10,000 workshop "for a select few" to be led by Master Dolphins in the Bahamas when Harald got up and left the room, severely annoying Dr. Delphini, the plain woman, and several members of the Society for the Protection of Creative Cretaceans.

In the hall, Harald moved his head back and forth and sniffed once in a long, slow, intake of breath. Months ago Nazra had sent him the fragment of a cup which Krazensky had used. Like a bloodhound—actually, far more accurately than a bloodhound—Harald recalled the odor and sought a match in the air around him. Krazensky was here and had moved on down the hall. Harald followed the invisible trail into a large room tightly packed with tables and people. Ignoring the offerings of psychic healers, tarot readers, massage practitioners, crystal clerks and aromatherapists, he scanned the room, trying to connect Krazensky's odor with a body. His peripheral vision picked up a small group of men going through a door to his far left and he knew his prey was one of them.

Paying no attention to the physically jostled and emotionally hurt people he brushed aside, Harald made his way to the same door and went through into another hallway, carpeted and quiet. With more care he followed the hall until he came to a closed door apparently guarded by a pleasant young man seated in a chair next to it.

"*Godmorgen*, good morning" said Harald as he passed by the door.

"*Godmorgen*," said the man politely.

A single glance told Harald that the young man was a trained bodyguard, that he was German, and that he was ready for any movement that Harald might make even though the man looked completely relaxed. The same glance showed Harald the handprinted sign on the door: "Healers International Board Meeting - members only." A single whiff told the blond Dane that Krazensky had gone into that room and that there were two others in there with odor patterns he had never encountered before; rather tropical they seemed.

Without a pause, Harald continued on. If he were lucky... He was. A short distance beyond the guarded door the hall branched to the left and opened up into a lounge area. Harald moved a chair aside, slipped off his Italian loafers, and sat on the floor in a meditative position with his back to the wall, which he judged had to be part of the room with the closed and guarded door. During a conference like this one it was highly unlikely that anyone would disturb him as long as he seemed to be communing with other dimensions. He leaned his head against the wall and let bone conduction bring him the vibrations he wanted. The first words he heard were, "...and so I turn it over to you, professor."

Inside the room, Feodor Krazensky stood behind the small podium and smiled at a strange assortment of people. On the other hand, he was the strange one to them. Big and bulky in his poorly-tailored Russian suit, he looked more like a fat wolf than a genial bear. The very fact that he was Russian made him strange, because they were still not often seen outside of their homeland. At least, his type wasn't.

50

In the audience of seventeen there was a representative of Interpol, three agents from German Intelligence, and a minor official from the Danish government. Krazensky's attention, however, was centered on the remaining twelve: five men and seven women. The best of their breed, he thought wryly. But would they be good enough? He cleared his throat and began speaking.

"My friends," he began in barely accented English. "First of all, I thank you for coming together to help us in this terrible situation. I do not know how much you already know, or have guessed, or intuited." He paused to smile and receive their return expressions of polite amusement. "So I will proceed as if you are hearing it for the first time." He paused and took a sip of water, not because he needed it, but because it looked good.

"Before the breakup of the Soviet Union my colleagues and I were researching the parameters of human capacity for extended sensory perception and influence. Our purpose, of course" (*of course!*) "was to develop training procedures for future astronauts" (*well, it could have been used for that*) "which would assist them in space travel and exploration. We had already achieved several important breakthroughs when the demise of the unwieldy Soviet system" (*inoperable is a better word*) "caused a disruption in our funding" (*or, to put it another way, I had to shut the operation down before the authorities found out about it*). He glanced down at his notes, another unnecessary gesture, but one that befitted a professor.

"Unfortunately, as we attempted to search for new funding sources our work came to the attention of a powerful group of religious extremists who thought that we were doing the work of the Devil" (*that ought to produce some sympathy from these people*). "To make matters worse, they succeeded in subverting one of our most promising trainees, a young woman of exceptional talent, and convinced her that that all those working on the project were demons in disguise and that it was God's will that they be destroyed. It may seem fantastic that such an idea could be accepted in today's world, but this is a case of a girl brought up in a remote part of Russia where superstitions still run strong, and all of you here must know how impressionable and confused a young, immature psychic may become in times of great change" (*that was very nicely put, if I do say so myself*).

51

"In short, this group of religious fanatics kidnapped the girl, brainwashed her, trained her as an assassin, and set her like a ravenous wolf upon the very people who wished most to help her develop her great potential for good."

Krazensky stopped to drink some more water and see how well the audience was accepting his fabrication. So far, so good, it seemed. The officials, of course, seemed uncaring, but the psychics seemed sympathetic, all but that young man in the back who looked afraid of something. His mind drifted again to the flash of panic that had nearly overwhelmed him when he received news of Gregori Balenkov's death in Berlin and the card found on his body. It was a Tarot card, the Hanged Man. He knew it well from many hours spent with Nazra in the early days of the project, observing the training of her intuitive skills. The Hanged Man was one of the Major Arcana, a portion of the Tarot deck with special significance in divination. In its normal position, with the man hanging head downward from a cross-like structure it represents the surrender of self to spiritual guidance. But the card that was carefully attached to Balenkov's forehead by a pin was in the reversed position, signifying someone with clairvoyant ability who lives by his own wits and uses his gift for selfish purposes. Krazensky also knew that in Tarot lore the person who was using or receiving information from the cards was called "The Seeker."

Until that news came he had accepted the report, like the rest of his colleagues, that Nazra had hanged herself and had been consumed in the fire set to the Institute. On hearing the description of the card attached to Balenkov, however, he knew with frightening certainty that Nazra was alive and seeking retribution. It wasn't logical and his colleagues laughed at him, but he knew it was so. Perhaps some of the intuition training at the Institute had rubbed off on him. His colleagues had laughed, until the death of Pyotr Lernov in Düsseldorf. Another card was found, this time in the victim's pocket. It was the card called Justice, reversed, signifying that the Seeker had experienced injustice in some manner. The fact that Lernov's eye sockets had been filled with tiny glass jewels helped to convince others that the killer was Nazra.

A few coughs and some shuffling of feet brought Krazensky

52

back to the present. He had been in reverie too long. "I apologize, my friends. I was mourning the loss of my com..., my colleagues (*have to watch my words with these people*). Gregori Balenkov, a research scientist in human behavior at the University of Berlin, was assasinated in a horrible manner by this deranged woman. I will spare you the details (*as much for my sake as for yours*). Pyotr Lernov, a professor of surgery at the University of Düsseldorf, was assassinated by the same woman in an equally horrifying, but different way (*poetic justice would be the term used in English, I believe*)."

Krazensky took another sip of water. "It seems that this woman is planning to assassinate all those who held responsible positions in the project. If this is her plan, that means she will be seeking out at least four more members of the project team: Boris Orlov, a professor of psychiatry at the University of Munich (*who subjected Nazra to many kinds of mind-altering drugs*); Ivan Mikalov, presently a sculptor in Freiburg (*who disciplined her mind and body to turn her into an assassin*); Dimitri Treffsky, a research fellow at the University of Tübingen (*and master of martial arts*) and myself, a mere retired senior citizen who is writing his memoirs in Hamburg (*for NATO*)." His eyes swept the room. They looked ready. "We are asking for your help in stopping this madness. We need your special abilities to help us find Nazra Narovskaya before anyone else is harmed. Only that. The generosity of the German government has allowed us to continue our work, and your assistance can assure that future developments can benefit future generations. Thank you." Krazensky stepped away from the podium to polite applause. His words merely set the background. Now they wanted to know what they could do.

The woman from Interpol stepped up to the podium and introduced herself as Madame Jeanne Villier. Her French-accented English confirmed her origins, and her severely cut blue suit and black hair pulled into a bun demonstrated her seriousness. She said that she was a liaison officer for the Pan-European Research Institute and similar groups who used psychic skills to help Interpol, and she thanked the present group for volunteering their services. She emphasized that their assignment was only to help track the woman known as Nazra, who had been given the code name "Seeker." The group would be divided into four teams of three persons each. The teams would then be assigned to one of the four remaining members of the former Soviet project and be sent to the city in which that person resided. Each team would work under the supervision of a control, or coordinator, from German Intelligence to whom they were to report their findings, or even their guesses. Under no circumstances were they to attempt any contact, even visual, with Seeker.

The German government would pay for all transportation and personal expenses as long as they were properly documented. To ensure a fair, or intuitive, distribution of resources, team members and agents would pick a marker numbered one, two, three or four from a bowl to be passed out immediately. The team members were also handed a bio sheet for Seeker which contained a police artist's rendering of her appearance based on Krazensky's recollection. It bore no resemblance to her current persona, but no one knew that yet.

As Keoki, uncomfortable in his new suit, waited his turn for the bowl he stuck a finger into the neck of his white shirt to loosen it and wondered why he was considered a potential team member, and what he was supposed to do if he was on a different team than Gramps. The assignment didn't sound so dangerous, but he wasn't a psychic. He had wanted to protest when the bowl had started around, but he had seen Gramps brush his lips with a knuckle—an old signal to be silent—and he had obeyed. Still, somebody might get angry when they discovered he was a fraud. He also wished he could take off his tie.

When the deep, ceramic bowl came to him Keoki shrugged and plunged his hand in. He sifted through the markers, but one seemed to stick to his fingers and he held on to it. The plastic disk was marked with the number three. Keoki turned toward Gramps who was smiling and holding up a disk with the same number. *Wow, what a coincidence*, was his first thought. *Oh-oh, I don't think so*, was his second.

After all the markers had been chosen, a recess was called to allow the team members to mingle and introduce each other. A blonde and blue-eyed angel with an impish smile came up to Keoki and Lani, holding a third disk with the number three stamped on it. "Hi, I am Karen Gunnarsen," she said in English with a slight Scandanavian lilt. "I am a member of the team with you. I hope we will be working well together." She wore a short, yellow dress, with a matching yellow sweater thrown over her shoulders. It looked like she was in her early twenties, and she could have been a model for "Victoria's Secret". She smelled like flowers.

Way to go, Gramps, thought Keoki.

After introductions, they found out that team three was assigned to Krazensky, so Lani, Keoki and Karen met briefly with him near the speaker's podium. Krazensky thought they should have an opportunity to "tune into my vibrations," as he put it with a smile. He was leaving for Hamburg the next evening, but he would like to meet them "somewhere in the open with a good view all around." Karen suggested *Jaegersborg Dyrehave*, the Deer Park north of the city near the Bakken amusement park. Krazensky consulted with a German agent and agreed to that, suggesting 10 am. at the hunting lodge as a meeting time. That was fine with everyone, and Krazensky left the room in the company of two German agents.

Lani went off to greet some old friends who were taking part in the project, and Keoki turned his attention to Karen. "So, why don't we have lunch so we can get to know each other better," he said as calmly as he could. "Since we're going to be working as a team." Karen smiled and he could feel the warmth of the smile penetrate all the way down to his groin.

"That would be wonderful," she said, "but I have to meet a friend for lunch. Why don't we have dinner later at Tivoli, instead?"

"Tivoli?"

"Tivoli Gardens, the oldest amusement park in the world, so they like to say. I'll meet you and Lani outside the main entrance at eight. Okay?"

"Okay," he said with forced enthusiasm. Karen smiled again, touched his arm, and made her way to the door with the grace of a dancer. Keoki looked longingly after her. What a *wahine*, a woman! Dinner alone with her would have been so nice... Oh, well. There would be time in Hamburg, in between the psychic snooping. That reminded him. He would have to ask Gramps what he was supposed to do on this project. Maybe just be an errand boy while Gramps and Karen did their psychic thing. He walked over to stand next to his grandfather, who introduced him to his friends.

In the lounge area, Harald also smiled, but it was not the kind of smile that would induce a warm response. He got up and sat in a chair just in time to see Krazensky and his guardians walk through the lounge on their way to somewhere else. No need to follow them. He knew where they would be tomorrow. When he told Nazra what he had heard she might even get him that illegal electric prod he wanted so much.

Six

The Inner Garden

Malu ke kula, koe ke'u pueo
(The uplands are quiet, except for the hoot of an owl)

Suits off and casual clothes back on, Lani and Keoki had lunch in the Garden Room of the hotel, an airy, glassy dining room that resembled a greenhouse. The other teams were on their way to various destinations, so the Hawaiians ate by themselves. When the waiter came Lani ordered for both of them in Danish. Keoki asked what had been ordered and Lani said, "Just a typical Danish meal. No pizza this time."

Keoki smiled. Helle Andersen had wanted so much to please the visiting Americans that she had taken them to a pizzeria for dinner the night before. It wasn't bad pizza, but Keoki had been looking forward to trying some Danish food.

Moments later a bottle of Tuborg beer was placed in front of each of them. Keoki took a swallow, decided it was okay, and asked his grandfather what he was supposed to do on the team.

Lani took a sip of beer before answering with a serious expression. "Oh, we'll think of something. You could answer the phone, take out the trash, stare at Karen to make sure she doesn't vanish. Important stuff like that."

Keoki made a disgusted face. "C'mon, Gramps. I know you arranged for us to be on the same team and for Karen to join it. And I know this situation is too serious for me to be just a tagalong. What's my role in this? Am I supposed to guard the door while you and Karen work, or something?"

"I did "arrange" for you to be on my team," said Lani, "but Karen did her own arranging. No coincidence that you were the youngest and most attractive male in the group." Keoki flushed

57

and both of them sat in silence, looking at the other tables of diners until the first course arrived.

"Ah," said Lani, his eyes lighting up as the waiter set the appetizers down. "*Sild marineret*, marinated herring, for you and *ål røget*, smoked eel, for me. Enjoy!" After one delicious bite, Lani asked, "would you like to try some eel?"

"I don't think so," said Keoki, looking dubiously at Lani's dish. "I do like the herring, though. It tastes kind of sweet and sour at the same time."

"Eel, or *puhi*, used to be a delicacy in old Hawaii," Lani said. "But then it was usually salted. What do you think of Karen?"

Keoki choked on some herring. Karen, in a lot less than a yellow dress, had been foremost in his thoughts just then. "Excuse me. Hmmn. Well, uh, she's very attractive."

Lani grimaced and took another bite of eel before commenting. "Don't be silly. She's a knockout. I mean beyond that. What do you think of her *hoaka*, her personal aura?"

Here we go, thought Keoki, putting down his fork. What had he felt besides instant attraction? Did he want to think about that? Once he started getting into this, would he be able to get out? "I don't really remember," he hedged.

They were almost finished with the appetizers when they were interrupted by the next course, what appeared to be open-faced sandwiches piled high with a large assortment of ingredients. "This is *smørrebrød*," said Lani, making room for it on the table. "The word means 'buttered bread,' but as you can see there's a lot more to it than that. Yours is *med makrelsalat*, with mackerel in a tomato sauce topped with homemade mayonnaise, and mine is *med rejesalat*, with shrimp, apple and celery in a tomato dressing." Lani took up his fork and focused on eating, without bring up the subject of Karen again.

As soon as they were finished with the *smørrebrød* the waiter brought the main courses—*blå foreller*, poached trout with boiled potatoes, melted butter, horseradish and lemon for Keoki, and *vinkogt laks med pikant sovs*, salmon poached in white wine with a spicy sauce and potatoes as Lani's dish. For the rest of the meal Lani told Keoki some of the history of Denmark, including its Viking heritage.

"The Vikings were Scandinavians from Denmark, Norway and Sweden," he said between mouthfuls of his savory meal. "Because of their different locations they developed somewhat differently and even their language differed somewhat, along with their sphere of influence and interest. The Danes raided Western Europe and Eastern England and were called *dani*, instead of Vikings, which was a Scandinavian word having to do with sea battles. Those raids terrorized Europe and parts of Asia for about 300 years, and many Danes settled in England and northern France, especially in what became known as Normandy, named after the Norsemen."

"I didn't know that," said Keoki, putting down his glass. "I've read about the Norman knights, but I didn't know they were originally Norsemen. Anyway, the Danes seem pretty peaceful now."

"Most people are peaceful when they're not driven by need or greed," said Lani. "As the Scandinavians became Christianized they took on the European feudal system and the king of Denmark ruled the whole of Scandinavia for awhile. Today, Denmark has a constitutional monarchy, like England still does."

"You mean Denmark has a real king and queen?" asked Keoki, a little excitement coming into his voice.

"That's right. We're in the Kingdom of Denmark. King David Kalakaua may even have visited Denmark during his world tour."

"Wow, we're in a real kingdom. That's cool." Most of Keoki's graphics work had to do with medieval role-playing games, and kingdoms had just seemed to be the subject of fantasy.

"What I like most about the Danes," said Lani, "is that they are basically romantics. Look at this coin." He handed Keoki a five *krøner* piece. "See there? They have hearts on their coins, and on a lot of their public monuments, too. And look at this," he gestured around the room. "Candles and flowers for lunch. Actually, you'll find them for breakfast, lunch and dinner, even at McDonalds." Conversation went on in this vein until dessert. Lani suggested that they forego the cheese and fruit courses and Keoki readily agreed.

Silence reigned again as Keoki plunged into his *æblekage*

med rasp og flødeskum, stewed apples with vanilla served with alternating layers of biscuit crumbs and topped with whipped cream, while Lani took delight in an old favorite: *bondepige med slør*, "veiled country maid," a mixture of ryebread crumbs, apple sauce, cream and sugar.

"Now to business," said Lani over coffee. His usually pleasant face took on a somewhat sterner look. "Your role in this affair is just as important as that of me and Karen. You have more talent than you like to admit, and it's time to give up your childish resistance to 'spooky stuffs.' That's kid talk, and you're a man, now. I need your help, these men whose lives are in danger need your help, and everyone, including Karen, will be counting on you to do your part." Lani went back to his coffee.

Keoki was shocked. This was the closest Gramps had ever come to giving him a verbal rebuke. His mind was in turmoil, racing between his fears and his hopes. They finished the meal in more silence.

After signing the check, Lani said, "Let's go for a walk." Keoki followed him out of the hotel and to the right. They walked for awhile along Skovshoved Street, enjoying the smell of the lilacs frequently overhanging the sidewalk, making the two men duck under the branches at times. An occasional bus or car passed by, but for the most part it was a quietly beautiful spring day. The silent walk continued past the U.S. ambassador's residence until they came to a wooded park. "Let's go in here and find a place to talk," said Lani.

The park was more like a natural woodland, with trails running between large oaks and elms and chestnuts bursting with fresh, green, leafy life, and around wild meadows where fragrant flowers engaged in beauty contests. Lani found a bench where they could sit facing a meadow. Birds unknown to Keoki flew in and out of the trees and across the open space and unfamiliar birdsongs drifted through the afternoon air every once in a while. Thousands of bees provided a faint, background hum. Two young women joggers in sweatsuits came by, and an elderly man with a dog was briefly visible at the far end of the meadow. Other than that they had this part of the park to themselves. Lani extended his *la'a kea*, his field of influence, to help keep them isolated. It wouldn't stop anyone who had an important reason for passing near them, but most people would simply feel inclined to walk or run elsewhere.

"So, *mo'opuna*, grandchild," Lani began, "tell me what you are afraid of." The acknowledgement of their relationship let Keoki know that Gramps was his loving self again.

Keoki gathered his thoughts. "Well, it's just that I get really nervous when I think about doing the stuff you do. About doing the stuff I used to do. I mean, I know it was fun when I was a kid, but now... I just get really nervous." Keoki was hunched over on the bench with his head hanging down.

"What would happen if you did do all the things I do? If you did follow our family tradition and become a kupua, a Hawaiian-style shaman?"

"What?" The question was so unexpected it jolted Keoki upright on the bench.

"You heard me, Kanoa. What would happen?"

Keoki took deep breath and trembled. A multitude of emotions whizzed through him. Finally, he said, "I'd be different from other people."

"How different do you think you'd be?"

"I don't know. It's just a feeling that I'd be really different somehow. That I wouldn't be able to have the same friends, or do the same things. It sounds silly, but I even have the feeling that I'd look different, that I wouldn't fit in."

Lani was quiet for a few minutes. Then he said, "Are you willing to try something? Nothing 'spooky,' just an exercise that will help you find out more about yourself. It's up to you."

Keoki thought about it. It was time to do something. He shrugged, then squared his shoulders. "Sure."

"Good. Then go to your *waena*, your inner garden, your center, like I taught you."

Waena was a word that meant both the center of something and a garden, as well as "to meditate." As Gramps used it the word referred to an imaginary place that you made up in your mind; a place where you could rest, solve problems, play games and do a lot of other things that Gramps used to hint at. Keoki had "gone there" a lot until high school. After that he did it only rarely, and finally stopped doing it at all. The last time had to have been five or six years ago. But some part of him had not

61

forgotten the technique.

Keoki took a deep breath and closed his eyes, holding the intent to be in his inner garden. To his surprise he was suddenly there. When he was first learning it he had needed Gramps' voice to guide him there and help him focus. but eventually he could do it himself with no effort. Now, after so long, the skill hadn't diminished at all. The inner garden that Keoki had constructed in his mind as a child was based on a hanging valley that he had seen on the slopes of Haleakala Volcano on the island of Maui during an airplane ride to Hana to visit an aunt. "Hanging valley" is the name given to a narrow depression at the base of a waterfall that is part way up the side of a mountain. They can range in size from a few tens of yards square to a few acres.

Keoki's imagined valley was small and cozy, like a secret hideaway. A gentle waterfall tumbled down a fern-covered cliff into a dark pool of water. Keoki was surprised at that. As he remembered it the pool used to be crystal clear. He noticed other differences, too. The soft, grassy places were now covered with tough *uluhe* ferns, and all the flowers were gone. "It looks different," murmured Keoki with his eyes still closed.

"Of course," said Lani softly. "As you change, so does your garden."

"It's not a good kind of different."

"Well, the garden just reflects your mind. When you change your mind about something, the garden changes, too. What's really interesting is that if you change the garden, with your imagination, then changes happen in your mind. But we can experiment with that another time. For now, just describe your garden to me." Keoki described the falls, the pool, the flowers, and the ferns. "Alright, what can you hear?"

Keoki hadn't been paying attention to sounds in his garden, but now that Gramps had mentioned it he could suddenly hear the falling water, and the faint cry of an *'alala*, a Hawaiian crow. He told that to Gramps.

"Good. Now, how does the water feel?"

In his mind, Keoki reached a hand into the water of the pool. It was icy cold, like mountain water usually was in the islands. He also felt the ferns by the side of the pool. Again he described the experience to Gramps.

62

"Very good," said Lani. "Remember now, when you want to connect deeply to the inner world all you have to do is focus on some visual detail, some kind of sound, and a physical touch. But right now I want you to look around and find a nice, flat stone that you can stand on."

It didn't take long for Keoki to locate such a stone, not far from the pool. It was about a yard across amd roughly circular. Under Lani's direction he stood on it and imagined a door appearing in front of him. This was a door to the future, Lani told him. A symbol would appear on it shortly that would represent the path he was already on. When he walked through it, in a moment, he would find himself five years in the future along that path. Lani asked him to describe the door and the symbol as well as he could.

"The door is just a plain, white door with a brass knob. The symbol is in the middle. It's...hunh! It's a dollar sign."

Lani smiled a little. "Take hold of the knob, walk through, and find yourself five years from now along that path. Look around and see what you see, hear what you hear, and feel what you feel."

Keoki did that, and his physical body twitched as he instantly found himself in the noise and bustle of a high-rise office building. He knew he was in Los Angeles, and he knew he was doing digital illustrations for a large corporation. He was sitting in front of a computer in a cubicle, feeling very lonely and unhappy. An office colleague came in to talk to him. It was Dilbert. A startle reaction caused his eyes to snap open and he was disoriented for a moment, breathing heavily. Where was he?

"Easy, easy," said Lani. "Close your eyes and be back in your garden. It's okay. Take a drink from the waterfall and let yourself settle down for a bit."

Keoki did his best. His intellect wanted to deal with the implications of the experience, but he forced it to be quiet by putting all of his attention on details of the garden. He knew how to do this because it was often required in his illustration work when he had to choose intuition over logic. He also knew that suppressing his intellect wasn't good, so he just gave it a different task. In this case it was making plans to turn his garden into digital art. He was figuring out how many layers it would take for the final rendering in Photoshop when Gramps' voice came through asking if he was ready to go on. He nodded his physical head.

This time, when he stood on the rock in the garden, the door that appeared was an upright slab of volcanic rock with a petroglyph carved in the center. It was an image of the so-called Rainbow Man, a human stick figure with broad shoulders and an arched line going over his head from one shoulder to the other. There was no handle on the slab so Keoki pushed on it and it opened inward, revealing a lava tube cave. Keoki walked into it, feeling the rough floor and the slight dampness of the rounded walls. There was a light up ahead. Very briefly he thought of "the light at the end of the tunnel" and of accounts he'd read about near death experiences, but he brought his focus back to his inner world surroundings.

In a short time he was at the mouth of the cave, standing at the edge of a clearing in the midst of lush vegetation. In the clearing was a family of human-sized owls doing ordinary things like making poi, weaving baskets and sharpening stone tools. One of the owls stood up and spoke to him in Hawaiian.

"*Welina, e Kanoa. Pehea ko piko*? Greetings, Kanoa. How are you and your spiritual centers?"

"*Maika'i*," said Keoki. "Fine. Who are you?" Part of him was amazed that he was accepting this so naturally, but he didn't let that part interfere.

"We are your ancestors."

My ancestors are owls? part of him wondered. "Uh, where is this.?"

"This is *Po*, the spirit world, where all spirits live, even yours. You seldom remember, though."

He looked around. "What are you doing? It looks just like ordinary outer world stuff."

"Everything is different here," said the owl. Sweeping one wing toward the other owls, the creature went on, "We are preparing spiritual nourishment for your journey, baskets in which to carry your experiences, and tools that will help you accomplish your tasks."

"What is your name?" Keoki remembered now that he was following a ritual taught to him by Gramps years ago.

"*Kapueokamau*, The Eternal Owl," said the bird-man. It seemed to smile. "You may call me whenever you need help."

"Wait a minute," said Keoki. "I thought I was supposed to be seeing what my life would be like in five years if I followed the *kupua*, the shaman, path. What am I doing here?" All of the owls made a peculiar clicking noise, which Keoki knew was laughter.

The owl in front of him seemed to smile again. "You have always been on the shaman path. You never left it. You are *kupua*, you are one of us."

Keoki looked down and saw that he, too, had the body of an owl.

"WHOA! No way!" He was on his physical feet, eyes open but barely seeing, shouting, stumbling into the meadow. "No way!" he shouted again, and began running. He heard a voice behind him calling his name, but he ran away from it, trampling flowers, bumping into trees, until he reached a path where he could run full out and leave all the strangeness behind him.

Seven

Dinner at Tivoli

Me he makamaka la ka ua no Kona, ke hele la a kipa i Hanakahi
(Expressing a visit with a friend who dwells in a distant place)

Lani found him an hour later, curled up at the base of a great oak tree next to a duck pond at the far end of the park. The young man had his knees pulled up and his arms wrapped around them, and his eyes were red and puffy when he looked up as his grandfather approached. Neither said a word as Lani helped Keoki to his feet and they walked in silence back to the hotel.

Later, in their room, after both had showered and rested, Keoki said without looking at his grandfather, "I am different, you know. I always have been. I tried to cover it up by exaggerating it sometimes, but it didn't really help." He was staring out the window.

Lani spoke from the tiny bathroom without looking at his grandson. "I'm going to tell you a secret that probably won't help you feel any better. Everyone is different. They know it, but they don't know why, and it scares them. Some try to exaggerate it, some try to exploit it, most just try to hide it by attempting to blend in. None of that ever works, though." Lani slapped a bit of Old Spice cologne on his face. "The best solution is to make peace with it, because the only way not to be different is to become one with the universe, and that's no fun because then you don't have any friends to party with."

Keoki laughed in spite of himself and the tension between them eased.

Dressed in sweaters, wool trousers and warm jackets, partly because it was cold out as far as they were concerned, and partly because it was an informal dinner, they took a taxi to the center of town. They got off at Tivoli Gardens, which advertised itself as the oldest amusement park in the world, even though it was modeled after an older Parisian Tivoli as well as Vauxhall Gardens in London.

As soon as they got out of the taxi Keoki's breath was taken away by the entrance to the park. It had a Victorian look with bright lights outlining a cupola over the main gate, two side buildings, and the several entryways. Attendants in uniforms like doormen at a fancy hotel took tickets and guided visitors inside. The street was crowded with people waiting in line and music could be heard from inside the park.

Lani saw Karen near the entrance, waving to them, and he pulled Keoki with him to greet her. She was with another woman, also blonde, very good looking, probably in her thirties. The evening was somewhat chilly even by Danish standards, so Karen wore a dark blue three-quarter length wool coat over a lighter blue dress that matched her eyes. Her companion was all in black, including a black beret and black boots. All that black was set off by gold buttons on her overcoat and an abundance of gold jewelry around her neck and on her hands.

"*Godaften*, good evening," said Karen as they approached. "This is my friend and spiritual teacher, Lisbet Friedlænder. I thought it would be nice to be a foursome." Introductions were made and then tickets were bought, and they went inside the park.

Keoki was surprised at the spaciousness. He had expected a typical, old-fashioned amusement park with a midway and rides, but Tivoli reminded him more of Disneyland. It had gardens and pathways, and beautiful, exotic pavilions, and restaurants, and a lake, as well as rides. The place was ablaze with lights, along the walks and in the trees, that made it look like a fairyland in the soft light of the evening. The air was filled with the fragrance of flowers, speech and laughter, and sounds of music from every direction. Maybe this was where Disney got his ideas, Keoki thought to himself.

Karen gave the visitors some information about Tivoli Gardens after they passed through the entrance. It had been built in 1843, she told them, on twenty acres right in the heart of

Copenhagen. The land had been leased from King Christian VIII by an architect named Georg Carstensen on the condition that seventy-five percent of the space remain open. There were rides and games as in all amusement parks, but some of them had a distinctly Danish touch. "The merry-go-round, for instance," she said with a smile, "has tiny Viking ships instead of horses, and the ferris wheel carriages are made to look like hot air balloons." There were more than two dozen restaurants, plus parades, fireworks, practically everything you could want for fun.

"There are a lot of flowers, too," said Lani.

"One hundred and fifteen thousand," said Karen. "I counted them." Everyone laughed.

As they walked through the park they passed a large, open-air theater where actors were prancing on the stage in what was obviously a comedy. Karen explained that this was the oldest building in the park, the Pantomine Theater. It was also called the Peacock Theater because of the colorful curtain. One of the characters seemed out of place to Keoki. The others were dressed normally, but he was wearing an odd costume and make-up that made him look like a clown in tights and a pointed hat. When he asked Karen about it she said that the character was called *Pierrot*, a favorite of old and young alike throughout Europe. He was sort of trickster-fool archetype. She said they were very lucky because the actor playing the role was one of the best and most loved, and soon he would retire.

They watched the end of the play and joined in the wild applause, then continued on their tour. They walked by an ersatz Taj Mahal fronted by fountains and gardens and came to a fantastic pagoda covered in lights. "It's actually a Chinese restaurant," said Karen, "with a fine chef from Hong Kong. But I picked another place for this evening's meal."

They came to the edge of the area with the rides and Lisbet suggested that they'd better see that later so they could get their seats for dinner.

All agreed, so they headed for *Grøften*, the restaurant Karen had picked out. She said it was very famous. It was also very busy, very noisy, and very efficient. The foursome went in the entrance and waited in a short line, watching the speedy waiters maneuver skillfully between tables and around people. Most of the diners sat outside under the branches of linden trees amid hundreds of lights in the form of tiny hot air balloons strung through the trees and along the posts that provided a framework for the restaurant itself. Ivy screens gave a semblance of privacy to some areas.

Finally their reservations were acknowledged, they were immediately led through the crowd to a table in a corner, their orders were taken right away, and they barely had time to start a conversation before their drinks and food were on the table. The fare was simple. Both Lisbet and Karen had Jolly Cola with *rødspætte stegt*, fried plaice with boiled potatoes and parsley dressing. Lani and Keoki had the local porter with *frikadeller*, rissoles served with red cabbage and tasty potatoes.

Although the food had been served quickly, they took their time eating and getting to know each other better. Lani started it off by asking Lisbet about her work, since she had been introduced as a spiritual teacher.

"My purpose in life is to help others find and develop their own spiritual path," she said in British-accented English. "I teach small groups around the country, I do spiritual counseling, and I have a few special students like Karen," she smiled and patted the young woman's hand. She described her work further as one of helping people to identify their particular talents and to practice methods for refining them. She worked mainly with the aura, the unique energy field surrounding everyone and everything. By examining a person's aura she could determine a great deal about that person's past experiences, present state of mind and body, and future potential. "I recognize you, for instance," she said to Lani, "as a very old soul and a very wise one. Your future is clouded, that is, it doesn't appear clear to me. That sometimes happens when you're about to enter a period of great change. Your past has been filled with adventure. And great sadness. You are married?"

"I was," said Lani. "My wife died in childbirth with our second child." It had taken years for him to understand that it was not a failure of his skill as a healer, but a choice on her part to move onward. He smiled inwardly at the memory of all the adventures they'd had together since then in *Po*, the Inner World.

"I'm sorry," said Lisbet, although she wasn't. This Hawaiian man might be an old soul, and much older than her in years, but he had a youthful spirit and he was certainly good looking. "You," she turned to Keoki with her head cocked, "are a mystery. Your aura is very bright, but there is no detail. I don't mean to be rude, but are you purposely masking yourself from me?"

"No," Keoki said, laughing. "I wouldn't know how to do that if I wanted to." He took an odd pleasure in the fact that she couldn't read his aura, and felt a bit of disappointment at the same time. It was always interesting to hear people tell you things about yourself, as long as they were good things. He took a drink of beer to cover up his feelings.

Lisbet frowned briefly. "It's curious, nonetheless. I wish all of you good luck in your project. Karen has told me you are doing some work for the Pan-European Research Institute, which she prefers to call PERI. I don't know what kind of work and I'd rather not know, but I wish you luck, anyway." She looked back at the older man. "Can you tell us something of your own background, Lani?"

Lani took a bite of potato and a sip of beer before replying. He decided it would be best to keep it very simple. "Keoki and I both come from a tradition that primarily uses conscious dreaming, similar to what Jung called 'active imagination.' That's really a sideline for both of us, though. Professionally, I'm an ethnobotanist. I do research and teach about the use of plants in traditional societies. Tell them what you do, Keoki."

Keoki was glad that Gramps had saved him the embarrassment of trying to explain that he didn't know what he was supposed to do for the PERI. He grinned. "I'm an illustrator for computer games." That drew somewhat surprised looks from both women, but neither knew enough about computers or games to ask any questions, so Keoki said, "What about you, Karen?" He was also glad that this gave him a chance to look directly at her for awhile.

Karen flushed prettily as they all turned their attention to her. "I practice as a conscious medium," she said. "I receive information, words and pictures, from my spirit guides. Every since I was a little girl I was aware of invisible friends who would help me or comfort me. Once, when I was sailing by myself and got lost in a storm, they told me exactly how to get back home.

However, it was Lisbet here who taught me how to get information from my guides to help others. So now I do readings for people and I am a consultant to businesses and sometimes government offices. I also use the Tarot because it inspires me and because ..., well, because it seems to impress people more than just speaking. It's a good life, I think. I get to travel and meet interesting people, like you two." She smiled at Keoki, who tingled.

They finished their meal with more casual conversation. Over dessert of *karamelrand*, caramel custard, Lani, Lisbet and Karen were talking about the difference between conscious and trance mediumship and that didn't interest him, so Keoki just looked around. He was in the corner chair and some movement in his peripheral vision caught his attention. He looked a little further to his right and saw that there was a crack in the wooden wall. Beyond that he saw the actor who had played *Pierrot* taking off his make-up in a tiny dressing room. While Keoki stared in surprise, the man turned his head slowly and looked directly at Keoki for what seemed like a very long moment. Keoki felt a strange sensation of kinship and, even more strange, a sense of an old, old friendship. The man winked at him and turned away.

Lani's hand on his arm brought his attention back to the table. "Are you ready? We'll walk through the rest of the park and find a place by the lake where we can watch the fireworks."

They walked through the midway area and around the lake, and were lucky enough to find empty seats on some park benches close to shore a half hour before the fireworks were supposed to start. The walkways and bridges all around the lake quickly filled with people happily awaiting the spectacle. Across the lake from where they sat they could see the lighted outlines of a what looked like a pirate ship.

On the deck of the pirate ship, hidden in the shadows, Nazra scanned the party of four. Since Harald made his report she had put most of her attention on finding out more about the Pan-European Research Institute and the teams of psychics assigned to track her, particularly the one that was going to meet with Krazensky the next day. A standard computer search turned up a bland website that said nothing substantial, but a deeper search of Interpol records breached by a hacker contact showed a surprising number of arrests and preventive missions in which PERI teams had played an important role. The teams worked by focusing on a particular target, cross-checking the psychic information received by each team member, and cross-checking the team's results with conventional sources of information. The sixty-five to seventy-five percent success rates of the Institute's teams gave Interpol a significant edge in their war on crime. The more she discovered about them, the more Nazra realized that these psychic trackers had to be taken into serious account.

She had had far less success in gaining any information about the individual team members that were supposed to be tracking her. Given time, of course, she could find out more about them than they knew themselves, but she didn't want to take that time. Krazensky was her next target and she knew where he would be tomorrow. Harald had heard the names of the members of this team spoken, and was able to tell her that they would be coming to Tivoli this evening. So she had tracked them to Tivoli to learn what she could about them.

The girl Karen was a lightweight, Nazra decided, using a form of internal information accessed by symbols defined as "spirit guides." Nazra had experimented with such a system years ago and had discarded it as inefficient and limited by personality and secondary characteristics attributed to the guide figures. Also, it tended to make one dependent on sources that, by their very nature, acted in an unsuitably independent fashion. Nazra preferred to use her own, controllable, sensory channels. Since the girl was dependent on such sources, Nazra felt confident that she could manipulate or scramble the information Karen received from what she thought of as her spirit guides.

The other two members of the team were a different matter. The young one bothered her because she could not read his energy pattern. It was more like the pattern of an animal than a human. There were surface emanations that were normal and easily interpreted, of course, with the usual content of fear and doubt and pride and sexual obsession that young men had, but the core was a blur. All she had to do was find a key to his pattern, though, and she would be able to read him like a book. So she was not overly concerned about the young one.

The older one, however, made her deeply afraid, more afraid

than she had been for many years, ever since she had first been kidnapped off the streets of Minsk and taken to the Institute. She recognized his pattern as being the same one that had connected with her so briefly the day before. Then she hadn't known it well enough to be afraid. It was not a fear of being hurt, because there was something in the older man's pattern that subtly reminded her of her barely-remembered grandmother, and that part was almost comforting.

No, the fear was that of being in the presence of an authority with more power than she could ever hope to have. At the beginning of her enforced training she had felt so helpless and alone that she had feared everyone, even the janitorial staff, and had cried herself to sleep for a month. Then she had overheard a doctor saying that he was afraid of her talent and what she might learn to do with it. She was completely astonished that one of her feared authority figures should be afraid of her! From that moment on she strove to conquer her fear, to develop her confidence, to be the one who inspired fear in others.

But now she was afraid again. This man had such a calmness in his pattern. Like the eye of a hurricane. Wind was a good metaphor. His energy was as soft as air, yet she knew it could be devastatingly powerful if focused and directed against her. There had to be some weakness that she could exploit. Perhaps some area of compassion that could be used against him. She tested the idea that the young man might be the weak point, but although she could tell there was a bond between them, the older man seemed to have no fear at all on behalf of the younger one.

Keeping her own energy well masked, she continued to study them from the deck of the make-believe pirate ship. The older woman she dismissed completely. One of those spiritual types with a bit of talent who oozed love and goodwill to cover up a core of weakness. She didn't want to draw the attention of the older man at all, so she made herself more comfortable and shifted frequencies to a level that ought to open up a pathway to the younger man's core, where she could plant some seeds to give her an advantage if it were ever needed. It wouldn't be necessary to define the blur. She would use the most basic of all connections. Nazra waited for the fireworks to distract his consciousness and let her in.

Eight

Night Vision

He ho'ike na ka po
(A revelation of the night)

"They are about to start!" said Karen, a bit of little girl excitement coloring her voice. The large crowd around the lake hushed in eager anticipation. To some degree they all shared the human fascination with lights, sparks, flames and explosions. Perhaps it was an atavistic response to the dangers of volcanic explosions and forest fires that their ancestors had to deal with, or perhaps it was just the contrast between light and dark, silence and sound, that held their attention. Regardless, all eyes but two followed the fiery streams and and starbursts, and most of those made moans and groans of pleasure at the display. Perhaps it reminded them of some other forms of excitement, forms more personal and intimate.

Keoki, leaning back in his chair and sitting close to Karen, enjoyed it more than any fireworks show he remembered, even though it wasn't all that spectacular by U.S. standards. There was something different about experiencing it here in a foreign country, in such a romantic setting, in the company of beautiful women. He looked at Karen sitting next to him on the edge of her seat, her face turned up and shining with delight. Keoki admired her profile. Such a doll! He was very glad they would be working together. He hoped it would last a good while. It would be so nice to hold her close and kiss those lips ...

Wait a sec. What's that bump on her forehead? Keoki adjusted his focus and realized that what he saw wasn't on Karen's forehead. It was much further off, across the lake. He shifted in his chair to get a better look and found himself staring into the glowing eyes of the most lovely and seductive woman he had ever seen. He could see her clearly on the deck of that pirate ship, a vision that aroused in him an intense desire, and for the moment he didn't even wonder how he could be seeing what he saw. Then suddenly she vanished.

Across the lake a shaken Nazra withdrew her energy back into herself and moved out of sight behind the deckhouse. *Holy Mother!* she thought, forgetting all her years of indoctrination. Keeping her energy under tight control, she walked quickly down the gangway of the ship and moved virtually unseen through the crowd toward the exit. On the way, while part of her mind blended her pattern with those of the people she passed so as not to be noticed, she berated herself for nearly ruining all her plans. It had been working well. She had established a subtle connection with the younger man and was inserting a program to make him susceptible to emotional manipulation when she touched an unexpected memory complex. Before she could do anything it linked to a complex of her own and energy ran both ways as if the switch to start up an electrical generating plant had been turned on. The man glowed from within with a light so bright that she could see every detail of his features. The worst part was that she felt an instant desire for him that was stronger than she had ever felt for any other man. An absurd and powerful urge to join with him had nearly caused her to jump up and shout.

Fortunately, she was saved by her disciplined training. As soon as the energy started to go out of control a part of her mind automatically disengaged the connection and stopped the outward flow. Now, as she fled from the park, her body still tingled with lustful feelings. She used a form of slow, yogic, whole-body breathing and let the feelings continue without allowing them to influence her nervous system. It was like quietly standing in the rain and letting it flow over you, fully aware of its wetness, but not tensing up against it. Still moving out of the park, she created a mental structure that redirected the emotional energy into more useful channels without suppressing it. She could feel her overexcited genitals calm down and her brain begin to clear. She willed herself to set aside the evening's experience for analysis at another time. She would spend the rest of the night preparing for the next day's encounter.

Lani had known they were being watched from the time they had entered the park. The watcher was very skilled, however. Lani's awareness had ranged widely around them since their arrival and he knew there was a presence focused on them, but he could not locate it with any certainty and he could not tell if it were a man or a woman. He had stayed alert during the fireworks and had even assumed the watcher was gone when he noticed a surge of energy in Keoki's *hoaka*, his aura. Keoki had appeared to be looking intently at something across the lake, but Lani hadn't been able to see anything. Perhaps the boy was having an inner vision. He would ask him later.

Now it was time to finish the evening and get ready to answer his grandson's questions, of which there were bound to be many. Karen was a sweet girl with a strong *hoaka*. Her talent would be useful when they got to Hamburg. She was also young, pretty, healthy and Danish, so he would not be surprised if she and Keoki found some enjoyment together. Probably at her initiative, if she didn't want to wait for Keoki to build up his courage. Lisbet was intriguing. There was a subtle invitation there, in spite of his age, but she didn't have enough passion for his taste. No doubt he would remain celibate until he got back to Hawaii.

"It's been a wonderful evening," Lani said when the fireworks were over and people began moving toward the exits. "Thank you for suggesting it, Karen."

"Would you like to stop somewhere for an after dinner drink?" asked Lisbet." She hoped he would.

Lani smiled at her. "No thank you. We are still adjusting to the time difference and we need to be sharp for a meeting tomorrow." A small deception to ease the parting. He noticed that Keoki didn't object.

"Then I'll pick you up at nine a.m. tomorrow," said Karen. "It will take us a while to get to the meeting point."

With that agreed to they all stood and walked away together, chatting about their impressions of the park and the fireworks. Even Keoki managed to join in with a few words. On the sidewalk they said their goodbyes: Lisbet regretfully, Karen warmly, Lani politely, and Keoki more distantly.

Neither man spoke much during the taxi ride back to the

hotel. Once inside, Keoki asked Lani if they could talk for a while. In the small lounge area to the right of the hotel entrance there were two men at the bar having a quiet discussion, but no one else. Lani and Keoki sat at a small table in a corner. The waiter came over and Lani ordered a Cherry Heering for each of them.

When the drinks came Keoki took a sip of the cherry liqueur and found it delicious, but distracting, and set the glass down. Lani took a sip of his own and waited patiently.

Keoki's mind and emotions were whirling like the clouds in a speeded up movie sequence. The experience with the figure across the lake was too strong to deal with just yet, so he chose a safer subject to begin with. Karen's spirit guides. He fingered his glass without picking it up.

"Okay," he began. "The aura I understand. At least it's familiar to me. It's like the *hoaka* you taught me about, right?" Lani nodded. That was close enough for now. "Okay," Keoki went on, "so Lisbet can get information from the aura. I can accept that. Radio waves carry information. Why not auras, once you accept them as being similar?" Lani didn't say anything. "But spirit guides? Uh, hey, I know the ancestors can help out sometimes, or at least I don't have any problem with that idea, but I don't think that's what Karen was talking about. Was she?"

Lani leaned back into his "talk story" posture while Keoki took another sip of liqueur. "No, Not exactly," Lani said. "There are a lot of different ways to think about things in this world. Experiences can be very similar, but look at all the languages used to describe them, all the philosophies and religions used to explain them, all the political systems invented to regulate them. What we might call 'spiritual' experiences are the same." Lani rubbed his jaw to give his *ku*, his subconscious self, time to organize what he wanted to say.

"Let's say that there are four people who have the same experience," he began. "We'll call them *Kahi, Lua, Kolu* and *Ha*." Keoki smiled at his grandfather's use of the Hawaiian words for 'One, Two, Three and Four.' Lani continued. "Let's say that all four have seen a vision, an internal image, of something happening at a distant location. And all four come from different backgrounds." Lani paused to sip his drink. He took four coins

77

out of his pocket, each a 10 *krøner* piece, and lined them up on the table. He touched the first one. "*Kahi*, here, comes from a scientific background in which this kind of experience is pathological. It obviously can't be true because there is no known medium by which such knowledge could be transmitted to the mind directly. If the vision happens to match what is actually happening somewhere, that's merely a coincidence or, possibly, *Kahi* learned about it in a different way and either forgot or is purposely engaged in a deception. So he decides to go into therapy."

Lani touched the second coin, moving it slightly. "*Lua* comes from a family with a spiritualist tradition. To oversimplify it, spiritualism teaches that when humans die they often maintain an interest in this world, and the better ones try to communicate so they can help. They are often called 'guides' because of this. Some people are more sensitive to this kind of communication and act as mediums for the messages. Again, I'm oversimplifying, but one of the beliefs of this system is that all psychic phenomena-telepathy, clairvoyance, psychokinesis-are carried out by these spirits of the dead. So when *Lua* gets a vision, the automatic assumption is that it was brought to him by a spirit."

"Now for *Kolu*." Lani picked up the third coin and put it back down. "*Kolu* comes from a culture in which it is accepted that everything is alive, aware and responsive. In *Kolu's* world it is possible to communicate with everything-trees, rocks, stars, people-regardless of distance in time or space. When *Kolu* gets a vision he acknowledges it as a communication from something or other. The message is more important than the source. The vision could be of an actual happening or it could be symbolic. Depending on *Kolu's* role in the culture he would either call on a specialist, or he would work with the vision himself in some healing or creative way."

"That's us, right?" said Keoki. Then, as a realization of what he had just said crossed his mind, he frowned and corrected himself.' Uh, I mean you." He had almost gotten drawn in that time. He took a swig of the cherry stuff to hide his nervousness.

"Whatever," said Lani, purposely ignoring Keoki's reaction. He picked up the fourth coin and tossed it in the air a few times before setting it back down. "Our last example, *Ha*, believes that everything comes from God, and that he has been especially chosen by the Lord of Heaven for some very important mission. For him, the content of the vision is less important than the fact of it. That is, he treats it as a sign of God's favor and of his own importance in the great scheme of things." Lani paused to take another sip of his drink.

"Which one is right, then?" asked Keoki.

"You're missing the point, *mo'opuna*. Each one is right from his own point of view." Lani leaned forward. "What really matters is not which one is right, but which one is most effective for what you want to do."

"I don't understand," said Keoki.

Lani decided that this was not the time or the place to follow through with that thought, so he revised his intent. "Think of it this way. When someone explains something in a way you don't agree with, just remember that he or she is only expressing a set of beliefs. Let them believe what they want and keep your own counsel. Explore their ideas if you wish, but don't feel obliged either to accept theirs or defend your own. Karen has her own way of thinking about what she does, and as long as it provides the information we need it doesn't matter how she believes it happens. Now, was there anything else you wanted to know?"

Keoki still wasn't ready to bring up the incident with the woman across the lake, so he said no, and thanked Gramps for his help. After they finished their drinks Lani paid the waiter and they went up to their room. He had decided not to bother Keoki about whatever had happened to him at Tivoli.

That night Keoki dreamed about the woman he'd seen so clearly and had felt so strongly about. The dream began with the same scene that had appeared during the brief encounter. He and the woman were walking hand in hand, naked, down a path on the side of a steep hill that led to a lake. The woman looked different, but Keoki knew who it was. He looked different, too. Both of them were young, blond and happily heading for a swim. The area they were in was heavily forested. The lake was large and somehow Keoki knew it was connected to the sea. It was a sunny day, but he also knew that the water would be very cold. At the edge of the water, he and the woman, really just a girl in

79

the dream, stopped to kiss before plunging in.

Suddenly rough hands pulled them apart and held them captive. The dream-Keoki had a fearful thought: *Raiders!* The girl screamed as the three men holding her laughed and fondled her body with coarse delight. Dream-Keoki struggled and shouted as his two captors did the same to him.

A sixth man appeared from around a curve on the shore. He was clad in the same sort of ragged garments as the others, with the same kind of axe and sword at his belt, but he had an air of authority about him and he wore a gold chain around his neck. He looked at the scene and gave an order in a language that Dream-Keoki did not understand. One of the men holding the girl let go and ran back along the shore out of sight. The man, who was obviously their chief, came closer. He looked the girl over carefully, and did the same to Dream-Keoki.

Just then a large rowboat came around the curve with more men in it, and landed next to them. The chief gave another order. All the men cheered and the two holding the girl began dragging her to the boat. She screamed and struggled furiously to no effect. One of the men holding Dream-Keoki knocked him down with one back-handed slap, then he and his companion walked to the boat and got in. Only the chief was left on shore, ready to enter the boat. Dream-Keoki grabbed a nearby rock, jumped up and ran toward the chief, intending to bash his head in.

Several of the men in the boat shouted and the chief whirled around, his sword drawn. Dream-Keoki couldn't stop his forward rush and expected to be skewered. Instead, the chief lowered his sword at the last instant and stopped Dream-Keoki with a massive hand around the boy's throat, bringing Dream-Keoki's face close to his own. The boy noticed that the chief did not look cruel, nor did he look kind. The chief's intense blue eyes searched his own for a few moments and Dream-Keoki could hear the girl crying and calling out to him. The chief raised his sword hand and struck Dream-Keoki in the face with the hilt, knocking him to the ground where he hit his head against a large stone. The pain was so real ...

Keoki woke up, the back of his head throbbing painfully from a close encounter with a nightstand. Images of the dream remained clear, interfering with his awareness of the room he was in. There were a few moments when he wasn't certain where he really was. Then the dream slowly faded and he became more aware of his bed in a room in a hotel in Copenhagen in Denmark with Gramps. But the other experience had seemed just as real when he was in it. He shook his head, bringing back the pain. It was just a dream. He had hit his head against a nightstand, not a stone. That made him feel better, a little.

Nine

The Deer Park

*'Ikea mai la, ua ha'ale i ka wai li'ula
(One notices the waters of the mirage)*

Karen arrived by taxi just after nine in the morning. Lani and Keoki were waiting in front of the hotel, dressed in their suits, with sweaters under their suit jackets, because the day was overcast and cold. Karen wore a bulky knit sweater-jacket in a rich pattern of blues, greens and purples, and black ski pants with boots. To Keoki she looked almost irresistably cuddly. Karen chattered away about nothing in particular during the short ride in the taxi to the Deer Park.

Jaegersborg Dyrehave, "Hunterstown Deer Park", was a nature preserve about seven miles north of the city center. In the eighteenth century it had been a royal hunting preserve, but now it was open to the public. Because of its out-of-the-way location it was mostly visited by the Danes themselves.

The PERI trio went in by the south entrance, which led first to the Bakken, "The Hill," which was truly the oldest active amusement park in the world. Karen took them on a tour of the park within a park, telling Keoki and Lani that it had been created thirty-five years before the Pilgrims landed at Plymouth Rock in America. The rides and restaurants opened at noon, but it was open to walkers at this hour. As an amusement park Keoki didn't think it was very impressive, but Karen assured him that many people liked it more than Tivoli. Keoki thought that was probably because it was away from the city and cheaper. They stopped for hot chocolate and coffee at a small eatery that catered to the early crowd. Karen looked thoughtful for a moment and then turned to the others. She had a tiny frown on her usu-

82

ally smooth face.

"I had a premonition this morning. About *Herr* Krazensky. But I'm not sure what disturbs me more, the premonition itself or the form it took."

"What do you mean?" asked Keoki while Lani quietly drank his coffee and waited for her to continue.

"It's just that ... I told you I'm clairvoyant. My guides give me pictures. They always give me pictures. They might be about the past, present or future, and they might come when I ask or by themselves, but it's always pictures."

"And?"

She fiddled with her cup of chocolate before continuing. "Early this morning I was given an image of Krazensky, but it didn't hold. That is, it broke up. That's never happened to me before."

Keoki put down his coffee and looked at her curiously. "Broke up?"

"That's what it seemed like. The picture appeared and then ... it broke into little pieces that faded away and all that was left was darkness." She was frowning at the memory.

"Sounds like it could be a symbol that Krazenzky's in imminent danger," said Lani.

"But that's not how my guides work," said Karen. "I always get a picture that points me to something specific to look out for, either an object or a part of the body. Sometimes it's so specific that it takes a lot of figuring out to put in a proper context, but it's never just a picture that just breaks up like that. If *Herr* Krazensky were in immediate danger I should have seen a gun, or a bullet, or a knife, or a speeding car, or something like that. So I don't know what the picture means."

"Well," said Lani, pouring some more coffee from the little pot on the table. "we know that Krazensky's in danger. That's why we're here. And there's no reason why the assassin has to wait for him to get to Hamburg. We don't know much about her, yet, so let's just stay alert, and inform Krazensky of anything we pick up, including your premonition. Perhaps he'll be able to make some sense out of it."

There being little else to say about it, they finished their beverages, left the amusement area, and began the long walk to the center of the park to meet with the Russian.

They followed a dirt road that passed between thick stands of trees and brush. Karen pointed out a sign that described the various kinds of deer that could be found in the park, and shortly after they saw a small herd of does and fawns to the left of the road, peacefully munching a late breakfast. Lani extended his spirit as they walked, seeking out anything unusual, but everything around them seemed normal.

There were very few people out this early on a weekday, so it was a quiet walk. Birds called out to potential mates and spring flowers lightly perfumed the air. Once the quiet was broken for a few minutes by the harsh buzzing of a chain saw as park personnel did some necessary clearing of winter debris, and one jogger went crunching by, but other than that everything was still. Even the air barely moved, for which Lani and Keoki both were thankful. Karen told them that there were also horse-drawn carriages to take people through the park, but they weren't available at this hour. As they approached the great central crossroads another herd of deer became visible, this one on the right, in the corner. It was larger than the first one and there were two bucks with it. None of the deer paid them any attention because humans were so common and non-threatening. They quietly munched on the grass around the trees, hardly even bothering to look up.

At the crossroads itself Keoki was surprised at how broadly the space opened up. To their right another road stretched out toward the eastern gate. Directly in front of them, on the right of their own road, stood Ermitage Castle, the old royal hunting lodge, looking more like a smallish, square, stone palace, with gardens and fields behind it bordering the north side of the eastern road. The southern road that they were on continued past the lodge across open ground for a considerable distance before entering a wooded area again. Most surprising to Keoki was the golf course on the far left. There were golfers out, but they were paused in their game while another small herd of deer made their way slowly across a fairway.

The trio still had twenty minutes to wait before the meeting, so Karen took them on an outside tour of the closed lodge. Although supposedly a hunting lodge, much of the statuary and carving was erotic enough to suggest that its major purpose was as a trysting place. Karen pointed out various architectural features as they walked slowly around the building, and Keoki found quite a few that she didn't mention.

At five to ten they made their way back to the crossing point of the southern and eastern roads and looked east. The deer were still in the woods near the corner on the right, moving around a little more than before. On the road they could see four men in suits and overcoats heading toward them, still too far away to make out faces, and beyond them a good distance were scattered groups of other people on their way in.

The group of four had to be Krazensky and his guardians. One was behind, frequently turning around and walking backwards for a few steps to survey the rear. One was on the left side, from the trio's point of view, watching the gardens and fields, and one was on the right, checking the woods. Krazensky had to be the one in the middle, of course, striding forward as if he hadn't a care in the world.

As the four men approached the crossroads, Lani noticed that the deer had stopped grazing and were all looking toward the men. The two bucks moved in front of the does and fawns as if to protect them, and Lani thought that was odd. Why should the deer feel threatened by those men? Were the humans giving off such a strong scent of fear? Lani couldn't detect any. They seemed confident and competent. They had no scent at all. And their auras ... they had no auras! Something was very wrong. Lani saw the bucks lower their heads and paw the ground. Looking back at Krazensky with strong intent he saw a brief flash of a wolf's head. The Russian started to raise his hand in greeting and a smile began forming on his lips.

Xorosho, good, thought Krazensky. *The amateurs are here. Well-meaning, but not much use, I think. Nazra is too clever for them. But not for me. In Hamburg ...* Krazensky whipped his head to the left as he heard sounds of breaking twigs. *What were those deer doing?* His face froze in a mask of fear. Behind the deer, seemingly floating above them, was Nazra's head, with eyes of green fire and smiling mouth dripping blood. It was his moment of doom.

"Stop! Watch out..." Lani's cry was lost in the crashing sound

85

of stampeding deer. The herd rushed out of the woods and onto the road, the does in a panic, knocking down the man on the right and the one in the rear, and the bucks swinging their antlers threateningly. The man on the left crouched and drew a gun, but didn't know what to shoot at and had to move away quickly to avoid being trampled by the apparently crazed deer. In the middle, Krazensky screamed as both bucks moved to attack him directly. The gored him repeatedly and struck at him with their hooves, as if he were some wild beast trying to make off with one of their females or young. Lani ran forward and tried to reach Krazensky, but the milling herd kept him away and he could do nothing to calm them down. Karen was paralyzed with horror. The screams went on and on. People from other parts of the park came running.

Keoki, meanwhile, had his eyes fixed on the woods. He saw a woman there, looking straight at him with glowing eyes. She was obscured by brush and branches, but he knew with absolute certainty that it was the same woman he had seen at Tivoli on the pirate ship, the same woman he had dreamed about the night before. He didn't know what to do. Amidst all the noise, and shouts, and screaming, and terror, he could only look at her in confusion.

Impossibly, he heard a voice speaking to him. It was as clear and loud as if the person were standing next to him in a quiet room, but he was not in a quiet room and there was no one next to him. It was the woman in the woods. It couldn't be, but it was.

You can hear me. Then there is a deep connection between us after all. I may have loved you once. No matter. You cannot harm me. You don't know how. The Danish girl and the old man have to die.

Keoki glanced at Karen. Her face grew pale and she fell to the ground, her multi-colored sweater and blonde hair making her look like a dying flower. Through the noise and confusion he heard his grandfather cry out and when he turned his head quickly he saw the older man clutching his head and sinking to his knees. Keoki swung back to the woman in the woods and shouted "Nooo!" Without thinking about it he drew upon sub-conscious memories of computer game battles and willed a blazing fireball toward the glowing eyes. He was not even aware that he had his hand thrust out like one of his wizard illustrations. In his minds's eye he saw the fireball fly out of his hand in into the woods. The eyes of the woman grew wide in surprise and then she blinked out. Disappeared as if she had never been there at all.

Surprised himself, Keoki took a few stumbling steps forward and looked around to get reoriented. First he looked at Gramps, who was sitting down on the gravel roadway and shaking his head, but otherwise seeming okay. Then he turned to Karen, who was still lying on the ground. He rushed over there and as he knelt beside her and took her hand her eyes opened and her color started coming back. She took a deep breath and tried to get up and he helped her to her feet. He held onto her as they looked around the area.

The deer were calm now. They had moved off the road and into the field. The bucks were scraping their antlers on the grass, trying to wipe the blood off, but otherwise the herd looked normal. One of the bodyguards was trying to keep a growing crowd away from Krazensky's mangled body. A second was speaking into a cell phone and kneeling by the third, who was apparently injured. Lani got up and went to speak to the first guard. They conversed quietly for a few moments, and then Lani came back to Karen and Keoki were standing and holding each other.

"Let's go," he said, taking Karen's arm.

Keoki was stunned. "What? We can't just leave here like that without doing anything!"

"We've been told to," said Lani as he gently nudged them back to the southern road. "They don't want us involved. Don't want the local police to know about us. We're to go back and wait for further instructions." He waited until they were about twenty yards along the road and then said, "However, we need to talk with each other about what went on back there. Karen, do you know some place where we can talk about this in private?"

"My flat," she said promptly, leaning against both men for support.

"Are you okay?" asked Keoki worriedly.

"Fine," she said, weakly smiling at him. "Just...just a bit shaky still, that's all."

"Alright," said Lani. "Let's organize our thoughts on the

way and save the talking for when we get there."

Karen's flat was in the picturesque little waterfront town of *Dragør* ("pronounced Drah-wer," she told Keoki) on Amager Island south of Copenhagen and beyond the airport. The flat was small, but bright and cheery, with flowers everywhere and candles in many places that she lit as soon as they came in. Since they had not been able to get a taxi and had to walk to *Lyngby* and take an S-train, it was close to noon and she insisted on fixing something to eat first. "To give energy to their brains," was the way she put it. Two windows by a sitting area looked out on a quiet, tree-lined street. A third, in the tiny kitchen area, had a view of a little garden with lawn chairs and an umbrellaed table that was shared by all the tenants of the building.

The center of the flat's living area was taken up by a round table covered with a colorful, shawl-like cloth, and surrounded by four chairs. On one wall was a bookshelf and a small television set. Most of the books were in Danish, but there were some books on psychic phemenomena published in London and an American edition of an art book featuring the works of Maxfield Parrish. On another wall were the doors for the bath and bedroom. Between the doors was a space with a framed photo print of the Dalai Lama's palace at Lhasa, Tibet, shining golden at sunset. Below that was a small table with a telephone on it. Most spare surfaces had quartz crystals on them, either singles or clusters. There was a faint trace of sandalwood incense in the air.

Conversation was kept light while Karen prepared the meal. Keoki and Lani sat at the table.

"You obviously live alone," said Keoki, looking around as he undid his tie and pulled it away from his neck.

"Yes," said Karen with an amused tone. "I prefer it that way. Men are always so messy."

"No boyfriends?" asked Keoki.

Karen laughed and turned around to put a plate of open-faced sardine sandwiches on the table. They were topped with bits of onion and some kind of herb. "Oh, plenty," she said. "I just don't want them underfoot all the time." She added a bunch of grapes, sliced apples, and a plate of cheeses. She also set down glasses of orange juice. "No beer," she said. "We need to think our best." She sat with them and they ate quietly for awhile.

When the sandwiches were gone and everyone was just nibbling at the fruit and cheese, Lani began the serious conversation.

"We've had our first encounter with the assassin, sooner and closer than we expected. What happened to Krazensky was terrible, but none of us was in a position to do anything about it. Mainly because we were so closely involved, however, I think we have an important role to play in protecting the rest of the people who are in danger. Whatever information we can glean from this experience may prove valuable later on." He drank some orange juice.

"If I hadn't suggested the Deer Park ..." began Karen.

"And if cows had wings ..." added Lani.

"All right," said Karen resignedly. "I understand what you mean. So what do we do now?"

Lani wiped his lips with a napkin. "Let's each describe the experience from our own point of view. I'll start." He leaned back in his chair. "I first realized something was wrong when I was looking at Krazensky and his bodyguards, just before the deer stampeded. I could tell the deer were restless because of something that had to do with the men, so I checked their auras ... and they didn't have any. The lack wasn't an illusion—actually, even an illusion would give off energy to some extent—so the only conclusion I can come to is that someone, undoubtedly the assassin, was doing something to suppress my awareness. I tried a sharper focus on Krazensky and saw a symbol of a wolf's head. That leads me to believe that the assassin may have been able to get the deer to think that Krazensky really was a wolf and a danger to the herd. That would certainly explain their behavior."

"You really think someone can have the power to do that?" asked Keoki. He was holding a glass of juice halfway to his mouth and had, in fact, been holding it that way for quite a long while.

""Let's deal with that later," said Lani, leaning forward. "I couldn't reach Krazensky because of the deer milling around, and I couldn't even calm them down. Normally I can communicate very well with animals, and I'm glad only you two are here to hear me say that, but it was as if the deer wouldn't listen or couldn't hear me. Another possible indication that my abilities were being suppressed." He paused and looked out a window. "Then I felt as if someone had hit me on the head with a rock, was continuing to hit me, and would continue until I was dead. I fell to the ground and tried to resist, but the pain was intense and everything was going black. Then, suddenly, it was gone. The pain, the sensation of being hit, all of it. My head was clear and I felt normal again. That's when I got up and talked to the guard who told us to get out of there. That's my story. Karen?" Lani leaned back in his chair and looked at her.

Karen clasped her hands on the table and kept her eyes down. "I could not think. I could not move while all that was going on. It was terrible, yes, but in addition I was ... 'blocked' is the best way I can put it. Your mention of having your abilities suppressed, Lani, makes me think that that's what happened with my vision of Krazensky this morning." She changed the position of her hands and took a deep breath. "At the park, I was watching the stampede, feeling very helpless, and then it was if all my energy drained out of me. I don't remember anything else until I saw Keoki above me and realized that I was lying on the ground. As he helped me up I felt my strength returning and then I was okay again." She and Lani both looked at Keoki.

During their recitals, Keoki's mind was a jumble of confused thoughts. He didn't know what he should and shouldn't say about his experience. If he just related the outer events they could miss some vital information about the assassin. If he related the inner events, he would be stepping over the line into the psychic world of Karen and Gramps. By giving voice to the impossible he would make it real, and he was afraid that if he did that he would never be able to get back to his old world again. On the other hand, he knew with a deep knowing that Karen and Gramps had almost died back there. And that there was no reason to think that the assassin would stop trying to kill them as long as she felt they were a danger to her. Funny, he thought, way down inside I always knew that I would have to make this choice someday. And I always believed that it would be during some great event in the middle of a wild storm or something. Instead, it's after lunch in a friend's apartment. A flat, rather. That's appropriate.

90

Karen spoke. "Keoki?"

He sighed dramatically, stretched, relaxed, and plunged over the line. "At Tivoli last night, during the fireworks, I saw someone across the lake, on the pirate ship. I know it was dark, but I saw her anyway, clearly. Just for a few moments. Then she disappeared. Just flickered out, like a light." He glanced at Gramps and Karen to check their reactions. Both seemed fascinated, rather than skeptical. "Later that night I had ... I guess I had what you might call a sort of a lucid dream about her and me in, uh, I guess it was like a past life." No one laughed, so he went on with his tale.

"Today, I didn't notice anything until just before the deer charged out of the woods. Then I saw her again, behind the deer. It looked like her eyes were glowing. She spoke to me, uh, sort of telepathically, like. She said you two had to die. When I looked at you Gramps was holding his head like he had a bad headache and I saw you fall down, Karen, looking pale as a ghost." He paused for a moment, looked around, and down. "This next part sounds crazy, I know. I got really upset, and I think I shouted at her. Then, it was like some old memory took over, like something I used to know how to do well and had forgotten, or hadn't done it in a long time. Like riding a bike or sailing. And then when I had to do it the memory, the skill, came back. Without thinking about it or planning anything. Anyway, I ... wished, I guess you could say, that something would stop her from harming you. I even imagined a ball of fire like from one of my games flying out and blasting her. At any rate it seemed to stop her. Or she stopped for some other reason. She disappeared again, and you guys were okay."

There was a long period of silence while Lani and Karen just stared at him. Karen finally reached over and took his hand. "You saved our lives."

Keoki flushed. "I just did what I did. If I had anything to do with helping you, then I'm glad."

"She's right," said Lani. "I'm amazed at how often you amaze me without even realizing it, Kanoa."

Keoki was saved from further embarrassment by the phone ringing. Karen got up to answer it. She spoke in Danish for a few moments, then hung up and turned back to the others. "That was the director of the Institute. We've been asked to meet with Interpol and representatives of the German government in one hour. To be interviewed about this morning. And to be reassigned in some way."

"We'll have to continue our analysis later," said Lani. "I suggest we tell them everything they want to know, and nothing they don't ask about. Visions and dreams and telepathy and psychic battles are not likely to be well accepted. Since we've been recruited for our paranormal abilities, they will probably be satisfied if we tell them that we are now better prepared to help in locating the assassin. Agreed?"

Both Karen and Keoki agreed that was the best course. Keoki noticed that none of them had even brought up the idea of quitting. It would take them nearly an hour to get to the meeting place, so Karen called a taxi and then helped Keoki put his tie back on.

Ten

Symbols and Shops

Ua ahu ka imu, e lawalu ka i'a
(Everything is ready, let the work proceed)

The meeting took place in the center of Copenhagen in a
smallish room in an unassuming building off *Gammel Strand*
near the Ministry of Cultural Affairs. The director of the Institute was there, along with Madame Villier from Interpol, the
Danish government official who had been at the Skovhoved
meeting, and one other man.

The room was richly paneled in dark oak, and the few places
where a wall was visible were covered in what looked like faded
green silk. The ceiling was high and composed of more dark
oak framing faded paintings of Greek gods engaging in various
debaucheries which no one had looked at for at least twenty
years. Light came from three Georgian-style windows with a
view of trees partially obscuring another building. In the center
of the room was a long, oak table lined with chairs. A plain
white ceramic pitcher of water on the same kind of plate sat at
one end of the table and seven filled glasses of water waited on
the table, ready to quench someone's thirst or to give someone
time to think while they were sipped. The table had many lighter
water rings and darker cigarette and cigar burns. No ashtrays
were in evidence today.

Lani, Karen and Keoki sat on one side of the table, facing
the windows and the others who were present. The director of
PERI was nominally in charge of the meeting, so he opened it
by thanking everyone for coming and then he introduced the
third man, whom the group had not met. "This is *Herr* Nichts of
Department Five, the Security and Defense Department of the

93

Bundesnachrichtendienst, The German Federal Intelligence Service, or BND," he said, and stated that the purpose of the meeting was to clarify details of the unfortunate incident of that morning, and to determine what to do next. Then he turned the proceedings over to Madame Villier.

The Interpol liaison still looked severe, but now she wore a gray suit with subdued pinstripes. She looked cooly at the members of Team Three. "It is my understanding that *Monsieur* Krazensky asked you to meet him at the Deer Park this morning. Is that correct?" All three nodded. "Then will you please tell us what you were doing and what you saw when he was attacked and killed? First we will hear from *Madamoiselle* Gunnarsen, then *Monsieur* Müller and then *Monsieur* McCoy."

Karen told about watching Krazensky and his men approach the intersection. The suddenness of the deer stampede completely surprised her and the horror of what was happening caused her to faint. Lani added that he noticed the deer becoming agitated shortly before Krazensky drew abreast of them, but he didn't make any connection at the time. During the stampede he had tried to reach Krazensky, but the milling deer had prevented him from getting closer and he had been knocked down. Keoki's account included the fact that he thought he caught a glimpse of a woman, in the woods where the deer had been.

"That is what we want!" said the German. "What did she look like?"

Those glowing eyes. "I didn't see her features," said Keoki truthfully. "It was dark in the woods. It just seemed like a woman."

"How tall was she?" asked the man.

Keoki recalled the tree she had been standing next to. "Oh, about five foot five to five foot eight, I'd guess." *And thirty-six, twenty-two, thirty-six?* he wondered to himself as he drank from the water glass in front of him.

"Any distinguishing features?" Keoki shook his head. "Too vague," said the German, turning aside in disgust. "That's useless."

"The very fact that it seemed to be a woman is useful information," said Madame Villier. "Especially considering the Tarot card that was found."

Karen leaned forward. "You found a Tarot card?"

"An odd-sized playing card of some kind," replied Herr Nichts. "It was attached with a type of sticky paste to a tree near the place of the incident. Obviously it was a calling card of the killer."

"Why obviously?" asked Karen.

The German looked at her as if gauging whether she was worth answering. He shrugged as if to imply that he didn't think so, but was willing to give it a shot. "A similar card was found at each of the previous assassinations."

"Was it the same card?" Her interest was evident in her tone of voice.

"I don't know that. I've only seen the reports and they merely speak of an unusual playing card without giving a description." The German took a drink of water just for something to do.

"Could I please see the card?" persisted Karen. "I sometimes use the Tarot in my work and if it is from the Tarot deck it might give us more information."

The man from the BND shurgged again and reached for a briefcase on the floor next to his chair. He opened it, took out an envelope, and from that he allowed a large playing card to slip onto the table, face down. The back of the card featured a multi-colored rosette on top of a multi-colored cross on top of a twelve-pointed star on top of an eye-boggling pattern of swords, disks, cups and wands or staves. Karen's eyes opened wider and her skin became slightly pale.

"What's wrong?" asked Keoki, worried that she might faint again.

Karen continued to stare at the card. "It's ... it's from the Crowley deck," she said.

"Which means?" asked the German, only mildly interested.

Karen tore her eyes away from the card and took a deep breath. "Aleister Crowley was a famous, or rather, infamous, ceremonial magician, or occultist, in the early part of the twentieth century. He and a man named Harris produced this deck in the 1940s, but it wasn't published until twenty-two years after Crowley died. It's the most emotionally disturbing of all the Tarot decks. Crowley had a reputation for dabbling in black magic."

"I've known that some of the PERI members use the Tarot,"

said Madame Villier, "but I didn't know there were different kinds of decks. If so, then the deck chosen by Seeker would be significant." Her hands were clasped as she leaned forward.

"Oh, there are many kinds of decks nowadays," said Karen. "The Tarot is a hobby of mine so I keep up with the latest news. There's the old Marseille deck that Gypsies like, and the Rider deck that most readers use. Among the newer ones are the Russian Tarot of St. Petersburg, very beautiful, and," she glanced at Keoki, "a new Hawaiian deck that's very good, too."

"Fine, fine," said *Herr* Nichts, impatiently tapping a finger on the card that lay on the table. "What does this one tell us that's of interest?"

Lani looked at 'Mr. Nothingness' for a moment and decided that the man would be more insulted than pleased by a Hawaiian speaking fluent German, so he said in English, "The choice of the Crowley deck tells us about the state of mind of the assassin. It's complex, convoluted, arrogant, fearful, and she wants us to think she has vast realms of mysterious powers at her command."

"Are you also a Tarot expert?" asked the German, looking at Lani skeptically.

"I just know something about Crowley," said the Hawaiian.

Keoki gazed at his grandfather in amazement. The old man sure got around.

"We'll know more if we turn the card over," said Karen in a small voice.

For a moment no one seemed to want to touch it. Finally the German growled, "It's only a card," and flipped it over. For another moment everyone held their breath without realizing they were doing it.

The face of the card held a picture, framed in blue. In the top of the frame was the Roman numeral for thirteen. In the bottom of the frame was the word "TRUMPS" in faded capitals, and behind that, making it hard to see, was the somewhat darker word, "Death." Prominently in the foreground of the picture was a skeleton with a horned helmet in what seemed to be a frenzied dance while holding a scythe. The rest of the picture contained a variety of symbols scattered about in apparently random order, including a scorpion, a fish, an eagle, some human-like forms, and a number of serpents. The whole thing had a strange, twisting effect on the mind. Madame Villier reached out and turned the card over.

"Crowley had a real knack for disturbing people," said Lani dryly.

The intelligence man swept his gaze from Lani to Karen. "Did you learn anything from that, other than the obvious relationship with death?" It sounded like a challenge.

"The Death card may imply disaster, the death of a political figure, political upheaval, or even revolution," Karen said stiffly. "The political figure could be *Herr* Krazensky himself, as well as possibly giving notice of more assassinations to come."

"We have the other members of Krazensky's team under constant protection," said the German, "PERI has its own teams in place. We didn't expect an attack here in Denmark, but now we are on alert and very well prepared. With Interpol, German security forces and PERI all on her trail, Seeker doesn't stand a chance. What more is there to do?"

The fate of PERI Three hung on what was said next. They could either be disbanded and sent home because the other teams were already in place, or they could receive a new assignment on the current project.

"There is something," said Lani. All eyes locked onto him as he continued. "From a psychic point of view, this card has Seeker's vibrations recorded on it. As Madame Villier knows, PERI members often use such objects for what they call 'psychometry,' tuning into whoever was last in contact with the object and possibly getting a location."

"Can you do that now?" asked the German.

Lani grimaced. "Tuning in accurately requires a different kind of physical and emotional environment. With this card, which was probably handled directly by Seeker, and with the nearness to her aura which we experienced this morning, I think the three of us stand the best chance of using our psychic abilities to locate her. So ..." he paused.

"Yes?" asked Madame Villier.

In spite of his earlier decision, Keoki still felt a jolt at being included as a psychic.

Lani went on. "I suggest you station our team in some fairly central location and provide us with good maps of the areas you want to cover. We don't have to be physically close to locate her, as long as we have someone in each area that we can contact."

"That sounds like a good idea," said the Frenchwoman.

"We don't want to deal with a lot of false alerts," said the man from BND in a doubtful tone. It was bad enough having to deal with a so-called "psychic assassin," without including sooth-sayers and fortune-tellers in the investigation.

Madame Villier gave him a long look. "PERI is very experienced and practical about this sort of thing. Any information that a team provides is correlated with all other known data before it is acted upon. In an emergency our office makes the decision as to whether an alert is appropriate. With your permission I myself will be the contact for this team."

"Of course, *Frau* Villier," the German said courteously. It wouldn't do to antagonize Interpol unnecessarily, and besides, it meant that he wouldn't have to deal with the crazies.

After a great deal more discussion it was finally agreed that the German government would provide a place for PERI Three to stay and transportation to the location, while Interpol would cover all other expenses. Keoki was surprised at all the financial bickering involved.

Heidelberg was chosen as the central location for PERI Three since it was within easy reach of Freiburg, Tübingen and Munich and also because there was a safe house there that was not currently in use. The German called someone from a phone in another room and then returned to announce that a courier would pick up the PERI team in front of the Central Station at 10 am the next morning and would take them to Heidelberg by car. Madame Villier made arrangements with the PERI director to provide funds for expenses. In a short time the meeting was over, perfunctory goodbyes were said, and PERI Three was out on the street with the director.

There were no objections when the director formally acknowledged Lani as the leader of the team. "I will send someone to your hotel by 9 o'clock tomorrow morning with money for your expenses and train passes for your travel in case it is needed. Are you all prepared to stay for one month? It should be over by then. One way or another." The three said they could do that. "Then I wish you Godspeed and good luck. I will let the other teams know how to contact you and give you their numbers as well so you can keep in direct touch and exchange information. And feel free to go where you think you are needed, even if they don't contact you." He shook hands with each of them, turned, and walked briskly down the street.

"So what do we do now?" asked Keoki. He checked his watch. "It's a little after four."

"We could visit the *Strøget*. Or perhaps *Nyhavn*," said Karen, smoothing out her sweater.

"What're those?"

Lani said, "The *Strøget* is a pedestrian shopping area, and *Nyhavn* is a very interesting area along a canal. Why don't we shop the *Strøget* first. We can get some souvenirs for the family. Then we can go to *Nyhavn* for dinner."

"That would be fine with me," said Karen.

"Sounds good," said Keoki.

Keoki managed to stay next to Karen as they made their along the streets to where the *Strøget* began, keeping her on his left or his right. He thought he was being cooly unobtrusive, but although the others gave no sign that they noticed, Lani was amused and Karen was pleased.

Karen pointed out various landmarks along the way and Keoki realized that she knew a lot more about her home city than he did about his. He made a mental note to learn more about Honolulu when he got home. Copenhagen was a lot older, of course, but he would bet that Honolulu could be every bit as interesting.

Soon they reached the *Rådhuspladsen*, the Town Hall Square, and turned right onto *Frederiksberggade*. They were immediatcly part of a crowd of people filling the street from side to side except where sidewalk cafes or benches for the weary intruded on the space. Such crowds have been likened to a moving sea, but Keoki thought they were more like schools of fish feeding on a reef, some plain and some bright, some looking and some eating, some going in different directions and sliding past each other with intimate unconcern. There were some who were lurking, too, as if waiting for unaware prey to come in closer. This was the *Strøget*, famed thoughout Europe and much of the tourist world.

99

The windows and stores were lavishly packed with goods for every taste and pocketbook, from furniture to art to souvenirs to pastries and practically anything else that one could desire. Karen introduced Keoki to Italian ice cream, an act which transformed her from a woman he was pursuing into a lifelong friend. The names of the flavors were unusual and the scoops were small, but when he tasted the bright red *jordbaer*, strawberry, packed tightly into a tiny cone, he couldn't help exclaiming, "Where in Heaven's name has this been all my life!" And the *hasselnødder*, hazelnut, was so good it almost made him cry.

In a souvenir shop further on Keoki bought a Tuborg t-shirt and a photo book of Copenhagen for himself and, on impulse, a little Viking figure with a horned helmet and fuzzy red hair to put on top of his computer. He started loading up on other small items for family and friends until Lani reminded him they they would be in Germany for quite a while and there would be a lot of stuff there, too.

They meandered happily along the way, enjoying the shops and each other's company while *Frederiksberggade* changed into *Amagertorv* without anyone noticing. Just before it changed into *Østergade* Lani steered them into the Royal Copenhagen Porcelain store. Keoki was reluctant to look at dishware and ceramic statues until he was well inside. Then his artistic side became totally fascinated with the beauty, craftsmanship and creativity around him. He marveled at the delicacy of porcelainware almost as thin as fiber netting, was moved by scenes of farming and social life that wonderfully captured the emotional states of the people, and nearly blushed at some of the more plainly erotic pieces.

Karen told him that the factory which produced the porcelain was started in 1775 and that it originally belonged to the royal family. She pointed out the company's world-famous trademark of three blue wavy lines and suggested that he move away from the naked nymph so that other people could look at it, too. Meanwhile, Lani, who had been there before, wisely went upstairs to where the seconds were being sold and picked up a virtually perfect serving dish with a lilac pattern for Lily, Keoki's mother.

By the time they left the porcelain store it was seven o'clock and all three were starting to get hungry. Even in May it didn't get dark until quite late in Denmark, so there was still plenty of light as they continued along *Østergade* to the big square of *Kongens Nytorv* and across to the small, busy, and colorful harbor of *Nyhavn*.

Eleven

Sheep and Swans

Ho'onóhonoho i Waineki kauhale o Limaloa
(Plans have been established)

Outside of the small town of *Jungshoved*, well south of
Copenhagen, Nazra parked her car on a dirt drive near a country
church. Since the events at Deer Park she had kept her mind
tightly sealed against any intrusion, using the image of an ancient Russian stone fortress with its defenses enhanced by modern weapons and detection systems. The rest of her attention
was centered on driving and nothing else. She had to find a quiet,
isolated place to rethink her strategy and plans. Harald had told
her of a place he had been to on a school outing when he was
younger. "Utterly dull and boring," he had said, which was exactly the kind of place she wanted.

Nazra got out of the small, gray, Renault rental car and
glanced at the church as she started walking. It was a typical
Danish design, a white, stuccoed building about twenty feet wide
by forty feet long with a high false front that looked like a flat-
topped, stepped pyramid. A low, stuccoed wall surrounded it.

Within the wall Nazra could see well-tended flowers, shrubs
and gravestones. She knew that all the churches in Denmark
belonged to the State and that the Protestant ministers were government employees. Harald had told her that most of the churches
were empty most of the time because the free-thinking Danes
had less and less interest in religion, but Nazra didn't know how
much of that to believe. People needed an organized religion,
something to believe in that was larger than themselves. Otherwise their lives would feel useless and confused. That was because humans were basically tribal, like apes. Without a tribe of

some kind they were lost souls.

Marx was right as far as he went, she thought as she walked along, subconsciously following the directions that Harald had given her. Religion was the opiate of the people. But Marx didn't understand two things about that. First, that people needed an opiate, to shield them and comfort them and create dreams for them so that they wouldn't be overwhelmed by a chaotic, infinite, incomprehensible world. And second, that religion didn't necessarily have anything to do with a church or an invisible God.

Your religion was whatever provided you with the benefits of an opiate. It could be an organized set of beliefs like Christianity, or Buddhism, or Islam, or Communism. It could be your family or tribe, country or race. It could be Money, Power, Love or Nature. It could be anything that, in your mind, did the job of an opiate. It could even be opium, or another drug. They were all drugs, all addictions. She smiled ruefully to herself. Her religion was Revenge, carefully planned and well-executed. When she ran out of people in her current crusade, she would find other ways to practice her peculiar religion.

Her walk took her along a dirt path through a grassy field to a wooden gate that was part of a white-painted fence separating the field from a low hill that jutted into the sea in a gradual slope. The path continued beyond the gate and around the point of the slope. There was a light, onshore breeze that carried the mingled smells of the ocean and of sheep. On her right, just a few yards away, was a bay, perhaps a half mile across, where white and black wild swans fed, rested and flew back and forth to land on the slightly choppy water. From where Nazra stood, for as far as she could see in any direction, there were neither buildings nor people.

Nazra passed through the gate and closed it behind her. It and the fence were probably there to keep the sheep on the point, although none were presently in sight. To the left of the path was the hill which Harald said had been the site of a small Viking castle. Nazra walked up the hill, now covered with grass and trees. From the top she had a good view of the bay, the sea, and the surrounding lands. She could easily imagine it as an ideal location for the castle of a local *jarl*, lord, in those ancient days.

103

There were no traces left of such a life except for a shallow, moat-like depression surrounding the hill. On the bay side, Nazra made her way down to a wooden bench placed beside the path and sat facing the water.

First she sent out a "scanprobe," a mentally-constructed, flying robotic eye that acted like a remote viewing device, to "see" with her mind's eye whether anyone else was already on the point, but out of sight. Some people would say that she just imagined such an object floating over the area, but the energy and focus that she was able to put into it went so far beyond ordinary imagination that it was like a different talent altogether. She knew that she had created the probe in her mind, but she also knew that such constructions could be invaluable in helping to extend and focus the ordinary senses.

As she extended her awareness over the point through the probe she determined, with an estimated ninety-five per cent accuracy based on experience, that there was a small herd of sheep, fifteen or twenty, grazing at the far end, and that there were no humans around. Someday, when she met Harald again in Heaven or Hell, she would have to thank him for recommending this place. It was shameful the way he had wasted his talent. And what he had done to those children was intolerable. At least he wouldn't be doing that anymore. Or anything else in this lifetime, for that matter.

To ensure privacy she set up a psychic barrier just beyond the fence, another mental construction, or "thoughtform" as some liked to call it. She imagined it there as a foul-smelling, squishy-surfaced garbage dump, and willed energy into it from her brow center. Though it would be invisible and undetectable to all but a highly trained clairvoyant, it would subtly influence any but the most determined visitors, nevertheless. Without realizing why, most people would simply not feel like approaching. Any who did could be dealt with more directly.

With her location clear and her perimeter reasonably secure, Nazra allowed herself the luxury of some careful analytical thinking.

First, a review of the killing of Krazensky. That had gone very well. Harald's report had allowed her to set it up perfectly. Too bad Harald's peculiar talent wouldn't be available any more, but there was plenty of underused talent in the world and many ways to do the same thing.

Back to Krazensky. She had arrived at the Deer Park at dawn and had located just the right herd of deer shortly after. Enough does and fawns to provide cover and confusion, and two strong males to do the job. She had not had a lot of experience with deer, but the process she had learned to use with other animals worked just as well with them. She had observed them for awhile and then she had modeled their movements, even to feeling the sensations of twitching her ears and a tail. When she was comfortable with that she mimicked their smell. She knew that most animals identified members of groups and sub-groups primarily by smell. It was highly probable that humans used to do that as well, but over time humanity came to rely more and more on sight until most people were barely aware of any but the strongest odors in their environment.

With most animals, how you smelled was far more important than how you looked. You might look like a deer, but if you didn't smell right you wouldn't be accepted. On the other hand, even if you looked like a human you would be accepted if you moved and smelled right. Using the same yoga-based technique that had produced the smell of death at the Institute, Nazra had altered her body chemistry until she was giving off the same group smell as the deer around her. She had projected an image of herself as a deer so that her imitative movements only had to be suggested, not carried through. She hadn't had to get down on all fours and chew grass, for instance. It was enough to maintain the same approximate height and to move her head in the direction of the grass while making the appropriate sounds. Deer habits also allowed her to frequently raise her head and look around at her environment.

In this way she had become an accepted member of the small herd she had chosen for her task. Once integrated, she was able to influence their movement through the forest with gentle nudges of will and imagination until they reached the southeast corner of the crossroads by the hunting lodge.

The memory of the three psychic trackers arriving at the crossroads came to mind, but she shoved that thought aside for later analysis. For now she would concentrate on Krazensky.

Once settled in at the corner of the woods, she had sent out a T-probe, her mental shorthand for a thoughtform probe, to watch for the arrival of Krazensky. When her inner senses, in the form of the probe, alerted her that the former KGB officer was coming with three bodyguards, she began to get ready. She had ignored the guards and projected the form, sounds and smell of a hungry wolf onto Krazensky, and as he approached the deer became agitated. From within the herd she had created the expectation that the wolf was after a fawn. The herd shifted, moving to protect their young, and the males took a forward position as Krazensky came closer. When he was opposite the herd she had generated powerful feelings of attack and escape, and the herd had reacted instantly. As Krazensky looked toward them she had projected an image of herself as Death so he would have a few moments of knowing what was happening and why and by whom.

When the first male had pierced Krazensky's body with its antlers she had felt a surge of joy and had turned to place the Tarot card on the tree beside her. But then ... no, that was for later. Krazensky had died, suitably horribly, knowing who had made it happen.

Analyze the use of the Tarot card, she instructed herself. Originally it had been to let Krazensky know that she was alive and after him. It had been unnecessary to leave it on the tree this morning, so why did she do it? The card made it clear that she was behind the incident and that would increase the intensity of the search for her. Where was the benefit? Hah, of course. She wanted, needed, recognition. She wanted her talent to be appreciated. And she wanted, needed, the challenge.

The more difficult it was, the more each success proved her skill. The question was whether the risk was worth the benefit. Is it? She thought seriously about it and decided that it was. The emotional charge of succeeding fueled the motivation to continue. It might end with her own death, but then every life did. Better to live dancing on the edge of life than cowering in the middle from fear.

Nazra stopped thinking, got up and stretched. A white swan had paddled up to the shore, wondering if this human might provide a free handout of bread crumbs. To the left a few sheep were slowly grazing their way toward her. The breeze had picked up a little and there were more whitecaps in the bay. She put her hands in the pockets of her coat and decided to tackle her analysis of the trackers while walking. She felt a curious reluctance to do it, but her disciplined will had no trouble in overcoming that.

First, the girl. She was quite good at what she did, but it had been easy to distract her by planting a subconscious thought of danger to her if she focused on Krazensky.

Nazra took a deep breath, barely aware of the grazing sheep as she walked among and beyond them. Now the old one. Power unlike any she had ever encountered. Confidence as solid as steel. No, wrong analogy. As solid as granite. It felt like a natural confidence, not a manufactured one like hers. No way she could tell to shake it, so she had used it.

She had known immediately when he had entered the park. She had felt his energy seeking her own. Fortunately, the ruse that she had devised had worked. In addition to blending her energy with her environment, she had added a layer attuned to him alone, essentially giving him the pattern of a false park to lull his senses. She hadn't had to recreate the whole park, of course. Just the small area she was in. There she overlaid a pattern of peaceful deer with her absent. His very confidence made him assume that his sensing was accurate. She had had to suppress the energy fields of Krazensky and his guards to keep their natural sensitivity to danger from detecting that anything was wrong. That was probably what had finally alerted the older one. She smiled to herself. Too late to do any good for the Russian, however.

Her inner smile vanished abruptly. She stopped, now feeling the chill of the ocean breeze and a fluttering in her chest. Grimly, she brought her will to bear. These feelings were unacceptable. Her confidence might be manufactured, but it was even stronger than granite. She imagined a roaring fire and drew energy from that to infuse her aura with a warmth that erased the chill of the wind. She imagined her heart as a finely-tuned machine at the center of an efficient factory that was her body, and the fluttering stopped. She imagined her mind as a computer and began her analysis again.

Item: there was some kind of deep connection between her and the boy. His youth and inexperience made it easier for her to think of him a boy, and it helped to control her feelings as well. She knew about such connections from her research, but had never experienced one personally before this. Most people who did thought it was proof of reincarnation. Perhaps, but that was irrelevant. Such ideas were not of any use to her unless she could use them against someone. She would keep this one in reserve in case the boy could be swayed by it.

Item: the same connection enabled the boy to penetrate her normal layers of concealment. He had seen her at Tivoli and at the Deer Park when no one else did. In both cases she had been able to shift to an alternate pattern and evade his awareness. In the future she would confine herself to those patterns if she needed to conceal herself from him.

Item: she had successfully triggered near-death memories in the older man and the girl. There was a temptation to refer to the former as the "old" man, but that involved a potential danger of not taking him seriously enough. She didn't have to know exactly what the memories she triggered were about. During her training she had discovered a generic pattern of thought and feeling that would evoke such memories in anyone who had them. The more sensitive a person was to outside influence, the stronger the recall. Then it was only a question of energizing the thought until the person literally killed himself. It was particularly effective with psychics, especially if they had no time to put up a mental shield. It had worked very well with the girl and the older man.

Item: she had underestimated the boy's power. He was not a trained psychic and his energy was undisciplined. However, in a crisis he was able to send her a psychic blast of tremendous power. Enough to startle her, distract her, and send her into flight. There was no intent to kill her, though. Only to stop her. What he did was brought on by his concern for the others. The fact that he did not intend to harm her might also prove useful later on. The fact that he was able to do what he did indicated a well-developed skill of imagination. That could also be used against him if necessary.

Related conclusion: avoid the older man and the boy if possible; if not, lure them away from each other and eliminate them in isolation by turn.

Looking outward, Nazra found herself on the farthest end of the point, with water on both sides of her. To her left was a small beach that ended in an outcropping of rocks and thick brush. She took a deep breath, held it long enough to get the right carbon/oxygen mix to increase the amount of oxygen absorbed into her blood cells, and went back inside herself.

New item: there were now experienced psychics searching for her as well as German intelligence agents. This would certainly make the game more interesting. Killing Balenkov and Lernov had been far too easy.

Item: she would need help for the next three kills. Probably Graben, from Berlin, would enjoy helping her again. And she might pull in Marta from Basel, too. They could take point and rear or shield positions. And if they were caught or killed it didn't matter, of course.

Item: It would be necessary to change appearance again. Perhaps an Italian look this time. Something very feminine. Someone men would wish to impress and to protect.

Related conclusion: the revised plan goes forward, right on schedule.

Nazra came out of her analytical state and blinked her eyes. She took a deep breath of sea air and looked at the clouds, the water, the trees, the sheep and the land. She let the chill of the wind reach her skin again. Then she turned and headed back to the car. Time to prepare for death.

Twelve

The One-inch Punch

'A'ohe e loa'a, he uhu pakelo
(She will not be caught, for she is like a slippery parrotfish)

Nyhavn, or "New Harbor," is a short canal that was built in 1673 as a seaman's quarter. Today it is one of the most famous landmarks of Copenhagen, lined with multi-colored eighteenth century houses and filled with quaint old sailing vessels. What also makes it so popular are the numerous bars, cafes, restaurants, and open-air jazz events. Karen led Keoki and Lani straight to a boat on the canal with a sign, *Restaurant Gilleleje*, at the gangway. She stopped and turned to the men before entering. "Since this is your last night in Denmark—I assume you will go straight home when we're done with our assignment—I made reservations here. It's one of the best places to eat in the whole city and we were very lucky to get a table, even at this early hour."

"When did you do that?" asked Keoki, barely noticing the anchored boat or the narrow buildings on the other side of the canal that reminded him of a similar row of buildings that he had seen in San Francisco. Karen was more enjoyable to look a than they weret.

She touched his arm and smiled. "While you were ogling the erotica and your grandfather was shopping for bargains." She became brisk, as if she expected an argument. "Now, this is my treat and you are my guests. I won't have it any other way, alright?"

"No problem," laughed Lani.

"If you're really sure ..." began Keoki.

Karen grinned at him and led the way onto the boat. More

110

eyes than his followed her shapely form.

The interior was richly decorated with old-time nautical artifacts and decorations. Even the tables were made from oiled, inlaid and brass-fitted remnants of old sailing ships. Candles were on all the tables and there was a wonderful smell of spicy food. They were seated next to a porthole in an area that gave them a lot of privacy. Karen suggested they order dark *fadøl*, draft beer. "Many Danes think it tastes better than the bottled kind," she said. Still following her lead they all ordered *rijsttafel*, rice table, which meant curry-flavored rice with all kinds of meats, fish garnishes and spices.

While the three companions settled in, Nazra watched them from a corner of the bar. She had tailed them from the time they had entered the *Strøget*. Their energy fields hadn't been hard to locate. Her plane wasn't leaving until very late, so in spite of her earlier resolution to avoid them she gave in to a compulsion to study the opposition.

She kept her own field very passive, cloaking herself in a mental aura of gray fog. She'd had to poke the barman to get him to notice her, and now she nursed a glass of Italian white wine to go with her changed persona. She programmed her senses to receive data from the trio and not to give any out. Nazra didn't have Harald's extended aural perception, but as part of her training she had learned to read lips. The lighting was dim, so she willed her pupils to dilate and went into observation mode. She had chosen her location to be able to see the faces of the older man and the girl, and to not have to look at the boy.

"So," said Lani, after swallowing some of the dark, rich-tasting beer from the tap, "we still have some things to consider. Like how the ... let's just call her Nazra to keep it simple. Calling her 'Seeker' just distances her too much. So, like how Nazra was able to suppress or divert our awareness and how she was able to directly attack Karen and I."

Karen put down her fork. "I've thought a lot about the last part. It was the strangest feeling, just as if all my energy was draining away. It reminds me of a time when I was a little girl and I had taken a big drink of some preparation my father had made for poisoning rats. The feeling then was very much the same. They had to rush me to a hospital to pump out my stom-

111

ach and I nearly ..."

"That's it!" said Lani excitedly, causing some nearby diners to stare at him. He softened his voice. "She used our own memories against us! While you were talking I suddenly remembered a time when I was caught in a rock avalanche. After I was knocked down the rocks kept hitting me on the head until I was unconscious. A friend saved my life by covering me with her own body. We were both badly injured and almost died."

Keoki interrupted, waving a spoon around as he spoke. "Wait a minute, wait a minute. What do memories have to do with it. Didn't she just zap you with some psychic energy or something?"

Lani leaned back in his chair. "It doesn't exactly work like that, Kanoa."

"I don't follow you," said Karen. "Are you saying that it really wasn't a psychic attack?" She had already realized that "Kanoa" was his grandfather's pet name for Keoki.

"The whole idea of psychic attack is a myth," said Lani, leaning forward again. He ate a bit of fish before continuing, very aware of the sceptical looks of his companions. "I know that there's a lot of folklore about psychic attack, and there are a lot of psychics and occultists who thoroughly believe in it. I also know that there are those who profit from making you believe that they can either do it or protect you from it. But the whole thing is a myth, like those virus hoaxes you've told me about," he said, smiling at Keoki.

"That's a very strong statement," said Karen. "I personally know people who have been under psychic attack. And what about possession? That's another form of it that certainly exists." Her voice and face were almost belligerent, as if she were defending an article of faith.

Lani raised his glass and took a drink of the dark, draft beer. "I'm not trying to question your beliefs or your experience, Karen," he said softly. "Let's just deal with the case at hand. Nazra didn't use a psychic attack on Krazensky. She got the deer to kill him. We know that she is a powerful psychic, so why didn't she attack him directly? Let's explore the idea that, for whatever reason, she couldn't, or can't. Now, in our case, we each had a different experience. You felt an energy drain and I felt painful blows to my head. And both your experience and

112

mine were linked to actual experiences that we've had before. I'm suggesting that, instead of psychic attack, maybe she knows how to trigger a victim's memories, and to stimulate his or her imagination. Maybe she finds that easier and more effective than a psychic attack. According to what we were told she has had a lot more training in the area than most professional psychics would ever have. If she can get people to kill themselves, or to be unaware of danger, that saves her a lot of effort." Lani went back to eating.

Karen was looking down at her plate and stirring the food around with her fork. "That makes sense," she said.

At the bar, sipping her wine, Nazra was filled with admiration and dread. She admired the skill with which the man had moved the conversation away from a confrontation of beliefs to a discussion of alternatives, thereby allowing the girl to keep her beliefs intact and still be open to new ideas. At the same time, Nazra thought, *This man knows far too much.*

In a brief flashback she recalled her own struggles with the concept of psychic attack. The literature on mental powers was full of dark references to it, yet a parade of supposedly powerful psychics, shamans, witches, occultists and hypnotists brought to the institute had failed to produce a single instance of a psychic attack phenomenon. They blamed their failures on everything from unusually strong auras, to electromagnetic influences, to guardian spirits, to opposing forces. But the glaring fact was that all their supposed powers had no effect on subjects who were unsuspecting strangers.

When she herself was the subject she noticed that, in response to the efforts of certain of the practitioners, she would feel an increased energy flow and the appearance in her mind of images related to her own personal experiences. Some of the imagery stimulated emotional responses of fear and anger, but muscle relaxation and the merest act of will disengaged the emotions from any equivalent action on her part. Likewise, an occasional subject would become anxious or irritated, but would be otherwise unaffected. The potential for influence was there, but it could hardly be called an attack.

The results during fieldwork, however, were amazingly different. In their own environment, among people who knew and sometimes feared them, the experts in psychic attack were outstandingly effective, even at great distances. This aspect of her research made it clear that telepathic influence was real, but highly dependent on factors of expectation and prior experience. This made psychic attack per se unfeasible as a tool for assassination. It taught her, however, the importance for her trade of extensive training in psychology.

As for assassination itself, she had discovered that the most dangerous and successful death-dealing sorcerers around the world first induced as much fear as possible in the victim and then added a generous helping of whatever else was necessary for the deed, including poison, arranged accidents, and outright murder. Of course, they also made sure that the whole event was organized to enhance their own reputations as dangerous sorcerers, because that was good for business.

While Nazra was indulging in her flashback, Keoki turned away from the conversation at the table and casually looked around the room. He saw her immediately, and almost dropped his beer glass. He didn't recognize her physically, though. What he saw was a dark-haired woman at the bar with glowing eyes, and what he felt was the same feeling of connection that had so entranced him at Tivoli. He knew who it was without any doubt.

At that same moment, Nazra became aware of the attention from the outside and a sharp surge of deep longing from the inside. Suppressing that viciously, she tried at first to change the frequency pattern of her aura. To Keoki she appeared to blur for a moment. Without thinking about it, he shifted his internal perspective, the way an artist might who is looking at the features of a person and then looks at the play of light and shadow that makes up the features. To Nazra it seemed as if Keoki were able to follow her frequency changes, and for a moment she was stunned because she didn't think he had that ability.

A moment was all Keoki needed. He was up and walking toward her without a conscious decision to do so. Lani and Karen were startled when he got up, and just followed him with their eyes.

Nazra experienced something she hadn't felt since her early teens—uncertainty. The boy would be right in front of her in seconds and she had to decide quickly what she would do. The

114

room was too crowded to run effectively and she didn't want the boy to grab her because she didn't know how she would react to that. For the same reason she didn't want to stay and speak to him. If she tried to ignore him he would probably persist and might even draw the older man over, which she definitely didn't want. Keoki was right in front of her now. She made her decision, and for the first time in many, many years her strange eyes filled with tears.

"Hi," said Keoki.

Nazra gathered all of her energy and attention into her right fist. Among all the forms of martial art that Dimitri Treffsky had drilled into her, her favorite was the Wing Chun system of Bruce Lee. And out of that system, what she practiced most diligently on her own was the one-inch punch. With enough energy and concentration, taught Lee, you could move your fist against an opponent only one inch and produce enough power to explode his internal organs and knock him clear off his feet. The main element, though, was the ability to move the physical fist only one inch while projecting your energy six inches further.

Nazra slid off the stool and stood close to Keoki. He smiled, and she struck. There was a look of total amazement on Keoki's face an instant before he flew backward through the air a good ten feet to land on a table laden with food and drink and surrounded by a very surprised party of six Australians from Sydney. The table turned over, spilling rice and fish and beer, and Keoki, on the wooden floor of the restaurant, and the noise drew the attention of all the patrons and staff. Chairs and diners fell over in every other direction. Drinks were spilled on other tables as diners stood up abruptly, their eyes riveted on the mess and Keoki's inert body. Lani and Karen rushed to his side. The space where a dark-haired woman had stood by the bar was empty, and no one noticed or even remembered that she had been there.

Keoki's look of amazement was not a result of what Nazra had done. It came from what was happening inside him. He had said "Hi," the woman had slid off the stool to stand close to him, and then he had felt a tremendous charge of energy coursing through him. Half a heartbeat later it felt like she had gently pushed him and he had flown backwards through the air to land softly on a table and then on the floor. He was lying on broken

115

dishes, sticky food and spilled drinks, too surprised by the whole experience to move a muscle. Then Lani and Karen were bending over him, feeling for his pulse, prodding for broken bones, and anxiously asking if he was all right. He took a shuddering breath and started to get up.

"Don't move until we get an ambulance," said Karen, trying to push him back down.

"I'm okay, I'm okay," he said, pushing her hand away and rising. Lani leaned back and stood up, looking very thoughtful. Karen was so astonished she remained kneeling on the floor, looking up at Keoki who was standing and starting to brush food off his clothes. By this time the diners had picked up their chairs and were brushing themselves off and restaurant staff had gathered around, some already beginning to clean up. Keoki apologized profusely to the diners and to the *maitre d'hotel* and thanked a couple of waiters who were helping to clean him off. Lani helped Karen to her feet and suggested that it was a good time to leave. She began the process of paying the bill while Lani and Keoki moved toward the door.

A curious thing happens sometimes when a group of people are faced with an inexplicable phenomenon that occurs in an ordinary situation. The more strange the event is, the more people seem to come to an unspoken agreement not to pay any attention to it. If reptilian aliens landed in a spaceship on the White House lawn, that would provoke an enormous reaction, but if those same aliens materialized in a supermarket, bought some Captain Crunch cereal and then dematerialized, the other shoppers would tend to pretend that it never happened. So when Keoki flew through the air in plain sight of diners and staff and crash-landed to cause a messy ruckus, the diners straightened themselves up, the staff cleaned up the mess, Karen's credit card was accepted to pay for the dinner, and the event was quickly ignored. By almost everyone.

When they were well away from the restaurant and on their way back to *Kongens Nytorv* square, Karen couldn't hold herself back any longer. "Well," she demanded, "are you going to tell us what happened?"

Keoki shook his right foot to loosen a wet trouser leg and looked at her. "What did you see?"

116

"I saw you suddenly get up and walk to the bar, and then you jumped backwards like an acrobat and landed on that table. I was sure you must have broken something."

Keoki looked inquiringly at Gramps.

"That was quite a leap," said Lani. "The way you landed it should have hurt, but obviously it didn't. Maybe it's time for you to teach me some things about the powers of mind and body, Kanoa."

"So you didn't see her." It was a statement.

"See who?" the others asked at the same time.

On their way to find a taxi stand Keoki explained that he had seen Nazra, or at least he had seen a woman with glowing eyes who triggered the same sensations he had felt at Tivoli and the Deer Park. He had gone over to confront her and ... yes, he knew he should have told them first, but it wasn't something he had thought through, he just did it on impulse. Then he told of her getting off the stool, the rush of energy, and her sort of pushing him through the air. He was aware of landing on the table, but it felt like hitting a mattress, and the same when he hit the floor. He didn't have any explanation for any of it.

The three walked on in silence until they found a row of taxis. Lani took Karen's hand in two of his own. "Thank you for a delicious dinner and exciting entertainment," he said with a half grin. That got an amused smile from her. "Rest well and keep your psychic doors locked. We have a long trip tomorrow and a lot to talk about and prepare for." He signaled to a taxi driver who came over and opened a door for her.

Karen gave him a peck on the cheek and turned to Keoki. "You are certainly a strange one," she said, and kissed him lightly on the lips. "*Vi ses i morgen*, see you tomorrow." Then she got in the taxi and left.

Keoki was still happily recalling the kiss when Lani said, "I've done a lot of things to impress a girl in my time, but flying backwards is one I never thought of." Keoki gave an embarrassed grin. "We'd better get back to the hotel and see if we can clean up your clothes," his grandfather suggested.

On the way to the hotel in the taxi Lani remarked, "I remember something that happened to me at the university, but I never thought much about it until tonight. I was sharing a flat

117

with two other students. One of them was okay, but the other was a real pain in the *okole*. One night I was trying to study for an exam in our shared living room and he sat down next to me to read a book. That was bad enough, but then he started to munch potato chips and slurp beer. I swear he was going out of his way to make as much noise as possible. First I asked him to stop, and he refused. Then I asked him to study elsewhere, and he refused. Finally I jumped up and shouted at him and he jumped up with his fists raised. He was a lot bigger than me but I was too mad to care. Anyway, he threw a punch and hit me square in the chest and I suddenly found myself about five feet away, still raring to go. He looked at me strangely, said he didn't want to hurt me, and left the room. The oddest part was that I wasn't hurt at all. His punch felt light as a feather. I also remember that I felt so charged up it took me a very long time to get to sleep. It sounds a bit like what you experienced."

"It sounds just like it!" said Keoki excitedly. "Only Nazra, that woman, didn't really hit me. She just sort of poked at me with her fist."

"Hmmm," said Lani. "I'll have to think about that." They made small talk for the rest of the trip. Once in their room, Lani helped Keoki to clean his clothes and then they packed and went to bed.

Thirteen

The Safe House

Aia no i ke au a ka wawae
(Whichever current the feet go in)

The ruined castle was the color of gold in the light of the setting sun. It looked like a scene from a fairytale, or the object of a magical quest from one of the sword and sorcery novels of Fritz Leiber. Keoki was awestruck by the beauty of Heidelberg Castle and its surroundings. Baroque and Gothic church spires rose up from the medieval Altstadt, Old Town, of the famous German city reknownced among university students the world over, mainly because of the rousing drinking song from The Student Prince.

From where he stood on the terrace of the safe house, drinking a glass of local white wine, he could see the lush green hills above the castle to the right, the old city right in front of him, the Neckar River on the left, and the lower hills on the north side of the river. It was so gorgeous, and so exotic from his point of view, that he found it difficult to accept that he was really here. As he was finding other things difficult to accept, too.

The trip from Copenhagen in the limousine had been comfortable, but very long. First they had crossed lots of farmland going south across Zealand, the island on the Baltic where Copenhagen was situated. They had taken a ferry across to Funan, Denmark's 'Garden Island,' had driven through the city of Odense, taken another ferry to Jutland, and then had gone south to the German border and on to Hamburg. It was late when they had arrived and they spent the night in a small, nondescript hotel. There was no time to go sightseeing the next day, but from what Keoki could see as they drove through the city it was just

119

urban sprawl with a great deal of traffic.

From Hamburg they had gone south again through Hannover and Kassel on their way to Frankfurt, passing industrial areas, farmland, mountains and rolling hills with many little villages. They spent the night at another small hotel in a suburb of Frankfurt and waited around most of the next day while the driver took care of some government business. It had been midafternoon by the time they left for Heidelberg. When they arrived there the government driver had given Lani the key to a two-bedroom apartment and dropped them off on a tiny street with very old-looking buildings and cars packed as tightly as possible, half on the sidewalk and half on the street.

After locating the right building, Lani had opened an ancient door to a narrow foyer with stairs right in front of them. Their apartment, or flat, rather, was at the top. There was no elevator and it was five flights, or eighty steps by Keoki's count. Used to the bare stairwells and hallways of Stateside apartments, he had been suprised to see that the landings in front of each flat were highly personalized, with paintings, photographs, posters and knick-knacks.

The door to the safe-house flat had opened onto a short and narrow hallway leading to the left, with one door on the right leading into a very small bedroom and a door on the left for the very small bathroom. The end of the hall opened up into a rather largish living, dining and kitchen area. An extended space on the right held a floor stereo system with cushions around it. On the left, past the dining/kitchen area, was another door that led to a roof terrace.

There were dishes and silverware, but nothing to eat in the cupboards or refrigerator. Karen's German was better than Keoki's, so he was assigned to find the linens, make the beds and stock the bathroom while she and Lani went out to shop. Any protest Keoki might have made quickly faded out when he realized that the shoppers would have to go down five flights and come all the way back up with the grocery bags.

After a lot of searching he finally found the linens and started playing housekeeper. The small bedroom was easy, and so was the bathroom, but it took him another long time to find the second bedroom. He was just about to give up when he noticed a rope hanging from the ceiling to the left of the kitchen counter. He pulled on it and down came a staircase. Climbing up he found a large loft area right under the peak of the building's roof. Other ropes formed a sort of railing around the stairwell and he had to use them to pull himself up into the loft itself. As he faced down the stairs there was a bedroom area on the right with one great big double mattress lying directly on the floor. On the left was an office area with a desk and a computer. Three small windows let in air and light.

Now he knew why some of the sheets and blankets were so large. There would be plenty of room for him and his grandfather, although it would be strange to sleep in the same bed with him. Keoki hoped he didn't snore.

After making the bed he had explored the office. It was very basic, as was the computer, an old Macintosh 6100/66 PowerPC. He sat down on the single wooden chair and turned it on, and he was happy to find that it worked, although it was way slower than his G3. The hard drive contained only the system software and a German version of Netscape 3.0. There wasn't any modem, though, so he wouldn't be able to connect to the internet unless he bought one himself. And if the phone line worked, too.

When Lani and Karen returned he was typing a storyline for a CD-ROM game in SimpleText. Doing illustrations was good, and he was good at it, but someday he wanted to be a writer of games, and maybe books, as well.

Lani shouted his name and he called them up to see the loft. They both climbed the stairs, one after the other, and each of them complimented him on his bed-making abilities. Then he joined them downstairs to help put away the groceries. That didn't take long, because none of them had any intention of cooking meals. There was wine and beer, chips and crackers, two boxes of chocolates, fresh bread and cheese, a box of breakfast cereal, a carton of milk, and a bottle of orange juice. Plus butter, jam, fresh strawberries, apples and bananas, and a small jug of *Obstler*, a mixed fruit brandy.

When everything was put away, Lani opened a botte of Neckar Valley white wine that was still fairly cold and poured three glasses.

"*Prost!*" Cheers!," said Lani, clinking glasses with his two

PERI partners.

"To success!" said Keoki.

"To love!" said Karen. "May it someday fill the world." They all clinked glasses again and drank.

When he had drained his glass, Lani picked up his suitcase and said, "Since I have seniority I have first choice for accomodations. And since I like to sleep alone, I'll take the room down the hall. You kids work out your own thing." With that he went to his room, leaving Karen and Keoki just staring at his departing back.

Karen was the first to recover. "What a sweet old man, Keoki, what would you like to do?"

He didn't know what to say. He finally came out with, "Uh, I could sleep on the couch."

Karen put down her glass, stepped up close, and put her arms around him. "Now that would be silly. That's a very big bed up there and we are two very healthy young adults. Of course, if you have problems with the idea of sleeping next to me, we could always find an old sword in an antique shop and put it between us to make sure nothing happens." She was grinning just like a mischievous child.

Fortunately, she would never know that Keoki seriously considered it. Like most men with a certain degree of insecurity he experienced anxiety when confronted with a confident, assertive woman, expecially one who was beautiful, besides. It had nothing to do with dominance and submission. That was a kind of game that could go both ways. No, what was scary to him and men like him was the assumption of such a woman that she was not only his equal, she expected him to act like an equal to her. He didn't have any roles rehearsed for that kind of relationship. He could be a flirt, a seducer, a protector, a victim... but what Karen wanted was different. She wanted a lover who was also a friend. He wasn't sure he could do that.

By now Karen's grin was fading. She dropped her arms and looked deeply into his eyes for a moment. Then she turned away with a rueful smile. "I guess I'd better take the couch."

What in hell's name was he doing? If he didn't act now he deserved the Stupid Award of the Century! Using something he had learned from Gramps a long time ago, he recalled a hero

122

from some of his favorite movies: he imagined himself to be James Bond, the most confident male figure he could think of at the moment. He let the sense of being Bond enter his bones, his muscles, his skin, and then he touched her arm. "Wait a minute, Karen. The thought of sharing that bed with you just made me speechless for a moment. I can't think of a better way for us to get to know each other. And to improve our psychic communication," he added with a smile.

Karen turned back to him in surprise. His voice had changed, his posture, even his eyes. She had hoped he would turn out to have the strength of his grandfather. He seemed to have it now. Could he really be the kind of man she was searching for? Down, girl. Take it easy. Let it flow in whatever way it flows. She smiled brightly, "Okay, Keoki, let's be bedmates and see what happens. Do you snore when you sleep?"

He chuckled. "Nope. Do you?"

"Just a little," she laughed. "Help me get my bags up and then you go do something manly while I get ready for dinner. A little bit of mystery is good for a relationship. And please don't ask why women have to carry so much stuff on a trip."

So it was that Keoki came to be contemplating the setting sun's reflection off the red sandstone walls of Heidelberg Castle. He had found a role model, had played the role, and it had worked. At least, it had pleased Karen and he had felt good while doing it. But it wasn't really him.

Whoops! He remembered what Gramps would say to that. "Who do you think you are?" Gramps would say, meaning it seriously. "Which set of habits, expectations and beliefs are you?" his grandfather would say. "Which pattern of behavior that you've learned defines you?" he would say. When Keoki had asked him how he defined himself Gramps had answered, "I use the Popeye definition of Self," and had refused to say any more. Keoki had no idea what his grandfather meant until late one night he had flipped on the Cartoon Channel out of deadly boredom and had seen an ancient, black and white Popeye cartoon. When the sailor man sang, "I am what I am and that's all that I am" Keoki suddenly understood. Or thought he did. Now, here on the terrace of a flat in Heidelberg he tried the sentence out on himself. "I am what I am." What did it really mean? Then, in his mind, he heard

Popeye sing the words a bit differently: "I am what I am, whatever I am." The force of that insight made Keoki go back inside
to refill his glass.

He was at the dining table pouring the wine when he saw
Karen in a bathrobe and a towel wrapped around her head come
out of the bathroom and rush up the stairs. "The bathroom is
yours,' she called. "Lani's already done."

Keoki gulped down the wine and went to the bathroom to
take a shower. Afterward he used the toilet, but couldn't figure
out how to flush it. After five frustrated minutes he had to call in
Gramps. His grandfather came in to where the separate toilet
stall was, reached into a hole in the wall, and flushed it. "Only
took me two minutes to find it when I used it," he said with a
tone of pride in his voice.

Because of its particular geography, Heidelberg was warmer
than much of the rest of Germany, so they only needed light
jackets when they went out. On the street Karen and Keoki agreed
that they wanted something German, but not too heavy. Lani
warned them that the phrases "German food" and "not too heavy"
didn't fit together very well, but he had something in mind that
they might like. He led them along narrow streets for several
blocks until they reached *Hauptstrasse*, High Street, the main
thoroughfare of old Heidelberg. It was primarily a pedestrian
mall and on this early Spring evening the tourist shops and cafes
were open, but it was not at all crowded.

Although Karen had been here before on student jaunts she
didn't know much about the city beyond the pubs, so it fell to
Lani to play tour guide. As they walked along he pointed out
some of the university buildings, informing them that there were
four separate university complexes in the town.

He showed them the *Haus zum Reisen*, the Giant's House,
named for the bigger-than-life-sized statue of the original owner
who'd built it with stones from the castle in 1707. Further on
was the *Kurpfälzisches* Museum where they could find a replica
of the jaw of Heidelberg Man if they really wanted to. Neither
Keoki nor Karen expressed any interest in that, so Lani led them
on to the *Heiliggeistkirche*, the Holy Ghost Church, that stood
on Marketplace Square across from the *Rathaus*, the Town Hall.

Lani told them that the church was built in 1399 and that it

124

was very common in Germany for the main church or cathedral and the Town Hall to face each other on a square in the center of town. He wasn't sure, but he thought it was probably a result of the Protestant Reformation and a desire to create a clearer distinction between spiritual and material matters. He had also noticed in his travels through Germany that the decorations on the Town Hall were often not only secular, but so radically opposed to the church's spiritual symbols that they frequently included cavorting Olympian gods and erotic nature spirits.

"Very interesting," said Karen. "When are we going to get something to eat?"

"Right now, hold on, it's just a little further." He guided them along to another square and announced, "This is it. My favorite hangout when I came to visit. *Zum Sepp'l*. It's a student drinking club."

Keoki found it hard to imagine his grandfather as a student drinking with a rowdy group of friends. Karen said, "Oh, I've been here. I like it."

The interior looked every bit like a student hangout. Photographs of former students covered the walls and nearly every available surface had someone's initials carved into it. There were a fair number of early drinkers, if not diners, and noisy conversation blended with the clinking of beer mugs and the odors of sausage and sauerkraut and things more mysterious. There were also lots of shelves with a fascinating array of memorabilia, from Berlin street signs to Alabama license plates.

They sat at a booth and a waiter brought them a menu and took their drink orders. Lani suggested *Altbier*, "old beer," a rather dark beer originally from Düsseldorf with a mild, creamy taste, so they each ordered a glass and in a little while they had made their choices. Karen ordered a local Swabian favorite, *Maultaschen*, a sort of ravioli flavored with onions and spinach and filled with spiced meat in a soup broth. Lani had a hearty bowl of *Eintopf*, a thick beef and potato stew, and Keoki chose a plate of *Bauernwurst*, farmer's sausage, on a bed of sauerkraut.

Their conversation during dinner was casual. Lani told them more about the history of the area, including how and why Louis XIV had sacked the town and destroyed the castle twice near the end of the seventeenth century. All of them commented on how

125

good the food was. Keoki kept raving about the sauerkraut, which was unbelievably better than any he'd ever eaten before, either at home or in a restaurant.

The meal ended, the bill was paid, and they left to return to the flat. On the street Lani said, "Well, we've successfully avoided the topic of Nazra for three whole days now. I called Madame Villier while you two were getting ready and everything's quiet so far. None of the other teams have picked up anything, but as we know from experience that it doesn't necessarily mean that Nazra isn't close to one of the remaining, hmmm, let's call them 'subjects.' Tomorrow we have to go to work. Karen, I don't really know how you like to operate. Do you prefer to integrate our efforts from the start or do you like to work by yourself?"

"I need quiet isolation to tune in properly," said Karen. "Then, once I have some data to work with we can get together and compare notes. If that works for you, maybe I could do my work in the loft while you two do your thing in the living area."

"Actually, Keoki and I work best outside, on the move. I thought we'd go up to the castle gardens first, and then over to the Philosopher's Walk. So you can have the whole place to yourself for most of the day. Is that all right with you?"

"Sure," she said. "I've seen the sights before. You guys go out and have fun and I'll stay at home and work."

"You'll probably be shopping while we do the work," said Keoki.

Karen punched him in the shoulder. "Only to take a break, smart guy."

Lani slowed his pace imperceptibly and let the other two walk ahead. He watched them walking side by side, bumping into each other frequently, knowing it was their *aka* bodies, their auras as Karen would say, magnetically attracting each other. He hoped they would enjoy their mutual appreciation, regardless of where it led or how long it would last. The world could always use more genuine loving. Every little bit added to the healing of the whole.

Fourteen

Anything Is Possible

He 'ike papalua
(Dual knowledge)

Back at the flat Lani turned down the offer of a nightcap and started getting ready for bed. Keoki located two small glasses and poured some brandy for himself and Karen. Then the two of them went out to the terrace and sat down on two deck chairs that they moved close together. Keoki merged again with his version of the Bond persona and just let the pattern take over.

Tentatively, they kissed, they stroked, they fondled. Eventually they got up and went back inside, holding hands. Karen went into the bathroom while Keoki had another shot of brandy and washed the glasses. When Karen came out she smiled at him, and went upstairs. Keoki used the bathroom and went upstairs, too.

When he got to the top Karen was waiting for him, sitting on top of the sheets, completely nude and so lovely it made his heart ache. A small candle was burning in a dish beside the bed, filling the room with its soft, magical glow. He almost made a smart-alecky remark, the kind that he used to make to cover up his nervousness and that almost always destroyed a romantic mood. The Bond persona nearly flickered out, but Keoki noticed and willed it back in. Wordlessly he undressed as he stood there, letting Karen see his full nakedness before he knelt down on the bed and went to her. Then youth, health, desire, friendship and Nature combined to make it a highly energized and very sleepless night.

Morning came early. It's a silly phrase because morning never comes late, but on this morning it seemed apt. Lani came up the stairs to the loft, banged a pan and its cover together, and had the satisfaction of seeing the sheets jump like an earthquake had hit the bed. "Rise and shine, children! Dawn has come and gone, noon is on its way, and work awaits! There's also breakfast on the table to refresh your batteries."

"Noon is still one heck of a way off," grumbled Keoki a little later as he dug into a bowl of cereal. Karen, looking fresh as a rabbit, just grinned at him as she munched on bread and butter and cheese.

Lani and Keoki were out the door before nine, leaving Karen to her isolation. Before they left, Lani had made sure that she had Madame Villier's phone number in case she had an important connection to Nazra.

The day was fair and bright and a bit crisp. Lani had told Keoki to wear a sweater and a short-sleeved shirt, though, because it would probably warm up quite a bit later on. They followed *Plöck* Street toward the castle in silence, ignoring the medieval buildings around them, until Keoki asked, "So what am I supposed to do now, Gramps? You made it sound to Karen like we do this sort of thing all the time and I have absolutely no idea how to go about finding Nazra with my mind."

"Have you forgotten everything I taught you?"

"Not everything," said Keoki, "but I don't remember much. And nothing about finding people."

Lani sighed and patted Keoki on the back. "First things first, then. Do you remember when you were fourteen and we were hiking the slopes of Mauna Loa and you willingly agreed to follow the *kupua* path?"

"Yeah," replied Keoki almost sullenly because he felt guilty about not having done it, "but I really didn't know what I was saying then. What it meant."

"Granted. But that was then and this is now. Here you are with me, and with Karen, and we've been assigned to find a dangerous assassin, one who almost killed all three of us. Your help is needed, but in order for you to do us any good I have to train you, or retrain you, in some of the *kupua* ways. And I can't, I won't, do that unless you're willing to take up this path of your ancestors without any reservations. It's not an obligation, and I won't love you any less if you decide not to. But it is time to

128

decide whether you are willing or not."

Keoki looked around. They were just passing the *Universitäts-Bibliothek*, the University Library. How weird to be making a decision on following a Hawaiian shaman path in the middle of a medieval German city. Still, he knew that he had already made the decision in his own mind and that Gramps just wanted to verify it. "Okay," he said.

"Good," said Lani. "Then we have to do a crash course on basic assumptions and techniques so you can start pulling your weight ..."

Keoki interrupted. "Hey, hey, wait a minute!. That's it? One word and that's it? I'm commited for life?"

Lani let a smile play on his lips. "You want an initiation ritual? Hmmm. For that I'd need *kava*, *ti* leaves, a cloak, my special coconut bowls... How about if I accept your word now and we do the ritual when we get home?"

"Okay, okay." Keoki shook his head with a half grin on his face. Let's go to work."

"Fine," said Lani. "We'll start with a review of basic assumptions." As they walked along Lani said that in the *kupua* tradition of the *Ke'alapunia* family line, their ancestral lineage, there were several different assumptions made about the nature of the universe. Their particular cosmology, as an anthropologist might call it, started with a basic assumption that the universe is infinite. "*Ana'ole, ke ao, ka po*, in Hawaiian. "'The inner world and the outer world are without limit.' It sounds reasonable at first," said Lani, "but taken to its logical conclusion it means that the whole universe is everywhere and that there is no separation between the spiritual and material sides of life."

"Something like the hologram idea," said Keoki. He had seen something on TV, on The Learning Channel maybe, where someone had said that the universe was a hologram and the whole thing was in every part. He wasn't sure he understood it, though.

"Something like that, yes. The two practical sides of that assumption are, in the first place, that in an infinite universe anything is possible if you can figure out how to do it, and, second of all, if I knew how to do it I could find Nazra by connecting with her through this building here, or even through my little fingernail."

129

"Do you know how to do that?"

"Later," replied Lani, contiuing along the street. "According to the next assumption, everything is alive, and that means everything. People, animals, plants, rocks, stars, buildings, cars, computers..."

"Now, computers, that I believe."

"...and every part of every thing as well: cells, claws, leaves, molecules, light, bricks, tires, electricity, everything is alive, as a whole and in its parts.

"So these buildings right here are alive?" asked Keoki skeptically.

"That's right."

"How do you talk to a building?"

"You say, 'Hi, building.'"

Keoki had a coughing fit and had to lean against a wall for a moment. "Thanks, fella," he said to the wall when he had calmed down and was ready to start walking again. "All right. Go on.".

"The Hawaiian phrase for this idea would be *Ola i ka mea nui, ola i ka mea iki*, life is in big things, life is in little things. This assumption isn't just arbitrary. It serves a purpose." By now they had gone past the funicular station that went up the mountain to the castle and beyond, and had reached the corner of the *Fussweg*, the footpath that led up to the back of the castle, and the *Kurzer Bucke*, the much steeper short path of stairs that led to the front. Lani took the footpath and continued talking.

"In general, the scientific community assumes that only a small portion of the universe is alive: plants to some extent, animals to a greater extent, and, at the top of the small heap, us. Everything else in this whole vast universe is considered dead matter or non-living energy. The thing is, there is no way to prove that the assumption is true, even if you make up strict rules about what constitutes life. It has its uses as an assumption, though. For instance, it gives you permission to do whatever you want with dead matter and non-living energy without any ethical considerations other than its potential effect on living matter. The downside is that there's a whole lot of the universe that you have no communication with."

Keoki was listening, but he was also aware that the so-called

130

footpath looked more like an old carriage road, and that it was pretty steep.

"By contrast," his grandfather went on, "the shamanic community generally assumes that everything is alive. However, this assumption cannot be proven, either. The advantage is that you can communicate with everything, as long as you learn the right languages,and that means you can learn from the universe and you can teach the universe."

"Teach the universe?" That was a new concept to Keoki.

"We'll get into techniques later," said Lani. Meanwhile, I just want you to know that these assumptions I'm giving you all serve a purpose. They allow you to do things more easily that other assumptions would make much more difficult or even impossible." Lani noticed that Keoki was starting to pay more attention to climbing the path than in listening to him, so he found a nearby stone bench where the two of them could sit for awhile.

Keoki sat down gratefully. He wasn't in bad shape, but heavy thinking and hill-climbing at the same time could wear a guy out. "Right, the universe is infinite and it's alive. Anything is possible and everything can talk. So why can't I fly and why doesn't that tree talk to me?"

"The answer to your first question is that you don't know how. Remember, I said that anything is possible if you can figure out how to do it. You just haven't figured out how to do it, yet. As for the second question, the tree is talking to you, but you don't know tree language. It's no different than if you were to ask directions from someone along this path and they answered you in Chinese. The answer would be there, but you wouldn't understand it."

"How do I learn tree language?" asked Keoki.

"Give me a drum roll."

"What?"

"Give me a drum roll", said Lani again.

Keoki suddenly remembered how his grandfather had always asked him to do that when he was a kid so he would pay attention to what Gramps had to say next. Feeling a little silly, Keoki rapidly slapped his thighs to simulate the sound of a drum roll, hoping that no one would see him.

"*Makia ke ali'i, ehu ka ukali*, concentration is the chief, activity is the follower. The way you learn anything, do anything, create anything, change anything is to put your attention on it. A little bit of concentration produces a little bit of activity; a lot of concentration produces a lot of activity."

"I remember that one!" said Keoki, somewhat excitedly. "I should. It's the one idea you drilled into me most whenever we met. Every exercise I did would start with me having to focus on what I wanted, and the experience would follow from that. I still use it, when I play basketball or when I'm at the computer and I need an idea. It even helps me fix problems with the computer. I just sit there, wanting to know what to do without efforting, and suddenly I just know what keys to hit or what sequence to change."

Lani smiled. "Remembering that is going to speed up this training considerably. So concentrate on your *la'a kea*, your *aka* body, expanding and helping you to get up and start walking again. I'm serious." Lani got up and began moving uphill.

It took Keoki a moment to recall how to imagine his *aka* body like an energy field, filling him and surrounding him. He imagined it expanding and sending out thread-like lines of force to connect him to his environment. Then he mentally directed it to lift him to his feet and carry him up the hill. He moved his physical body in line with his intent, of course, but he was amazed at how easy it was, how light he felt, and how available the memory was of what to do. He noted that Gramps was already a ways ahead of him, so he directed his *la'a kea* to bring him to Gramps' side. With hardly any effort he was soon walking alongside his grandfather. Wow! Cool!

A little further on the broad, cobbled "footpath" continued up toward a round-topped opening in the castle wall and what looked more like a regular footpath went left through some woods. Lani directed them to the left. "We'll visit the castle later," he said. "For now, just let your *la'a kea* touch the trees and plants around us."

Keoki imagined extending his field further out and, to his surprise, he actually seemed to feel the texture of leaves and bark and to feel the movement of leaves and branches in the light breeze. His first inclination was to call that imagination, too, but then he realized that if it was imagination it was not intentional and had far more vividness than the regular kind.

He picked out one tree up ahead and played with the idea of surrounding it with his field so that he could feel the other side. As he did that the sudden thought of a butterfly came to his mind. He wondered why until they passed the tree and a real butterfly flew off from the side of the tree that had been out of view before. A feeling of excitement infused him.

Soon they came to a stone stairway. Keoki directed his field to carry him up and the climb seemed very easy. At the top he saw that they were in a vast, park-like area with trees, flowers, pathways, fountains and benches. Solitary people, couples and families were scattered throughout the park, walking or sitting on the grass. It was bordered by a low, stone railing on the sides that rose above the woods, by sheer rock on the side that abutted the mountain, and by a large stone wall where it ended below what seemed to be another park or garden area on a higher level.

Keoki followed Lani to the left, where the stone railing formed a corner that looked out over the city and the river. They were higher than on the terrace of the safe-house flat, and seeing the view from a different direction. In the distance, to the west, the tall buildings and hazy air of the new part of the city were visible. More directly below, the rooftops and courtyards of the old city with its romantic charm were laid out before them. On the river near the center of town the *Alte Brücke*, the Old Bridge, crossed over the Neckar River, and just below where they stood was a newer bridge with locks. Lani told Keoki that you could take a boat down the Neckar all the way to Stuttgart. Across the river the multicolored dwellings contrasted beautifully with the green-cloaked hills.

Lani let Keoki remain entranced for ten whole minutes, and then gave him a nudge. "Back to work, Kanoa," he said, using Keoki's nickname. "Let's take this bench over here." When they were seated he said, "Onward and inward. Here's another assumption: *Noho ka mana i ka manawa*, power resides in the present moment. You already know that *mana* isn't energy."

It was almost a question, so Keoki nodded. His grandfather had drilled that into him enough times, too. Gramps had told him that you couldn't really get a good sense of the Hawaiian spirit without a proper understanding of *mana*. Westerners tended

133

to have a terrible time with the concept. Some thought it was magical energy and equated it with things like the Chinese *qi*, the Japanese *ki*, or the Hindu *prana*, none of which it equated to at all. Others thought that it was some kind of mysterious fluid that permeated the universe, which was really closer to the concept of *aka*. Still other Westerners thought it was just a superstition without any basis in fact.

The real meaning was so simple that it escaped most people, even some Hawaiians. *Mana* was no more and no less than a concept of influence. Whoever or whatever had influence of any kind had *mana*. The more influence, the more *mana*. The word 'authority' was sometimes used as a translation because it implied influence. So *mana* could come from strength, skill, position, responsibility, authority, wealth, charisma and even energy. The *mana* of something or someone corresponded exactly to the degree of influence it had to motivate, activate, modify or change the state or behavior of something or someone else. There was nothing mysterious about it at all, and although it might seem magical at times, it was just a practical observation.

"Are you saying that all influence only exists here and now, right in this moment?" asked Keoki.

"Right," answered Lani.

"What about things that happened in the past?"

"Thay happened in the past. They're over."

"But a lot of the things you taught me still influence me. And so do a lot of the things that happened to me."

"Not really," Lani said. "Not any more than yesterday's sun is warming you now. Whatever happened in the past isn't happening here and now. Give me a drum roll. Go ahead."

Keoki slapped his thighs, hoping again that no one was looking.

"Here comes a big one," continued Lani. "The only things about the past that are influencing you right now are your present moment memories of the past. It is what you remember about the past, with your mind and body, that influences you today. The best news is that you can choose the memories that you want to be influenced by, or change the memories whose influence you want to change. If you remember different memories, or remember memories differently, you can change the state of your body, mind, spirit and environment today."

There was a long pause. Then Keoki said, "That's pretty heavy duty."

"Very heavy duty," Lani agreed. "So let's just walk for awhile and let it settle in. Then we'll go through the castle, have lunch, and head across the river to start practicing some techniques.

Fifteen

The Philosopher's Walk

Heaha ka puana o ka moe?
(What is the message of this dream?)

Lani gave Keoki one more assumption before they reached the castle. They were on the upper level of the *Schlossgarten*, the Castle Garden, when he said, "*Ke aloha, ke alo, ke oha, ka ha*, love is being in the presence of someone or something, sharing joy, giving life."

"That sounds like a very present moment thing," said Keoki thoughtfully, glancing around. The grass of the garden area was almost glowing, the brightly-colored flowers were almost laughing, the fresh, green leaves of the trees were practically vibrating. Nature seemed full of joy, at least.

"It is very much a present moment thing," said Lani. "You can't love yesterday and you can't love tomorrow. You can only love today."

"And how long does that kind of love last?"

"As long as you keep loving."

They walked on a few steps along a concrete path bordered by purple petunias before Keoki spoke again. "I'm missing the point. Oh I understand the idea. Mom has said the same thing in different ways and so has Aunty. But so what? I mean, what does that have to do with what you're teaching me now? How is that very noble ideal going to help me in dealing with Nazra?"

Lani couldn't help laughing. "Why do you think you tried to save Karen and me?"

"Well, I guess you could call that love. Sort of."

"Why do you think you're still alive?"

Keoki was startled. "Huh?" He stopped in his tracks.

136

Lani stopped also and faced his grandson. "In the restaurant in Copenhagen, Nazra was really trying to kill you," Lani said patiently. "At least consciously she was. I figured out that she was using a kind of martial arts punch that probably could have scrambled your innards. But it didn't. Because the love between you modified the effect."

That made Keoki highly agitated. "What love? I don't even know her! She's an assassin!" He waved his arms.

Lani said, "Easy, easy now. I'm not saying you love her in any conscious way. But there's something between you. You saw her when she was trying to be invisible, and you could see her when I was trying very hard to and couldn't. And you were able to drive her off at the Deer Park because she didn't want to attack you. And you have dreams about her. Don't tell me there's nothing between you."

Keoki waved his arms some more. "And you're calling this love? Jeez!"

"In a very broad sense of the word, yes."

"A very, very broad sense," said Keoki roughly, starting to walk off again.

"Let's take a bigger look at this." Lani looked around, saw a nearby tree, and steered Keoki over to it. "In a way, since the universe is infinite, love exists between everything. Since the universe is alive and love gives life, then love connects the universe. Let's take the idea down a few notches. Any connection between a man and a woman is a love connection. The stronger the connection, say emotionally, the stronger the love. Of course, there may be a good deal of fear and anger mixed in there to distort the love, to make knots in the connection, you could say, but the love is there, nevertheless." He leaned against the tree.

"Okay, so Nazra and I love each other," said the young man, shoving his hands in his pockets. "Just don't tell Karen, please. And how does that knowledge help us anyway?" Keoki was half upset and half thoughtful about the idea.

"I'll give you a couple of ways," answered Lani. "First, look at where we've come to with the assumptions. Anything is possible, everything is alive, concentration moves energy, it's all happening now, and love connects. What can you think of to do with that?"

137

Keoki turned away and gazed out over the gardens, not seeing them this time. In a few moments he turned back. "How about this? If I skip over any ideas or feelings that it's impossible, and if I knew how to do it, I could put my hand on this tree here, concentrate on Nazra, and ask the tree to use whatever connects us to find out what she's doing right now wherever she is."

"*Maika'i no!* Excellent! Why don't you do it?" Lani moved to stand a few feet away.

The young man's expression showed that he hadn't expected to follow through with his analysis, but he gamely put his hand against the tree, closed his eyes and did the...non-impossible. At first it was only the bark of the tree that he felt, rough and cool in the Springtime air, but then a warm and comfortable feeling flowed up his arm and into his body. It felt like the tree was reaching out and connecting with him. He thought of lines of energy connecting everything in the universe, of the tree being older, more experienced and more connected than he was. He thought of the tree as a friend. And he asked it to search out the connection between him and Nazra and to give him whatever information it could about where she was and what she was doing right now.

There were a few moments of pleasant warmth and amorphous colors. Then, with startling suddenness, he was in a room, looking over Nazra's shoulder toward a window with a view of a church. His vision moved down with his intent and he saw that Nazra was holding a map, but he couldn't tell what it was a map of. At that moment, just as suddenly, Nazra whipped her head around and looked straight at him.

Keoki literally leaped back from the tree and fell to the ground on his rump. A lady passing by pushing a baby carriage stopped and asked in German if the young man were all right. Lani assured her that everything was fine. The young man was just trying out a martial arts technique. The woman shook her head at the foolishness of men and went on. Lani helped a trembling Keoki to his feet and over to a bench near the walkway. Lani waited until Keoki was ready to speak again.

"It... it was weird. Exciting and scary at the same time. I connected with the tree. Made friends with it like you used to

138

taught me to do with plants and animals. Then I asked it to find Nazra. The really scary part is that it did." Keoki paused before continuing. "I found myself in a room, I don't know why I felt like I was there. Anyway, it was like I was behind Nazra, looking over her shoulder, like I was taller than her, or floating in the air. I could see a window, and a church. Then I noticed that she was looking at a map, but I couldn't see any details. Then she looked at me and I just freaked out."

Lani didn't say anything for a bit. Then, "It was probably a good thing that you did 'freak out.' That got your focus away from her very quickly. I don't know the extent of her abilities, but she has already shown some interesting limitations. She may have been able to trace the connection to the tree, but I don't think she could have gone beyond that, both because of the limitations I mentioned and your friendship with the tree. It's even possible that she didn't recognize you, but let's not pin our hopes on that."

"But how..." began Keoki.

"*Pau!* Stop! Give it a rest, said Lani. "You did very, very well, but we have to move away from that area now. Time to get out of *Po*, the inner world, and shift to *Ao*, this outer world. Your connection to her is even stronger than I suspected. First we'll get something to drink and then we'll see at least a part of the castle. Keep your attention on what's around you, here and now. It's important."

Leisurely, they moved out of the garden toward the castle entrance at the garden's west end, passing along the edge of the old castle moat, now dry and grassy. Lani pointed out the 'Thick Tower' with its twenty-five-foot thick walls leaning at a crazy angle over the moat, an example of how seriously the castle was damaged by the French troops of Louis XIV. They stopped at a refreshment stand near the ticket booth for some bottled water, then bought tickets and walked through the entrance tower on a drawbridge across the moat and into the castle courtyard. There weren't too many visitors yet; a few individuals and families like in the gardens, a company of school children giving their teachers a hard time, and a well-organized group of Japanese. In summer it would be jammed.

Keoki was very interested in the statues of knights and bishops and kings on the inner palace wall of Friedrich IV who reigned in the fifteenth century. He went into the castle shop and picked up a couple of souvenir books as references for his graphics work. They didn't have time for a full tour, so Lani steered him into a room on the west end of the courtyard and let him gaze with wonder on the Great Cask built in 1751 which had been used to hold more than 55,000 gallons of white wine gathered as taxes. Lani gestured toward a statue of Perkeo, the well-dressed dwarf and court jester who was said to have drunk most of what was collected. "He was supposed to have been the biggest drinker in Germany. They say he died when he drank a glass of water by mistake."

Passing by the wine bar they went back into the courtyard, made a sharp left, and took a downward-sloping, brick-lined tunnel to the back of the castle which opened onto the top of the footpath they had taken earlier.

On the way back down into town Lani started teaching again. "Tell me what you think of this saying: *Mai ka po mai ka mana*,"

"Let's see," said Keoki. "*Mai ka po mai* is a stock phrase that's used in a lot of prayers and chants, I know that. It means something like 'from Heaven,' or 'out of the unseen world,' or 'from the realm of spirit.' *Ka mana* is 'the power,' or just 'power.' So, 'Power comes from Heaven,' or 'Power comes from spirit.'"

Lani said, "Not bad. Heaven is a missionary translation, however. *Po* means 'the unseen world,' or 'the invisible world.' That's why the same word is used for 'night.' Actually, *Po* could refer to Heaven, as well as outer space, the mind, or your innermost being. In this context, and context is supremely important in Hawaiian, the intention of the phrase is that the source of your power is inside you, not physically, but spiritually. And the same thing is true for anything or anyone. There isn't any power outside of you."

As Keoki grappled with that he stumbled on a cobblestone and Lani helped him regain his balance.

"Okay, look at what just happened," said Keoki. "I stumbled and you caught me. I can accept that the stumbling came from me, but the power to catch me came from you."

"That's only one way of looking at it," said Lani. "It's equally valid, if you accept different assumptions, that your spirit ar-

140

ranged the stumbling and my catching so that you could learn more about the nature of power, and that my spirit arranged the stumbling and the catching so that I could teach you more."

"Which came first, the chicken or the egg?"

Lani laughed. "That's a good Western *koan*, an enlightenment riddle. The answer is 'neither and both.'"

"Oh great!" said Keoki in mock disgust. Neither said any more until they reached the end of the footpath. Keoki opened the discussion again. "You seem to be confirming the popular New Age idea that we create our own reality, is that right?"

Lani grimaced. "No, but that's because I like to think of creativity as a conscious act. To use the Christian story, the universe wasn't created because of some random belch of God. He purposely, willfully, consciously said 'Let it be done!.' I think it degrades the whole idea of creativity to think of it as something that happens without any awareness of the one doing the creating!" Lani stopped speaking, took a deep breath, and chuckled. "I'd better stop before I start ranting."

"You were getting pretty close," said Keoki. They were heading up *Burgweg* toward the Market Place. "Tell me how this relates to what we're supposed to be doing."

Lani smiled and patted Keoki on the shoulder. "In terms of our present situation, it means that it could be extremely useful to accept the idea that no matter how much power Nazra has, she has no power over you unless you agree that she does or fail to question that she does. The more you accept or believe in her power to influence or control you, the more power you give her to do that. As long as we're involved in this, we'd be better off not philosophizing about this assumption. We can do that later, when it's over, providing we both get through it. She's very clever and very skilled, but any power she has over you comes from you. The more you refuse to accept that she has such power, while remaining aware of her skills and knowledge and counteracting them with your own, the more you reduce her influence. Consider this: I'm giving you these assumptions to use as tools for when you actively start seeking her out. We're not playing an intellectual game. This is a very serious, very dangerous situation we're in and I'm trying to squeeze a lot into a few hours to help you get ready for her. If I start wandering off into theory again, please bring me back again. Now I'll shut up and let you think while we find a place to eat."

What Keoki thought about mostly before they found a place was that Gramps was making it sound more and more like this was a personal contest between Nazra and himself.

What Lani thought about mostly during the same period was about the outcome of this affair. He had explored the future probabilities and he knew that Keoki's role would be critical, but at this point there were still too many variables to make an accurate guess about the events to come.

They had lunch at *Hackteufel*, a former student club on *Steingasse*, the street that led straight to the old bridge across the Neckar River. It was a very cozy place, with rough wood tables and lamps hanging low from dark overhead beams. They sat at a table against a wall which was decorated with a mural of some famous professor and his students.

The chef had a spring special that day, *bärlauchsuppe*, bear-leek soup, a light soup made from the tops of fresh, young wild leeks gathered in the woods. Tradition held that it was the favorite food of bears when they came out of hibernation. It was one of Lani's favorites, too, and both he and Keoki ordered it along with two glasses of Pilsner. For his main dish Lani had *Sauerbraten mit Rotkohl*, braised beef marinated for days in a spicy vinegar and cooked in red wine, along with red cabbage, cooked in a similar way. Keoki had *Bratwurst mit Bratkartoffeln*, a thick, fried pork sausage with fried potatoes and smoky mustard. Keoki was surprised to learn that they didn't have any catsup, but Lani assured him that lots of places did, just to cater to American tastes.

They were midway through the meal when Lani asked, "Are you ready for one more more assumption?" Keoki's mouth was full of sausage, so he just nodded. "Then here it is: *Ana 'oia i ka hopena*, Truth is measured by results. For our purposes right now it means that there's always another way to do anything. I'm going to teach you a number of techniques, but don't think that they are the way you are supposed to do things." He ate some beef and drank some beer. "It's okay to be creative and make up your own ways of doing things, and it's okay to borrow from what other people have done. What matters is how well

142

they work for what you want to do." He ate some more beef and drank some more beer. "On the other hand, whatever you do has to be *pono*. That is, it has to be right and good. Not right in the sense of being according to someone's standard, but right in the sense of being ethical, or just and proper for the situation and the people involved."

Keoki swallowed and put down his fork and knife. "You mean that the end doesn't justify the means?"

"I mean that the means determines the end. If Nazra were to hurt me and you went after her singlemindedly for revenge, without consideration for anyone who got in your way, that wouldn't be *pono*. Not only would it not be proper, but it wouldn't be effective in terms of the overall results. You might hurt her back, but in the process you would have hurt yourself and others." He continued to eat.

The young man considered this. "If she hurt you badly, I don't think I'd be able to simply take that kind of goody-two-shoes approach."

"I'm not talking about sweetness and light," said Lani, putting down his silverware to emphasize what he was about to say. "I'm talking about being effective. To keep on with our current example, you could go after her just as intensely, but for the purpose of stopping her from hurting anyone else, or to bring her to justice or whatever else would produce a further practical result. And along the way you would take others into consideration, bypassing them, using them, or moving them aside with the least amount of possible damage. That would conserve your energy, reduce resistance from others, and help lead you more quickly to your goal."

Keoki sat back in his chair. "Whew! That really sounds like cold-blooded ethics to me."

"Not cold-blooded at all," said Lani with a hint of a smile as he went back to eating. "Not hot-blooded, either. Warm-blooded."

They didn't say much for the rest of the meal. Both of them turned down dessert and coffee. Lani paid the bill and they went outside and walked toward the *Alte Brücke*, the Old Bridge from the Middle Ages that crossed the Neckar River. The entry to it was flanked by two towers and covered by a windowed chamber which had once housed well-to-do prisoners. An evil-looking portcullis hung just below the chamber, as if still ready to skewer unwanted intruders. As they neared the passage Keoki noticed a bronze statue of a baboon on the left of the entry. He went closer, but there was no explanatory plaque. He looked quizzically at his grandfather.

"You know," Lani said, "in all the times I've come here all I could learn was that some rich man put it there. I never did find out what it meant." They walked onto the bridge, which was only for pedestrians now. "Start revving up your *la'a kea*, your energy field, Kanoa. Extend it out to connect with your surroundings and make it strong."

They were a quarter of the way across when Keoki asked, "Gramps, I've always wondered what the difference was between the *kino aka*, the *aka* body, and the *la'a kea*. They seem to be pretty much the same thing."

"Well, now that you've wondered out loud I can tell you," he said with a smile. "The *kino aka* is close to what some people call the aura. It's your natural energy field that's in you and around you. It extends out to infinity, because if the universe if infinite, then so is everything in it. However, its intensity and influence depend on your physical, emotional, mental and spiritual state at any given time. When you consciously work with it we call it the *la'a kea*, the 'sacred clear light of awareness'. Then its intensity and influence depend on your awareness, your focus and your intent."

"Heavy," said Keoki, imagining that his energy was expanding out over the bridge in back of him, in front, and off to the sides. Just to make it more interesting he colored it a light blue and added golden sparkles.

There were no more words until they had crossed the bridge and reached the *Schlangenweg*, the Snake Path, a narrow, steep, twisting pathway that led up the mountain. As they stepped onto it Lani said, "Take it slow and easy. We're not in a rush."

On the way up they passed several overweight American tourists who had decided that whatever lay at the top wasn't worth the climb. Keoki realized that he really hadn't seen any overweight Germans so far. With paths like this and no elevators he didn't think it was so surprising.

At the top of the *Schlangenweg* they both stopped to catch

their breath. They had come to the *Philosophenweg*, the "Philosopher's Walk," a long, broad trail on the side of the mountain where, according to tradition, philosophers from the University used to come and think their deep thoughts. Lani turned left, westward and generally downhill, so that the Spring-green forest was uphill on their right and on their left the land sloped down past woods and residences to the river. As they walked without haste they passed several semi-private spaces with benches on the left of the trail, like lookout points where the medieval professors probably spent some time in isolated meditation. Lani took Keoki to one of these and they sat down. Lani silently greeted the spirit of the space and asked it to ensure their privacy during their stay. In return he offered a blessing that the next visitors would be people with happiness to share.

Below them the river flowed westward to their right and beyond it the whole of Old Town was spread out before them. It was warm, but a river breeze kept it from being uncomfortable. Lani let all the spirits settle down. It was fifteen minutes before Keoki showed signs of restlessness.

"Here's the plan," said Lani. "We're going to take an indirect approach because we don't want to set off any of Nazra's alarms if we can help it."

"She has a psychic alarm system?" wondered Keoki.

"Just assume she does for now. You and I will each go to our gardens. We'll call up a favorite animal spirit... you remember how to do that?" Keoki nodded, so Lani went on. "First we'll ask it to visit each one of the subjects and try to find out which one is attracting Nazra first. That will help us avoid a direct link. While the animal spirit is on its errand we will stay focused in our garden, doing anything that interests us. Don't, for any reason, put your full attention on Nazra. If she comes to mind, just move on to another thought or action as casually as you can. Got it?"

"Got it."

"Good." Both men closed their eyes and began to breath in the special way that Lani had taught Keoki thoroughly when he was a child.

Keoki was a little nervous about going to his garden again after the owl experience, but he was determined to go through

145

with this even if it got uncomfortable or scary. After relaxing, he held the intent to be in his garden and very soon the little hanging valley faded into view. He remembered to listen, to see, and to touch. He heard the waterfall's gentle burbling as it tumbled down the mountainside and into the pool. He saw lacey ferns growing on the damp cliff wall. He felt the spray of the water as a light breeze blew it onto his face.

Looking around, the first thing he noticed was that the valley seemed a bit bigger. Also, there was more clear space even though the *uluhe* ferns were still dense. It was so pleasant he almost forgot why he had come, but the chuckling of a gecko on a rock reminded him. As a child his favorite spirit animal had been a monkey, modeled after one he had seen at the Honolulu Zoo. He called the monkey spirit now to help him out.

Keoki waited for what seemed like a long time, looking toward the jungle beside the waterfall. Then he heard a sound behind him and he turned. It wasn't the monkey. Instead, it was a small *pueo*, a Hawaiian owl, that had just landed from the direction of the greater valley below. Keoki felt his muscles clench, but the owl ignored him, preening its feathers as if no one else was around.

Gradually Keoki relaxed as he realized that this was not a man-owl like the others, but just a regular owl of the islands. He waited for the owl to say something or do something, but it just went on preening. Then Keoki remembered that this was his garden and he was the host, so it was up to him to give the first greeting. "*Welina, e ka pueo hoaloha. Aloha kaua. E komo mai.* Greetings, friend owl. Love to each of us. You are welcome here." The thought struck him that he always seemed to speak better Hawaiian in his garden than in the outer world.

"Greetings, friend Kanoa. Love to each of us. Thank you for your hospitality," said the owl. "Did you call me?"

"I called my monkey friend," said Keoki.

The little owl looked at him and blinked once, slowly. "I used to be a monkey. And you used to be a child. We've both grown up."

Keoki was surprised at first, but he had to remind himself that the rules were different in this world. "Well, then. I need some help. I would like you to visit the spirits of certain men I am thinking about and find out which one of them is attracting the spirit of a woman called Nazra. I need to know which one she will go to first. Can you do that for me?"

"We'll soon find out," it said, and flew away, down into the great valley.

Now Keoki had to occupy himself until the owl returned. He looked in the direction the owl had flown and realized for the very first time that he had never, ever peeked over the edge of his hanging valley. Next, he realized that he wasn't going to do it now, either. He looked at the *uluhe* ferns and decided he would do some weeding.

Lani's inner garden was at the bottom of the sea, and it was a busy place. The main part looked like a sunken city that had been restored to glowing beauty, with temple complexes and thoroughfares and markets and many buildings of various kinds. It was a portion of ancient Mu, but instead of being peopled by humans the inhabitants were vast numbers and varieties of sea creatures swimming or crawling their way around, although these did include a good number of quite humanoid sea nymphs. However, the most human-like form was that of Lani himself, who in this world strongly resembled an old comic book character known as Aquaman. Quite close to the underwater city was the mouth of a huge lava tube that led upward to the distant surface of a volcanic island.

The best friend that Lani had in this inner world was hovering in front of him now. It was *Kamohoali'i*, the brother of Pele herself, who could take the form of a shark or a dolphin or a human at will. At the moment he was in his shark form after listening to Lani's request. With a flick of his giant tail he disappeared on the errand, causing a carriage full of starfish children pulled by a violet seahorse to rock in his wake. Lani swam over to calm them down and set about checking the condition of his underwater city.

The sun was a lot lower when Lani opened his eyes. He was seriously troubled, but he waited patiently until Keoki opened his eyes a half hour later. He looked troubled, too. The two men looked silently at each other for awhile, reluctant to say anything at all.

It was Keoki who finally broke the silence. He faced the

river as he spoke. "My spirit animal was an owl, who used to be my monkey. Anyway, he went to get the information and it seemed like a really long time before he returned. I weeded the whole mountain, practically. Anyway, he didn't look so good when he came back. He told me that each of the men was surrounded by huge ravens who attacked him and he almost didn't make it. Could they have really killed him?"

"Let's save that for another time," said Lani. "My experience wasn't any better. My spirit animal started out as a shark and came back after a long time as a dolphin, looking as if he had barely escaped from a fishing net. All he said was, 'Watch out, this one's tough.' The he left, dragging his tail." Lani paused. "Okay," he said. "Since that didn't work we'll try something else. Are you ready?"

"I guess so."

Lani reached out and gave Keoki's knee a reassuring squeeze. "This time, imagine that your field is expanding out to the whole universe, to connect with the spirit of the universe. And ask the universe, in terms of our present purpose, where is the best place for us to be."

Both men closed their eyes again. And opened them simultaneously less than a minute later. "Tübingen!" they said at the same time.

They were still a long way from the flat, so Lani led them quickly down the trail to the west, toward the new town. He projected his *la'a kea* ahead and directed it to bring a taxi to the right spot at the right time. The taxi was there when they reached *Brückestrasse*, at the base of the mountain. "I don't know why I stopped here," said the driver. "I usually do all my pick-ups on the other side." The bemused taxi driver took them across the busy *Theodor-Heuss* Bridge, west of the Old Bridge, and along *Sofienstrass* to *Friedrich-Ebert Anlage*, where the driver made a left and soon dropped them off right on the corner of their street. Lani gave him a generous tip and they rushed to the flat and up the stairs. The closer they had come to the flat the more anxious both had felt.

"Karen! Karen!" Keoki called. There was no answer so he headed for the terrace door.

Lani found the note by the phone before Keoki had reached

148

the terrace. "Wait!" he said. Keoki came back and waited for Lani to read the note. Lani dropped his hand that held the note and let out a hiss of air. "Karen's gone to Tübingen."

"What!"

"Here, read it."

Keoki took the note. In Karen's gentle script it said, "Had an extremely hard time tuning in, so I turned to the Tarot cards. Had just drawn the Moon as the outcome when the phone rang. It was Madame Villier. She said that something terrible had happened at Tübingen and that we must get there as quickly as possible. Don't know how to find you so I'm leaving. Join me as soon as you can. I'll be at the *Hotel Am Schloss*. I think the Moon means that they really need my psychic talents right now. Love, Karen."

"Is that what the Moon means?" asked Keoki.

"It could mean that," said Lani. "It could also mean unforeseen peril and deception." Lani picked up the phone and called Madame Villier. She was astounded to learn that someone had located them and had impersonated her. She could not imagine why the girl had been sent to Tübingen because there was no problem or danger that she was aware of. She would put the agents in Tübingen on alert, but she had no one in that city to intercept Karen. She suggested that Lani and Keoki stay put and she would try to get more help from Munich. Lani put down the phone after she had hung up and looked at his grandson.

"Well?" asked Keoki.

"Pack," said Lani.

Sixteen

Memories

Kala kahiko i au wale ai ka la
(The sun went down a long time ago)

Graben looked at the message that had just been delivered to him by private courier and felt like wetting his pants. The message itself was not so bad. "Meet me in Tübingen soonest" it said. The implications were worse: it meant that Nazra wanted him for another job. That was bad enough, but still not enough to cause sensations of extreme fear. No, it was neither the message nor the implication of having to do things he detested. What caused the fear was the aura of death and the accompanying visions that came with the message. This was a natural consequence of any contact with Nazra, but this time the visions were of his death.

Shaking his head, he reminded himself that his visions of the future were often mistaken. That is, they may have been accurate when he first got them, but things had a way of happening that usually changed the outcome. No, he reminded himself, his specialty was the past. He was always accurate about the past.

Graben sighed and absently fingered the deep scar on his right cheek that gave him his nickname. He was not exactly an ugly man, even with the scar. Nor was he particularly pleasant to look at. His features were regular, but his face seemed to have been roughly molded with lumps of flesh-colored clay. Thin, dirty-grey hair lay limply on his head and his ears were too small to look right. He was rather short, five foot six, and he was neither fat nor thin, neither strong nor weak. His clothes were neat and well-cut, like those of a moderately prosperous businessman. At present he was wearing his blue suit trousers and a white shirt, unbuttoned at the neck. The courier had arrived before he had finished dressing.

His appointment at the *Kronprinzenpalais*, the former crown prince's palace in Berlin used as a government guest house, wasn't for another two hours, so he decided to forego his usual morning coffee at *Cafe Bach* on *Unter den Linden*, the street called "Under the Linden Trees," across from the lavish *Deutsche Staatsoper*, the German State Opera House. With the message in hand Graben went over to his favorite chair, facing the large parlor window of his comfortable flat on *Prinzenstrasse*. A big delivery truck rumbled by and he remembered how quiet this street used to be before 1990 when they tore down the part of the Berlin Wall that ran across it only two blocks away. And then he remembered more...

Soviet agents, KGB as he learned later, had recruited him several years before the Wall came down, when he was thirty-one and a minor functionary in the purchasing department of a state-controlled furniture factory in East Berlin. His odd ability to determine the exact provenance of virtually anything he handled was noted in his personnel file, but was not given much importance. From time to time he was trotted out by the factory manager for the benefit of this or that privileged bureaucrat or military officer to provide information on some supposed antique, but otherwise he merely filled out forms all day and went home to a cramped and cold flat that he shared with three other men he barely knew.

When he was suddenly told to pack and accompany two dangerous-looking Russians he feared for his life and wondered what official or officer he had offended. Was one of his provenances wrong, or was it retribution from someone who had presented a fake? The worry upset his appetite and his sleep all the way to the Narovskaya Institute and even after he had been told of the part he was to play in the great plan to overthrow the capitalist West.

After a year of intensive development of his skill he had been returned to East Berlin and given a post as an assistant curator at the *Deutsches Historisches Museum*, the German Historical Museum. Care was taken to begin establishing his reputation as an expert on provenences, the assessment of data relating to the origins of art and artifacts. Although he only needed to touch something to know its origin, he had learned to make a good show of being an exceptional researcher with abundant contacts in the upper and lower worlds of art. Finally, he received word that it was time for him to cross over into the West. This was still part of the original plan, which had been for him to work his way into a position of easy access to the high and mighty and help pave the way for the assassinations to come.

So one day strangers had come to his office at the museum and had given him a secret sign to prove they had come from Narovskaya. In an alley he had been ordered into the trunk of a car and shortly thereafter, by means he had never learned, he found himself at a police station in West Berlin requesting asylum. Being in the trunk the whole time he knew nothing of the details of the escape, but the driver of the car was apparently convincing enough that before long Graben had his own flat and had set himself up as an independent art consultant. His reputation was already known in the West and soon he had a thriving business as a consultant.

A year after the fall of the Wall he had been taken back to the Institute, which was still operating, for a two-month reorientation. He was still extremely nervous about what he was supposed to do, until he had met beautiful Nazra of the opal eyes.

Her eyes appeared blue when they met, but the moment they shook hands he had "seen" her real eyes and had fallen instantly in love. In the two months he spent at the Institute becoming acquainted with her as his control, that love had remained, almost entirely and against his desire, platonic. Then, the night before he was to leave, Nazra had come to his room and had given herself to him with full and passionate abandonment. At least, that was how he remembered it, and his memory was very good. Now, of course, he knew that it had just been a way of binding him to her, but it had worked for a very long time.

Except for an annual and impersonal reminder of his commitment from Nazra, nothing had happened to interfere with his prosperity or his growing reputation or his occasional visits to the special houses of pleasure that his new influential friends directed him to. So much time had passed that he ceased to believe the plan would ever be carried out.

He had been shocked into a different perspective only recently, while on his way to meet a client at a gallery in one of his favorite locations, the famous Pergamon Museum.

The Pergamon is one of Europe's greatest museums. It sits with other outstanding museums on an island in the River Spree where one of Berlin's original settlements dating from the thirteenth century, *Cölln*, was located. The Pergamon Museum takes its name from a massive Greek temple built on a mountaintop in what is now Turkey in 180 BC. In the nineteenth century German archeologists had it shipped piece by piece to its present location. Graben never failed to experience a deep thrill whenever he entered the great room that held the huge temple altar with its frieze depicting the battle between the gods of Olympus and the Titans.

The same thrill was there that day and he couldn't help smiling as he made his way across the room toward the right to meet his client in the gallery housing the stolen remnants of the great Babylonian Processional Way. Before he reached the door to the gallery, however, he was stopped by a lovely blonde woman with green eyes who spoke to him in German with a perfect Prussian accent.

"Excuse me, *Herr* Graben. I know this is an imposition, but would you please tell me what you think of this artifact?" She held out an object of some kind toward him.

Graben looked her over. She was wearing a trim, cream-colored suit with shoes and purse of the same color, and a green blouse that matched her eyes. She was probably the wife or mistress of one of his friends who had bought a present for her husband/lover and wanted to make sure it was authentic. He smiled and was about to tell her to check with his secretary for an appointment later that day when he suddenly realized she had used his nickname instead of his professional name. Instantly wary, he reluctantly held out his hand.

Without touching him, the woman dropped the object into his open palm. His brain barely had time to register recognition before he was overwhelmed by a vivid memory of himself and Nazra trying to merge themselves into one being on the bed in his room at the Narovskaya Institute the night before he left.

Part of that vivid memory was that, when the love-making was over, he had given her a small wooden angel he had carved for her during his months of pining, a token of love that he hadn't had the courage to show until then. It was the same angel that this woman had dropped into his hand. And the hand that dropped it was the same hand that he had given it to those many months ago. Nazra had come to him.

"*Herr* Graben? Are you all right?"

He opened his eyes. The angel was gone from his hand and he was sitting on a bench next to a wall in the great room of the Pergamon. The woman sat on his right and he slowly turned his head toward her.

"If you are all right, please nod your head before you speak," she said. He nodded. "My name is *Frau* Blitzen," she said firmly, looking into his eyes to make sure he understood. Then, more gently, "It is good to see you, Graben. I thought you were going to pass out, so I helped you over here. Are you sure you are quite all right?"

Graben straightened his shoulders and cleared his throat. He knew what was expected of him and what to do. "I'm fine, *Frau* Blitzen. How good to see you again. What brings you to Berlin this Spring?"

"You, of course," she said with a wickedly seductive smile that threatened to send him into overwhelm again. She reduced it to a friendly grin and said, "In addition to that I need your help. I want an introduction to a certain professor at the University of Berlin."

"Is this... is this...?"

"Yes, it is."

Graben swallowed hard. It had happened. The plan was in operation, even though the great Soviet Union no longer existed. When Nazra told him the name of the target he was surprised and puzzled because he had met the man at the Institute and he had received orders directly from the KGB to assist him in developing contacts when he defected to the West. Graben had assumed the man was a spy and had no idea that the Institute had been closed and that the government had ordered its personnel placed under arrest to await trial. One did not question one's control, however, and so Graben had made preparations for the

154

introduction after leaving Nazra at the museum.

Two days later, Graben, accompanied by the lovely young widow, *Frau* Blitzen, attended a cocktail party at the home of a very wealthy art collector to celebrate the acquisition of a rare Japanese teapot whose provenance had been confirmed by Graben himself. He wore the formal attire required of men at parties given by wealthy Berliners, and she wore a new Paris creation: strapless, low cut bodice, ankle-length with a slit halfway up her left thigh, of a new material so darkly green that it looked almost black, which shimmered with emerald highlights when she moved. Her thick blonde hair swirled around her bare shoulders, matching exactly the color of the antique golden girdle she wore around her waist. She stood out like an orchid in a field of beautiful roses.

Moments after they had each tasted the delicate champagne served them by a waiter, a tall, very handsome man appeared, standing quite close to Nazra, but speaking directly to Graben.

"Good evening, Schultz," he said, using Graben's given name without the honorific, thereby putting Graben down into a servant's class and implying his own higher status. "Ever a fine judge of fine art, I see."

With smiling lips and admiring eyes, Nazra looked over the man who had taught her the science of verbal, postural and gestural manipulation, while her hidden side plotted his murder. How truly attractive he seemed in his formal attire and his kingly pose, with Smile #14 that ran along the border between contempt and invitation. He held his champagne glass like a prop, glanced at her appraisingly, then back at Graben while raising his eyebrows slightly. Knowing he would notice, Nazra transferred her glass to her left hand, fingered the bottom curl of her hair with her right hand for a moment, then brought it up to her chin in a thoughtful gesture, making sure that her open palm flashed briefly toward this handsome 'stranger.'

"Of course, of course," sputtered Graben. "Forgive me. Permit me to present *Frau* Blitzen, who is visiting Berlin to sell some of the African pieces from her late husband's estate." Well done, Graben thought to himself. In one sentence he had shown reluctance to make the introduction, which would increase the man's interest, he had made it known that she was a recent widow,

155

and that she had art, probably very good art, of a kind that the man collected. The jealousy that sprang up in his breast was ruthlessly suppressed. "*Frau* Blitzen, may I present *Herr Professor* Gregori Balenkov from Moscow, presently attached to the department of social anthropology at the University of Berlin."

As the two people touched hands they each had very different reactions.

Balenkov felt a hand that was warm and ever so slightly moist, exerting a bit more pressure than mere politeness called for. Connecting that to her grooming behavior, the showing of her open palm, her barely parted lips, the hint of body movement toward him and the faint odor of *Reality*, he concluded that this was an experienced woman looking for a worthy man to bed, and who had just found one. All of that, coupled with her stunning beauty plus the possibility of other treasures that he might be able to procure at little or no cost, made him decide to definitely follow up on her subtle invitation.

Nazra felt a hand that was warm and strong, yet gentle, giving an impression that this was his character as well. The pupils of his blue eyes were somewhat dilated, indicating an erotic interest in her. Nazra had a flash recall of the hundreds of hours he had forced her through until she had mastered the technique of dilating and contracting her pupils at will, 'rewarding' each step of her progress with the privilege of pleasuring his body. He had on Smile #5 now: sincere interest in her. She gave him back Smile #12: arousal and promise.

Graben cleared his throat to get their attention. His present role was merely to introduce them, let them spend a few minutes alone together, and gether information on Balenkov. "Here, let me refresh your glasses. The champagne is too warm now." He took the glasses from uncaring hands and moved toward the bar. As quickly as he could he passed by the bar and found a quiet corner on the outside terrace overlooking some of the woods left in the *Charlottenburg* district. There he sat on a stone bench under the stars and put his full attention on Balenkov's glass.

Touching Balenkov's forearm with slender fingers, *Frau* Blitzen laughed softly at a rather long and amusing story that he told involving Soviet snowplows and certain sexual practices among the natives of the West African country of Mali which he had visited on a field trip. "The story is amusing, but so is the coincidence," she said. "I think my late husband's collection includes some pieces from Mali, but I'm not sure."

"I'm somewhat familiar with the area," said Balenkov so casually that his interest was well masked. "Perhaps I could come over and have a look at them for you. I have no plans for the rest of the evening." How he would love to see those green eyes in the throes of passion. They even seemed to have dancing lights behind them.

Smile #6: if only it could be so. Nazra touched his arm again, let it linger briefly, then let the hand itself seem as if it were reluctantly backing away. "You are so very kind, but," she sighed, "my plans for this evening cannot be changed. I could give you a private showing of what I have at my place, if you think you could come tomorrow afternoon." The double meaning was so blatant that she was very nearly ashamed of herself. "*Herr* Schultz has kindly assessed the entire collection and had the best pieces delivered to my suite at the *Esplanade*. When he returns he will be able to tell you whether there are any pieces from Mali or not."

At this point Balenkov would have made the visit even if she only had a collection of plastic cups, but it wouldn't do to give her as much as a hint of such an intense interest. With the air of a man of the world who hasn't yet decided whether to indulge a woman's whim, he asked, "If I were able to visit you, what might be a good time?"

Nazra turned her body so that her left shoulder made contact with his arm, looked up at him sideways, and lowered her voice tone a full notch. "I think two is always a good time for meeting in the afternoon, don't you?" At the same time she increased the intensity of her energy field, visualized a roaring fire in the area of Balenkov's groin, and slowly brushed the back of her head with her right hand.

Graben, who had been hovering nearby waiting for her signal, plucked two fresh glasses of champagne from a passing waiter's tray and joined them.

"Ah, Schultz," said Balenkov, glad of the diversion. It must have been this woman's voice that triggered such an embarrassing erection. He took a glass of champagne and sipped, imagining that the chilled liquid was going down further than his stomach. Without any thanks, he said, "*Frau* Blitzen tells me there may be some pieces from Mali in her collection."

The much smaller man handed the second glass to Nazra, who thanked him, and then he looked up at Balenkov. "That is correct, *Herr Professor*. Several in fact." From his contact with Balenkov's first champagne glass Graben knew exactly what would interest the Russian the most, and he would make sure that the right pieces would be in Nazra's suite before noon the next day. "I have already delivered the best examples from Mali to her hotel: a Bambara protective spirit mask and a Dogon altar. Along with other fine pieces, of course."

Balenkov was suddenly aroused in a different way. "You are, uh, certain of their authenticity?" Graben had the deep satisfaction of looking straight into the Russian's eyes, silent and expressionless. Realizing his *faux pas*, Balenkov muttered, "Naturally, I apologize for questioning you."

Graben hid his great satisfaction at forcing an apology from Balenkov, looked at his watch and turned to Nazra. "I'm sorry, *Frau* Blitzen, but we must go. The solicitor will be waiting." There was no solicitor, but it sounded important enough to justify a quick exit. There was no more to be gained from prolonging the contact.

"Always attending to business, *Herr* Schultz, but you are right. We must go." Nazra extended her hand. "It has been a pleasure, *Herr Professor. Auf Wiedersehen*."

"The pleasure has been mine, *Frau* Blitzen." Balenkov took her hand and bowed slightly. "Bis morgen, until tomorrow."

Seventeen

Masks

O ka mea ua hala, ua hala ia
(What's gone is gone)

In the long taxi ride across the city from the suburb of *Charlottenburg* in the east toward *Lützowplatz*, where her hotel was, Graben filled Nazra in on Balenkov's personal tastes and behavior. She had known him professionally, during her training, but even the sexual 'reward' sessions had nothing personal about them. Graben's special talent saved her many days and possibly weeks of background research time. She learned, among other things, that Balenkov was inordinately proud of his size, his stamina, and his strength. Although not inclined to physically hurt his women, he did like to use his strength to force them into doing anything they might show reluctance about, expecially if they were young and inexperienced. The more she heard, the more Nazra looked forward to their next encounter. When they reached the *Grand Hotel Esplanade*, Nazra got out of the taxi, leaned in the window to give Graben some final instructions, and waited until his taxi was out of sight before entering the lobby of the hotel.

The following day was bright and clear, not too warm, and filled with the colors and scents of spring. It was the kind of day that makes Berliners believe they live in the best place on earth.

Gregori Balenkov arrived at *Frau* Blitzen's suite promptly at two. The concierge of the *Grand Hotel Esplanade* had been given instruction by the beautiful widow to direct him there.

The *Esplanade* is a modern hotel, strongly resembling in many ways a museum of modern art. On disembarking from a taxi the guest is greeted by a waterfall cascading down a massive sheet of concrete. The interior is just as dramatic, with an air of high sophistication. Nazra's suite had a light and cheerful aspect, and featured a number of Warhol reproductions, including Marilyn Monroe, who graced the living area. The furnishings were modern, but comfortable, and vases of Spring flowers were abundant. On and beside a table in front of a large window that looked out on the *Landwehrkanal*, a navigable canal that passed through the center of the city, were a dozen pieces of African art. Beyond the canal could be seen the woods of *Tiergarten*, the park so beloved by the citizens of Berlin, and their dogs.

Nazra, as *Frau* Blitzen, met Balenkov at the door to her suite in a forest green caftan with gold Senegalese embroidery around the neck, chest and sleeves. He was dressed casually in a lightweight tan silk suit with an open-necked, light blue silk shirt. They stood for a moment looking at each other without speaking, each trying to make it into a dramatic moment. Finally, Nazra stepped aside and let him in. "The art is by the window," she said. "I'll get you some wine."

Balenkov strode to the table by the window and immediately spotted the Dogon altar and the Bambara mask. The altar was on the left of the table, sitting on the floor. It was made of cast iron pieces, bolted and welded together and painted black. Two crossed pieces at the bottom were formed into a base, and attached to that was a long vertical piece shaped at the top into a crested man with upraised arms. A crosspiece just below it had a similar figure on each end, so that the three formed a unity. Below that more crosspieces had cups or bowls attached to them, ten in all, designed to hold lamp oil and offerings. It looked authentic, but then this type of thing could easily be forged. Schultz had verified it, though, so it was probably genuine.

The Bambara mask lay in the center of the table, its beardlike raffia streamers hanging over the edge. Balenkov lifted it for a closer look. It had been carved by a master. The demon-like horns and features were evenly balanced and skillfully rendered and it had the deep brown color and sheen of old hardwood polished with natural vegetable oils. What a find! It was easily worth ...

"Do you like them?"

The Russian turned and took a glass of white wine from

Nazra. "They are interesting, and they do look like artifacts I've seen in Mali. Do you have any idea what you are going to do with them?"

"Oh, I don't know," she said, looking at the table pensively. "Keep them, sell them, ...or perhaps give them to someone I like."

Balenkov took a sip of wine to keep from shouting, "Me, me, give them to me!" Instead, he said, "The wine is delicious. What is it?"

"*Sancerre*," she said, looking back at him with her pupils fully dilated.

"But you look even more delicious."

"Why thank you, *Herr Professor*."

"In a situation like this you may call me Gregori."

"What a fine, strong name for a man. Then you may call me Moira."

"What an exotic name."

"My mother was a romantic."

"And are you a romantic?"

"I am," she said as she put her wine glass down and moved close to him, "rather more than romantic. How long before we stop playing this game and go on to a much more active and enjoyable one?"

She was his already, and soon the art would be, too. Gregori put down his glass, took her into his arms and crushed her to him to give her a foretaste of the strength that would soon be used to possess her. Her full lips joined to his and her tongue sought his eagerly. He kissed back roughly, letting her know who would dominate this encounter. Her arms wrapped around his broad shoulders and her nails dug into his back. Somehow, though, she had inadvertently stuck one of her nails into a nerve center and it hurt. He shoved her away from him, holding her tightly by her upper arms. She looked properly frightened, so he growled, "Do we play here, or elsewhere."

Passion came back into her eyes and he released her. "Elsewhere is too far," she breathed, then turned around and lifted her hair.

What a hot little animal, Gregori thought as he unzipped her caftan and watched it fall to the floor. What a perfect body, he thought again as she faced him, and truly a blonde.

Nazra began undressing him, doing it with apparent eagerness, but being careful not to tear anything because they would need to go out in public later. He was indeed as large as she remembered. She pressed her naked body close to his amd murmured strange, erotic-sounding words in his ear as she fondled him and ground her hips against him. She whispered in Hindi and said over and over, "Rats piss in your soup, cockroaches crawl in your salad, flies swarm over your meat."

One of the revelations that Graben had produced from the champagne glass was that Balenkov had a deep-seated, debilitating fear of vermin, stemming from a highly-suppressed childhood experience of having been thrown into a garbage dump as a punishment by his father and forced to spend the night there. Like many behavioral scientists he had pursued that profession in a subconscious attempt to resolve his own behavioral problem. Because of that uncontrollable fear he had been recalled from his prestigious position in Africa and had been transferred to the Narovskaya Institute. From her own research and training, Nazra knew that the subconscious could respond to the meaning of emotionally-triggering words no matter what language they were spoken in, as long as a person's logical defenses were down.

Gregori's logical defenses were down and, very soon, so was the rest of him. Nazra slowly stopped rubbing against him and backed away, a look of hurt in her eyes. "Have... have I done something wrong?"

"No, no, of course not," said Gregori, looking down at his limpness in surprise. "This has never..., that is, I, uh."

"Never mind, darling," she said, hugging him warmly. "It happens. But I know what to do. Come with me." She led him into the bedroom, made him lie on his back, and with mouth and hands soon had him virile again. He smiled in satisfaction as she straddled his hips and got into position to lower herself onto him. In getting herself ready she pressed on a little-known acupuncture point about halfway between the outer hip joint and the uppermost point of his left inner thigh which has the function of causing blood to flow from the lower part of the body to the upper, and virility rapidly became debility. "Oh dear," said

Nazra. "Not again."

With a shout of anger Gregori threw her off him and onto the floor. He jumped to his feet, picked her up and threw her back onto the bed. Anger would work, he thought. Anger always worked. "I will have you woman!" he shouted. "I will have you like the animal that you are!" He shouted very loudly and Nazra was glad that the rooms of the *Esplanade* were so well sound-proofed. Gregori forced her onto her stomach, gave her bottom some resounding slaps, and proudly saw himself rising once more. Grabbing her hips he was about to thrust himself into her when Nazra caused her skin to emit a very faint odor of rotting meat and very softly made intermittent buzzing sounds. She heard a cry of forlorn rage and then a thump. When she looked, Gregori was curled up on the floor at the foot of the bed with his face hidden in his hands.

Nazra got up and left the room. She went into another bed-room and calmly dressed in light green slacks, cream-colored blouse, emerald pendant, and sturdy shoes. She brought Gregori's clothes into the first bedroom, lay them on the bed, and knelt down by him. "My darling," she cooed," you must be under terrible stress. The same thing would happen to my late hus-band, all too often. I discovered, however, that if we would spend some relaxing time together everything would be all right again. Please get dressed and forget about what happened. I want you, and I know you want me. Let us not waste this beautiful day. We will have a drink, and perhaps take a walk. Then we will come back and make lazy love, and I will give you whatever pleases you." Nazra waited in the living area, sitting on the sofa and holding the Bambara mask in her hands. It took Gregori ten min-utes to pull himself together, use the bathroom, dress and come out as if nothing had happened. Nazra gave him a smile she had made up herself, #19: all is forgiven; let's look toward the fu-ture. She put down the mask, took his arm, and they left the suite.

They stopped first at the *Eck-Kneipe*, the hotel's beer pub that featured a genuine Wurlitzer juke box. Gregori had *Pils*, a bitter beer, and Nazra had a *Berliner Weisse*, a wheat beer with a dash of raspberry syrup that is a spring favorite of the locals. They talked about art and travel, and then Nazra suggested a walk through the *Tiergarten* woods, not far away.

Leaving the hotel they followed *Lutzowuferstrasse* to *Lutzowplatz*, then turned right onto *Klingelhöferstrasse* until it became *Hofjägerallee* and they were inside the park. Hardly anyone was about at this time of day and Nazra casually led them onto a narrow dirt path through a thick stand of trees. As they walked, Nazra extended her field of awareness until she was sure that there was no one else within a hundred meters of them. She stopped and faced Gregori, smiled, and stomped on his right foot, crushing his instep easily.

Before he could howl with pain she dealt him a careful chop of the hand to his throat, just enough to stop him from screaming, but not enough to stop him from breathing. Gasping, Gregori fell to his knees and Nazra took the time to remove her contacts. Then she bent to grab Gregori's collar and look him in the eyes. She smiled again, another one she had made up, Smile #13a: you poor s.o.b. With great pleasure she saw his eyes dilate involuntarily with fear. "Hello, Gregori," she said in Russian. "Surprised? I learned a lot from you. And I endured a lot from you, as have too many other women. You are a rat of a man, a cockroach of a man. May a thousand flies lay eggs in your eyes and may their larvae devour your brain!"

Gregori tried to rise and she kicked in both of his kneecaps. Gagging, he fell face downward, writhing on the ground. Nazra withdrew a length of 50 kilo test fishing line from one pantleg and bound his wrists. Then she drew out another piece of line from the other pantleg and tied him to a tree. As planned, there was enough left over to bind his ankles to a dead branch she had placed there earlier so that his legs were forced apart. She knelt between them and with a simultaneous blow from each fist she broke each side of his jaw. From a thin leather sheath attached to her calf she pulled out a slim dagger and spun it before the man's agonized face. She gave him Smile #8: devoted love. Using quick, skillful strokes, she detached several vital parts of his anatomy and stuffed them down his throat. As he began to suffocate she took a small nail and a Tarot card of the Rider deck and attached it to his forehead. It was The Hanged Man, reversed.

Brushing her hands, she got up and walked a few meters away to where she had previously stashed a backpack. She emptied the pack first, then undressed and put those clothes into it. With moist disposable towelettes she wiped off all the blood, putting each one of them into the pack, too. Also into the pack went a blonde wig, false eyebrows, the green contacts, and an uncomfortable mouthpiece that had given a different shape to her face. The knife was wiped clean and went back into her calf sheath. False fingerpads were stripped off, rolled up into insignificant lumps, and buried in the dirt.

From the plastic bag she had taken out of the pack she removed and put on jeans, a navy blue sweatshirt with "University of Pennsylvania" printed on it, a blue windbreaker, socks and hiking shoes, and a wallet stuffed with *Deutschmarks*, American Express travelers checks, credit cards, and a new identity. From a last small packet she took out brown contact lenses, properly moistened, and put them in. Finally, she put on the pack and began walking to the central train station, not even bothering to look back.

Graben would send a professional to break into the suite and "steal" the African art, which would be returned to its rightful owner. He would leave half a dozen messages at the hotel for *Frau* Blitzen and then file a lawsuit against her for uncollected consulting fees. Balenkov's body would be found and a hushed-up police investigation would be launched. The hotel staff would eventually enter *Frau* Blitzen's suite and find clothes, money and jewelry still there, which they would claim as payment for unpaid bills. The police might or might not make a connection between her and the unsolved death of *Herr Professor* Gregori Balenkov, but in any case, *Frau* Moira Blitzen would become a permanently missing person, and Nazra would continue her quest for revenge.

Eighteen

Deceptive Voices

Li'u na maka o ke akua i ka pa'akai
(The eyes of the spirit have been filled with salt)

After Lani and Keoki had left the flat in Heidelberg to visit the castle, Karen cleaned up the remains of sleeping and eating and set up a special place to do her work. She used the stereo room because it was somewhat apart from the rest of the flat, it was more informal, and she liked to have music during her "accessing," as she called it.

She piled two cushions so they made a seat of the right height for meditating in a semi-yoga position. From her shoulder bag she took a CD that she carried with her called *Nature's Drums*, by Marc Anderson and Jai Bunito Aeo that combined drums of all kinds with sounds of Nature and that helped her get into the right mental space. She was glad to see that the stereo had a setting for repeat play and she pressed the button.

Around the floor area in front of her she arranged her favorite power objects to give her energy and protection. First, a clear quartz crystal about an inch thick and six inches long, cut flat at one end and and polished to a silky smoothness. This lay directly in front of her with the point facing outward in order to energize her aura and and prevent negative energy from entering her space.

Close to her feet she placed an amethyst crystal of the same size and shape, with its point facing toward her. This would strengthen her soul and guide the spirits to her. On the left she placed a small hawk feather with a red beaded stem that she had received from an American Indian shaman who had given a workshop in Denmark. It's purpose was to call on the protection

166

of the animal spirits.

On the right she put a small, silver Viking hammer, symbol of Thor, to call on her own ancestral spirits. In the very center she placed a polished, heart-shaped piece of Labradorite, roughly two inches square. It was golden brown with areas of brilliant opalescence. This was to call her own band of spirit guides. She picked up the remote from behind her and turned on the music. Now she was ready.

Resting the backs of her hands on her thighs with thumbs and forefingers connected, she softly chanted a sacred word that had been taught to her by her spiritual teacher, Lisbet. In a short time she was chanting in time to the drums, and felt herself being carried along a familiar river that she couldn't see. There were no images, just colors, flowing and glowing.

This went on longer than usual, though. Most of the time, as soon as she felt the river she would hear one of her guides speaking to her out of the mass of colors. But the flowing just went on and on. Finally she shouted the mental equivalent of "Hey. I'm here!. Speak to me." That got a response at last, to her vast relief.

"Greetings, beloved one." It was Dariel, the guide who had been an Egyptian priest ten thousand years ago. Her guides took turns at being the one to greet her in the spirit world.

"Greetings, Dariel. I have come again for your help."

"We are always here to help," said Dariel.

"I seek a woman. Her Earthly name is Nazra. I need to know where she abides in the earthly realm."

"Then I will show you."

Karen waited. And waited. And waited. What's going on?" she thought. Usually an image would come bursting out of the colors right away. It wasn't always easy to tell how the image connected to her question, but the image was always clear and it always came. Except for that time with herr Krazensky, of course. But she was better prepared and protected now. No one could enter and distort her perception. "Hey," she shouted with her mind again. "Is anyone there?"

The colors swirled and another voice spoke. "Greetings be unto thee, fair daughter of Light." This was Clestera, a priestess of the Goddess from ancient Delphi. "What is thy bidding?"

167

"I bid thee seek Dariel, and seek also the location of the Earthly spirit called Nazra."

"At once, O Fair One."

And Karen waited. And waited. And waited. She didn't know whether to be angry or afraid. This had never happened before. Was she no longer worthy? Were the spirits abandoning her? Were the spirits themselves in trouble? How could that be? She would try something else. With all her determination she focused her attention on Nazra herself. "Where are you? Where are you? Where are you?" she chanted into the ethers. She would not give up until she got an answer from someone.

It may have been five minutes, it may have been ten or more. At last a space in the colors appeared, like a transparent window. Through this window she could see a dark-haired, beautiful woman, gazing at her with a look of such utter peace and love that Karen felt herself opening up completely to her. "I'm seeing the Goddess herself," thought Karen. But then the image seemed to break up into little pieces and fade away.

Feeling extremely frustrated, Karen brought herself out of trance and back to awareness of the room. She shut off the music and thought a bit. There was no point in continuing right now. Maybe she really should do some shopping first. She put her power objects back in her bag, stood up, and stretched. She felt awfully stiff. She went into the kitchen for a glass of water and looked at the clock. It was just after eleven. She couldn't believe it. She had been in meditation for two hours! She definitely needed a break from this.

On impulse, she picked up her Tarot deck and went out onto the terrace. She sat down in a lounge chair, pulled out the stack of cards, and shuffled them idly. Instead of doing a full reading, she decided to pick a single card for whatever guidance it could give her. It was The Moon, with its image of a face in profile, eyes closed, inside a bright moon; a path running between two towers; a dog and a wolf sitting on either side of the path; and a crayfish crawling out of a body of water onto the land. Still holding the card, Karen got up and walked to the railing of the terrace, wondering what the card could mean in her present circumstances. Leaning on the railing, she looked over the town to the castle and and began thinking of Keoki. Such a man. And such a boy. He was so good in so many ways, but not quite the ideal she had in mind. Oh well, back to the card...

A sound broke through her reverie. It took her some moments to realize that it was a telephone, the one in the flat. She rushed in and picked up the receiver. It was the voice of Madame Villier, sounding very agitated. "You must come to Tübingen at once," she said in her strong French accent. "We need you here right away. Leave immediately and come to the *Hotel Am Schloss!* I will have someone there to meet you." And then she hung up.

What to do? Karen felt should get Lani and Keoki, but she didn't know where they were or how to find them. They could be at the castle, or in the town, or across the river. It could take hours to find them, and Madame Villier had made it sound very urgent.

Karen was not one to hesitate when a decision had to be made. She gathered her things, wrote a note, and left the flat. The train station was within walking distance, so on her way she stopped in a bank and exchanged *krøner* for *Deutschmarks*. She would have to purchase a ticket on her own because Lani held the train pass, which was for three people.

In Tübingen, Nazra attuned her energy to the person she had just spoken to and smiled, satisfied that her plan was proceeding well. It had taken considerable effort and financial inducement to find someone who could and would hack the Interpol computer system a second time, but it had been done and the information was worth far more to her than the money it had cost. She now knew the names and locations of all the German security agents assigned to the case and the locations of her quarry, as well as the names, locations and backgrounds of all the members of the PERI teams. She even knew how to contact them and why Team Three was in Heidelberg.

What bothered her was that she still knew hardly anything about the young man called George McCoy, except that he was related to Anton Müller. The Interpol records contained no background information on him at all and a Web search only turned up his email address and his physical address in Honolulu. The Interpol records for Müller were somewhat more extensive. He had graduated from the University of Munich, was fluent in

169

German and Spanish, and was a founding member of PERI who was consulted often. He lived in Kona on the island of Hawaii where he had family, but he was a widower. He was not a professional psychic, however, and there was no information on how he came by his esoteric skills. She wished Interpol would improve its record-keeping.

In Heidelberg, Karen checked the schedule and saw that the next train to Stuttgart left at 12:10. There was a local from there to Tübingen at 1:30. She could make it easily.

Karen got off the train in Tübingen at 2:00 pm. She could have walked the dozen blocks to the hotel, but the situation was urgent so she took a taxi from *Europastrasse* in front of the station to *Derendinger Allee*, then right across the *Alleenbrücke* that spanned the Neckar River, now shrunk to a modest stream. After the bridge the taxi took a right onto *Neckarhalde* and brought her right into the *Altstadt*, the Old Town, of Tübingen. Vehicle traffic was not allowed to go any further, unless she wanted to visit the castle, so the taxi made a U-turn and left.

She was at a kind of crossroads. The road she had entered on was fairly straight, but in front of her the narrow, winding streets branched off in four directions. She had told the driver she wanted to go to the *Hotel Am Schloss* and he had dropped her off here. She assumed that was because he couldn't go any farther and she was about to ask directions of someone when she noticed that the hotel was right on one of the corners where there was a sign that said, "To the Castle." She went to the entrance of the hotel and entered the lobby. In contrast to its very medieval exterior the interior was modernized, apparently recently. A German man seated in the lobby got up as soon as she entered and approached her.

"*Fraulein* Gunnarsen? My name is Hans Koenig. I am with security." The form of address he used would have seemed old-fashioned to a modern German woman, but Karen didn't notice. He flashed her an official-looking identity card with one hand and held out his other to grasp hers in a warm, strong grip.

Karen was a professional psychic on an assignment, and she couldn't help picking up information about people she met under such circumstances. "I am pleased to meet you, *Herr* Koenig. I hope you'll excuse me, but I sense that you have a

170

great interest in art."

The man looked startled, almost fearful for a second, but he recovered quickly. "You are right, *Fraulein*. It is a hobby that I do not speak about much in my profession. I'm sure you understand why."

Karen smiled understandingly. He was a pleasant enough man for a German security agent. Not very tall, rather nondescript as a matter of fact, except for the deep scar on his cheek that made him look curiously vulnerable.

For his part, the man who called himself Hans Koenig had picked up a great deal of information about Karen from their brief contact. She was very psychic, but also very trusting. She had a deep need to help people arising from a deprived childhood. She took her own beauty for granted and tried to seek the beauty in others. She had an intimate relationship with the young man that Nazra had seemed so upset about and who was still alive. Nazra knew that now, but it had been a shock to her when she found out. This girl was very familiar with the Tarot and had an eclectic, 'New Age' orientation. The man took out a cell phone. "I will let the team leader know we are coming. She will tell you everything." He turned away, spoke some words, and put the phone back into his pocket. We can go now, *Fraulein*."

Koenig led Karen out of the hotel and onto *Kronenstrasse*, which took them deeper into the Old Town. Tübingen was built among hills by the Alemanians in 1078 A.D., so many of the streets were not only winding, they could also be rather steep. Passing a wide variety of tiny boutiques and retail stores they soon reached *Münzgasse*, a small street right across from the *Stiftskirche*, a beautiful Gothic church also known as St. George's Church, that was associated with the *Stifts*, a boarding school for Protestant ministers-in-training that was founded after the Reformation reached Tübingen in 1534. On *Münzgasse* Koenig took Karen into the upper floor of what was once a famous printing house.

As they entered the fair-sized room with a window looking onto the church, an elderly lady looked up sharply from a map of the city spread out on a table that she had been poring over with a magnifying glass.

Koenig helped Karen off with her coat and made the intro-

171

ductions. "Mrs. Sothby, this is Karen Gunnarsen of Team Three. *Fraulein* Gunnarsen, this is Mrs. Matilda Sothby, leader of Team Four." The members of PERI seldom knew each other well and the membership changed often, so it was not so very unusual that they hadn't met before.

"Well, my dear," said Mrs. Sothby briskly. "You have come at just the right time." She did not offer to shake hands with the younger woman.

To Karen, Mrs. Sothby was a stern-looking woman in her late sixties with blue-grey, frizzy hair and a clipped British accent. She exuded an air of competence and efficiency. "I am pleased to meet you," said Karen. "*Herr* Koenig said you would tell me what is going on, but first I am wondering why neither of you were surprised that my fellow team members were not with me." Karen was trusting, but not stupid.

However, the question had been foreseen. "We have agents at the train station," said Koenig, as he hung up the young woman's coat. "When you arrived alone I was informed and I told Mrs. Sothby when I called. I assume you'll let us know the reason when the time is appropriate to do so."

Relieved, Karen said, "Yes, well, the reason is simple enough. They were out when I got the call from Madame Villier and I was unable to reach them. The situation seemed so urgent that I left a note for them to come as soon as they could and I left immediately. By the way, where is the rest of your team?" Looking around the room Karen could see signs that other people had been working there. There were hats and coats hung on a rack, probably for the cool mornings and evenings. Two used teacups and the remains of biscuits were on a coffee table in front of a sofa. A third cup, still half full, was sitting on a napkin on the map, next to a pendulum, so someone, probably Mrs. Sothby herself, was a map dowser. Another table with a chair held a crystal ball, old-fashioned, but workable, and a third table held some pieces of paper with drawings on them, probably the signs of a remote viewer.

"That is one aspect of the urgency, my dear," said Mrs. Sothby. "Someone, we assume now that it was someone helping Seeker, called here and asked us all to go to where Mr. Treffsky was being guarded, right here," she pointed to a place on the

172

map. "The caller identified himself as a security agent and said that Mr. Treffsky had important information that would help us find Seeker quickly. I did not believe that it was prudent for all of us to leave, so I elected to stay here and sent my colleagues. Mr. Koenig called soon after to say that he found two of the men guarding Mr. Treffsky unconscious in his flat and Mr. Treffsky was missing. When I asked him about my colleagues he said that he had not seen them. So it appears they are missing, too. I trust you see why the matter is urgent."

"I was picking up some lunch for the other men," said Koenig, "and when I returned the flat was a wreck, the guards were unconscious, and *Herr* Treffsky was gone. We do not want to bring the police into this and so I had Madame Villier call you. We need to establish first whether *Herr* Treffsky is alive or dead, and whether he is still in Tübingen. Then we must search for the missing team members and after that we will look for Seeker. I have already alerted our main office, of course, but the sooner we can find out where they are, the sooner we may be able to save some lives. If Seeker had only wanted to kill *Herr* Treffsky she could have done it in the flat, so there is a possibility that she kidnapped him for some other reason and that he is still alive."

Karen turned back to Mrs. Sothby. "And you have had no luck so far?"

"None at all, I'm afraid. There is something blocking me. Perhaps a psychic shield. Will you see what you can get, my dear?"

Karen did not feel comfortable in this room with the other two, but she could not tell why. Still, she had to help. "I need a quiet space to work," she said softly.

"Of course," said Mrs. Sothby. "Mr. Koenig, would you mind stepping out. Perhaps you could guard the door. And I will be quiet as a churchmouse." Koenig left and Mrs. Sothby sat down in her chair with her hands primly in her lap and her eyes closed. "Go ahead, dear. Whenever you are ready just begin whatever it is that you do."

The young woman felt only slightly better with Koenig gone, but this would have to do. For some reason she did not want to put out her power objects, even though Mrs. Sothby had her

173

eyes closed, so she sat on the sofa and visualized her objects in front of her in position to do their work. She closed her own eyes and the colors came right away, followed quickly by the river feeling. Then a familiar voice said, "Greetings, beloved one. How can I serve you?"

It was Dariel!. Karen felt immensely relieved. "And warm greetings you, Dariel. Where did you go before?"

Without a pause the voice said, "We are always here."

Well, she didn't have time to argue. "I have need of your help to find the spirit of a man named Treffsky. Will you seek him for me?"

"At once."

The colors swirled, the unseen river flowed, and in a very short time three images burst forth out of the swirl in quick succession: a castle on a hill, a cage being struck by lightning, and a child running behind a tree. The images were repeated in the same sequence three times.

Karen was so excited about receiving the information in her usual way that she opened her eyes and cried out, "I have something!" Then she remembered her manners and closed her eyes to thank Dariel for his help. When she opened them again, Mrs. Sothby was still sitting quietly on her chair, but her eyes were open, and seemed strangely bright.

"What do you have, my dear?"

Karen took a deep breath to center herself. "I usually get images, and this is what came to me. Three of them, repeated, which is a good sign. I don't understand them, but that's not unusual. They generally have to be correlated with other information before they make sense."

"And what were they?" Karen described them. "Hmmm. A castle on a hill. There happens to be a castle on a hill very close by. Could it be that Mr. Treffsky is being held right here in Tübingen? And a cage being struck by lightning. That's difficult. Do your images ever happen to involve a play on words, my dear?"

"No, never. They are always quite literal, even when they are symbolic."

Mrs. Sothby brushed a hand in front of her face as if she were clearing away a web. "We'll get back to that one. The third one seems clear. A child playing hide and seek. That could mean that they... Seeker and her accomplices, that is, are hiding him in the castle. But if the second image is equally important we have a puzzle. I'm going to ask Mr. Koenig to join us in case he has some knowledge that will help." She went over to open the door and call him in.

After describing the images and her tentative conclusions, Mrs. Sothby asked Koenig if he could add anything. He could. As a young man, Graben, whose strange abilities were just becoming known, had been required to participate in a series of experiments to determine the limitations on his perceptions. In one of those he was placed in a wire enclosure, given several objects, and told to determine where they came from. It was a terrifying experience for him, especially since he had been told nothing about what was going on, and for all he knew the enclosure was a new type of prison cell. In any case, he had been unable to get information from any of the objects. For the first time it felt as he were holding dead things in his hands. When he described his experience to the man whom everyone called *Herr Professor*, the man had laughed delightedly.

Ignoring Graben, he had told another man that this proved his theory of subtle perceptions of electrical waves. Graben was removed from the enclosure, taken home and promptly forgotten. "It sounds very much like a Faraday cage," he said, with knowledge gained since the incident. Such an enclosure, made of wire mesh on all six sides, had been discovered by a Dr. Faraday to have the property of completely blocking the passage of electrical radiation.

Mrs. Sothby tapped her pursed lips with a pencil. "It does seem to fit the circumstances," she said. Inwardly, as Nazra, she did not like the idea. It implied that she should have been looking for a cluster of German security agents, rather than Treffsky himself, and that there existed a simple device with the potential to thrwart her talents. Nevertheless, it was time to be practical instead of resentful. "Let us test the hypothesis," Mrs. Sothby said, moving over to the table.

Bending over the map of Tübingen she lifted her pendulum and let it hang over the symbol of the castle. Map dowsing was something she had practiced assiduously at the Institute because of its far-reaching applications. She could reach out with her mind and energy to seek something, but map dowsing allowed for great precision when there was time for it.

In ordinary dowsing the practitioner uses a pendulum or a rod of some kind—experimenters had determined that neither the style nor the material really mattered except to the practitioner—and walks, drives or flies over a physical location until a particular movement of the device indicates the presence of whatever the dowser is looking for. Amazingly, the same thing can be accomplished by dowsing a map of the same location, without having to leave the comforts of home. An American named Vern Cameron was so good at this that after locating the correct positions of the US submarine fleet during World War II he was officially designated a national security risk and he was forbidden to travel overseas.

As Mrs. Sothby held her pendulum over the image of *Schloss Hohentübingen*, the Renaissance castle solidly entrenched on a hill overlooking the Neckar River, she felt a positive response to her focused thought of a Faraday cage with German security agents around it. Reaching for a pile of booklets, she drew one out that contained a fairly detailed map of the castle. Carefully she directed the point of her pendulum over every room of every floor. Five minutes later she stood up straight and arched her back. "He is in a storeroom on the dungeon level," she announced. "An obvious choice, but one must be certain." Then, in German, she said to Graben, "Go and reconnoiter the area. I will meet you on the castle terrace later."

Nineteen

Transformations

Lele au la, hokahoka wale iho
(I fly away, leaving behind disappointment)

Karen just had time to register the fact that Mrs. Sothby had stepped out of character when the older woman turned to her and smiled sweetly. "That was nicely done, dear. Your clairvoyance has helped us trememdously. Now I think it would serve us best to remove you to another location in preparation for certain other events."

"What are you talking about? Who are you really?" Karen suddenly felt very nervous.

"Why my dear, I'm just an old woman trying to find an old friend." Mrs. Sothby walked to the coat rack and took an arm sling from underneath one of the coats. She put it on and then reached into her handbag and took out a small handgun. Karen stepped backward and Mrs. Sothby smiled. "That's good. It's very healthy to have respect for one of these. The bullets are small, but they are specially designed to break up when they enter the body and tear your inner organs to shreds. Also, they make a small hole going in, but a great, gaping, bloody one going out. Do you understand, my dear?" It was always easier to control people who had vivid imaginations if you gave them something to think about. "There's a pen and paper on the table. I want you to write a note for me. 'Meet me in the tower of St. George Church.' and sign it, 'Karen.' There, that's a good girl."

After putting Karen's note into her handbag she fitted a false cast over the arm and hand that held the gun and slipped it into the sling. The barrel of the little gun was covered by a very thin strip of gauze that made it very difficult to see for anyone not

177

looking for it. "Now, my dear, would you please be so kind as to help an old lady across the street?"

Mrs. Sothby held tightly onto Karen's arm as if leaning on her for support and led her outside. After a short walk the two of them entered St. George Church from *Holzmarktstrasse*, and the old woman guided Karen to the left, near the elaborate marble tombs of the *Württemberg* princes. The church was dark and cool and there were few people about at this hour. With complete confidence, Mrs. Sothby steered Karen to a door marked *Eintritt Verboten*, Entry Forbidden, and made her open it and close it behind them. No one in the church seemed to notice.

In front of them now was a narrow, winding stairway leading up, way up. Mrs. Sothby took off the cast and the sling and motioned for Karen to climb. It was a very long, dizzying climb up the bell tower of the church, through masses of wooden framing and past huge bronze bells. Twice they had to walk across a wooden floor to access stairs on the other side. Finally they reached a small room at the very top. The view of the medieval Old Town and the Neckar River was spectacular, but neither of them was in a mood to appreciate it. "Turn around," said Mrs. Sothby quietly.

Karen was trembling with fear and tears came to her eyes. She was afraid that she was going to die now. She was not a coward and would have fought for her life if there had seemed to be the slightest chance of overcoming the other woman. But she kept thinking of that nasty little gun and what it could do to her with just the slight pull of a trigger, and so she did nothing. She turned, waiting for the pain that would end her life.

As soon as Karen turned away, Mrs. Sothby grabbed her in a choke hold and pressed down on her carotid artery. In a few moments Karen had slumped into unconsciousness. Mrs. Sothby took some cord from her handbag and lashed Karen to some wood uprights, lifting the young woman as easily as if she were made of straw.

Karen came to in a few minutes, feeling her face being slapped. When that ended she became aware that she was spread-eagled against some posts, her hands and feet and waist tied so tightly that she was unable to move them. Then she became aware that she was also tightly gagged. In front of her Mrs. Sothby

178

began a slow transformation. Karen's eyes widened in shock as she saw the older woman start removing things from her face and body.

Mrs. Sothby's wrinkles disappeared, her jawline changed, her teeth became straight and bright, her hair became dark and straight and short, and, when she had taken off her dress and walking shoes, her figure became slim and smoothly muscled. The former Mrs. Sothby, clad only in black briefs and sports bra, smiled at Karen in a different way, and spoke with a very different voice.

"So you are one who thought to pit her skills against mine. It didn't work, as you can see. It never does. However, it was useful when I couldn't find Treffsky myself, even with my friend's help. For that I may just possibly spare your life. Perhaps." Nazra reached into a black leather bag that she must have already hidden here, and took out a very slim, very sharp-looking knife. Karen tried to cry out, but it sounded like a muffled whimper. Nazra stood close and said softly, "I want you to feel totally helpless. You are, of course, but I want you to feel that way." Taking her time, Nazra sliced through Karen's clothing, from the crew neck of her white cashmere sweater down through everything to the bottom of her blue cashmere skirt.

With the thoughtfulness of an artist, Nazra made more slices until she was satisfied with the result. Another thing that she had learned during her training was that people both looked and felt more naked when their sexual parts were completely exposed, especially if they still had on some clothing.

Nazra went back to her bag and retrieved a flat, leather object that was bulbous at one end. When she returned Karen's eyes were squeezed shut, but they opened at the touch of Nazra's leather sap. The touch encompassed every part of her body and that was all she could think of until Nazra said, "I wonder which part of you I should leave intact for your lover."

The pain was excruciating, and it didn't stop. It was unbearable for what seemed like a very long time, and then it was bearable, because she no longer felt anything.

When Nazra was finished she changed appearance again. With thick lashes, pouty red lips, a slight upturn at the corners of her eyes, black boots, black tights, black miniskirt, black knit

179

blouse and black vinyl jacket, Nazra looked like a Eurasian model, or perhaps a call girl, on holiday from the big city. Leaving Karen to suffer alone, the assassin quickly left the church, walked to the *Hotel Am Schoss*, and followed the path to the castle.

On reaching the the castle terrace she sat on a bench next to Graben for a full minute without him recognizing her until she tapped him on the shoulder. "*Wie geht's?* How's it going?"

Graben was getting very good at regaining his composure. After a minor startle reaction he replied, "*Gut*, good. Or perhaps not so good." He knew that Nazra did not like small talk so he got right to the point. "The storeroom is two levels down from where we are. There are two guards at the bottom of each of the main stairways. They cannot see each other, but they do keep in touch by radio. Two more guards with radios are outside the storeroom door, and two are inside as well. Treffsky sits in a cage in the center of the storeroom, very restless. Apparently the guards have recently been placed on emergency alert."

Nazra raised an eyebrow. "You picked all that up by yourself?" She crossed her legs and leaned one arm on the back of the bench.

Graben smiled and rubbed the first three fingers of one hand together. "Ah, well, I had to use some additional talent to get all of that."

"Other ways in or out?"

Graben struggled to keep from looking at her legs. "A third stairway, unguarded, accessed only through the janitor's cleaning supply room, one floor down on the far side of the castle. It leads to a narrow hallway past old cells to a door that gives onto the main hallway which the storeroom is on. I am not sure whether that doorway is visible from the main stairways. Oh, the storeroom is connected by a thick door to to a cell at the bottom of that tower over there, and it has a small, high window that opens onto the wooded area between the castle and the town. The window is quite visible from the outside, though."

"Is it barred?" A small part of Nazra's mind was aware of admiring glances from passing tourists, both male and female.

"I don't know."

Nazra thought for a moment. "Storeroom access?"

"The guards inside the storeroom hold the only key. There are air vents leading into the storeroom, but they are only fifteen centimeters wide and my informant did not know the source of the air. The door to the cell has been locked for many years and no one remembers what happened to the key."

After a minute of silence Nazra said, "Fine. I have my plan. What time do the Hawaiians arrive?"

"6:10." Graben had also made good financial connections in the German Railway service.

"That will give me at least an hour." She pulled a piece of paper out of her black leather bag. "Give this to the younger Hawaiian and say that a young Danish girl gave it to you for them. You can describe her well enough. Then go home.

"Home?" In that one word was a mixture of relief, hope, and despair. "And what about you?"

Nazra reached out and stroked his chin. Here was one person, probably the only one, who truly loved her. "It is likely that you will not see me again, dear Graben. And that is best for you. Take this back in memory of me." She handed him a carved wooden angel, stood up, and walked briskly toward the exit through the elaborate castle gate, leaving Graben looking after her with a strange mixture of wistful longing and the sense of dropping a heavy burden.

Among the many, many things that Nazra had learned in her study and practice was something called "casting a glamour." She first ran across it in the works of Helena Blavatsky, found it again in the works of Annie Besant, and then in various other occult writings. The ability of the Polish Jew turned Soviet citizen, Wolf Messing, to pass for Lavrenti Beria, head of the Soviet secret police, and to enter Stalin's well guarded dacha without any disguise suggested that he knew something about it as well.

Not until she came across secret research files of the British Order of the Golden Dawn, however, did she find anything of practical value. Essentially, the files she read detailed a technique for hiding your true form. It was different from blending in with your surroundings, which required a fair ability to remain still. A "glamour" was more like a cloak that enabled you to move around while looking like someone or something else.

It required a high degree of skill at condensing and shaping your aura, which Nazra had developed, and, in addition, exceptional skill at keeping your focus, which was her forte. So when she climbed the tower wall with the aid of spiked gloves and toe pads, right out in the open, she wasn't noticed by anyone.

The window to the cell was not barred: it was filled with leaded glass. That meant, very likely, that the cell would be reasonably clean and not covered with bat guano. Hanging on with two toes and one hand, she reached with the other into her bag and brought out a tool that she used to loosen the edges of the window pane. She attached a suction cup and a cord to the pane and lowered it gently into the cell. The window was small, but she was slender, and very shortly she had wriggled though the frame.

The cell was quite dark after the sunlit exterior, so Nazra widened her pupils to see better without delay. The cell was completely empty and apparently well sealed, too, for there was just a light covering of dust. The door looked like it was made of very solid wood planking, the kind that would be five to ten centimeters thick. The hinges were on the other side, of course, and the lock was an old one of thick, black iron. Being inside like this it had probably, and hopefully, not rusted shut. It was bound to be stuck, though, if only from grime. Nazra took out a sturdy lockpicking tool and a small spray can of WD40. With a slender, flexible tube she sprayed the inner mechanism of the lock with scarcely a whisper of any sound.

She employed the pick and added the help of another one of her abilities to it. Her trainers at the Institute had all wanted her to develop the talent of psychokinesis, the ability to move objects with one's mind. They had envisioned her being able to lift a knife from a table behind the victim and hurl it into his heart from behind, with no one ever suspecting that she was the culprit. Or, better yet, having her able to clamp down on someone's artery or heart valve and cause death instantly and invisibly.

Unfortunately, it didn't work out that way. First, it was discovered that lifting and/or moving an object with the mind took a tremendous amount of emotional energy. Poltergeisters, those around whom objects flew in many directions without their apparent participation, produced their effects with short, extremely intense, emotional bursts that often left the person mentally and physically exhausted. Even poor Ninel Kulagina, who had achieved a certain measure of fame and neo-Stalinist censure for her psychokinetic ability, was only able to cause a few objects to roll around a table. As for using psychokinesis to stop someone's heart, no one had ever been able to do it with a "cold" subject, someone without a heart problem and who had not been psychologically set up. The trainers had felt that those conditions were too limiting, and so they had dropped that line of Nazra's research and training.

Nazra, however, had been fascinated with one aspect of psychokinesis which the trainers had disdained: spoon-bending. As she practiced with it and accumulated a sizeable collection of bent silverware and other assorted objects, she discovered two very useful bits of knowledge: one, that the more electrically conductive a material was, like copper or silver, the easier it was to bend it with focused intent and, two, that anything could be moved or altered more easily by adding focused intent to physical action.

So, in opening the old lock on the heavy wooden door, Nazra not only exerted physical pressure on her pick, she also willfully imagined that her energy was doing the actual moving and that the pick was only helping. The lock was stuck, and there were some moments when the assassin wondered whether it would work or not, but finally it did begin to move after two minutes of concentrated effort and, thanks to the penetrating oil and her will, it moved silently. When the lock was fully open she stepped back from the door and entered into a different state of consciousness.

Now it was critical to get some information about what exactly lay in the other room, using another talent she had been trained in: remote viewing, Directing her attention beyond the door, she drew a rough sketch of the room in her imagination based on Graben's description, and let her extended perception fill in the rest. She neither expected nor needed total accuracy. She just wanted a general sense of who and what was where. Keeping her muscles relaxed to allow what was really there to take precedent over what she wanted to be there, she saw in her mind's eye a semblance of a cage in the middle of the room with someone in it lying on a cot, and beyond that, two men sitting at a table, perhaps playing cards.

Pulling her awareness back to the cell, Nazra had to choose between a tactic of "distract and attack" or "attract and attack." She chose the latter.

Inside the storeroom the two agents and Treffsky heard an impossible sound coming from the heavy, locked door at the other end of the room—impossible, because they had been assured that the door had been locked for years and that there was nothing behind it but an empty storage area.

"*Bitte, hilfe!* Please, help!" cried an anquished little girl. "I'm lost, please help me!"

"It's a trick!" shouted Treffsky, backing up to the end of his cage and going into a crouch.

The two agents ignored him as the pleas for help continued. They unholstered their guns and moved toward the door, cautiously. One moved to the side and motioned for the other to try the handle so that only one was at risk and the other could cover him from safety. The one not in charge tried the handle, found the door was moveable, opened the door ninety degrees and quickly crouched. At first there was only an opaque blackness. Then out of that formed a very pale image of a young girl looking very much like the waif in the posters for *Les Miserables*, only even more pale and skeletal. "Help me," said the girl.

The crouching man's mouth dropped open, the hairs on the back of his neck stood up straight, and his gun hand lowered. The other man, seeing his partner's reaction, could not help but look around the door and be transfixed by the apparition. When Nazra had them both well in her sights she used a pair of silenced pistols to drop each of them with a shot to the head. Then she stepped into the room as the Eurasian model and said, "*Nasdarovya*, Comrade Treffsky."

Dimitri Treffsky was not a weak man, but it took him a minute to gather his wits again. When he had finally assimilated the fact that this strange woman was actually the person who was trying to kill him, he leaned against the back of the cage with one leg bent and the foot resting against the wire. "Nazra," he said, shaking his head as if in wonder and admiration, "You always were amazingly unpredictable. Am I to be slaughtered

184

like an animal, then?"

"Yes," she said simply, walking forward, "but not like a caged animal." She searched through the clothing of the dead men, found the key to the cage, stepped up to it and opened its door wide.

Treffsky smiled, and attacked. Using his bent leg as leverage, he shot forward in a horizontal lunge, hands poised to break through tissue and bone. Nazra fell flat on her back and kicked upward, contacting Treffsky's hip and increasing his forward momentum. In one twisting motion she was up and moving toward him even before he fell.

The Russian tried a rolling fall, but it was interrupted by a wall he hadn't expected to meet so soon, so he used the bounce off the wall to help him roll sideways, thereby removing his neck from the point where Nazra's boot struck half a second after. With no neck to cushion her leap Nazra bent her leg and used the friction of the wall to jump upward as Treffsky's foot lashed out at the empty space where her head would have been had she fallen to the ground.

They scrambled to their feet and faced each other in a semi-crouch, all advantage of surprise gone for both of them. They each understood that this was the most dangerous point for skilled martial artists. Unlike in the movies, where masters would rain ineffective blows on each other for ages, a really deadly encounter didn't last long at all. One or two of the right strikes at the right moment and it could be over in less than a minute. The trick, of course, was in making the right strike at the right moment, when the other person wanted to do the same. It was positioning oneself for the strike that took the most time.

Nazra feinted. Treffsky feinted back. Then Nazra "fainted." She just collapsed totally, falling to the floor as if unconscious. In the second of time it took Treffsky to wonder what had happened, Nazra kicked him in the chest, breaking his sternum and puncturing a lung. He collapsed back against the wall and she leaped up to pin him there with her left forearm against his throat.

She smiled into his eyes. "Never trust a woman, Dimitri. But then it's too late for that advice, isn't it?" Treffsky smiled and blood oozed from his lips. With her right hand Nazra chopped down on the bridge of his nose and slowly pushed the gristle into his brain, ignoring the shakes and shudders of his dying body. Before leaving she pinned the Tarot card "Strength" to his chest in a reversed position. She like the meaning of "Too much attention is given to the material at the expense of the mental and spiritual."

It didn't take long at all to return from the storeroom to the cell, climb out and down, rush back along the streets to the church, and make her way up to the top of the tower. By the time she heard the sounds of two men climbing the wooden stairs she was rested and ready for them.

Keoki was the first to come out of the stairwell and into the small room. He saw Karen's bruised and battered form instantly and cried out, "Oh, my God!" He rushed straight to her without any other thought. Nazra could have killed him so easily, but he wasn't the one she wanted first. Where was Anton Müller, the older one?

"Right here," said a voice beside her.

Nazra was so startled she let go of the swinging beam she had been holding in readiness to smash Lani's head the moment he appeared. How had he evaded her? She turned toward the voice, red hot anger burning inside her. Too much anger. She forgot that the beam had to swing back when it didn't hit anything in the doorway. On the backswing it struck her in the legs, knocking her off her perch and onto the big bronze bell below her. She grasped for a handhold, but there wasn't any and she slid down until she was only holding on by the raised rim, her legs dangling out over more bells and hundreds of feet of space. She looked up and saw Lani looking down at her. "You could have killed me," she said.

"I don't kill people. I help them. Do you want some help?" He reached a hand down toward her.

"You old fool!" she grated. Nazra dropped down to the next bell and used it as leverage for a jump to the stairwell. The jump caused the bell to start swinging and its deep tones accompanied Nazra's descending footsteps.

Lani glanced at Keoki who was untying the cords that held Karen, and he dashed down the stairs after Nazra. There was no time to even regret that they hadn't called German security before coming to the church. He risked life and limb several times

186

jumping over stairs in an attempt to catch up with the woman known as Seeker.

The rush and noise of the chase startled the couple of dozen visitors in the church. When Lani erupted out of the church doorway onto *Holzmarkt* he didn't see Nazra, but he heard the sound of shoes running on cobblestones to his right. He ran that way and caught sight of her sprinting down the pedestrian passage of *Neckargasse* toward the main thoroughfare of *Mülstrasse*, dodging between people so as not to slow down. At that crossstreet she turned right and Lani followed her, actually jumping over a little girl who cried out in fright.

Nazra headed across the *Eberhardsbrücke* and in the middle of the bridge she made a sharp turn to the right and down some stairs to the pencil-shaped, artificial island that split the Neckar for about eight hundred meters. On the straightaway of the *Platanenallee*, the Avenue of Plane Trees, she picked up her pace in a dead run for the other end of the narrow islet.

Lani had been only twenty yards behind her until then, but on the straight avenue he began to lag behind. It wasn't so much a matter of his age and her youth. He could still outrun most people younger than him. She was simply a faster runner. But where did she think she was going? He knew that the island didn't connect to any other bridges.

Ah, thought the man in the small motorboat, at last here comes the lovely *junge frau* who wants to play games with her lover. As Nazra came running up he started the engine and she jumped into the front of the boat resting on the sandy bank at the tip of the island that faced upstream. She told the boatman to wait until her lover got closer, and the boatman smiled with amusement at the strange games played by the lazy rich.

Lani was about sixty yards behind her when Nazra jumped into the boat. She just stood there while he got closer: fifty yards, forty, thirty... When he was twenty yards away she gave a signal and the boat backed away from the island. Before the boatman turned the craft to head upstream she blew Lani a kiss, unsmiling. On the sandy spit at the tip of the island Lani bent over with his hands on his knees, panting heavily as he watched the little boat and its passenger disappear around a bend in the river.

Twenty

Inner Guidance

Loa'a ke ola i halau a ola
(Healing is obtained where healing is taught)

Keoki was drunk and Lani was disgusted.

Once Nazra's boat was out of sight, Lani had made his way to the public phone at the end of the bridge near the corner of *Mühlstrasse* and *Gartenstrasse* and called the number for the BND contact that Madame Villier had given him. He told the contact that Seeker had escaped by the river after having badly injured a female PERI member from Heidelberg, and he requested an ambulance to pick her up from the tower of St. George Church. Then he crossed *Mühlstrasse* to *Neckargasse* and walked uphill past the shops and restaurants to the church. He climbed the tower again and found Keoki bending over Karen, whom he had laid on top of Mrs. Sothby's discarded dress. Keoki had covered Karen with the black vinyl jacket that Nazra had left behind, and had put the assassin's black bag under the girl's head. Now he was sitting beside her, weeping. Karen was still unconscious.

Lani sat on the other side of Karen and told Keoki that he had called an ambulance. He started to lift off the jacket and Keoki said, "What are you doing?"

"I'm going to start a healing process that will ease the pain and help her recover more quickly."

"Can you really heal her?" Keoki asked, his eyes grown wide. This was an area of Gramp's knowledge that Keoki knew nothing about. He had heard a lot of unbelievable stories, and once when he was young and had injured his knee on a rock while crossing a stream, Gramps had done something with his hands that had taken away the pain and swelling in minutes. But

188

it was still an area of mystery to his mind.

"Given enough time I could help her to heal herself completely," said Lani, taking off the jacket with great gentleness, "but I'm afraid we don't have the time. When the ambulance comes she'll go into the modern medical system, so I'm going to help her get ready for that and do as much for her as I can right now. Let me concentrate."

Lani's soul ached to see the damage that Nazra had done to this kind and beautiful young woman. Clearing those thoughts from his mind, he he centered his awareness at his *piko*, his navel, which also served as his meeting point for the center of his being and the center of the universe. He did a special kind of breathing that caused his energy to flow and expand and encompass the woman before him. Using a technique called *ha-ha*, he let his hands move slowly over her entire body about five inches above her skin. This initial series of passes was for gathering information from her energy field about her physical condition. In addition to the visible bruises that covered nearly every inch of the front portion of her body, with the notable exception of her face, Lani sensed three broken fingers on her right hand, a fractured right collarbone, two fractured ribs on her left side, a fractured tibia on her left leg, and a broken toe on her right foot.

The second series of passes was for increasing the circulation of her blood and activating her lymph system to help relieve muscular and cellular tension, bring more oxygen to assist her own body's repair work and reduce the pain, and start carrying off the toxins built up around the injuries. Lani also spoke to the spirit of her body, as if it were something apart from the spirit of her mind. He used words that would have seemed totally irrational or even insane to someone else if they could have been heard; words like, "I'm glad to see you're healing so quickly. Good thing you're young and strong. In a very short time you'll be looking and feeling good again. Get some more oxygen over there, will you? Relax those muscles, please. Take away those dead red and white blood cells in this area more quickly, okay?"

While part of him dealt directly with the spirit of her body, another part went off in search of the spirit of her mind. This part of her had sought refuge somewhere from the pain and the horror of the experience. If it weren't brought back, there was a chance that Karen might spend the rest of her life in a coma.

This other part of Lani went to a place which has been described as an altered state of consciousness, a dream, another dimension, another world, a figment of imagination, a psychotic state, and other things less kind. Lani would have called it *Po*, a term rather difficult to describe, but which, in its simplest form, could be translated as "a place invisible to outer sight."

To Lani's inner perception he was flying in the form of an *'io*, a Hawaiian hawk, over a fantastically shaped and colored mountain range. He was looking for a particular valley that he knew existed, but that he had never been to. A sensation of pulling on his right led him in that direction and soon he swooped over a perfect valley, hidden between a cluster of peaks. He saw perfect waterfalls, perfect trees and flowers, and perfect animals roaming around, mostly of the cat family. In a clearing at the center of the valley was a white, domed temple with a pool nearby and he headed toward it.

On the ground he changed into an ocelot, because he wanted to be exotic without being too large and it was a form he used for other purposes from time to time. He padded up to the temple and looked around, but he didn't see anyone among its alabaster columns. Then he pricked up his ears as a harp cast its notes upon the balmy air and he padded over to the pool. When he arrived there he immediately recognized it as a replica of a Maxfield Parrish painting. The pool and the columns around it had a sort of classical Greek look to them and the whole area, including the lush vegetation around the pool, was bathed in the glowing colors of a fading sunset, even though the valley had seemed to be in morning light when he was flying above it.

A young Adonis in a short, white tunic was seated on a stool at one end of the pool, his fingers producing rich, rippling melodies from a simple lyre that he held on his lap. On the side of the pool opposite Lani-the-ocelot a young Karen, looking to be about fifteen years old, lounged on a padded bench in a long, white robe trimmed in gold. She was eating grapes from a bunch that was held by another young Adonis, twin to the first.

Lani dove into the pool, swam across, pulled himself up on the other side, and shook himself dry. He knew that he didn't really have to shake himself dry, but he liked the sensation. Karen didn't pay any attention to him until he brushed his head against a dangling hand.

"Well, hello there," she said. "My, you're a pretty one. What's your name?"

"Lani," purred Lani.

She didn't act like it was odd that a cat should speak. "Lani...," she said thoughtfully. "That sounds so familiar. But it's a nice name. Do you like the music, Lani?" It was Pachebel's *Canon*.

Pretty good for a lyre, thought Lani. "It's beautiful, just like you are," purred Lani.

Karen just smiled and ate another grape.

Lani purred, "I bring greetings from Keoki. And Lisbet. And your landlord, because the rent on your flat in Copenhagen is coming due."

Karen frowned and pushed the grapes away. "You can't talk about things like that in this place."

"Why not? They miss you. Don't you care about them?"

Karen sat up, still frowning. "Stop that! I don't want to go back there to...to... I just don't want to!" She sighed, relaxed, and looked around. "It's so nice and peaceful here, isn't it? I could stay here forever." She smiled at the Adonis twin and stroked his hand.

"It's very nice," agreed Lani, licking his fur as if he didn't really care what the place looked like. "Your body needs you, though. It's trying to heal itself, but it really needs your help. You could always come back after you've helped it to heal."

The girl looked concerned. "Can't my body get along without me?"

"Not very well," said the ocelot, pacing a bit before sitting back down. "If you don't return to help your body some other people will have to pay for keeping it in a hospital, your landlord will lose money on your lease and will have to sell all your things, your clients will have to find someone less talented to help them, and the man you are going to meet and marry will go unloved. But it's your choice, of course."

She chewed on her lower lip. Adonis One had stopped playing and was just looking at her. Adonis Two had disappeared. "My body... hurts," she said finally. "The pain is so terrible... I

191

was so helpless... why would someone do that to me?" The last was the cry of a very little, bewildered child.

Lani looked intently into her eyes. "Most of the pain is gone, now. No one is there to hurt you anymore. A lot of people are helping you to recover and your body is doing its best to heal itself completely, but it still needs you, and they need you. Besides, like I said, you can come back here and visit any time you want to."

"I can?"

"Any time."

Karen lifted Lani into her lap. Adonis One had disappeared. "How do I go back?" she whispered.

"First, I have to tell you what to do when you do get back," purred the ocelot. "In order to help your body to heal as quickly as possible, you'll have to forgive the person who hurt you and you'll have to forgive your spirit guides for not being able to protect you."

The girl stiffened. "I don't know if I can do that."

"Sure you can, because you're a healer. The best way would be for you to think of that woman as a very lost soul, hurting you only because she is hurting so much. She wasn't attacking you personally, she was attacking everything that had ever hurt her. Can you forgive her for hurting inside so much?"

Karen nodded slowly. "I could forgive her for that."

"Good," said Lani. Remember that. Now let's talk about your spirit guides..."

"Why didn't they protect me!"

The ocelot licked her cheek once. "They're not supposed to protect you from being hurt. That's not their role. Their supposed to protect you from being taken over by negative entities, negative beliefs, and they did that very well. Poor Nazra doesn't have any protective spirits, and so she got taken over. Think about this," Lani purred, "Nazra is an assassin and she didn't kill you when she could have, Perhaps your goodness, and the help of your guides, has helped her just the tiniest little bit." Karen's face brightened at this idea. "So can you forgive your guides for only doing what they were supposed to do?"

"Yes, I can do that, too" said Karen, musingly. "So now what do we do?"

Lani wriggled out of her arms and sat on the bench, looking up at her. "You make yourself very, very small and I'll change into a bird, and then you can ride on my back while I fly us home."

"Oh, that sounds like fun," said Karen, clapping her hands.

Lani turned back into a hawk as Karen shrank to an appropriate size. Then he let her mount his back before spreading his wings and lifting off into the multi-colored sky. He swooped once over the valley so she could get a good look at it from above, and then he took her home.

Back in her body Karen opened her eyes, searched for Lani's and found them, and managed a ghost of a smile. "That was fun," she said so softly that only he could hear.

"Karen!" cried Keoki.

She looked at him and tears came to her eyes. She mouthed the words, "Thank you."

"Let her rest," said Lani. "She has work to do. Karen, do you know how to help your body to help itself?" There was the barest of nods. "Then go to it." She closed her eyes.

"Will she be okay?" said Keoki.

"She'll be fine," said Lani, and brought his full attention back to her body. The worst of the swelling had gone down, some of the bruises had actually disappeared, and the ribs were solid again. The pain had been dulled to an overall ache. The rest was healing and would heal more quickly with medical help and Karen's fully conscious cooperation. Nevertheless, Lani kept working with her until the medical team arrived.

When Karen was safely in the hospital and arrangements had been made for Lisbet to come down and stay with her until she was ready to be taken back to Denmark, Lani and Keoki were summoned to a borrowed room at the *Deutsches Institute für Fernstudien*, the German Institute for Foreign Studies on *Konrad-Adenauerstrasse* on the south bank of the Neckar, for a debriefing with Madame Villier and *Herr* Nichts.

"This would be a good time to strengthen your *la'a kea*, fill it with harmony, and keep your muscles relaxed," he told Keoki when they got the command. It was obvious that Keoki was still in a state of semi-shock, but he did nod agreement.

At the Institute a BND agent led them to the tiny room that

193

only contained a table and four chairs and a half open window that opened onto an empty, enclosed garden. They were left there and the door was closed by the departing agent. Lani sat down in one of the chairs at the table and motioned for Keoki to take the one opposite. A half hour passed. "Where are they?" asked Keoki. "I thought this was an important meeting."

"It is," said Lani, "but there's protocol to follow. We wait for them to show that they are more important than we are. The longer we wait, the more important it shows that they are, up to a point. Past a certain point the wait starts to be an insult, but there's a sort of transition period just before that which means they are angry at us but don't wish to be outright insulting just yet because that would be counter-productive to their ends. It's a fine art. By my estimate they should be coming just about..."

The door opened abruptly and *Herr* Nichts and Madame Villier entered without a word. Nichts looked around, clearly upset with the room itself. Not only was it too small to be intimidating, but Lani had purposely chosen to sit across from Keoki, rather than next to him, thus forcing a split in the ranks of authority, unless they wanted to make an issue of it. However, that would mean acknowledging that Lani and Keoki had the power to diminish their authority, even if they were able to take it back. The conundrum was that if they forced a reseating their authority would, in fact, be diminished. It was a very fine art.

Nichts and Villier sat across from each other, Nichts slapping a dossier of some kind on the table and Villier placing a briefcase on the floor right next to her chair.

Nichts stabbed a finger at Lani and said, in German, "You were told to stay in Heidelberg."

Ignoring the finger, Lani said, also in German, "If we had, the young lady would be dead and you would not have the wealth of clues that you found in Seeker's bag."

The German leaned back with a mocking smile. "Very good. Your accent is hardly noticeable."

"Yours, too," said Lani calmly. "Swabian, is it?" Nichts' face reddened.

"Gentlemen," Villier said in her French-accented English. "The rest of us do not speak German as well as you. Please continue in English."

Nichts turned on Keoki. "Do you always obey your grandfather in everything he says to do?"

"I do whenever I believe it's important to do so," said Keoki quietly.

"You could be in a great deal of trouble. You might even go to jail for intefering in a State security matter."

"We did the right thing," said Keoki stubbornly. Nichts gave an exaggerated sigh and threw up his hands. Keoki knew then that it was an act. He wouldn't have been able to prove it, but he could feel it. He strengthened his field and relaxed his muscles a little more.

The BND chief's attempts at intimidation were going nowhere, so Villier entered the fray. "I don't quite know what to do with you two. Your participation in this affair is becoming entirely too active. PERI members are supposed to stay behind the scenes, not run around the countryside chasing after assassins and getting in the way of an official operation."

"Excuse me, Madame Villier." Lani kept his tone neutral. "It's only one assassin and it seems she was chasing us, not the other way around. Somehow she breached your security measures," Lani kept his eyes on Villier, "and went out of her way to locate us in Heidelberg, when she could just as easily have ignored us and continued with her plan. That indicates she believes that we are a danger to her. Isn't there any way to exploit that?" Lani could think of a dozen ways, but it was important that any solution come from the authorities.

Nichts leaned forward again, his eyes gleaming. He had seen the potential immediately because he was always looking for ways to use people to serve his ends. The ends of the State, that is. He acted as if he disliked the Americans, but that was just an act. He really didn't have any feelings about them. They were merely tools. Now, however, he saw a way to make the tools more useful. "I can think of a way," he said. "It would be dangerous, but no more so than now, if she really is after you. In fact, it would be safer because you would be working inside of our organization instead of outside of it."

The others looked at him, waiting for him to continue.

195

Twenty-one

Trust Gramps

'Ai no i ka 'ape he mane'o no ko ka nuku
(He who eats a poisonous plant will have an itchy mouth)

Nichts tried a friendly smile. He wasn't very good at it. "I would like to ask the two of you to serve as bait to help us capture Seeker."

"Ah, non!" said Villier. "Absolutely not! I will not allow you to put civilians at risk, even with their consent."

"Let us hear what he has to say, first. Please?" Lani made his tone as conciliatory as possible, but Villier huffed some more anyway.

Nichts stood up and paced one side of the small room, apparently thinking better on his feet. "The way I see it, if we assigned each of you to one of the remaining PERI teams, Seeker would be drawn to one or the other. That's assuming she finds you important enough to continue chasing you. If not, then perhaps the teams will find you useful. If so, then we can arrange a trap associated with each of you. She will be expecting increased security around the Russians, but not around the PERI teams. When and if she comes for you, we will have her!"

"And if she avoids the trap?" asked Lani.

"Don't even think about it," said Nichts reassuringly. "We will have a dozen good men and women around each of you. I can guarantee your safety."

Lani didn't think so, but it was a better deal than they currently had. He wasn't too worried about Keoki. In the tower Nazra had been after him, not his grandson, although she might have gone after Keoki if she had been able to do away with him first. He had no intention of letting that happen, so the boy should

196

be safe enough on his own. Actually, safer away from his grandfather than close to him, at least until this was over.

Now they were at a critical juncture, in terms of protocol and power. He and Keoki were part of PERI, and the well-being of PERI members on assignment was the responsibility of Madame Villier. She could veto any proposed use of their services by the BND. And even if she did allow it, as long as they were civilians she would be overprotective and Nichts would treat them with contempt, especially if he and Keoki agreed to do it without any tangible benefit. Nichts was not about to put much trust in a civilian acting out of an altruistic sense of social duty, and Lani wanted to know as much about what was going on as possible to decrease the risks to himself and Keoki. Suddenly, Lani got a really offbeat inspiration. Would they buy it? Only one way to find out.

"We would like to help," said Lani, speaking for both Keoki and himself and trusting that Keoki would be too numbed and too surprised to object. "However, it would have to be done in a way that would benefit everyone."

Villier had a bemused look and Nichts looked interested. "What do you have in mind?" asked the agent.

"We will do this for you if the two of you will use your influence to get my grandson and I hired as operational crime analysts in Subdivision Four of Division Two of Interpol."

Villier and Nichts were stunned. Keoki was, too, but for different reasons.

When Lani had first been approached by a friend to work with PERI and Interpol, he had researched both of them thoroughly before making a decision. Interpol, he found, was an independent, international police organization. Under its General Secretariat were several divisions, including the Liaison and Criminal Intelligence Division, also called Division Two, that Villier worked for. She was specifically part of Sub-Division One, which dealt with international liaison related to crimes against persons and property. Sub-Division Four dealt with criminal intelligence, both strategic and operational. Technically, what Lani and Keoki were doing for Interpol and German Security as part of PERI could also fit within the latter part of Interpol's organization.

Nichts looked at Lani with new respect, more for his knowledge than anything else. "You really want to be a policeman?" he asked with a small smile of amusement

"That's what I'm proposing," said Lani.

"And you want this, too?" the agent asked of Keoki.

When Keoki was a lot younger he had made up a proverb for himself. He thought of it now. *When in doubt, trust Gramps.* "Sure," he said, not knowing at all what he was getting into.

Villier blustered, "There are training, procedures, interviews, contracts to consider, protocol to follow..."

"I'm counting on the two of you to speed things up," said Lani. "We are already trained for the kind of intelligence gathering that we do. We would probably have to go through some kind of orientation to become familiar with your policies and procedures, but that could wait until after this affair is over. The real question is whether the two of you have the connections and influence to make this happen."

"Why would you want to do this?" asked Nichts, ignoring the implied challenge.

"Three reasons," said Lani, thinking fast. "We like to use our talents to help the good guys; we would no longer be 'civilians' in relation to you; and both my grandson and I could use some supplemental income, me for my retirement and him to invest for his future."

The last two reasons made the most impression on Nichts. In addition, the agent reasoned, it would actually be better if they were not civilians because then the risks they would take would be part of their job and less a concern of his. And the very last reason the old Hawaiian had given was a practical one that he could appreciate.

"Well?" asked Lani.

"Well?" added Keoki.

It took two days of pulling a lot of strings and calling in a lot of favors, and it only succeeded because of the high priority of the Seeker operation within Interpol and the BND, and the fact that everything that had been tried so far to prevent the assassinations had failed miserably, in spite of knowing about them in advance and knowing who the assassin was. It wasn't until Lani and Keoki had identity cards in their hands naming them officially as "Special Operational Crime Analysts" for Interpol and they had filled out piles of forms that the two were provided with the details of what had happened at Berlin, Düsseldorf, and the castle in Tübingen. No new attempts by Seeker had been made since then. Nichts thought she was being more cautious because of the increased security measures; Lani thought she was waiting to see what he would do.

Since the Interpol computer records had apparently been accessed from outside, everything related to Operation Seeker had been taken offline and stored on un-networked servers, and any information that had to be shared was to be transmitted by voice code over scrambled lines.

During those two days Keoki sank further and further into a black depression, and he had the time to use more and more alcohol to ease his inner pain. Beer was too slow and hard liquor was too fast and too expensive, so Keoki was numbing his heart and brain with the cheapest wine he could find.

Lani tried to talk him out of it and that didn't work. He tried to reach Keoki through the inner world and met angry resistance to any communication. Something entirely different was needed.

Lani's view of depression was that it was triggered by a situation in which a person felt both frustrated and helpless. The person tried anger to solve the problem, and if that didn't work the person began to experience the state of helpless anger called depression, where the anger was turned inward instead of outward. Some people, with or without help, got out of depression by changing their mind about the situation in a way that made anger unnecessary. Some were able to move their attention elsewhere so that depression was relieved. Some alternated between depression and mania in an endless cycle that made the situation tolerable for them and intolerable for everyone else. And some made their way beyond depression into hopelessness and apathy. Lani knew his grandson well enough to see that he had a tendency to go in that direction.

Drugs could be a help, but by themselves all they did was to alter the chemical state of the body so that false information was provided to the cells and thence to the subconscious mind. There was also the danger of creating a dependency on that false information in order to lead what other people liked to call a "normal" life. Based on his experiences with helping himself and others, Lani believed that what a depressed person really needed was to feel effective in some way related to the situation that caused the frustration.

Keoki was frustrated because he had been unable to prevent Karen from being hurt, had been unable to get back at Nazra for hurting her, had been unable to help Karen when she was hurt, and had been unable to make her love him the way he thought he wanted her to. Her last words to him in the hospital, which Lani had overheard, were "You are very sweet, Keoki. I will always remember our time together. Please remember me once in a while when you go home." What he had wanted her to say was, "My darling, go forth and capture the evil witch and then return to me so I can love you and worship you forever and ever!" But she hadn't. She had, essentially, dismissed him.

So frustration had turned into helpless anger and he was growing more and more depressed. Alcohol was a drug that, in small amounts, relaxed the body and the anger and helped a person to cope. But in larger amounts it lied to the body, saying, "See, it doesn't hurt at all." In those larger amounts it also made communication between the conscious and subconscious minds more difficult.

On the third morning of their stay in Tübingen, in a comfortable room at the *Hotel Am Bad*, a rambling, yellow structure in the middle of a park by the Neckar River and the Sports Plaza, Lani removed a half glass of Reisling and the empty bottle from the end table next to Keoki's bed and replaced them with an icy glass of cold water. Then he sat in a chair near the bed and patiently began sketching with a pen on a pad of paper.

Keoki woke up about ten, hitched himself up a bit and reached for the glass on the end table. He took three swallows before he noticed that it wasn't wine, and then he noticed Lani in the chair. "Where's my wine?" he said in a surly tone.

"In the refrige," said Lani without looking up. "It was warm so I put it in to chill." Sketch, sketch.

The need to know was irresistible. "What are you doing with that paper?"

"Laying a trap for Nazra."

"Huh!" said Keoki. He took a sip of water, made a face, and

200

took another sip. "She's the one who's laying a trap for you. She's too smart for any of us."

Lani didn't reply. He was too busy sketching.

"What kind of a trap?" Keoki tried to make it sound as if he were not really that interested.

"A psychic trap," said Lani without looking up.

Several things happened in Keoki at once. A habitual reaction of fearful disdain came up, but it was weaker than before. A newer reaction of curious interest came up, based on a subconscious reminder that he had made a commitment to the *kupua* work. And a brand new reaction of professional interest came up because he was now a Special Operational Crime Analyst for Interpol and it was his job to know about psychic traps. So interest democratically won out over fear. "What is a psychic trap, anyway?"

Lani handed the pad to Keoki. "It's a symbolic trap, based on the concept of a maze. The outside of the trap represents wherever the person is that you want to trap, in this case Nazra. At the opening you put a symbol of something that would interest her and in the middle you put a symbol of something she wants very much, plus whatever you are going to use to make her want to enter the trap."

Keoki looked at the drawing. It was badly done, even though Lani had drawn it over a dozen times while waiting for Keoki to wake up, and even though he was quite a good sketch artist in his own field of ethnobiology. "I sort of see what you're trying to do," said Keoki, not able to look at the drawing with a totally uncritical eye, "but I don't understand how it works as a trap. You've got a drawing, but how does it trap her?" Keoki took another drink of water.

"Psychically," said Lani. "The drawing is just to help me focus. Once I have the drawing done I recreate it in my mind and energize the symbols. Then I hold it in my subconscious and let the pattern do the work. If it's effective, she won't even be aware that she's in a maze and she won't be aware of the trap until it's sprung."

Keoki tapped the end of his nose with a forefinger, like he did when he was thinking deeply. "Wait a sec." He went to the litte refrigerator and poured another glass of water. When he returned he said, "You haven't really drawn a maze, you know. It's a labyrinth."

"What's the difference?" asked Lani from the desk, genuinely puzzled. "I thought they were just different names for the same thing."

The young man picked up the pen Gramps had been using, sat on the edge of the bed and drank some more water from the glass. "'Sokay, Gramps, most people think that, but they're not." Keoki put the glass down on the end table, uncovered a fresh sheet of paper on the pad and quickly drew two patterns side by side. "Mazes and labyrinths are the basis for all computer games," he said. "Basically, you start somewhere and you have to go somewhere. In a typical maze, like this," he tapped his pen on the left pattern as he showed it to his grandfather, "you start here, you encounter a lot of dead ends, and you end up somewhere else." He tapped the exit point of the maze. "In a typical labyrinth," he said, tapping the right hand pattern, "you start here, wander around for a long time, reach the middle, and wander back to the same place you came in. There aren't any dead ends, but the time it takes can be discouraging."

Keoki skillfully drew some images of treasure chests and monsters, and made lines from them to various parts of both patterns. "In a game," he continued. "there has to be a good reason for entering the maze or the labyrinth, and something you want at the far end or in the middle. And in a good game, there has to be something interesting to do or find along the way, like problems to solve, treasure to collect, or monsters to slay. You've got symbols for the reason to enter and the thing Nazra might want, but I think it's too simple for her. She'd be suspicious. In some simple games, like 'Duke Nuk'em,' the maze is obvious and the player accepts it. In others, like 'Riven,' which is more like a labyrinth, by the way, the underlying pattern is hidden so that the player gets more involved in the adventure."

"And doesn't realize the pattern is guiding him," said Lani, thoughtfully.

"Right. Your choice of a labyrinth was a good one because she would probably feel safer even subconsciously knowing that she could return to her starting point. It's just not challenging enough. What kind of symbol were you going to put in the middle?"

"Me," said Lani.

Keoki got up and walked over to the window, still dressed in just the briefs he'd slept in. He looked down on the red flowers lining the sun terrace of the hotel, the lawn beyond, and the Olympic-sized pool of the Sports Plaza beyond that. When he turned around he was frowning. "Do you really think we can stop her?"

"If I didn't, I'd go home," Lani said.

"She's so powerful," said Keoki.

Lani came over to the window and turned Keoki around so he could look him in the eyes. "She's a skilled assassin with psychic abilities. She's very dangerous. She's also a human being under a lot of stress and she can make mistakes. It's our job to analyze her behavior, find a way to amplify those mistakes, and lead her to where she can be captured. Maybe by creating something that looks like a labyrinth to her and is really a maze leading to prison. We are not going to seek her out, remember? We are the bait. We are going to get her to come to us and then the BND will pounce on her. It's their job to make it seem like it's safe for her to get to us and get out, or at least make it seem like it's possible. We play a strictly passive role, now. No more risks by either one of us."

"What about this?" Keoki waved the pad of paper that he was still holding.

"I'm going to think about what you said. I suggest that you start working on a game in your mind that she can't resist. The sooner you can get her to come for you the sooner she can be captured. Make it like an Inner Garden place, a new one in some fantasy land where she'll feel like Xena or something. Remember that whatever you do in there will have its reflections out here. Use your own skills plus what I've taught you. We'll do what has to be done and then we'll go home and go hiking in Kohala. And I'll teach you the healing skills."

Keoki looked at Gramps, saw the great love and wisdom in his eyes, and stepped up closer to give his grandfather a long, warm hug.

Later that afternoon, when the final meeting with Villier and Nichts was over, Lani and Keoki took a train to Stuttgart

203

together. At that busy station they said goodbye for awhile. Keoki boarded a train going north in order to turn south again and reach Freiburg. Lani boarded a southbound train for the city of Munich.

Once he was settled in his first-class compartment Lani thought of Nazra. *It's just you and I, now, Distorted One.* Then he thought of Keoki, and that thought brought him pleasure. Getting him to think in terms of using his gaming skills against Nazra had quickly brought him out of his depression so that he was actively involved again in a positive way. Actually, it was a good concept, though he had no intention of using it himself.

He should have.

Twenty-two
A Meeting Of Friends
'Akahi ho'i ku'u 'ono i ka uhu ka'alo i ku'u maka
(I long for the fine thing my eyes see)

Keoki and Marta left on the same day for Freiburg, a charming little town in the southwestern corner of Germany. It was a five-hour trip for Keoki, but only one hour for Marta.

Three days before this trip, Marta Brunn had been sitting in St. Elisabeth's Church in Basel, Switzerland, having a cafe latte and negotiating with a Japanese gentleman for her services, when a young girl of about twelve came up to their table, handed her a note, and left without a word. Marta read the note, smiled broadly, dropped some Swiss francs on the table to pay for her beverage, and also left without a word. The Japanese man was totally confused and remained a long time at the table vainly trying to figure out what he had done to offend her.

Marta left the old Gothic church, which was turned into a cafe during the week to help pay its expenses, barely glanced at the pyramidal glass skylights of the *Stadt-theater*, the City Theater Complex on which the church now stood, and turned left for a bit on *Elisabethenstrasse*. Instead of taking that route all the way into Basel's Old Town, she took a short cut that passed by Tinguely's fountain with its array of fantastic machines spraying water in equally fantastic patterns. Auburn-haired, sultry-eyed, pouty-lipped, long of limb and slim of hip, Marta caught many eyes of both sexes as she confidently strode along through the little park, lovely thighs flashing through convenient slits in the skirt of her rust-colored suit.

Though Swiss by birth, she had spent much of her young life in Japan. Her father was the representative of a Swiss consortium of business interests in Tokyo. Her mother had been a frail artistic type who had succumbed to pneumonia during a severe Japanese winter when Marta was thirteen. Marta's father had neither the time nor the inclination to either care for her or send her home, so he paid a geisha handsomely to take care of the girl and see that she had a proper upbringing. Then he forgot about her. The geisha was a good woman, but she could not control a precocious girl just entering her teens and Marta's proper upbringing began to take the form of sex, drugs, and gangs. In desperation, the geisha turned to a brother for help, a brother who was the very last person whose help she had ever wanted to ask for.

The brother did help, though. He got Marta away from the drugs and the gangs, at least. He took her to a mountain retreat and kept her as a concubine at first, and as he got to know the young girl he became impressed with her intelligence, her agility, and her intuitive skills, so he began training her in his profession and tradition. By profession he was a thief, and by tradition he was what Westerners would call a ninja. Marta was such an excellent student that by the age of sixteen she was helping him on all his major jobs. Then one night as he was traversing a narrow ledge on an office building fifteen stories up from the ground a sudden storm came up and a freak gust of wind knocked him off the ledge and down to his death.

With nowhere else to go, and unwilling to carry on the life of a ninja thief without her mentor, Marta went back to the geisha. This time, however, she was highly disciplined, loaded with new skills, and wise in many of the ways of the world. Seeing what a beauty she was turning into, and realizing that Marta would have to make her own way in the world fairly soon, the geisha taught the girl what she knew best - how to please men. In the course of learning that art, a compound of ancient psychology and genuine artistic skill, Marta discovered that a relatively minor part of the training was actually the area she was most adept at. In learning various way to please men erotically, Marta also discovered that sex was a completely difference experience when she was in charge of the action, rather than being a submissive participant. She found that she liked being sexually aggresssive, and she became aware that there were men who

206

liked playing a submissive role so much that they would pay very well for the privilege.

Marta made the additional discovery that some of her ninja skills were very useful in her new profession, skills such as tying unusual knots, the ability to influence thoughts and feelings, and the use of knives. Marta had an almost mystical connection with knives, swords, and other sharp instruments. When she played with them an observer could easily get the impression that they obeyed her unspoken commands like faithful servants, cutting or not as she willed, appearing and disappearing like magic, and flying wherever she desired without any effort on her part.

In time she came to the attention of agents working for the Narovskaya Institute. When she was eighteen she was brought to Russia to meet and train and have an affair with Nazra. At nineteen she was sent to Basel, Switzerland and attached to an escort service as their resident dominatrix. In the next two years she became fluent in French, English and German, in addition to Japanese and her native Schweizedeutsch. She did freelance work as a call-girl and thief and spent most of her time enjoying life while she waited for the order to participate in the final revolution. She had killed on occasion and was ready to do so again if it were necessary.

Now she walked briskly down *Steinenberg* in eager anticipation, for the note was from Nazra herself. She turned right past the outdoor cafe of the *Stadt-Casino*, the City Casino which actually housed restaurants and concert halls, onto *Barfüsserplatz*, a busy square named after the barefoot Franciscan friars who built the high Gothic *Barfüsserkirche*, the Barefoot Church, which had been turned into the city's Historical Museum. Marta made her way through the crowded flea market on the plaza in front of the church, and into the church itself, a cool and quiet haven after the heat and activity outside. She ignored the displays of secular and religious antiques from Basel's past and went downstairs to the cases that held the rich regalia of the city's former guild masters, they who had kicked out the bishop of Basel and had kept an image of his crozier as the symbol of the city in high mockery of his ouster. The caps of the masters glittered in their cases, being almost as finely and lavishly made as the crowns of kings.

Marta stopped by the case housing the cap of the guild master of the fishermen, made of velvet embroidered with gold and pearls and displaying a silver fish on its crown. This was where she was to meet Nazra, but the Russian wasn't anywhere in sight. While she stood there a neopunk-rocker in faded denims with close-cropped green hair, multiple earrings, and a nose ring attached by a silver chain to a silver pin that appeared to pierce her cheek, wandered into the same aisle, peering intently at the items in the cases. Marta was about to turn away when the girl looked at her, waggled her tongue, and smiled. The end of the girl's tongue was pierced by what looked for all the world like a tiny silver dumbbell.

With a small shudder Marta began to turn away again, then stopped. There was something about that smile ... "Nazra! It's you! Oh, my God!"

Nazra laughed and took Marta in her arms, kissing her with passion. They kissed for a fairly long time, uncaring of the shocked stares of the few older tourists who could see them through the glass cases. Or, perhaps, wanting to shock them on purpose.

They finally broke apart, both laughing. Marta felt inside her mouth with her tongue. "Interesting," she said. "That silver thing adds a piquant quality to the kiss. Does it hurt?"

"No more than pierced ears," laughed Nazra. Then more soberly. "Hold me again, and caress me. It will keep people away. I will give you details here and then we can go and talk in general at a cafe. And then... We'll see."

Fifteen minutes later the two women walked out of the museum arm in arm, chatting animatedly about everything and nothing. Men and women envied their obvious friendship. A few advanced souls wished the two of them well.

As they passed through the flea market Marta stopped and bought a perforated disk of lapis lazuli with a black cord and hung it around Nazra's neck. "It goes with your image," she said, smiling.

Nazra grinned and strolled through the market until she found and bought a curved Moroccan dagger with a chased silver handle and sheath. "For your image," she said, presenting it

208

to Marta.

They stopped at a sidewalk cafe on the square and had Heinekens while they talked some more. After a time they were just looking at each other. Marta took a deep breath and said, "There's an empty office nearby and I have the key. The boss is on holiday. It has a beautiful red leather settee."

"I have an hour," said Nazra.

A little more than an hour later, Marta smiled and waved to Nazra as the Russian woman boarded a tram which would take her from *Barfüsserplatz* to the *Hauptbahnhof*, the main train station. Sighing, Marta left the square and crossed *Freiestrasse* to *Münsterplatz*, the square in front of the great cathedral of Basel. She took a path that led behind the cathedral and down to the bank of the Rhine River. There she took the *Münsterfähre*, one of the ferries that carried passengers across the Rhine from *Grossbasel*, Big Basel, to *Kleinbasel*, Little Basel, where she had a flat.

It was a short, but peaceful trip, because instead of an engine the ferry was attached from its prow to a cable that looped over another cable that crossed the river. The force of the river current against the boat played the same role as the wind for a sailboat. By turning the rudder one way or another the boat could "tack" across the river in both directions without the need for an engine and without polluting the river. Marta started laying her plans with no distractions.

Twenty-three

A Friend In Need

Hapapa hewa ka malihini makamaka ʻole
(A stranger without a friend feels lost)

On the morning of the third day after Nazra met with Marta in Basel, Keoki was on a train leaving Stuttgart and bound for Karlsruhe. This was only his second train ride in his entire life, or his fourth if you counted the short roundtrip between Stuttgart and Tübingen. Still, it would be his first and longest one alone. He felt naked in a way without Gramps, but excited to be on his own in Europe, on a dangerous mission, as a real international cop. He didn't have the authority to arrest anyone, of course, but that was just as well. He was really more like a detective for a huge agency.

He was sitting in a first class open car because all the compartments had been reserved on the busy run between Munich and Frankfurt, but at least his seat was next to the window and facing forward. He was able to get this seat only because it was unreserved between Stuttgart and Karlsruhe, where he would change trains for Freiburg. His suitcase and shoulder bag were over his head on the rack that ran the length of the car above the windows, and his jacket was on a hook between his window and the window by the seat behind him. On a little fold-up table next to his right knee was a cup of coffee and a tasteless sweet roll that he had ordered from a man who rolled a food cart down the aisle shortly after they left the station at Stuttgart.

Before he finished the coffee a conductor entered the car to check and punch tickets. Keoki reached into his jacket pocket and pulled out his ticket and reservation slip, both of which were the size of airline tickets. He thought it was odd that you had to pay separately for the reservation, but he had learned that many people just took their chances on finding an unreserved seat, even in first class, and that a reservation was considered an extravagant luxury. He had had to buy a ticket because the rail pass given to Lani in Copenhagen had been for three people, since it had never been anticipated that the team would have to go separate ways. Keoki had been told that he would get his own Interpol pass in Freiburg.

"*Guten Morgen, fahrkarten, bitte*, Good morning, tickets, please," said the conductor as he came up to Keoki's four-seat section. Two other passengers and Keoki presented their tickets for inspection and punching. Before leaving them the conductor removed two slips from a reservation plaque on one of the aisle seats.

One of Keoki's seatmates was a middle-aged woman immersed in a novel. The other was a young and friendly man in a business suit. The man leaned forward, "*Bitte, sprechen Sie Deutsch?* Excuse me, do you speak German?"

Keoki smiled. "*Ja, ein wenig*, Yes, a little."

"Ah, good," said the man in German. "Are you an American?"

"Yes, I am. I'm... here on holiday."

"A student, then?"

What to say? Keoki decided to go undercover. "I sell computers. What about you?"

"I sell books," the man said, "on audiocassette. I'm on my way to a book fair in Frankfurt to sell a lot of them."

Gramps had once told Keoki that the easiest way to make friends was to share a little about yourself and encourage the other person to talk a lot about anything. Most people enjoy talking about themselves and anything else they think they know something about, Gramps had said. If they think you are really interested they'll usually talk a lot, and you will usually learn a lot. It wouldn't always be accurate or true, but you would always get some good out of it if you were a good listener. Besides, Gramps had told him, it's good practice for studying people's behavior, learning about beliefs systems, and for getting information.

So Keoki expressed interest, and during the rest of the trip to Karlsruhe he learned a lot about the book business and one man's opinion on the German economy ("It's in serious trouble because of the Japanese"), German politics ("The former East Germany has an influence all out of proportion to its population") and German social problems ("We have too many immigrants on welfare"). Keoki also learned a lot he didn't know about regional foods ("You have to try Swabian *spätzle*, a kind of noodle; Bavarian *weisswurst*, a veal sausage that should only be eaten between midnight and noon; and, of course, *Schwarzwälderkirschtorte*, the famous Black Forest chocolate cake").

By the time they reached Karlsruhe Keoki was glad to say goodbye and get off the train. It had been interesting, but exhausting. The conversation had been incessant, and it had taken all of his concentration to understand what the man was saying. As it was, he probably only got about seventy-five percent of it. On his way to the next track he realized that they had never even exchanged names and, to his surprise, he found that okay.

He found the track for the train to Freiburg, but it wasn't leaving for a half hour, so he wandered around the station. He stopped in the bookstore and was surprised to see so many magazines dealing with computers. There were American and British mags, as well as German; many more than in a typical US bookstore, and more of them had CDs included. He was tempted to buy a few, but decided to wait until he was ready to leave the country. He did buy a copy of *Der Spiegel*, just to brush up on his German. Gramps had given him two thousand *Deutschmarks*, close to a thousand dollars, and he felt good about paying his own way for a change.

It was close enough to noon for him to buy a ham and cheese sandwich on a long roll and a can of St. Pauli Girl beer. In talking about food, the man on the train had said that ham and cheese sandwiches were an American innovation. No one in Europe mixed ham and cheese until American tourists clamored for the combination.

Ten minutes before his train was due Keoki walked out to the platform with his bags and checked the train map. This was a large, glass-enclosed chart placed in the middle of the platform which displayed moveable cut-outs of each arriving train in relation to the alphabetized sections of the platform. In order to know just where to wait for a particular car, all you had to do was look at the map. Keoki's car was number nine, next to the dining car, and it would stop in Section A.

Keoki went to the right position and waited with the other passengers. This train would not be as crowded as the first one because the run was not as popular, the man on the last train had told him. Finally the train pulled into the station and Keoki felt a thrill of anticipated adventure rising up from his subconscious. He had very little personal experience with trains, so he must have been programmed for it by all those movies from the thirties and forties that he had watched in his cinematography classes.

The non-smoking half of his car was on the left, marked boldly by the big red circle with the cigarette slashed in half. He climbed on board, found his compartment, and stashed his bags on the rack above him. He waited to see who else would be sharing the compartment, but no one entered by the time the train pulled out of the station, so he had it all to himself.

He just gazed out the window until his ticket was punched and he had bought a can of Coke from the food cart. He picked up the magazine and read one article on Claudia Schiffer, then put it down. He was restless. Maybe he ought to practice some of his kupua skills before he joined the team in Freiburg. Keoki settled back and used the special breathing that got him deeply centered. While in that state he decided to explore the train.

He sent his awareness forward through the next two cars to the engine. He was careful not to try and pay attention to details. Gramps had told him that *Po*, the inner world, was like a stack of photographs of different places, with each photo being like a different layer, or zone, of experience. It was difficult to keep your focus in one zone without slipping over into another zone, perhaps many layers away. The trick to staying in one zone was to keep your focus moving within a certain range of experience related to the zone you wanted to stay in. Gramps had said that the same thing applied to *Ao*, the outer world, but Keoki hadn't really understood until he read somewhere that fighter pilots had to be wary of focusing too intently on a single target or they would go into a trance.

So Keoki let his consciousness drift along within the range

of the train experience, no more than a few layers away from *Ao*. At the engine he let himself feel the electricity pouring into the engine itself, and followed its transformation into the mechanical movement that drove the wheels. When he tired of that he drifted back, through his own car and over his own body, into the dining car. He observed how it was set up and made a mental note to check his perceptions when he got back to his body. He kept moving, into the second class cars, until he came to the bicycle car.

He was riding a red velvet bicycle along the narrow ridge of a purple mountain range that crossed the center of an island from sea to golden sea. The air was filled with rose petals that kept obscuring his vision and he was afraid he would ride straight off the edge of the ridge. He batted them away with one hand, causing his bike to wobble dangerously. The bicycle told him to stop that before the ogre-dance caused a mass rift in the cicular plenifold and...

The bicycle told him what? What was he doing on a bicycle anyway? He remembered something Gramps had said: If you're ever lost in inner space, return right away to your body. Keoki willed himself back and woke up in his compartment on the train to Freiburg. He looked around, moved his hands and feet, touched the seat cushion, and stood up. Now he knew what had happened. He had been caught by an *aka* thread connecting the bicycles of the layer he'd been in to another *aupuni po*, another inner realm, so fast he didn't notice it. He knew what had happened, but he didn't understand it. *Po* was a complicated place.

He decided that that was enough practice for the time being, so he left the compartment and went to the dining car, bouncing from side to side in the corridor as the train rocked on the tracks. The dining car turned out to be more narrow than he had seen it in *Po* and it had waiters instead of waitresses. There were flowers on the tables that he hadn't seen on his inner journey, but he did get the shape of the chairs right. Chalk up a bit of success. He found an empty table and ordered *ein bier vom fass*, a draft beer.

The train arrived in Freiburg just after two in the afternoon. It had followed the Rhine Valley south, with the Black Forest on the left and the Rhine River and France on the right. Keoki didn't think the Black Forest looked very black, but maybe the name referred to the deep woods of long ago. He knew it was associated with a lot of fairy tales of ogres and trolls and elves and witches, and that the area was probably part of the inspiration for the Hobbit series by Tolkien.

At Freiburg he got off the train with his bags and walked beside the track to the Inter-City Hotel which bordered the platform. There was a prepaid reservation in his name for one night and the male clerk gave him a large envelope along with his key. Once Keoki had settled in his small, but comfortable room he sat on the bed and opened the envelope. Inside were three sheets of paper and his Interpol rail pass.

On the first paper was a list of the three PERI members assigned to this area, with a brief background on each. On the second was a telephone contact number for the BND agent in charge of security for Ivan Mikalov, and instructions on what information could and could not be shared with the PERI team. For instance, the fact that Mikalov had been moved to Triberg without their knowledge could not be shared. Their role had been reduced to the monitoring of Nazra's presence on railways and roads in the area. Keoki thought that was dumb, but he guessed that the security forces didn't have much faith in PERI's resources after having lost two of their charges while PERI teams were on the job. The fact that they had lost those men while they themselves were on the job apparently didn't count. The third sheet was an Interpol form for reporting expenses. The necessity for attaching receipts was mentioned three times.

Keoki put the sheets back in the envelope and was considering what to do next when the telephone rang. "Hello?"

"Hello, old chap. Finished reading your instructions?"

Old chap? "Uh, yes, but..."

"Hah! Got it right on the button, what? Jeffrey Boggles here, resident geo-astrologer for PERI 2. Not much happening on the Seeker front, so the teammates sent me along to pick you up and hide you off to the old hideout."

"Uh, Jeffrey Boggles?" Keoki was pulling out the paper to check the PERI list. There he was, geo-astrologer, whatever that was. British. He had several books published.

"I expect your reading my bio right now, what?" said the

215

man on the phone.

"I am," said Keoki.

"Hah! Knew it. I'm getting rather good at this psychic rigamarole, even though I operate along more scientific lines as a rule. So, I'll show you the town, won't take long, we'll have a good meal, perhaps a do, sleep a nice sleep, in separate rooms, of course, hah-hah, and in the morning it's off to good old Kirchzarten. Up for that, are you, chappie?"

"Good old where?" Keoki was getting confused.

"Kirchzarten, old chum. That's where we're bunkered. Out of town a bit. No one's in Freiburg. Too difficult to espy and protect, you know."

He didn't know, and was somewhat upset about it. "I'll need some time to get ready..."

"Three o'clock, then. Should be ample. Meet in the lobby by the front desk?"

"That'll be fine." Jeffrey hung up and Keoki let out his breath. He didn't know if he could keep up with that kind of energy. He unpacked the bare necessities, took a shower, and redressed. Then he called his German contact, who confirmed that Jeffrey had been sent to pick him up and take him back to Kirchzarten the next day. Keoki didn't bother to complain about the lack of communication. He just hoped that the rest of their plans were better organized. He was going to be bait, and he didn't want to be gobbled up because someone had forgotten to put the hook on the line.

When he arrived in the lobby he knew instantly who Jeffrey was. He was the man with the unruly abundance of brown hair that hung six inches below his shoulders, bug eyes and overbite, dressed a silky gray shirt, zodiac pendant, and beige, pleated trousers. He looked like a British hippie from the sixties.

"Ah, there you are, old chap." The long-haired man stretched out a hand. "I'm Boggles, you're McCoy, right?"

Keoki shook his hand. "That's right, but my friends call me Keoki."

"Kay-oh-key," Boggles said slowly. "Would that be a last name or a first?"

"First."

"Oh, I see. Must be an American nickname for George. Like

216

Bob for Robert, what? Hah-hah! I'll go along with it, since we're neither here nor there. Jeff's my handle, pahdna."

Keoki cringed. "Uh, okay, Jeff. You said you were going to show me around?"

"Right-o! Let's be off." and he practically bounded out the door.

He actually said 'Right-o!, thought Keoki. He hadn't thought that people talked like that outside of the movies.

They crossed *Bismarckallee* in front of the station and walked along the pleasant, tree-lined *Eisenbahnstrasse* toward the center of town. Jeff pointed out Colombi Park with its museum that was running a display of Celtic culture, but Keoki wasn't that interested. They passed the *Rathaus*, the Town Hall, crossed *Kaiser-Josephstrasse*, the main commercial street loaded with shoppers, and followed a short street to the *Münsterplatz*, a busy square surrounded by shops and restaurants. In the center of the square was the great, mostly Gothic, Cathedral of Freiburg. Actually, Jeff told him, the real name of the town was *Freiburg im Breisgau*, meaning "Freiburg on the Breisgau River."

Jeff fairly danced around the ancient, sandstone Cathedral, pointing out items of interest. He seemed particularly delighted with a carving of a nude man and woman apparently being married by a priest which was over one of the doorways to the church, and high on the other side of the building, another carving of an amazingly erotic figure of a naked woman whose butt was thrust outward with an appropriately-placed hole serving as a rainspout. Keoki was truly shocked to find something like that on a church. Jeff softened the blow a little by mentioning that according to local lore there was a time when most of the men had been killed off in wars and the Church saw this as a subliminal way of stimulating marriage and procreation.

Jeff took Keoki inside the cathedral to see the elaborate interior with its beautiful stained glass windows and the self-portrait of the main sculptor peering out from under the stairs leading up to an intricately-carved pulpit. Keoki declined an offer to climb the tower, so Jeff led him out another door into a tiny sort of courtyard. "You've got to experience this," he said. "Stand there, look up, and tell me what you feel."

Keoki felt rather foolish with all the other people around

looking at them and wondering what they were up to, but he stood on the spot indicated by Jeff and looked up. He was looking straight up between the towers of the cathedral and it was naturally dizzying, but suddenly he felt a rush of energy coming up from his feet that almost pulled him over backwards. "Whoa!" he said as he caught his balance. "What was that?"

"Try it again," urged Jeff, "just so you know that it was real, and not a fluke."

Keoki stood back on the spot and expanded his *la'a kea*. He could definitely sense a strong field of energy here now that he was paying attention. He looked up and the rush hit him and nearly threw him backwards again. "Whew! That's enough for me," he said, stepping back. "Why does that happen?"

"You'll have to ask God for the details, old chum," said Jeff, leading him back inside and then out through another door. "The ancient Druids had a sacred oak grove here on this very spot. I've a bit more to show you and then we'll stop to refresh ourselves."

As they walked away from Cathedral Square, Jeff said, "The ancients knew a lot more about earth energies than we do today, you know. The Druids, the Celtic priests, were specially good at that. When the Catholics defeated the Druids they built their churches on old Druidic holy places whenever they could, so there were obviously Catholic priests who knew a lot about earth energy, too."

Keoki was a little familiar with the concept of "power spots" because of the research on medieval magic and magicians that he did for his computer games, but he never considered it as more than research material. Also, Gramps had taught him about the energy fields of stones and trees and certain special places in Hawaii, so he wasn't entirely skeptical. Not entirely. "Maybe the Catholic priests just wanted to take advantage of local habits. You get used to going to a particular place for spiritual things. It would have been smart to make use of that."

"Hah! Good point! If," the Britisher waggled a finger in Keoki's face, "they had done no more than tear down the old to build something new. But they did much more. A lot of older churches and cathedrals incoporated Druidic energy symbols, and some were designed to protect or enhance major energy points. The Freiburg cathedral, which was started in the year 1200 A.D. and took four hundred years to finish, was not only built on a Druid holy place, the builders went out of their way to protect that spot you stood on, and even the baptismal font was placed over an ancient spring. Some cathedrals, like the one at Chartres and the one at Cologne, incorporate labyrinths in their design and..."

"Labyrinths?" Keoki perked up at that. "What for?"

Jeff patted him on the shoulder as they walked along. "Labyrinths are more than just intriguing patterns, old sod. They collect and concentrate earth energy so it can be used for healing and conjuring up spells."

That broke the spell. "Oh, right, spells," said Keoki disparagingly.

"Listen to the unbeliever!" Jeff said to the world. Then to Keoki, "Dear me, don't you know what spells really are?"

Keoki hated the condescending tone, but he bit the hook anyway. "Probably not. So, what do you think they are, Jeff.?"

"What spells are," said Jeff, implying that this was not open to question by any reasonably sane man, "are merely thoughts strengthened by energy and activated by intent. You undoubtedly conjure spells all the time, only you probably have a different name for it. I think a lot of Yanks use the word 'programming' for that sort of thing. Sounds more high tech, what?"

The Hawaiian was surprised by Jeff again. He had never thought of the things that Gramps had taught him to do as having anything to do with spells. That was for magic in games and stories. On the other hand—another thought hit him—if throwing that fireball at Nazra in the Deer Park wasn't casting a spell, what was? "I hadn't thought of it that way," conceded Keoki. "Maybe there's something to that."

"Hah! A concession! Careful, chappie, your mind might open in spite of your best efforts." Jeff halted in mid-stride and grimaced. "Sorry. Didn't mean that. No offense intended. Apologies?" He held out his hand.

Keoki thought it was odd, but he shook hands and said, "No offense taken. What else do you want to show me?"

Jeff brightened and said, "We're there!" With a grand flourish he pointed to a tall, very medieval clock tower that straddled

219

the street. "The *Schwabentor*, a fully restored architechtural masterpiece. Formerly one of the city gates when it was surrounded by walls. But what I really have to show you is on the other side of it. Come along, old chap."

They walked under the tower, leaving the Old Town, and continued for several tens of yards until Jeff made Keoki turn around. On this side of the tower was a large painting of St. George in full armor slaying a dragon. "Thought you might like to see how your namesake is portrayed here," said Jeff. Amazing likeness, what?"

Keoki grimaced. "Right. By the way, why is he here? I mean, I thought he was an English saint."

"Hah! You and too many others. But this opens up a line of inquiry that may be more than you can handle. Shall I cease forthwith or dast ye leap into the breach eyes open?" Jeff raised his eyebrows, which made him seem even more bug-eyed.

Keoli looked puzzled. "Are you asking if I want to hear more about it?"

"You could put it that way, yes."

Gramps said to listen, so he would listen. "Okay."

"Jolly good! But let us hie to yon mountain for a cooling drink first." Jeff led the way to a set of stairs which took them up a slope to a kind of grotto. "There's an elevator up to the restaurant in there, but the walk is better for you." They passed by the grotto and walked up a path which eventually brought them to the entrance of the *Schlossle* Restaurant. They went inside and through to a terrace with a gorgeous view of the whole city of Freiburg, the Rhine Valley, and a range of mountains in France. They ordered a half carafe of the house white and Jeffrey began pouring out words after the first sip of the wine.

"First things first. To the surprise of many, including you, George the saint was a Roman soldier born in Cappodocia who lived toward the end of the third century A.D. and just a bit into the fourth. The exploit that really made him famous took place in Libya. Seems there was this village, or kingdom perhaps. Don't really know if it started out as a village and grew into a kingdom with the telling, so we'll call it a kingdom and be done with it. This kingdom was sorely beset by a large serpent or, more likely, a giant crocodile. After they had fed it all their goats to keep it away from the important folk they started tossing people into its maw, but that didn't work, either. Someone came up with the brilliant idea of handing over the princess to the monster, for surely it would be satisfied with royal blood. The king and queen must have figured better her than them, so off they marched her to her doom and, hopefully, their salvation. Fortunately for the princess, George happened to be about and decided that princesses were more valuable than crocodiles, so he offed the beast with his spear."

Jeff paused briefly to soothe his throat. "The next time we hear anything interesting about George he is at the court of the emperor Diocletian in Rome. George declares for Christianity; Diocletian doesn't like competition; George is tossed into the Roman equivalent of the Tower of London and gets badly beaten about the head and shoulders. According to the Catholic Encyclopedia Christ appears and heals him. Diocletian tries poison and a particularly nasty crushing device. Same result. Finally, in the year 303, when Christ isn't looking, Diocletian has George beheaded and he becomes a saint. Actually, sainthood takes place about the middle of the thirteenth century. Finally, in the fifteenth century, more than a thousand years after he lost his head, good old George takes England by storm and becomes its patron saint. That's in the history books."

"Wow," said Keoki. "I didn't know any of that."

"Don't let it get you down, old chum. Most Catholics don't, either." After another refreshing pause, Jeffrey said, "Now it gets more interesting. Shall I go on?" Keoki nodded. "Excellent. At this point our story takes a curious twist. The word 'dragon' comes from the Greek drakon, with the double meaning of 'serpent' and 'sharp-sighted.' It can also refer to a seer, or a psychic. Biblically, the word is used for a serpent, a crocodile, and as an epithet for Satan." Jeffrey got so excited about what he was saying that he knocked his glass over. Fortunately, it was empty, so he refilled it.

"When we mix this into a stew combining the Dark Ages, Celtic culture, Druidic religion, and Christian expansionism, we get our mighty knight in shining armor, St. George, battling the wicked dragon to save the ravishing —or is that ravished?— princess. As well as other stories of knights killing dragons and

221

stealing their treasure." Jeffrey downed half a glass of wine in one gulp.

"Thus, Druids are identified by Dark Age Christians as dragons, both because of their abilities as seers and their supposed relationship to Satan. A great many of their sacred sites are given names that include the word 'dragon.' You'll find them scattered all over the British Isles and all over Germany, where the dragon is known as a worm, or *Wurm*. The most interesting part, however, is this: the Druids established two primary types of sacred sites, those on rounded hills and those on sharper peaks. All over Europe you will find that towns that are on or near rounded hills will have St. George as their patron, and those that are on or near peaks will have St. Michael as their patron. Both were legendary dragon-slayers, right? Some clever group of priests used those symbols to represent the two major types of earth energy power spots, which they had taken over from the Druids. Hah!" With a flourish, Jeffrey drank the last of the wine.

That was a lot for Keoki to handle. "Uh, I'm going to have to digest all that for awhile, Jeff. Let's head back toward the hotel, okay?"

Jeff smiled smugly. "Bully!"

Keoki paid the bill will little resistance from Jeff, and they went back out to the path. Jeff took them on a different route and Keoki could see lots of paths going up the gently sloping mountainside. They walked down to a footbridge that took them over a highway and back into the Old Town. Jeff led them past art galleries and the studio where he said Ivan Mikalov usually worked. "Got him hidden out in Kirchzarten now," said Jeff in a low voice, as if sharing a secret.

They walked through the theater area and along the shopping district, where Keoki bought some souvenirs for his family. Finally, Keoki announced that he was getting hungry.

"I have just the spot," said Jeff. "Very Germanic, but good nevertheless. I'm not a boiled beef fan, you know. Norman blood; mother's side. Prefer some taste on my board." Jeff marched them along *Eisenstrasse* to the *Kartcherstube*, a small and cozy restaurant very near the train station with a tiny outdoor seating area. They shared some house red wine. Jeff had the *Sauerbraten* and Keoki had the best sausage he'd had so far, with a side of

Käsespätzle, Swabian noodles with cheese, and *Zitronsorbet mit vodka*, lime sherbet drenched in vodka, for dessert. Keoki was glad the hotel was close by.

They parted in the lobby with an agreement to meet for breakfast at eight. "Ta-ta," said Jeff as he went to his room.

Ta-ta?

Twenty-four

Strange Attraction

He 'iwa ho'ohaehae naulu
(A bird that teases the rain clouds)

In the morning Keoki woke up from a nightmare in which he was a knight in rusty armor fighting a huge red dragon. He was riding a donkey and he charged the dragon at a trot, but his lance broke on the monster's scaly hide and the dragon ate the donkey. Then Dream-Keoki pulled out his rusty sword and struck a mighty blow, but the sword broke, too, and the dragon reached out to puncture him with a claw.

He awakened in a panic, wrapped in a sweat-soaked sheet with his heart pounding. When he realized he was in a hotel room and not in a dragon's belly, he breathed deeply and slowly from his navel to calm himself down and then disentangled himself from the sheet. He thought about the dream while he got out of bed, did some stretching exercises in the small space between the foot of the bed and the wall of the room, went to the bathroom, shaved in front of the smallish mirror, and took a shower in the very tiny stall.

One of the first things Gramps had ever taught him was how to deal with nightmares. As a kid he had had a lot of them, and at the time he had thought that the technique Gramps had taught him had literally saved his life. And it was kind of fun, besides. Gramps had told him when he was a child that a nightmare was a story that his inner self made up to tell him that there was some kind of problem he had to solve. Instead of trying to figure out what the problem was, all he had to do was to change the story. As a kid he didn't question this, so every time he had a nightmare he would redo the story in his mind so that he was the hero and it had a good ending. Besides being fun to do, he stopped having so many nightmares, and when they happened they didn't scare him so much. A few times he was even able to change the story while he was dreaming.

When he grew older and more educated he began to wonder if changing the story wasn't just suppressing the problem. When that kind of question came up Gramps told him that the images in dreams were a kind of language, a pictorial expression of beliefs that often could not be translated very well into words, any more than musical language could. By changing the story, Gramps told him, he was actually changing the beliefs that produced the story. That had been, and still was, hard for Keoki to understand. It became even harder when, later on, Gramps had tried to teach him the idea that dreams were real events, as real as any in the regular world.

"I thought dreams were just stories," Keoki had said skeptically.

"Life is a story, too," Gramps had replied.

At the time Keoki had just rolled his eyes and gone off to party with his friends. That was about the time he had begun to drift away from his grandfather's teachings.

Here and now, in Freiburg, in his new role as a psychic investigator for Interpol, he renewed his decision to take up the teachings again and tackled the nightmare in the way his grandfather had taught him. He recalled the nightmare to his conscious mind and the first thing he did was to change the donkey into a powerful black stallion worthy of a knight. That was easy enough. Then he changed his armor into silvery, elven mithril, borrowing a concept from Tolkein. Next he turned his lance and sword into the finest Damascene steel. Okay so far. Finally it was time to take on the dragon. When he looked at the dragon in his mind it was just sitting there with a smile on its face, patiently waiting for him to finish.

He tried to make the dragon look fearful, but that didn't work. He tried to make it smaller, but that didn't work, either. He tried other ways to change the dragon, but none of them had any effect. Even though it was his own imagination, the dragon seemed to have a power of its own. A little angry, the knight-Keoki charged the dragon head on. His lance hit the dragon and

225

skittered off, as if the dragon's scales were even too tough for good steel. With one giant claw the dragon plucked the lance out of his hands and knocked the horse out from under him. Wait a minute, this is my dream! thought Keoki. The knight-Keoki pulled out his sword and stomped toward the dragon on foot. He raised it to strike and the dragon pulled it out of his hands with its teeth. The knight-Keoki was shocked, but nimble enought to jump out of the way when the dragon attempted to bite him in half. For the next few moments the knight-Keoki kept dodging out of the way as the dragon tried to claw him and bite him. Finally Keoki shook his head and stopped the imagery. This was going nowhere. When you couldn't change a particular image, Gramps had told him, that was a sign that a core belief was involved, which would take a lot more work. Right now Keoki had neither the time nor the inclination to go any further with it.

At breakfast Jeffrey was his usual bouncy, ultra-British self and Keoki was not in a tolerant mood. During a particularly tedious and gossipy story about the time Jeffrey almost had an opportunity to actually speak with Princess Diana at some kind of rally in Kensington Park, a story liberally sprinkled with "old chum," "old sod," "don't you know" and the like, Keoki raised his hands and said, "Just stop it, will you?"

"Stop what, old man?" Jeffrey froze, his bug-eyes wide and a fork held high in the air in order to illustrate a point he was just about to make.

"That!" said Keoki through gritted teeth. "Your whole British act. It's too much. You're like a joke."

Jeffrey stared at Keoki and slowly brought his fork down to the table. To Keoki's amazement tears formed in Jeff's eyes and rolled down his cheeks. The Britisher picked up his napkin, wiped away the tears, dabbed at his mouth, put the napkin down and stood up. "Sorry to have offended you, Mr. McCoy. Bit of a rum do, that. Our train leaves at nine. I'll meet you at the station in Kirchzarten and take you to your lodgings." Then he walked away.

Oh Jeez! Keoki said to himself. *You're a real ambassador for the Aloha Spirit, aren't you?*

Keoki boarded the train to Kirchzarten at nine. It was all second class open seating and he had no idea where Jeff was, so he took a seat by a window. Earlier he had gone to the ticket booth to make sure his pass would be accepted and found that there would not be a conductor to check the tickets. Shorter routes worked on the honor system. Unless you had a pass you had to buy a ticket at the booth or at a vending machine, but you never had to show it to anyone unless an inspector boarded the train for a random check. It was easy to cheat, but few people did, partly because there was a high penalty if you got caught.

Now Keoki turned his thoughts back to Jeff. By this time he had stopped beating himself for being so rude and was trying to find a way to heal the situation. A plain apology would no doubt be politely accepted by Jeff, but it wouldn't improve their relationship. An abject apology would probably be received as a mockery. What could he do that would work? What would Gramps have done?

Thinking of Gramps brought up the memory of a time when he was getting into a series of fights with another kid in grade school. He hadn't wanted to fight anymore, but he couldn't think of any way to stop without breaking the other guy's arms and legs. One evening Gramps had helped him to imagine that he was playing catch with his enemy. At the beginning of the imagery he and the other boy kept trying to bean each other with a baseball, but by the time Keoki finished some five minutes later he was imagining that they were tossing the ball back and forth in a friendly way. In school the next day the boy glared at him, but didn't try to start anything. Within a couple days he even stopped glaring at Keoki. Within a couple of weeks they were playing football on the same team without any fuss. Keoki never did become friends with the boy, but neither were they enemies any longer.

What the heck, thought Keoki. *What kind of ball do Britishers play?* He thought of cricket, but he really didn't know much about the game. He knew they played rugby, but he also knew that it was a rough sport and that didn't seem appropriate. They also played soccer, he remembered. He would try that. In his mind he set up a soccer field where he and Jeff could practice. It took some effort to imagine Jeffrey in a soccer outfit, but he finally managed it. The next problem was that Jeff wouldn't play. Keoki would kick to ball to him, gently, and Jeff would simply

227

fold his arms and look the other way. Keoki was stumped for a couple of minutes. Then he got the idea to turn the soccer ball into a globe of the earth. That got the imaginary Jeffrey's attention and with a little exertion of will Keoki was able to get the ball going back and forth quite nicely. When his image of Jeff started to smile Keoki figured it was enough for the time being.

Keoki looked around and decided that his bag would be safe enough where it was, so he went looking for Jeff. He found the Britisher two cars away staring out the window. The seat next to him was empty so Keoki sat down in it. Jeff acted like he didn't notice.

After some moments of silence Keoki said, "I remember one time in Hawaii there was this visitor—that's what we call tourists—there was this visitor from the State of Illinois who got really mad at me when I had a summer job as a guide in one of our parks. 'You people are always talking like you're in the movie Hawaii. It's always *aloha* this and *kanaka* that, or *tutu* and *wahine*. Why can't you just talk like normal people?' That's what he said. Of course, he didn't know we were talking like normal people in Hawaii. The State, not the movie." Keoki paused. "I'm sorry for being as narrow-minded as he was."

Jeff turned around, but still looked away. "Actually, you were somewhat justified." Jeffrey brushed his nose with a finger. "Most of it was an act. I'm not very good with people, you know. I play the ultimate Brit to cover up my shyness. It's like a mask that lets me do things I couldn't do otherwise. Unfortunately, it often pushes people away that I'd like to know better." He was still looking down.

"Tell you what," said Keoki. "You go on playing the ultimate Brit and I'll play the ultimate Hawaiian. Maybe they'll cancel each other out."

Jeffrey looked up and smiled. "Tell you what," said Jeff, "let's don't. But if you're willing to put up with a few 'whats" at the end of a sentence on occasion, I'm sure I could tolerate an *aloha* once in a while."

"That's a deal." Keoki put out his hand and, after a moment's hesitation, Jeff shook it. "So tell me," said Keoki, "what in heaven's name is geo-astrology?"

"Hah!" said Jeff, and launched happily into an explanation.

228

According to Jeffrey, geo-astrology was the science of relationships between earth energies and stellar energies. Part of it had to do with a complicated formula for mapping currents of earth energy by establishing a correlation with patterns of planetary movement. Another part, the part that had to do with his being a member of the PERI team, consisted of doing astrological charts for landforms or population centers based on significant geological or social events such as earthquakes, the founding of a city, battles, or the building of an energy-related structure like a cathedral or a tower. Then one did a progressive chart representing the movement of planets from one of those dates to the current time and looked for significant patterns in the chart that indicated a potential event of the type one was looking for.

In the present situation Jeffrey was looking for correlations between Mars and Saturn in the progressed charts of Kirchzarten and his best approximation of Seeker's. But his favorite part of the science was researching ancient knowledge of earth energy. For instance, did Keoki know that the name George was derived from Greek and meant "tiller of the soil," and that some of the early meanings of "to till" meant to cultivate, to breed, and to bring into being? Or that the name Michael was a Hebrew word meaning "to be like God," but also meant "to be like expanding power?"

"I didn't know that," said Keoki, thinking that he had been saying that a lot lately.

For the rest of the trip Jeff proceeded to tell Keoki a lot of other things he hadn't known.

After disembarking at the tiny Kirchzarten station they took a taxi to *Haus Hubertus*, a kind of cross between a bed-and-breakfast place and a miniature hotel on *Dr. Gremmelsbacherstrasse* at the edge of town. The town of Kirchzarten itself seemed rather quiet, with curving streets and a mix of old and modern buildings of modest size all set in a farming area east of Freiburg. *Haus Hubertus* took its name from a local legend about a hunter named Hubertus who saw a stag with a glowing cross between its antlers and who was thereby converted to Christianity. It was very cozy inside the hotel and the friendly landlady showed Keoki to a comfortable upstairs room while Jeff went to his own room to freshen up. A half hour later Jeff knocked on Keoki's door.

"Time to go to work, old man," said Jeff.

Keoki opened the door. "Be right with you, *hoapili*. That means 'friend.'"

The Britisher grinned. "I see I'm going to get tit for tat for the rest of our time together, what?"

"*Ae*," said Keoki, and closed the door. He opened it again. "That means 'yes.'" He closed it again. In a few minutes he opened it once more. "Okay, let's go to work."

It had warmed up enough so that both men simply wore shirts and trousers. Jeff led Keoki outside and across the street. They turned left and walked along a weedy field toward a large, white two-story building on the right. As they walked Jeff waved a piece of paper. "There was a note in my room from Peggy, that's the clairvoyant I've been working with. Says that she and Charlotte, that's the pendulumist, were called away by Madame Villier for some other assignment and that they've been replaced by some bird named Brigid Meisterle. Too bad. Peggy was a nice sort. Of course, Charlotte fussed a lot. Hope the new bird isn't one of those German amazon types." They walked on a ways until they were in front of the white building. "That's the *Kurhaus*," said Jeff.

"Which is?"

"Where we work. Use to be a sort of spa. Now it's used as a community center and for seminars and classes, mostly health-related, sometimes metaphysical. We've let a room on the second floor. Ah, you would say 'rented.' Want to show you something on the other side before we go up."

As they walked across the parking lot to the left side of the building Keoki noticed a trailer park across the street. "Looks like a popular tourist spot," he said.

"Very popular, I'm told. We're quite close to the Black Forest. Lots of hiking and other outdoor nonsense. Look there!"

Keoki looked where Jeff was pointing and saw a kind of polished wood framework about thirty yards away in a grassy place apart from the main building. In front of the framework was a bench and next to it was a water trough fed by a spigot. While they were looking a car stopped on the nearby road and a man got out. He was dressed in a gray leather coat with matching shorts, knee socks and sturdy shoes, and a gray leather cap that reminded Keoki of what Robin Hood was supposed to have worn. The man walked over to the trough, took off his coat and laid it on the bench, and undid the collar of his white shirt. He turned on the spigot and rinsed his hands, then cupped them to take a drink and used more water to rinse his face, neck and forearms. Finally he buttoned up, put his coat back on, walked back to the car and drove away.

"Bit of luck, that!" said Jeff.

"Why?" asked Keoki.

"Intended to show you the site of the ancient spring," Jeff said as he turned Keoki toward the entrance of the *Kurhaus*. "Goes back to Celtic times. Reputed to have magical healing powers. Now you've seen it in action. That man we saw obviously follows some of the traditional customs of the area, including a partaking of the healing waters. I knew that the site of the spring had been maintained, but I didn't know it was still used for the old magical purpose."

They walked up the broad steps to the entrance and through the doors into an airy foyer. No one was about and Jeff led the way up a stairway on the left to the second floor and left again to a door with a hand-printed sign that said "Meeting In Progress." Jeff walked right in and said, "Glory to God, the angels are on our side. My name is Jeffrey Boggles. This is Keoki McCoy. Are you of the Cherubim or the Seraphim?"

On the far side of the room, standing next to a map of the region, was a vision. There are a great many pretty women in the world. There are a lot of beautiful women in the world. There are a considerable number of gorgeous women in the world. There are very few charismatic women in the world. Jeff and Keoki gazed with awe on a woman whose looks were on the border between pretty and beautiful, but whose energy filled the room.

It is a curiosity of human nature that the more good-looking a woman is, the more weirdly most men act around her. It is one thing to admire a very attractive woman in a magazine or on a screen. It is a different experience entirely to be in the same room with one if you are not used to it. The energy of certain women evokes a protective intinct in men. That of others induces a desire for companionship. That of a few provokes instant, powerful lust.

"I don't think I would qualify as angelic," said the woman in English with a light Germanic accent. She smiled deliciously as she brushed back a strand of auburn hair, touched a strand of pearls around her neck to bring attention to the low neckline of her off-white sweater, and made straightening motions on her dark brown mini-skirt which emphasized her slim hips and long legs. Then she stepped forward with her hand outstretched. "I'm Brigid Meisterle. I work mostly with energy."

"I'm, ah, sure you do," said Jeffrey as he took her hand. His eyes looked bigger than ever and he didn't seem to want to let go of her.

Brigid looked at Keoki and Jeff's hand fell away. It was the kind of look that said, "You're the one I'm really interested in." Some men would throw away their lives and values for that kind of look from that kind of woman. So Keoki was surprised that his own gut reaction was one of wanting to get away from her as quickly as possible. Don't be stupid, he told himself. Faintly, some part of him replied back with the same words, but he ignored them. "Hi," he said with a silly grin as he took her hand.

"Hi," said Brigid, making it sound as if the two of them were alone in bed. "Peggy and Charlotte said you were coming, but they didn't know anything about you." All they could tell her, after she had kidnapped them and Peggy had been forced to write the note, was that a Hawaiian psychic or shaman was being added to their team and Jeffrey had gone to pick him up. As sources of information they were virtually useless, but she had no instructions to harm them so she had left them tied up in a woodshed in one of the fields outside of town. If they were smart enough they would be able to free themselves in a couple of days or so.

However, Nazra had told her a lot more about Keoki. This was one of the men she was to kill, but not before he led her to Ivan Mikalov, the other target. Nazra had said that her information channel to Interpol had been cut off, but before that happened she had learned that the PERI team was based in Kirchzarten and that the Hawaiian was supposed to join them there. He also had some kind of special connection to Interpol that was unclear. According to Nazra, the Hawaiian was inexperienced, but he was supposed to have a strong, natural, intuitive talent. No matter.

After she and Nazra had made love in Basel she had shared a joke that one of her American clients had told her. After God made man he said to the new creature, "I have given you means to have dominion over the earth and to go forth and multiply, but there's a little problem." "What's the problem?" asked the man. "Well, to do that I had to endow you with a brain and a penis," said God. "What could be the wrong with that?" queried the man. God looked embarrassed. "The problem is that they don't ever work at the same time." Nazra had laughed so hard she almost fell out of bed.

"I'm, uh, from Hawaii," said Keoki. She had the hottest hand of any woman he had ever touched. He was almost glad when she took it away.

"How interesting! But what exactly is your specialty?"

"Uh ..." What was his specialty? Hawaiian-style shamanism? But that wouldn't mean anything in terms of a specific skill. What could he tell her? Impulsively, he said, "I, uh, I talk to spirits, sort of."

"Like a medium?"

"Not exactly." This was harder to explain than he realized. "I sort of talk to the spirits of people, places and things, and, uh, I get information that way." He didn't even know if that was accurate.

"Hmmm." Brigid walked back to the map and both men were prepared to just stand there all day and watch her walk back and forth, but she stopped and turned to face them. "I've been trying to tune in to our subject," she said, placing a hand over the Kirchzarten area, "but I don't get a sense of his presence at all." Nor did any of the dozen people that she had contacted in the town, from prostitutes to police inspectors. Mikalov was definitely not in Kirchzarten.

"He is supposed to be here, but we don't have a location," said Jeff. "Our assignment was only to monitor the entry and exit points of Kirchzarten, to see whether Seeker had entered or would enter shortly. Peggy scanned the roads, Charlotte monitored the railway station, and I did progressed charts for the town itself. Quiet place, though. Haven't charted any potential violence through next week, at least."

"And that could be due to the fact that the subject isn't even here," said Brigid with a slight frown. She sat down and crossed her legs, causing all kinds of male hormones to dance crazily through two sets of bloodstreams. "In that case we are just wasting our time." She fingered her pearls and the temperature in the room went up. "I think we need to expand our search area." Two minds were more than willing to expand the search area. "May I suggest that we start by locating our subject so that we may protect him properly? Gentlemen?" *Gott in Himmel!* God in Heaven! Men! She reduced her energy output and toned down the lust factor.

"Absolutely!"

"Right-o!"

"Good. Now, Jeffrey," she caressed the name with her voice, "I understand that you use astrology in some fashion ..."

"Geo-astrology, really."

"Geo-astrology, then. Can you use it to check the surrounding area for the location of our subject?" Without realizing it, both men had already accepted her leadership without question.

Jeff glanced at his IBM laptop on the conference table. "Actually, I'm not able to locate the subject directly. I can do a chart on a particular location and get some idea of the kinds of events that are likely to take place there. That's what I've been looking for, signs of potential violence associated with an attempt on the subject's life."

"And could you do that for other locations in, say, the Black Forest area?" asked Brigid.

The Britisher scratched his ear, rubbed his nose, and pursed his lips. "I did load a database for Germany before coming down here, but there are hundreds of locations in it. I suppose I could start with an expanding perimeter around Kirchzarten and see what happens. Would a one-week progression be sufficient?"

"That would be fine, Jeffrey." Her smile made him tremble. "For my part, I will send out the vibration of our subject's name into the energy field of the Black Forest and track the areas of greatest resonance." She had no idea what that meant, but she knew it would sound good. Her real intuitive talent had to do with a heightened awareness of changes in local physical and

234

emotional patterns, and an ability to influence or take advantage of those changes. "And you, Keoki," somehow she made his name come out as 'my love,' "will you check with your spirits for what they can tell you?"

"Sure!" he said, too brightly. He didn't know whether Brigid could read his mind, so he was trying hard not to think of where he knew the subject was. On the other hand, she was right. PERI's team here was wasting its time. On the other hand, he was really here as bait, not really to do psychic work. On the other hand, if he was bait and Nazra took the bait, who was going to protect him? He suddenly realized that he had no instructions about what to do if Nazra did appear, and no assurances that any BND agents were nearby to save him. He had probably been stuck out in the boonies because the local head of German Intelligence didn't think much of the bait idea and just wanted him out of the way. Still, he had an obligation to protect the information they'd given him, whether it was true or not.

Twenty-five

Beauty Is The Beast

He 'umu a pua'a
(A pig-strangling—treachery)

Brigid was watching Keoki's face carefully, as she had been trained to do. He knew something, that was certain. And he was nervous about something, too. Was he worried about Nazra? He needn't be. She looked at her watch. "Why don't we have an early lunch? That way we can get to know each other better and then we can get to work in earnest. Do you know of a good place to eat?" she asked Jeff.

"As a matter of fact, I do," said Jeff, glad of the attention. "Nice place, just out of town. We could walk there in ten minutes, actually."

"That's a lovely idea, Jeffrey." It would give her more time to study them, to better judge their reactions to questions.

They closed the office and went outside, taking a walkway that led past the site of the ancient spring. At the street they turned right and started walking out into the country. They came to an underpass that went beneath a highway that skirted the town and walked through. On the other side they were on a country road amidst flowering fields and lush trees.

Soon they crossed a bridge over a stream and on the other side was a traditional-looking inn with a big white horse painted on one wall below a sign in script that read *Gasthof Weisspferd*, "White Horse Inn." They crossed a gravel parking lot and went in, with Jeffrey continuing a conversation about sacred Celtic sites that were scattered throughout the Black Forest. The whole walk took just over ten minutes.

In that time Brigid/Marta confirmed her initial assessment

that Jeffrey was a highly educated and intelligent man with typical male insecurities. Keoki, however, remained somewhat of an enigma to her. That he was intelligent there was no doubt. His American education had enormous gaps in it, which was usual, and he seemed to have the male insecurities typical for his age. But all of that seemed to lie on the surface of something deep and impenetrable. She almost regretted that there would be no time to explore it.

The dining room of the inn was furnished in a kind of rustic elegance. The plain wood tables and chairs were substantial as well as old and well-polished. The few paintings and decorative objects were tasteful instead of touristy, and the waitress wore a semi-costume that looked like it was her everyday dress and not just for atmosphere. Brigid ordered for all of them and the men didn't object: a house white wine that was light and flavorful; *Geschnetzeltes vom Kalb*, lamb cut into strips and stewed to turn it into a thick sauce; and *Schwartzwälderkirschtorte*, Black Forest cake, for dessert.

As they ate and talked, Keoki's mind was divided between the delicious meal, the conversation, and his impressions of Brigid. She was by far the sexiest woman he had ever encountered, even if not the most beautiful. She was also more assertive and self confident than any woman he had ever met. At the same time he couldn't get over the feeling that she was playing with them. She just didn't seem to fit as a PERI member. It wasn't her looks. Karen was just as pretty. It was her style. Brigid was more the kind of woman you'd expect to find on the arm of a very rich man. Still, he wasn't going to complain about her being there. It was a rush just to be near her, and he had totally suppressed the part of himself that didn't want to be so close.

Brigid had just asked him a question and he only got the last part. "...places in Hawaii?"

What were they talking about? It was still about sacred sites. Keoki willed his subconscious to give him the first part of the question. *Do you have any sacred places in Hawaii?* He smiled. "We believe that the islands themselves are sacred," he said. "But there are special places like *heiau*, temple sites from the old days, and places that are important in legends, and places of special beauty and power, and there are the volcanoes, of course."

"By the by," said Jeff, "I've heard that the Hawaiians still worship Pele, the volcano goddess. Do you really?"

Keoki grimaced at hearing the popular misconception again. Patience, he told himself. It was asked with an honest intent to understand. "That isn't true," he replied. "The great majority of Hawaiians are Christians. However, there are a few Hawaiians with a special relationship to Pele who do worship her. And," he said with a grin, "it's always a good idea to have respect for the spirit of a volcano when it's in your backyard."

That subject was put off by the arrival of the cake. It looked like an ordinary chocolate cake to Keoki, but when he took a bite his mouth was filled with the rich taste of cherry liqueur that permeated the cake. "Wow!" he said. "I think I like that!"

When the meal was over and the cost shared between them, at Brigid's insistence, they walked back to their office and went to work. In reality, only Jeff went to work, using his computer to pull up data on the surrounding towns, formulate charts, and compare them to Seeker's progressions. Brigid sat where she could observe Jeff and Keoki and pretended to tune into energy fields. Every once in a while she got up to look at the wall map to make it seem like she was actually doing something.

Keoki took a few minutes to go to his garden and ask his owl spirit to see whether Mikalov really was in Triberg. The bird said he was, and since Keoki didn't have any other information to go by he accepted that and spent the rest of the time fantasizing about Brigid.

Fifty-five minutes later Jeff leaned away from his computer and broke the near silence. "I think I may have something," he announced. The others were instantly alert. "I have a correlated chart that shows a potential for violence in or near the town of Triberg within the next few days. Problem is the relation to Seeker's chart is minimal. Could be another type of event altogether."

While Jeff spoke Brigid observed Keoki very closely. She noticed a suppressed startle reaction and a flush on his cheeks. He knew something, but he wasn't sharing it. She moved closer to Jeff, which also brought her closer to Keoki, and decided to take a risk. "That's very good, Jeff," she said. "It matches what I got, too." She saw Keoki's pupils widen and some facial muscles twitch. He does know! Of course, he was probably informed by Interpol. It is Triberg. "How about you, Keoki?" she asked, wanting to see how he would respond.

"Uh, I got something, ub, similar. In the general area. I'm not sure of the exact location." *Jeez! What do I do now?*

He's lying! thought Brigid/Marta. *Got you now, young man.* "I think this much correlation needs to be reported," she said. "I'll go and call Madame Villier. I'll be right back." She hurriedly left the room.

"I say, this is exciting, what?" Jeffrey looked happier than Keoki had seen him so far.

"Where is Triberg, anyway?" asked Keoki.

Jeff got up and Keoki followed him to the wall map. He pointed to an area right in the center of the Black Forest mountains, just north of Freiburg's latitude. "Here she is, old chum. Never been there myself. Said to be charming. Famous for cuckoo clocks. Rather unsporting of the Germans not to let us know."

"It's still speculation," said Keoki. "We don't know for sure whether Mikalov is there or not."

Meanwhile, Brigid/Marta had found a pay phone downstairs. She called a friend in Basel and asked for a contact in Triberg. Since it was a heavily-visited tourist center it was no problem to find the kind of contact she required. Next she called Triberg and set up an appointment for that afternoon. With a smile she hung up and returned to the PERI office.

Jeff was at his computer showing Keoki how the positions of Mars and Saturn in Seeker's progressed chart fell within ten degrees of Mars and Saturn in Triberg's chart when Brigid re-entered the room, charged with sexual energy. Two brains came to a dead stop.

"Madame Villier wants Keoki and I to go directly to Triberg and warn the BND agents there. She said the local phones couldn't be trusted. Jeffrey is to stay here and man the office." She could have said, "Gabble, gabble, gabble," for all the men cared. *Men are so absurdly easy to manipulate*, she thought. She walked over to Jeff. "You've been a dear, Jeffrey. Take care of things while we're gone." She kissed him on the lips, giving him the most memorable feminine experience of his life. Then she took Keoki by the arm and guided him out the door.

As they descended the stairs Keoki asked, "How are we going to get to this Triberg place?"

"I have a car," she said. Keoki followed Brigid/Marta to the parking lot of the *Kurhaus* where she stopped on the driver's side of a yellow Mercedes SLK 230 roadster and unlocked the doors. She opened the door, slid in, and put the roof down. Keoki got in the passenger side and felt the sensuous thrill of very expensive leather. Brigid backed out and started forward. "Hold on," she said. And he had to.

It was a wild ride eastward through the town of *Himmelreich*, The Kingdom of Heaven, along *Höllental*, Hell Valley, and up to the resort town of Titisee. They raced on over a high mountain road where the temperature dropped radically and it even snowed for a short while. Keoki shivered in his shirt, but Brigid in her meagre outfit didn't seem to notice. Keoki noticed her, though. She concentrated on her driving like a professional, shifting and braking to get the maximum speed on the straightaways and the minimum reduction of speed on the curves. Most of all, Keoki couldn't help noticing the way her skirt kept riding higher and higher up her thighs till she might as well not have been wearing one.

A terrifying series of switchbacks finally brought them down into the valley where Triberg nestled like a gift in a leafy green package. It was warmer there when they parked and Keoki was glad of it, even though Brigid pulled her skirt back down when she got out of the car. She smiled at him and said, "Madame Villier gave me a contact. He's not far from here." Brigid began walking and Keoki followed.

The main street of Triberg sloped gently downhill and they had parked at the upper end in a lot between the buildings on one side and the street. They passed numerous shops featuring cuckoo clocks in more styles and sizes than Keoki ever knew existed. Brigid turned in to a very large shop and told Keoki to look around while she located their contact.

Keoki was awed by what he saw. Most of the stores they had passed displayed clocks that either looked like children's toys or factory-made tourist items. In this shop, however, the clocks were obviously made by highly-skilled craftsmen. There were small clocks with delicately-carved figures of men, women

240

and animals engaged in activities like sawing wood, picking flowers, and eating grass; there were larger clocks carved with game animals and some with a troop of dancers who performed every hour; and there were gigantic clocks over six feet high covered with beautifully-detailed images of hunting equipment, animals, flowers, fruits and faces.

Throughout the store there was a constantly changing chorus of cuckoos. On a sign Keoki read that the cuckoo clock originated in the seventeenth century in the Black Forest, where cuckoo birds still roamed, laying their eggs in the nests of other birds for them to take care of while the cuckoos lived a carefree life. Keoki decided to get a clock for his mother, and finally decided on an unusual design with the clock in a forest below and a chapel on top sitting at an angle. The salesclerk showed him how to work the weights that ran the clock mechanism and it was being wrapped when Brigid reappeared from a back room carrying a large shoulder bag that she didn't have before. She raised an eyebrow when she saw the package. "For my mother," said Keoki. "I think she'll like it."

"That's sweet," said Brigid.

"What's in the bag?"

"Goodies. We've been told to wait at a safe house for debriefing. Let's go."

Brigid left the store and Keoki followed again. This woman sure likes to take charge, he thought.

They returned to the car and Brigid drove them to a one-story cabin on a side road not far from town. She entered the cabin first and put the shoulder bag down on a sideboard by a window directly across from the door. When Keoki came in he saw that the cabin appeared to have only two rooms. The one they were in had a table and four chairs in the center and a kitchen area on the right. On the left was a roll-top desk and a stand with a telephone. There was also a doorway on that side. The door was open and Keoki could see a brass-framed bed inside the second room. Brigid was opening the shoulder bag when Keoki started to sit at the table.

"Don't sit down just yet," said the auburn-haired beauty.

Keoki straightened up and saw the barrel of a gun pointing at his stomach. He felt a cold chill in his gut. "What's this?" he asked shakily.

"I'm afraid I haven't been very truthful, *mein Liebling*, darling." She smiled broadly. "As a matter of fact, I've lied a lot. To start with, I'm not really a member of PERI. My name is not Brigid Meisterle, and I wouldn't know an energy field from an elephant. Now be a nice Hawaiian and go sit at the desk." She waved the gun a little to emphasize her order.

Thoughts crashed through Keoki's mind like storm surf. Could he rush her? She was too far away. Could he run? She would shoot him in the back. Who was she? Why was she doing this? Maybe it was a joke. Maybe it was a sex game. Maybe he was going to die.

His body moved him to the desk and sat him down. "What now?" he asked.

The woman came and stood behind him. She caressed the left side of his neck with one hand and pressed the muzzle of the gun to the right side. Like an intimate friend, she said, "Take that pen and a piece of paper and write down your mother's address so I can send her the clock in case you're not able to." She waited until Keoki had done so with a trembling hand. "Good boy. Now clasp your hands and put them behind your head." He was not in a position to do anything else, so he obeyed, knowing that he was making himself even more helpless. He felt her put something around his wrists. "Fine," she said, "now get up and go into the bedroom."

Keoki brought his hands back down and saw that his wrists had been secured with some kind of plastic handcuff. He got up from the desk and walked through the doorway into the tiny bedroom with the tiny adjoining bathroom. "What are you going to do?" he asked.

"Pull the bed out about thirty centimeters from the wall," she ordered, ignoring his question. "That would be about a foot for you," she added. Keoki took hold of the footrail and pulled the bed out. "Now lie down on the bed and put your hands over your head." Keoki hesitated. That would make him totally helpless. The woman he still thought of as Brigid made a disgusted sound and aimed the gun at his head. "You can lie on the bed with half an ear, a hole in your hand, with a shattered kneecap, or just as you are. Take your pick."

Keoki moved quickly around the side and lay down with his hands over his head. His mouth was so dry he croaked as he asked, "Are you going to kill me? Why would you do that?"

"All your questions will be answered shortly," she said. She moved behind him and did something that attached his wrists to the headrail, then came around to the foot again. She put the gun down and removed his shoes and socks. "My name is Marta Brunn. I'm a professional call girl." She stood up, amused by the look in Keoki's eyes, and kicked off her own shoes. "I'm also a very good friend of Nazra."

Oh shit, thought Keoki, and the picture of a kitten barely hanging on to a tree branch by its forepaws flashed clearly in his mind.

"I see that means something to you," said Marta, as she started to pull off her sweater. "Nazra asked me to do her a favor." She tossed the sweater aside and unfastened her bra. "She asked me to get you to help me find Ivan Mikalov." She dangled the bra in front of Keoki's face. "I only wore this for you and dear Jeffrey." She dropped it and began to remove her skirt. "I'm supposed to kill you and the Russian, but I'm going to wait until I can do you both at the same time." Her skirt was gone and she took off her panties. "My contact at the clock store helped me to find out exactly where Mikalov is being held, and helped me to locate some help."

Marta, clad only in pearls, reached into the shoulder bag she had brought with her and took out a pair of stilletos. She twirled them like miniature batons. "I love to play with knives," she said, a look of childlike happiness on her face. Then she turned her attention to Keoki, walked to the side of the bed, and jumped onto it with the same expression. "And I love to play with men." With one of the knives she sliced open a trouser leg. "We have hours before everything will be ready. What shall we do to pass the time, hmmm?"

Keoki felt extremely angry, utterly helpless, very afraid, and intensely aroused, all at the same time. During the long afternoon he discovered that, under the right conditions, it was actually possible for a woman to rape a man. Several times. In fairly rapid succession.

He must have dozed off, because when he awoke his hands

243

were free and the sun was very low in the sky. When he stirred the bed creaked and Marta came in. She was dressed in a black jumper with a black cap that hid her hair. She tossed a black bundle at him.

"Use the toilet and leave the door open. I can stand the noise and the smell if you can. Then put that on. Don't forget your shoes. You have five minutes." She leaned against the doorframe to wait.

Keoki removed the tattered remains of his clothing and used the bathroom to do what was necessary. The bundle was a black, polyester jumpsuit similar to what Marta wore.

When his shoes were on, Marta had the gun in her hand again and she motioned him out of the room and out of the cabin. "You will drive," she said. The top was up on the car and Keoki slipped into the driver's seat. He watched Marta keep the gun aimed at him as she walked around in front of the car and got into the passenger side. Then she gave him the keys. "Keep your hands on the wheel except to shift and follow my directions. If you try to run off the road or into anything I will simply kill you and trust in my survival skills. Start the car." There was nothing playful in her voice at this point.

After a very jerky start while Keoki got used to the manual shift, he drove them north for awhile as far as he could tell and then took a number of small dirt roads until they reached a clearing where two other cars were parked and a group of men were waiting, also dressed in black. Marta told Keoki to get out of the car and one of the men came over to them and took charge of the Hawaiian, binding his hands and tying a gag on him. He was shoved roughly into the clearing and held while Marta talked with several men a short distance away.

Keoki counted ten men and they all looked like his idea of hardened mercenaries. He noticed an array of handguns, rifles and automatic weapons, and two of the men even carried what appeared to be grenades. He caught a few words of the discussion from voices raised in excitement or emphasis. "One kilometer." "Two of them." "Upstairs." "Autos." Finally the discussion, or instructions, were finished. Marta headed off through the woods and the men followed in single file. Keoki's guard dragged him along at the end of the line.

It was the beginning of twilight when they stopped. Keoki's feet were bound and he was tied to a tree. Through a thin stretch of woods in front of him he could see and hear a stream, and beyond that a large open space with the strangest building he had ever seen. It looked like a rather large barn with a steep thatched roof that reached almost to the ground.

On the end facing the stream a large, triangular section of roof came halfway to the ground and Keoki could make out a balcony with flower boxes on it, but he couldn't see any people. Looking around him he realized that Marta and her gang had disappeared. As he waited for something to happen he thought he heard a cuckoo clock behind him. Who would have a cuckoo clock in the woods? he wondered. Then it hit him that it must be a real bird. He heard it going farther and farther away.

Twilight had deepened to grayness when Keoki heard gunfire—handgun pops, rifle hammer-blows, snare-drum automatics—mixed with shouts and screams. Then came two explosions, one right after the other, probably grenades, and all was quiet. It seemed like only a few minutes had passed.

Soon one of the men came for Keoki. He was released from the tree, his feet were unbound and he was forced to stumble past the trees, through the cold, shallow stream, and across the field to the building, which turned out to be a traditional-style farmhouse turned into the home of a country gentleman. Keoki was almost sick as he had to step over and around bodies that were still bleeding from knife and bullet wounds. One had to be dragged aside so he could climb the stairs and he felt a deeply painful regret that a man devoted to protection should be killed so easily and treated so carelessly. He caught a few snatches of conversation from the men he thought of as mercenaries. "All of them." "Two of ours." "Nice ass."

At the top of the stairs he had to move aside as two very young and very pretty blonde girls rushed by while still putting on their clothes. Keoki couldn't help following them with his eyes. He noticed that the mercenaries eyed the girls hungrily, but no one interfered with their escape. Keoki was pushed forward and into a room with an oversized bed occupied by a naked man holding his head very still so as not to get cut by the knives sticking out of the wall on either side of it. It had to be

Mikalov. Then he saw that the man was looking at Marta, who held another knife in her hand. She was still dressed.

"Ah," said Marta, "together at last. Get on the bed, Keoki, while I decide how to end the evening."

Sick at heart, Keoki didn't have any doubts about the ending. He climbed on the bed like an obedient child, trying to ignore the man next to him who reeked with the smells of recent lovemaking. *What a stupid way to* ... Keoki shook his head. *Wait a minute! What the hell am I doing? I'm just sitting here like a rabbit waiting to be slaughtered. Gramps would be ashamed of me!*

There was a time when he and Gramps had been caught in a rare lightning storm on the slopes of Mauna Loa. Keoki had been very afraid and Gramps had said, "You might as well enjoy the show. You'll never know if it hits you. You're not dead until you're dead." *I'm not dead until I'm dead.* Keoki looked around. Marta was sorting through a set of knives on a table beyond the foot of the bed and one of her men was near the door with a gun trained on him and Mikalov. It didn't look like there was much he could do at an ordinary level.

Keoki extended his *la'a kea* and used all his willpower to build up as strong an emotional charge as he could. He didn't know what he would do with it, but it was all he could think of. He started with anger and quickly decided there was too much tension in that, so he used a desire to live instead.

The man at the door asked Marta how long she was going to take and she just shrugged. "You've been paid for the whole evening, so I intend to take my time. It isn't often that I get a chance to ..."

She was interrupted by the wailing sound of European police sirens. It sounded like there were a lot of them. "*Die Bullen*, the cops," muttered the man at the door. He ran out and shouted to the men downstairs. There were sounds of rapid departure as the sirens got louder.

Marta held a throwing knife in each hand, ready to skewer either man if he tried to move, and she was angry. "There's no time to play, so farewell, gentlemen." Her left hand was raised halfway up in case Keoki tried to move, and her right hand was drawing back for a killing throw at Mikalov's head.

Memories provide the basis for all our skills. When a skill is called for, the memories involved with learning it zip through the brain and to the appropriate muscles so fast it almost seems instantaneous. Marta was about to throw a knife, and her intent called upon long hours of practice over many years, in many places, and with many targets. In those same moments an intent of Keoki's called upon his own memories of practice at throwing horseshoes with Gramps. Of course, Gramps had his own variation on the game. He taught Keoki that if you could build up your energy enough and concentrate your attention enough right at the moment when the shoe was about to leave your opponent's hand and if, at that moment, you could sort of will a twisting motion, you could often cause the person's hand to jerk slightly and the throw would be way off. Gramps also said that it worked best when the other person was not totally focused on what they were doing.

Marta's hand came forward and at just the right point Keoki willed a twist with his mind. Perhaps it was the strength of his desire to live; perhaps Marta was distracted by the sirens, but for the first time in her adult life, she missed her target. It wasn't by much, but it was enough. Instead of plunging into Mikalov's forehead where she was aiming, the knife veered slightly and merely cut his right ear. Marta was so shocked she stood completely still for a moment. That was just enough time for Mikalov to leap screaming off the bed and onto Marta, bringing her crashing to the floor. Keoki came off the bed to stand near them as they thrashed about. Marta succeeded in bringing the second of her knives to Mikalov's throat and Keoki did the only thing he could with his hands still bound. He kicked her in the head. She went limp and Mikalov grabbed the knife. The Russian put it to Marta's throat and it was obvious that he was going to kill her with it, so Keoki kicked him in the head, too.

The sirens had stopped and Keoki heard noises downstairs. He rushed to the door. "Up here," he shouted. "We're all up here!"

"That won't be true in a second, *mein Liebling*," said a voice behind him. He turned and saw Marta crouched on the sill of the open window. There was a visible bruise on one side of her forehead. "You made me miss my target. And you saved my life. I

247

won't forget you." She blew him a kiss and was gone into the night.

In the hours that followed Keoki and Mikalov were arrested and released and underwent a real debriefing with the BND. Not long after sunup, Keoki was dropped off at *Haus Hubertus* in Kirchzarten, still wearing the black jumper Marta had given to him and carrying his mother's cuckoo clock. He was dead tired and about to fall into bed when there was a knock on his door. Barely able to keep his eyes open, he answered it and saw Jeff with a piece of paper in his hand. "Thanks for calling the police, Jeff," he managed to mumble.

"My pleasure," said Jeff. "When I didn't hear from you by evening I decided to check in with Madame Villier. She's the one who actually made things happen when I told her about Brigid. But that's not why I came." Jeff waved the paper. "Sorry, old man. This fax arrived last night. Looks like a spot of bad news."

Keoki took the paper, thinking first that something had happened at home. What he read sent shock waves through his body and in the state he was in he almost fainted.

"Come to Munich immediately," it said. "Your grandfather has suffered a serious accident. He is at the Ramberg Clinic in Schwabing. Do not delay." The message included an address and phone number for the clinic.

Twenty-six

The Siren's Call

'Anihinihi ke ola
(Life is in a precarious position)

After saying goodbye to Keoki, Lani's train ride from the busy Stuttgart station to the even busier Munich station was short and uneventful. The Hawaiian man sat alone by the window in an open first class car, resting in a state of present moment awareness without any conscious thoughts. As always, he felt admiration for the orderly countryside where farms and fields and woods were so neatly arranged and cared for that they gave the impression of having been manicured.

He felt the energy patterns of the land and the people and knew without thinking about it that he was seeing a uniquely German blend of human and environmental energy that helped to shape both the productivity of the land and the thinking patterns of the inhabitants. At another time, in a more analytical state, he would contrast it uncritically with the wilder lushness of Hawaii and the free-spiritedness of the Hawaiian people.

Signs of city life grew more abundant as the express train by-passed Augsburg and Dachau and entered the suburbs of Munich at Pasing. While the train slowed down on its approach to the *Hauptbahnhof*, the main train station at the center of the city, his knowledge of this place where he had obtained his two university degrees floated freely in his mind.

The city of Munich had begun as a small monastery, established in the eighth century on the banks of the Isar River. The monastery and the small villages that grew up around it lay in a great and fertile plain bounded by forests to the east, north and west, and by the formidable barrier of the Alps to the south. In

249

1158 Duke Henry the Lion adjusted the the route of the salt trade between Salzburg, beyond the Alps in Austria, and Augsburg, to the north, so that it passed through *Münichen*, The Little Monks, the name given to the village that later became *München*, the German form of Munich. Because of the connection to the monastery, the city's coat of arms retained a monk as its symbol. However, the monk has his arms raised, and a joke at the university was that he was saying *"Mein Gott! Oh my God!"* about what had happened to the place.

As it became larger and more influential, Munich turned into the capital of the independent state of Bavaria, and from that into the third largest city in unified Germany, and, in the process, into a city with a reputation as a place of non-stop parties and festivals, with the best beer and the biggest drinkers in the world. A lot of other places might dispute that, but Lani was looking forward to getting re-acquainted with the golden Bavarian brews that were normally served in full liter mugs. As the train slowed to a stop in the huge station, Lani recalled a popular local saying that the German population was divided into two groups. Those who lived in Munich and those who wanted to.

Lani retrieved his bags from the open storage bins near the car's exit and stepped onto the platform into the noise of travel: arrival and departure announcements, friends and family greeting passengers, luggage carts and general train and people sounds. He walked along the platform, which was parallel to more than two dozen others where trains took people all over Europe, and headed for the main waiting area. Glass panes in the high, arched, hangar-like roof let in plenty of light.

At the end of the track Lani noticed that there were a lot more food booths operating than there had been last time he was here, and there was a Burger King restaurant on an upper landing that had to be relatively new. He felt a strange, nostalgic sense of loss to see that the twenty-four-hour blue movie cinema had been closed, even though he had only gone in once or twice when he was a student. He smiled to himself, noting again how the subconscious tends to dislike change of any kind and how the conscious mind craves it.

Apart from those differences and a few cosmetic alterations, the station was pretty much as he remembered it. With the trains

250

behind him he turned right and through the main doors, then left and into the small lobby of the Inter-City hotel where he had a reservation. The clerk handed him an envelope and a key card and he went to his third floor room. Designed for businessmen, it was small, comfortable, and soundproof. Lani kicked off his shoes and lay on the bed with the envelope in his hands.

There was an Interpol transportation pass inside, though he decided he would still use up the rail ticket he had because he hated to waste it. There was also a sheet with a contact number for the BND and an Interpol expense form. He noticed that the need for receipts was mentioned three times. He sat up on the edge of the bed and called the contact number. There were a lot of buzzes and whistles before he heard a live voice. Probably some kind of scrambling system. He and the contact conversed in German.

Lani learned that the Munich station chief was taking absolutely no chances on anything happening that resembled the disaster at Tübingen. There were two agents shadowing Lani in case Seeker tried to make another attempt on his life. He had taken on the risk of being used as bait, so it was his duty to wander around and give Seeker that opportunity. The contact suggested that he spend some time in *Marienplatz*, acting like a tourist. The BND had quite a number of agents in that area, ready to intervene if Seeker showed up. Lani also learned that Boris Orlov, Seeker's target who worked at the University of Munich, was being held in an undisclosed location. *Probably safer for him if I don't know*, thought Lani.

The train ride had been short and he felt no need to shower, so Lani left his bags on the bed, pocketed his key card, and left the hotel. Outside the hotel, he walked down the broad steps to *Bayerstrasse* and turned left past the taxis toward *Karlsplatz* a few blocks away. He could have gone by way of the underground shopping mall that started below the station, but he liked the atmosphere of traffic, shoppers and high-rise stores in a European setting, as least as a temporary change from quaint medievalism.

He extended his *la'a kea* as he walked, letting many thousands of impressions flow through his awareness without restriction. He spoke to his extended field as if to a friend, telling

251

it to alert him to friend or foe or anything else of particular interest, and by doing so he quickly located his shadows. They felt like two points of pressure in his field behind him and to his right. He knew that Nazra would be able to locate them with the same ease, and he wondered whether she really would come after him before going after Orlov. If she considered him a serious enough threat she just might.

Arriving at the busy intersection of *Karlsplatz*, also known as *Stachus*; by locals, Lani continued on through the *Karlstor*, the fourteenth century city gate that currently housed a children's toy museum, and on to the main shopping district of Munich. This area had been turned into a pedestrian mall since Lani was a student and it was a little disorienting to him now, but there was the Renaissance façade of *Michaelskirche*, the Church of St. Michael, on his left with its large relief of the archangel defeating still another dragon, and he got his bearings back.

Like a good tourist, he decided to have a beer at the *Augustiner Gastätte*, Munich's oldest brewery, that was across the street from the church. It was a hot and sunny Spring day and the interior of the brewery and restaurant was relatively dark and cool. The tour groups hadn't arrived yet and only hardcore customers were settled in to spend most of their day drinking their 'liquid bread.' Lani sat down at one of the empty long tables where he could see the door and ordered "*ein Helles Mass, bitte*, a liter mug of light beer, please," from the waiter. Light, of course, referred to color and not to alcohol. Lani looked around and admired the way the place had been decorated. A real tourist would have thought of it as typically Bavarian, but Lani knew from an art course he had taken because a girlfriend was taking it at the time that the style was *Jugendstil*, German Art Nouveau.

The beer arrived and the first swallow was a delight to his palate. For that matter, so were all the rest. He realized how much he had missed the curiously thick sensation on his tongue of Bavarian beer. There were a lot of good beers in the world, including Firerock Ale from Kona, but none were quite equal to the beers in southern Germany, in his opinion. He spent a half hour nursing his drink, scanning the center of the city without any effect, then paid the waiter and went back outside. What should he do now?

There was still a little more than a half hour before the noon event at the big square of *Marienplatz*. He looked around, thinking he might visit the *Frauenkirche*, the Church of Our Lady, which was Munich's cathedral and physical symbol of the city, when his eye was caught by a bronze statue of a wild boar that stood on the corner of the street that led to the cathedral. The statue was in front of the *Deutsches Jagd- und Fischereimuseum*, the German Museum of Hunting and Fishing. Lani was almost surprised to realize that he had never gone into that museum during all his student years. He crossed the street, entered the museum, and paid the modest admission fee of four marks.

Inside there were racks and racks of hunting and fishing gear from as far back as the Middle Ages, plus some purely killing weapons like swords and, toward the back, cases with stuffed animals that could be found in the German forests. In the last case against the back wall he received a startling surprise. The large display consisted of a section of forest populated by the strangest assortment of animals conceivable. All of them resembled rabbits in general, but they all had small sets of antlers. Some had clawed feet, some had webbed feet, some had fangs, a few had coxcombs, and the ones in the trees bore the wings of bats. Lani glanced at the sign that labeled the case. It was identical to those in the other animal cases, giving the name of the animal and a very brief description of its habitat. In this case it was "*Wolpertinger - Bayerischwald*, indicating that the animal in the case inhabited the forested areas of Bavaria.

Now Lani had always considered the *Wolpertinger* to be the German equivalent of the Texas Jackalope, a joke to play on strangers, but the animals in the case were so realistic and the presentation so matter-of-fact that for some moments he seriously considered the possibility that the animal was real. Then memories of the dry side of German humor flooded into his mind and he roared with laughter. What an exquisitely-crafted put-on. He would even bet that many Germans were taken in, at least for a little while.

He turned away, still chuckling, and then went silent. Maybe the hunting and fishing objects and the fantasy creature helped to create a resonance, but suddenly Lani was very aware of Nazra's presence in the city. He expanded his field and extended his awareness throughout the field, but he could not determine a specific location—just that she was near and aware of him. This awareness lasted for the time it took him to get back to the entrance to the museum, when it faded out and nothing he could do would bring it back.

He thought about that as he went back onto the mall. She must be able to alter her own field in very specific ways, something like changing the frequency of a cell phone, so that certain callers couldn't reach you. He knew how to get that effect by merging his energy with another pattern and he wondered if she did it in the same way. He also knew that he could fade out of her awareness if he so chose, but that would defeat the purpose of his being here.

He walked along the mall, barely aware of passing the *Frauenkirche* as he kept searching through his field for any trace of Nazra. If he could lock on to the core of her being he might be able to go beyond the limitations of frequency patterns. He thought of his ocelot helper and asked it to do the search for him while he kept his attention on his surroundings.

In a short time he reached the *Marienplatz*, where a large crowd had gathered in front of the *Neues Rathaus*, the New Town Hall, built in an elaborate Gothic style. The large square had been named in honor of St. Mary, and a tall column in the center supported a figure of her as the Queen of Heaven who had reigned over the city for three centuries. It had amused Lani and his student friends that many decorative elements of the statue included symbols of Isis.

The crowd, however, was more interested in the *Glockenspiel*, a chiming clock that was added to the Town Hall in 1904. At eleven in the morning and at noon throughout the year the chimes accompany two sets of colorful, life-sized mechanical figures that prance and dance to the delight of everyone. One set features jousting knights and chargers acting out a tournament held on the *Marienplatz* in 1568, and the other commemorates the end of the plague in 1517 with the lively *Schäfflertanz*, the Dance of the Coopers.

The attention of the crowd was occupied with mimes and jugglers until the chimes began. Then all eyes turned upward for the mechanical performance, but Lani turned away after a first glance. He had seen it many times and so it didn't distract him as he scanned the crowd. There! He felt something over to the left of the Town Hall. It was like a buzz in his field, quite unlike the pressure of his shadows. He suspected that the signal was intentional, but he followed it anyway.

He stood on the corner of *Weinstrasse*, which ran along the left side of the Town Hall toward the theater district, allowing his field to "hang loose." That is, he held a sense of it as being relaxed, like a cat, or an area of calm air, ready to move or respond to any disturbance. Ah, there. He felt a definite tug from the left side of the street. It came from a restaurant that had been one of his favorites when he was a student, the *Donisl*. Originally a customs house and reputed to be the oldest beer hall in Munich–it had been established as such in 1715–the *Donisl* specialized in inexpensive Bavarian food, which appealed to student tastes and student budgets.

Before going in, Lani scanned the area for BND agents and the numerous impressions made him feel more secure. After his previous experiences with Nazra he was not going to make the mistake of arrogantly assuming that he could best her in any encounter. If they were to deal with each other at purely psychic or dream levels he knew he would have no problem, but she was also a highly-trained assassin in physical means, and that was definitely not his area of expertise. With a sense of anticipation and trepidation, he entered the restaurant.

A hostess asked him if he had a reservation, and on impulse he said yes and gave his name. The woman checked a list. "Yes, *Herr* Müller. Follow me."

Twenty-seven

Into The Trap

He huaka'i paoa, he pili i ka iwi
(A dangerous journey puts the bones at risk)

His hunch was right and it disturbed him. As he followed
the hostess through the restaurant, already crowded with locals
and tourists, he scanned for any trace of Nazra, but found none.
They went upstairs to the balcony and he was seated at a table
on the left as one faced the entrance. He nodded politely to an
American couple who shared the end of the table next to the
wall. He glanced around at the decorations, which included coats-
of-arms from ancient German families, and settled down to try
different variations on scanning.

He kept that up even when the waitress came to take his
order. She was a youngish, buxom blonde with too much make-
up and a country accent, but she was friendly and set down a
basket of *Brezelen*, pretzels, the large, thick kind that Germans
and New Yorkers love, along with a little dish of spicy brown
mustard. Lani knew that he would only have to pay for the ones
he ate. He ordered *Leberkäse*, a thick slab of hot bologna that
came with fries, and a bottle of *Salvator*, a Spring bock beer he
liked that was very dark, very rich, and very strong.

Nothing unusual happened during the wait nor during the
meal. He caught the waitress' eye when he was finished and
when she came to the table he said, "*Die Rechnung, bitte*, the
check, please." She left and returned a few moments later with a
folded slip of paper that she laid on the table. Lani was scanning
and didn't even notice her walk away. When he brought his attention back to the table he picked up the paper with one hand
and reached for his wallet with the other, then stopped. It wasn't

a bill, it was a note.

"Dear Dr. Müller," it read in English. "with your mind so occupied I'm not sure you enjoyed your meal, but it was a pleasure to serve and observe you. Your grandson has been kidnapped. If you want to see him alive again, evade your escort and meet me at the *Monopteros* in exactly one hour. Your meal has already been paid for, so you may leave whenever you wish."

He couldn't help looking around, even while he knew she would no longer be there. He had been scanning the restaurant for her and she was waiting on him. How much she must have loved the mockery. As for Keoki, he would have known if the boy was in danger. Or was that a valid assumption any more? Nazra had suppressed his awareness in Denmark and had avoided his detection here in Munich. Was she capable of cloaking Keoki's energy in some way so that he could not make contact with his grandson? He didn't know for sure and he didn't have the time to do a deep scan to find out. For the moment he would have to assume the worst.

Lani left the restaurant and wandered back through the *Marienplatz*, past the Old Town Hall and the *Heiliggeistkirche*, the Holy Ghost Church that was his favorite because it was so full of Masonic symbols, and he wondered again, briefly, how the designers had gotten away with it. He entered the *Viktualienmarkt*, the Food Market, with its many booths and tiny stores, and paused at the booth with barrels and bowls of olives in a multitude of types and sauces, lingered at the booth with fresh bunches of lavender, and browsed in the honey shop, noting the honeyed beer for future reference. All the while he was gradually merging his spirit with that of the crowd, becoming less noticeable and, finally, less visible. By the time he left the Food Market he knew that the BND agents would be starting to panic because they had lost him.

He rushed back to the *Marienplatz* and went down the stairs to the Underground station that was across from the Town Hall. He boarded the next northbound train, passing the stop at *Odeonsplatz* and getting off at the University station which was so familiar to him. Then he loped two blocks east along Veterinärstrasse to one of the smaller entrances to *Englischer Garten*, the park known as English Garden.

This was Germany's largest city park, three miles long by a mile wide. Although it had been designed by Count Rumford, a refugee from the American War of Independence who was of English descent, the park actually got its name from the open style of rolling parklands so favored by the English aristocracy of the eighteenth century. Lani had spent a lot of time in the Garden, both at the beer gardens and with his friends at the officially-designated nude sunbathing spots.

Directly ahead of him now he could see the top of the *Monopteros*, a small copy of a Greek temple sitting on its own artificial hill about five hundred meters away. Lani looked at his watch. There was time enough to do it at a walk. He extended his field and scanned. No BND agents, at least none aware of him, and no trace of Nazra, but that didn't mean anything, as he now knew. He followed the path until it veered off, then kept going across the lawn.

The full summer season hadn't arrived, so the area wasn't very crowded yet. As he got closer he could see a few nude sunbathers on the hill where they weren't supposed to be. He knew that the law wouldn't bother them as long as there weren't too many and they didn't act too outrageously. He could hear what sounded like Ecuadorian panflutists, and finally saw a group of them at the foot of the hill when he got near. A smaller group of African drummers was sitting quietly nearby, smoking something. Curiously, it seemed like no one was at the top of the hill or in the columned rotunda, as far as he could tell. He still had fifteen minutes, so he walked around the base of the hill, attempting to scan in a different way because his normal scanning wasn't doing him any good.

Instead of scanning people, making contact with them through his field and letting information ripple back through it to his body and into his mind, he made contact instead with the grass and the flowers and the trees, asking their spirits if they sensed danger or if they sensed the presence of Nazra. The problem with that, of course, was that plants lived almost completely in the present moment and danger involving them would have to be imminent for them to be aware of it.

Apart from the expected concerns with grass being stepped on, flowers being picked or branches being broken, he didn't pick up anything from that scan. But the trees did have something to give him about Nazra. She was about, he could tell from their response, although her location was imprecise. Perhaps she was in the rotunda, blocking or discouraging access by anyone except him. He couldn't see inside the building from below, so he started up the hill. However, just in case, he strongly visualized a spirit body for his ocelot helper and sent it up the hill first.

At the top he stood outside the metal railing that surrounded the temple and looked between the columns. It was too small to hide anyone and it appeared to be empty. Maybe he was supposed to go inside and wait. He swung a leg up and was halfway over the railing when time stopped. He could clearly see the ocelot crouched in the center of the rotunda and it was snarling fiercely at him. Immediately, he pulled back and turned, focusing all of his energy in a tight cocoon of protection as he leaped down the hill, aided in his spectacular jump by the shock wave of a violent explosion behind him.

Lani curled up and rolled as he hit the ground, telling his body spirit to avoid any trees because he was keeping his eyes closed. When he finished his roll at the foot of a chestnut tree the sound of the explosion was still echoing through the park. Quickly, he calmed down his energy and blended into his surroundings so that anyone who had witnessed his leap would pay more attention to the smoke at the top of the hill.

Before he could even think about the situation he was hit in the shoulder by a rock with a note wrapped around it. In the direction that it was thrown from he saw a young woman pedalling away on a bicycle. He refused to let his mind think about what had almost happened, thereby allowing his body to begin healing the small cuts and bruises from his leap, and removed the note from the rock that had been thrown at him.

"Congratulations! Guess we're really subposed to talk. Sea you at the *Deutsches Museum*. No need to hurry. Don't forget to come alone."

That's very odd, thought Lani. Why would she make two such obvious spelling mistakes? He sat there for a bit, pretending to gawk at the site of the explosion like the other onlookers while he considered the note. The huge *Deutsches Museum* was on an island of its own in the Isar River and featured science and technology exhibits in thirty departments on six floors through twelve miles of corridors. How was he supposed to find ...?

Lani was ashamed of himself. There was a large section of the museum devoted to ocean technology which included some entire fishing boats. And, if he remembered correctly, there was even a whole U-boat, or at least part of one. Nazra had told him exactly where to go. But how had she known he would survive the explosion? She probably hadn't, and that meant she had prepared the note beforehand, to cover that possibility. And that meant she had probably prepared another trap, too, for the same reason. He could get agents to go to the submarine, but Nazra would undoubtedly evade them, and what about Keoki? The note had said not to hurry. He decided that he wouldn't.

Still refusing to dwell on the explosion in order to keep his stress level down, Lani got up and walked until he found an isolated spot under some trees near the *Eisbach* Stream that ran through the park and eventually into the *Isar*. He sat down with his back to a tree and his legs comfortably crossed. He allowed himself a few moments of amused thinking about all the modern spiritual teachers who insisted that you had to sit in meditation with legs uncrossed in order to let the energy flow. He didn't know of any traditional people who meditated that way, and the pretzel position that yogis used certainly didn't seem to interfere with their energy. Then he ceased all thinking and did the breathing that guided him to his center.

His spirit floated free, took the form of the 'io, the Hawaiian hawk, and sought out the physical focus of his grandson. As the hawk he soared directly westward, toward Freiburg, and while passing over the mountains of the Black Forest he felt a sudden downward pull. Letting it direct him he spiralled lower and lower until he was above a cabin in the trees. Was Keoki inside? He settled on a branch with a view of a window and used his hawk eyes to look in. The scene inside did not appear as it would have if he were a physical hawk or a physical person. The only way to get that accurate a representation would be to share the same frequency range as other physical beings. A spiritual visit always took place in a probable variation of the physical range.

As highly skilled as he was, Lani was able to keep the variation to a minimum, but what he saw chilled him even more than it might have had he been there in person. Keoki had the appearance of a skeleton bound in heavy chains and surrounded by flashing knives while a female demon danced around him. Lani knew that this was far from accurate in content, no doubt because of his emotional concern and the stress level of his physical body, but he also knew that it was quite accurate in concept. Keoki had been kidnapped and he was in deadly danger. Lani had no choice. He had to meet with Nazra no matter what the risk to himself.

Once he was reunited with his body, Lani set off for the *Isar* River, a few blocks away. At the river he turned right on *Widenmayerstrasse* and followed it along the riverbank through several name changes until he reached *Boschbrucke*, the short bridge that crossed over to the museum. The enormous façade of the museum was usually awe-inspiring, but right now he ignored it as he entered the courtyard. Still, he couldn't help glancing at the old Dornier Do 31 VTOL aircraft sitting on the left as he climbed the steps of the rotunda-like entrance. Inside the entrance hall he paid the eight marks for admission and took a map. His destination was straight ahead. In the Ship section, as it was called, he found himself in a large open area that was full of boats of every age and type, from primitive dugouts to a modern trawler, but no submarine. Checking his map he saw that there was another part of the Ship display area in the basement, so he took the stairs in the middle of the room and went below. The map didn't say where any of the particular displays were, so he wandered around and discovered that the U-Boat was in a separate section of the hall and that access to the conning tower was from a ramp.

The question now was, what kind of trap had Nazra set up? Would it be another explosive device? He tested the reaction of his energy field to that possibility and it didn't seem likely. A personal encounter? The reaction was very positive. Unless she changed her mind quickly or he walked away, that would be it, then. Was he up to it? Mixed reaction. Lani had no illusions about himself. He knew that he was physically tough in spite of his age, and he was skilled in *lua*, the Hawaiian martial art, though he was far from being a master. He also knew that Nazra was young, strong in body, mind and energy, and that she was a trained killer. This could very well be his last encounter of any kind. But there was a slim chance that she really wanted to negotiate, perhaps to offer Keoki in trade for Orlov. Anything that would keep Keoki alive for as long as possible was worth the risk.

Lani energized his senses, strengthened his field, and walked toward the submarine. When he got there he noticed that the U-Boat, usually crawling with children, was deserted and silent. Briefly, he wondered what her technique was for doing that, because he didn't think she worked with spirits the way he did. Tentatively, he extended his field into the sub and felt nothing but cold metal. He sent his spirit ocelot into the boat as a scout and it didn't return. Well, here goes everything. Then he did something that he hadn't done in a very long time. He asked for help. *E na aumakua, e ho'opakele ia'u*, Ancestors, protect me.

At the conning tower Lani looked down. There was only a ladder going below to an empty interior. He chose to descend as quickly as possible to gain as much advantage as he could. It didn't work.

As he was dropping freely for the last three feet he was struck in the right side by a terrible blow that knocked him sideways and left him gasping for air and with pain. Another hard blow in the same place broke a rib and sent it into his lung. He collapsed on the deck and looked up at a woman with kaleidoscope eyes. She was smiling at him. In spite of the nearly-blinding pain he recognized what she held in her hand. It was a *kombi*, a four-inch cylinder of black steel with a knob on each end that could maim or kill in the hands of an expert.

"Amazing," she said. "You knew this was going to happen and you came anyway. You must love your grandson very much." With surprising strength she threw him onto his stomach with one hand and delivered a crushing blow with the *kombi* to the base of his spine. Lani felt a moment of dazzling pain, then nothing at all from his hips down. Nazra rolled him over. "I've decided not to kill you. I just want you to suffer, permanently. Can't have you chasing me around any more. You're far too clever."

Lani raised his arms in an attempt to grab her, but she pulled him off the floor by his shirt front and reached around to smash a knob of the *kombi* against Lani's seventh cervical vertebra. His arms fell limply to his sides and he knew with horror that

262

she had paralyzed his entire body. "I'll make sure someone finds you before you die. And by the way, your grandson is dead." Nazra kissed his unfeeling lips, dropped him, and disappeared.

Twenty-eight

A Strange Encounter

Ahuwale ka nane huna
(That which was a secret is no longer hidden)

The doctor in charge of the Ramberg Clinic was clearly pleased with himself. "We have succeeded in repairing most of the damage, although the actual healing process has just begun. The doctor who first diagnosed him made an error and his condition wasn't as bad as originally thought." He spoke in excellent English. "A good thing the patient was in such robust health, really amazing for his age. I should estimate that he ought to recover most of his functions in eight to twelve months. I'm afraid he'll have to continue with the medication indefinitely, however, to control the pain and depression."

The doctor tried to look even more serious. "Of course, your grandfather was very, very lucky, you know. The broken rib only bruised his lung, missed going in by millimeters. And the blunt intrument used against his spine, well, I've been told that the person who wielded it was an expert, but I don't understand how she managed to avoid crushing the vertebrae. There was just enough pressure in each of the blows to induce paralysis, but not enough to do permanent damage. It was either greater combat expertise than I've ever seen, enormous luck, or heavenly intervention." The doctor smiled broadly to make sure it was understood that the last part of the comment was meant as a joke and nothing more.

Keoki was doing his best to control his impatience, something he could not have done a few weeks earlier. When he had arrived in Munich the day before he'd been met at the train station by a young-looking, female BND agent who told him that his grandfather was being treated at a private, government-sponsored clinic in *Schwabing*, a district just north of City Center, and that Keoki would be able to see him the next morning.

Although Keoki was extremely anxious to see his grandfather, part of him was relieved at the delay. As soon as Jeffrey had given him the news he had taken the first train out of Kirchzarten to Freiburg. With a few minutes to spare he caught a train north to Karlsruhe, and then had a half-hour wait for an Inter-City Express to Munich. With all of those good connections it was still a six-hour journey, during which he forced himself to stay awake for fear of missing a stop. He spent most of the time on the train remembering good times he had had with Gramps, because he had been told once that instead of worrying about someone you ought to think good thoughts about them to help them through their problem.

The female agent told Keoki that they had booked a room for him in a small hotel near the clinic, and while she drove him there she filled him in on what little she knew about what had happened. Apparently, Seeker had lured Gramps away from the agents who were supposed to protect him. It was unclear what his movements were after that because he hadn't been debriefed yet, but he was found inside the U-Boat exhibit at the *Deutsches Museum* an hour before closing the day before.

Fortunately, the police had been asked to watch for him, so when they were called they had immediately notified the BND. Lani was unconscious when he was found, and he was still that way now, although that was at least partly due to the surgery. He had been badly injured and the doctors said that his condition was critical.

At the hotel the agent helped Keoki through check-in because he was fuzzy with fatigue and stress, and she had helped to get him settled in his room. When she left he had just dropped on the bedspread fully-clothed and passed out. He woke up at nine in the evening and went out to one of the many inexpensive restaurants in *Schwabing* and had *ein Halbe und Weisswurst*, a half liter of beer and a white veal sausage. Then he returned to his room, showered, and went to bed properly. Half-awake, he murmured, "Okay, Gramps, meet me in *Po*." And then he passed out again.

The sea was green and the sand was soft and golden, almost like powder. Behind him was a stretch of dark green jungle, and behind that rose a line of narrow, emerald cliffs that resembled the folds of a gigantic curtain. In his hand was a fresh coconut with the top lopped off, and he was sipping its tangy water through a straw. He felt very content to just sit there in his shorts, watching a tiny speck on the horizon grow larger and larger.

Soon the speck began to take form. It became an outrigger canoe with a speck inside it, then a man paddling a canoe, and then it was his grandfather, pulling the paddle with long, hard strokes to catch a small wave that drove him into shore. In the shallows Lani bounded out of the boat and pulled it easily up onto the sand. He really looked good, thought Keoki, with his brown hair ruffling in the breeze and his familiar grin filling the boy with pleasure... *there's something strange here. Boy? Brown hair?* The scene shimmered slightly until Lani sat down next to him and touched his shoulder with a warm hand.

"Aloha, Kanoa!" said Gramps, using his nickname for Keoki. "I'm glad to see you! Are you okay?"

Of course he was okay. Why shouldn't he be? "Sure, Gramps. You're really looking good. I haven't seen you look like this since ..." *Since I was a kid. What's going on?* The scene began to shimmer and Gramps touched him lightly again.

"Stay here, Kanoa. I need to talk to you. Things aren't what they seem to be. We've both been through a lot and we need to talk. Please keep your focus and stay here for awhile."

Keoki looked around and decided that the surroundings were pretty, and also pretty strange. This wasn't normal sand, that wasn't normal water, and those weren't normal cliffs back there, although they looked something like the cliffs of northeast Molokai or the Na Pali Coast of Kauai. And yet, thinking of this place as not normal seemed familiar in a weird way. "What is this place, Gramps?"

The older man smiled happily as he also looked around. "In our tradition we call it *Na Pali Uli*, the Green Cliffs." He looked back at Keoki. "It's an in-between place, sort of a meeting place. We're not in our physical bodies now." He nudged Keoki's arm and thumped his own chest. "These are *kino akua*, spirit bodies, that we've formed so we can hold a focus and communicate more easily."

"I remember!" said Keoki. "I wanted to meet you, so that's why you came."

"I wanted to meet you, too, Kanoa," Lani said more seriously, "so that's why we came together. There's something I have to tell you ..." He looked away, then back again. "You're not in your physical body because..., because..." He stopped and began again. "Hold on to my hand and tell me the last thing you remember happening."

Keoki thought about it. "I fell asleep and then I woke up here in this place."

"Okay," Lani said carefully, "and just before that?"

The memories came easily. "Just before that I went out to a restaurant for beer and sausage, went back to my hotel, took a shower, and then I fell asleep and woke up right here."

His grandfather looked puzzled. "Where did that happen?" he asked.

"In Munich. Actually, in *Schwabing*. I came from Freiburg to see you in the clinic and ..."

The youthful spirit body of Gramps nearly faded away, but Keoki gripped the hand he still held and willed it back. "Stay here, Gramps!"

The body became solid once more. Lani's expression was unreadable. "You're still alive, then."

"Of course! Why shouldn't I be?"

There was a slight tremor in his voice when Lani spoke again. "Nazra said..., and I saw... I thought for sure you had been killed by her or someone else."

More memories came back. "Oh, right. Well, it was close. Nazra sent this other assassin and she was supposed to kill the Russian and me, but I got sort of lucky and Jeffrey called Villier and she called the police ..."

"So you're alive." Gramps had tears in his eyes.

"As far as I can tell," said Keoki cautiously. "How about you? I got news that you were injured."

Lani removed his hand from Keoki's and sat next to him on the golden sand with his arms wrapped around his knees, looking out across the lagoon. "I'm alive for now," he said in a very neutral tone.

"Don't give me that 'for now' jazz, Gramps. What's wrong with you?"

"I've lived a long life, Kanoa. A full life. I've seen a lot and done a lot. Right now I'm feeling tired. You can take care of yourself, the family's doing well, and I don't think my body's going to recover so well after this."

As Keoki watched, his grandfather's spirit body seemed to age rapidly. Then he got a sudden insight which would not have been available to him in the outer world. "I know what's wrong, Lani. You're just feeling sorry for yourself."

Lani twisted his head quickly and looked at Keoki with a startled expression. To his eyes Keoki had become much older and larger. At the same time, the sand had become grass, there were snow-capped mountains behind them, and a deep, misty valley opened up in front of them. Lani sighed. "So you remember, now."

Keoki stretched his arms and looked down at his body. It had the muscular form of a fifty-year-old athlete who stayed in shape, and he was wearing a short, brown, wool tunic. He looked at Lani, who appeared much the same and who now had black hair flecked with grey. "Not everything," said Keoki in a voice deeper than his normal one. "But enough to know that we've been friends longer than we've been relatives. And that you're feeling sorry for yourself. Probably because you got beat up by a woman."

There was a brief flush of anger, and then Lani laughed and stood up. "I never did get any sympathy from you. Since you're not going to let me fade into the sunset, I'll race you to the Runestone!" With that he took off into the air like Superman, with Keoki close behind.

An instant later they landed at the same time beside a tall monolith inscribed with a mass of Celtic runes and spirals. The Runestone sat in a small clearing in the middle of a dense forest of pines and firs and hemlock. "Go ahead," said Keoki. "I'm going to need your help for quite awhile longer in the outer world."

"You could do it and you wouldn't need me," said Lani, standing with his arms crossed.

Keoki smiled. "Not so, old friend. My outer Keoki-self doesn't have the energy capacity or the confidence yet to carry

268

on the work on his own. The time will come, but it isn't yet for that life. So quit stalling and do it."

The other man grimaced. "And I was looking forward to a very long vacation. Oh well." Lani turned to the stone and softly hummed a haunting melody. The monolith began to glow. Lani continued humming until the stone gave off a blue-white radiance. Then he placed his hands at the centers of two spirals and changed the tune he was humming to one that was lighter and more cheerful. The radiance seemed to enter his body and spread until he looked like a carved extension of the stone. That lasted for several minutes, and then Lani stopped humming and the glowing light gradually faded away. At last, Lani stepped away from the stone and said, "Well, that was refreshing!"

"Just remember not to jump out of bed when you get back," said Keoki. "The doctors can only handle miracles in small doses."

"And what will you remember?"

"Not very much," Keoki grinned. "I think it's much more fun that way."

In the hotel room in *Schwabing*, Keoki woke up to the ringing of his telephone. What was he dreaming? Something about Gramps. He reached over and picked up the phone. "Hello?" A recorded voice told him that it was nine o'clock in the morning. Keoki put the phone down. He didn't remember asking for a wake-up call, but he did remember that he would be picked up at ten to go to the clinic. He got up quickly to use the bathroom and realized that he felt pretty good. All he had needed was a good night's sleep.

In the breakfast room Keoki wolfed down a hard-boiled egg, some slices of cheese on pumpernickel, and a couple of sweet rolls with a glass of juice and coffee. He was on the sidewalk in front of the hotel a minute before the same female BND agent came to take him to the clinic.

It didn't look like a clinic and there was nothing on the outside to indicate that it was any more than a modest residence. It smelled like a clinic on the inside, though. Keoki was met in the foyer by a nurse who led him through several hallways to a room that seemed to be near the back of the house. She knocked and opened the door without waiting for permission to enter and let

Keoki follow her in. His eyes went first to Gramps, who was sitting up in bed with a brace around his neck and bandages around his chest. The nurse said something to Lani in German that Keoki didn't catch. His grandfather nodded and smiled at Keoki as the nurse left the room. "*Aloha, e Kanoa*, Hello, Kanoa. How are you doing?"

"How am I doing!" Keoki said, amazed. "I came here expecting to see you in a coma!"

Lani reached for a glass of water on the bedside table to his right and winced a little as he lifted it to drink. "Well, the doctors are calling it a miraculous recovery."

His grandson looked thoughtful. "Someday you've really got to teach me how you do that."

"I promise," said Lani, his eyes twinkling. "However, I'll still be bedridden for a few days. And it looks like I'll have to use a cane for quite awhile. Guess I'll finally have to act like an old man."

Keoki shook his head. "So what happened?"

Lani told him all about yesterday's events, giving his grandson more details than he had given to the agents who had debriefed him, particularly in regard to the explosion at *Monopteros* which had made the papers. So far everyone thought it was an unrelated, politically-motivated event. That suited Lani fine, since he didn't want to be associated with damage to a city landmark. After detailing the attack at the museum, Lani told Keoki that under no circumstances should he trust anything that Nazra would say to him. Then Keoki described the events at Kirchzarten and Triberg, leaving out his afternoon as Marta's sex slave.

When they had finished bringing each other up to date they just looked at each other for a few moments in silence. Finally, Lani said, "It's been quite an adventure, hasn't it, Kanoa?"

Keoki glanced around the room, noting half-consciously that it was a cheery place, with lace curtains and flowers on the dresser. "Do you think it's over?"

"I don't see why not. I can't do any more and you've saved one of the targets. The last one is hidden away somewhere and PERI has been rendered superfluous. Of course, we need Interpol's decision now to pull us off the case, but I don't know of any reason why ..." There was a knock on the door and the nurse walked in. She announced that there were two visitors. Lani glanced at Keoki and back to the nurse. "Send them in, please."

Madame Villier and *Herr* Nichts entered the room looking very solemn. Both changed their expressions to surprise at seeing Lani sitting up looking reasonably good considering the circumstances. They offered congratulations on his progress and praise to Keoki for his part in saving Mikalov. Each of them talked on for a few minutes about general aspects of the case until they fell silent.

"In American slang I would say that we're waiting for the other shoe to drop," said Lani.

Villier raised an eyebrow and Nichts said in English, "Other shoe?"

"It means that we are waiting to learn the real reason for your visit."

"Ah," said Villier, "you believe that there is an *arrière-pensée*, an ulterior motive for our coming here."

"Isn't there?"

"Let us call it an additional reason. *Monsieur* Nichts?"

The German Security chief did not look happy. "A full analysis of the Seeker operation indicates that hiding the target is not a viable long-term solution. The expense of moving Orlov from one hiding place to another and keeping him protected is not justified by his importance and it prevents him from serving in his professorial capacity, which serves the needs of Germany at least to some extent. At the same time, it is not politically appropriate to simply abandon him, either. The only feasible solution seems to be that of setting a trap for Seeker. For her own reasons she seems intent on carrying out her objectives as quickly as possible. That is fortunate in a way, because if she were willing she could simply wait us out and then strike at her own leisure."

"There must be an unsolved problem or you wouldn't be here," said Lani.

"There are two, in fact," said the security chief. "One is that we have no idea what she looks like. From Krazensky we learned that she is about 170 centimeters tall and weighs about sixty-two kilos ..."

"That's around five foot six and a hundred and thirty-five

271

pounds," whispered Lani in a quick aside to Keoki, who nodded silently.

"... and her eyes are multicolored due to some experiment they performed on her," continued Nichts. "However, we have also learned from experience that she has an excellent talent for disguises. According to the analysis, which includes debriefing information, *Herr* McCoy here is the only one who seems able to identify her. I have to assume it is due to your, ah, special abilities. In any case, for our plan to have any chance of success we need your help." He stared at Keoki as if waiting for a response from the young man.

Keoki glanced first at his grandfather, whose look seemed to say that it was his choice alone. Then he glanced at Madame Villier, who said, "Even though you work for Interpol you cannot be ordered to take a risk like this. She has already tried to kill you more than once. The assignment would be very dangerous. It is up to you."

"We would, of course, provide all necessary protection to ensure your safety," said Nichts.

That got a slight smile from Keoki. They had done a helluva poor job at protecting anyone so far. However, Nazra was a special case, no doubt about that. How do you protect someone from a psychic assassin who isn't afraid of using any method necessary, including the hiring of mercenaries? Nichts was right. Unless she could be identified she couldn't be stopped except with incredible luck. Not impossible, but not probable, either. She had to be stopped, nevertheless. "I'll help," said Keoki.

The relief that Nichts felt was obvious to everyone else in the room, though he tried to suppress it. "That leaves the second problem," he said, "and I don't know if there is a solution. We need ideas. How can we let Seeker know where Orlov is without making her suspicious?"

"I thought that had to be it," said Lani from the bed. "Are you willing to try an experiment that may give us an answer?" Nichts merely shrugged and Villier smiled. "All right, then. I would like to ask that you two think about a vacation, a holiday, I mean, that you've taken or would like to take. Just keep your minds occupied with that. And you, Kanoa," he turned to his grandson, "close your eyes and ask for a symbol of where Seeker is going to strike next."

"How am I supposed to know that?" asked Keoki with some surprise.

"Don't worry about it. Just ask for a symbol and pay attention to whatever appears, no matter how unimportant or silly it seems."

Keoki shrugged, looked around the room for a moment, and closed his eyes. He did the breathing process that got him centered and paused. Who was he supposed to ask for the symbol? He remained puzzled for a few more moments, then decided to expand his *la'a kea* out as far as he could imagine and ask it for a symbol, reasoning that it might be able to connect with Nazra, or the location, or Orlov or something.

Bands and streaks and clouds of hazy colors appeared behind his eyelids, and he was still aware of the sounds in the room. Then he started to hear a faint sound of music and he wasn't sure whether it was inside his head or outside. The music got louder and he could tell that it sounded like a marching band. With a suddenness that startled him he saw Mickey Mouse leading a parade. Gradually the scene opened up and his point of view was above the band, looking down Main Street toward Fantasyland. He let it go on a little while longer, then shook his head and opened his eyes, grimacing in disgust.

"Well, what did you see?" asked Lani.

Keoki looked at his grandfather, a disgusted look still on his face. "Disneyland," he announced.

Nichts was about to say something, but Lani stopped him with an upraised hand and said to Keoki, "What part of Disneyland?"

Realizing that Gramps was serious, Keoki carefully recalled the scene. "Main Street. Mickey was leading a band and it was marching toward the bridge that goes over to Fantasyland."

"Was there anything that stood out in the scene? Anything that glowed, anything that seemed to be a special point of focus?"

Keoki brought the image back clearly to mind. "Well, yeah. The band seemed to be heading straight for Sleeping Beauty's castle. I mean, you have to enter Fantasyland that way from Main Street, but it felt like that was the destination. Oh, yeah, and

273

there were balloons attached to the doorway, like somebody wanted to make sure they didn't miss it. What's that supposed to mean, anyway?"

Lani grinned slowly and turned back to Villier and Nichts. "Orlov is being kept at *Neuschwanstein*, New Swan Mountain, and if Keoki here can find out where he's hidden, you can bet that Seeker can, too."

Sometimes it can be a pleasure to shock officialdom.

Twenty-nine

A Vain Attempt

Ua pale ka pono
(Success was prevented)

Neuschwanstein, New Swan Mountain, is the name given
to the most famous castle of Ludwig II of Bavaria, often called
"Mad King Ludwig." Ludwig grew up in his father's neo-Gothic
castle of *Höhenschwangau*, Schwangau Hill, formerly called
Schwanstein, Swan Mountain, which in its pre-restored state was
the medieval castle of the Knights of *Schwangau*. This castle
sits on a hill above the town of *Schwangau* next to a beautiful
lake at the foot of the Alps, only five kilometers from the beginning of Germany's famous "Romantic Road" at *Füssen*.

In his formative years Prince Ludwig was surrounded by
paintings, tapestries and artifacts depicting famous Germanic
sagas such as that of the swan-knight *Lohengrin* and the
Nibelungen. He also ate in the castle's Hall of Heroes and visited his mother in her Turkish bedroom. It was in this castle that
Ludwig spent many hours with Richard Wagner, who may have
been influenced by the setting as well.

A portrait made soon after he became king shows Ludwig
as a rather effete-looking youth with perhaps a touch of melan-
choly. His first and only engagement to be married ended when
his fiancee jilted him without giving him a reason and he never
attempted another marriage. Having more of an artistic than a
political nature he spent most of his time, energy, and the
country's money building romantic castles. Ludwig was finally
declared mad and deposed in 1886 by his opponents in the government. Five days later he died under circumstances that remain a mystery. His political achievements were insignificant,

but his artistic legacy continues to help support the German economy by attracting millions of visitors, along with a lot of their money.

Of all the attractions in Germany, none can compare with *Neuschwanstein*. A true fairy-tale castle, inside and out, it sits on a rock ledge high above the narrow *Poellat* Gorge whose falls, starting well below the castle, plunge down forty-five meters, or one hundred and forty-nine feet. *Neuschwanstein* was built upon the ruins of an older castle, *Vorderhöhenschwangau*, translated as "in front of Schwangau Hill." In fact, this was what Ludwig called it; the name *Neuschwanstein* replaced it only after Ludwig's death. In addition to a royal architect, Ludwig used a theatrical set designer and it shows in both the interior and exterior of the castle. Its slim towers and magnificent, isolated setting, were the inspiration for Walt Disney's Sleeping Beauty castle, first for the movie and then for the park. The red bricks of the entrance contrast sharply with the white stone and green turrets of the rest of the castle, and the whole spectacle is both breath-taking and uplifting.

Above the castle, and a dizzying ninety-three meters, or three hundred and four feet, above the bottom of the gorge, is the fragile-looking *Marienbrücke*, Marian's Bridge, named after Ludwig's mother. And on this bridge little more than a meter wide, looking down at the castle, was Nazra. Before her she could see Ludwig's castle on its ledge, and beyond it the long ridge resembling a sleeping green dragon with *Höhenschwangau* sitting on its head like a crown, and a lake on either side looking for all the world like two blue wings. And behind all of that were the snow-capped ramparts of the *Allgäu* Range of the magnificent Bavarian Alps.

Nazra admired the view and considered the problem. Orlov was in there, she knew that. Psychic intuition and the torture of a BND agent had confirmed it. She had never been inside the castle, but she was familiar with its layout. The castle had never been completed and only a small portion was open to visitors, but even so, there were still many finished rooms that were used only for meetings, special guests, and staff quarters. Orlov had to be in one of them.

The problem was how to find out which one. The man she

had tortured hadn't known. Earlier that morning she had probed the castle from a distance, but the results were inconclusive. Somewhere in the center was all she could get. It was as if there were a psychic fog obscuring her inner senses, yet she hadn't detected anyone who could have produced such an effect. In fact, she didn't know anyone who was able to interfere with her probing except one man who was now permanently paralyzed and incapable of interfering with her in any way. Perhaps it was some sort of energetic anomaly of the terrain. She knew from her research that there were places on the earth where the natural energy could distort psychic perception, even though she had never encountered one personally before. She decided that it would be necessary to do a closer inspection of the premises.

Playing the part of a young, curly-headed blonde secretary on holiday, and dressed in tight-fitting slacks and sweater without any underwear, she found a young American man at the bus stop only too willing to leave his business associates and be her companion for the day. Although her get-up would attract attention, she knew it would be directed less on her as a person and more on fantasies about her.

Arm-in-arm with her new friend they walked up the steep trail that ran beside the high castle wall and to the main entrance. At this time of year it was not very crowded. A few weeks later it would take hours just to get into the courtyard. She and her companion purchased tickets at the booth outside the entrance and then passed under the round-topped portal and joined the line in the small courtyard that was waiting to enter the castle itself. Nazra used the time to send probes into the castle while she scanned the courtyard. The probes gave only vague results, but she detected five BND agents in the courtyard looking the visitors over while they pretended to be resting on the walls and sitting on the benches.

The line of people kept moving and soon they were inside, climbing the unpolished marble steps of the main staircase. At the top, on the third floor of the castle, they entered the oddly-shaped vestibule which was configured like a trapezoid because of a bend in the supporting ledge. Nazra projected her energy past the paintings illustrating the ancient Nordic saga of *Sigurd*, but found only empty rooms behind the inside wall.

The line was herded next into the throne room, where Nazra was momentarily dazzled by it's chapel-like appearance. Golden walls featured frescoes of saints and angels and Christ, while the floor was an expansive mosaic of animals from around the world. Marble steps led to an empty space in a circular apse below sainted kings where a throne should have been but never was. Before Nazra could recover from her amazement at such opulence the line was goaded onward, and she determined not to let her attention waver again.

.She kept up her probing and scanning through the study, with its scenes of the *Tannhäuser* saga; the king's bedroom, where Tristan and Isolde kept the king company on his lonely nights in his intricately-carved, Gothic-style bed; and even through the corridor designed like a grotto complete with stalactites that probably had given additional inspiration to Disney engineers.

It wasn't until they reached the fourth floor that she lost her concentration again. There they entered the fabulous Singer's Hall, modeled after the one at Wartburg Castle in Thuringia, where the legendary song contest recounted in the *Tannhäuser* saga was said to have been held. The huge and elaborate hall with its decorated oak-paneled ceiling and parquet floor featured scenes from Parsifal along its walls, and at one end there was a columned enclosure with an actual stage setting of Klingsor's play, "The Magic Forest."

However, the room was large enough that Nazra had time to regain her focus before leaving it. While clinging to her companion's arm and giving forth an abundance of "oohs" and "ahhhs" she continued her psychic search. Just before leaving the hall she began to suspect that she was being tricked. She had picked up an occasional agent, in the crowd or behind the walls, but no concentration of them. That didn't make sense if Orlov was here, which she was certain of. Additionally, every probe guided her toward the center of the castle, without giving her a specific location.

An energy anomaly was one possibility. So was an intentional diversion. Assuming that to be the case, she didn't know who it could be. Maybe it was another PERI expert brought in for the job. No matter. She had to get off by herself and do some more intensive work. When they were back outside the castle

Nazra gave her companion a passionate kiss and walked away, leaving him too dazed to call out or follow. She hiked down the hill to her hired camper van and changed into the jeans, sweatshirt, and unruly hair of an American backpacker. Slinging her pack over one shoulder, she went to a snack shop for a cheese sandwich and a can of beer and took them into the woods behind the castle.

When she was quite alone she sat under a large hemlock tree and ate her lunch, pondering which approach she should take to penetrate or bypass the anomaly or the diversion, whichever it was. When she was finished with the lunch, and the pondering, she brushed off her hands, drank the last swallow of beer, and belched. Then she was ready to do her thing.

Of all the hundreds of books that she had studied for her training, one that impressed her greatly was Power of Will, by Frank Channing Haddock, M.S., Ph.D. Put out by the Pelton Publishing Company of Meriden, Connecticut, USA in 1917, it was subtitled "A Practical Companion Book for Unfoldment of the Powers of Mind." It was written in a very old-fashioned style, but it was full of detailed exercises for developing willpower. The style made it difficult to read, but something about it compelled her to persist until she could understand every concept in the book.

Haddock's teaching consisted of three basic premises: that the goal of human evolution was to develop into a psychic being and willpower was the key factor in such evolution; that life was a play between inner and outer powers, and you either became subject to the outer powers or mastered them; and that willpower grows by directed exercise. The possibilities appealed to her.

At the beginning of each chapter the author had included one of his own poems, but Nazra had ignored these for a long time because they sounded too flighty and didn't seem pertinent. One day, however, the thought struck her that perhaps the author had included even more information in the poetry. One of her favorite chapters had to do with exercises in attention. In fairly convoluted language it started out by saying that whatever you fasten your attention on becomes a part of you, and develops within you the function that it represents. She finally memorized the chapter and it served her well. When she eventually

279

got around to studying the preceding poem, however, she discovered an astounding idea that led her to memorize the poem, too. Eventually she moved on to more exciting techniques, but she could still recite the poem by heart. Softly she murmured to herself:

> "WHAT SEEST THOU?
> The gracious light, in semi-sphere
> Created by the living soul,
> Encompasses the vision's whole
> Of worlds afar and atoms near.
>
> The vault of heaven, gemmed and deep,
> And earth and sea o'erwhelmed in light,
> Full complements of thought invite
> That soul may all its empire keep.
>
> And so the world within the flesh
> The larger gains, and grows apace
> To Truth's ideal and Beauty's grace
> With understanding ever fresh.
>
> Yet must the Wider Life emerge
> Within the lesser, welling up,
> If living spirit's wine-filled cup
> Reflect the Drama's drift and urge.
>
> What seest thou? Thy self alone:
> Thou art the world and all its parts.
> And this is being's Art of Arts:
> To know the Vaster Life thine own."

Tears filled Nazra's opal eyes, masked by dark brown contacts, when she finished. Haddock, like so many others she had read, had hoped that by teaching people to expand their psychic potentials they could help to guide humanity to a higher, more spiritual way of being and living. It was possible, too, Nazra knew that. She could have been a compassionate, loving wife and mother, as well as a creative and successful artist or entrepreneur. She still could, for that matter, especially now that her past ties were almost all gone. But she shook her head and wiped the tears away. She had made choices and she would continue to make choices that suited her and no one else. One of the side-effects of will training for her was the development of an immense stubbornness. She had picked her path and nothing would make her change it.

Her moment of self-pity over, she turned back to the practical insight provided by Haddock's poem. If she could expand her energy field and become the castle she would know it inside and out and could locate anyone or anything within or around it. She had never tried out this idea with anything like as a castle before, but if that wasn't a "Wider Life" then what was? She could do it. She would do it. She would will it so.

She moved to a place where she could have a good view of the castle from behind while still being isolated from other people. Then she worked on her energy, feeling it, intensifying it, expanding it. When it encompassed the entirety of the castle she willed herself to find the set of frequency patterns that would constitute the structure. With imagination as her guide she started with sensations of texture, and of the boundaries where different materials met and supported each other, or rested on each other, or connected to each other. From the awareness of stone, and concrete, and wood, and metal, and cloth, and glass, and paint she willed herself to sense these as a whole, as a container, as an enclosure, as a self-aware entity.

Like a yogi mentally exploring the organs, bones and spaces within his own body, Nazra-as-the-castle directed her consciousness through her chambers and halls. She was aware of people as points of formless vibration, some in movement and some at rest, but none with the particular quality that she sought. There was nothing in the center of the castle but a grey-black smudge of some kind that she couldn't identify, so she passed over it to explore further outward. There were spaces in her walls, but most of those were empty. She went downward, became aware of a kitchen space, and storerooms empty of human vibrations. Where to go next? She had explored the spaces in the center, along the outside, and those below. There was nowhere to go but up. No, that was ...

Why not? Ah! Surprise. There was a substantial attic. But it

281

was empty, too. She almost gave up, but there was a persistent feeling that there was still more to herself. She let her consciousness drift while still remaining Nazra-as-the-castle. She nudged her awareness upward, letting it find its own way, and felt the strange sensation of multiple, cylindrical risings. The towers! Of course! And in one, the highest, she found her quarry.

An hour later, once more Nazra-as-herself, she was studying the layout of the tallest tower from still another angle with a pair of binoculars. It rose from the center of the right side of the main castle building and was probably accessed from the Singing Hall on the fourth floor, as well as from stairs below. She was pretty sure she recalled a door on that side of the hall when she passed through. There was obviously a chamber of some sort just below the high and narrow conical roof of the tower, and a sort of semi-tower jutted out behind it like a room addition. Around the chamber was a crenellated balcony that looked wide enough to walk on comfortably. There was enough space in that part of the tower for a decent studio flat.

Another balcony three or four meters below held spotlights used to illuminate the castle at night for the benefit of guests in the local hotels. Their position and their angle indicated that they would cause the upper balcony to cast a strong shadow on the chamber, thus helping Orlov to get a good night's sleep. It would also hide anyone who could get up that high without being seen. Fat chance, she thought, using an American expression she had learned in her reading.

The stairway was out of the question. Too easily defended. A climb up the outside at night was perfectly feasible except for the lights, which were too strong for the camouflage of a glamour. And besides, she didn't want to take the chance that the tower would be unwatched from the outside. Climbing the tower was too obvious a ploy.

Nazra walked back and forth along the ridge behind the castle, ignoring the few tourists who had climbed the trail that far. A well-placed mortar round would do it, but the castle was too isolated for an easy shot and there wouldn't be time for ranging rounds. How about a guided missile? The SS-II shoulder launcher would work, but it would take time to obtain one. What if ... Her thoughts were interrupted by a shadow that flitted over

282

her. Glancing up she saw something that in former days would certainly have been called a dragon, only the modern name for it was a hang glider. She looked down and began pacing again, but stopped before she had gone five steps. A hang glider, she mused. Where was it launched from?

Nazra ran all the way down into *Schwangau*, and continued running until she found a travel agency advertising local tours. She burst into the office and demanded to know if there were any hang gliding or para-sailing activities available in the area. The woman at the desk was a bit put out at the brusqueness of the request, but she replied readily enough that there was a place in town that rented gear and she gave Nazra the address.

A few minutes later Nazra was asking an athletic-looking young man about the sport. He pointed his chin toward an array of hang gliding and para-sailing equipment in the back of his shop, and when she asked him where, he pointed the same chin toward the window. Looking outward, Nazra could see Ludwig's castle high on its ledge, and well above it a round-topped mountain which the young man said was *Tegelberg*. There was a tram that took one to the top, he told her, and it was designed to let one carry the proper flying gear.

She laughed so hard he thought she was a little crazy and he was reluctant to rent her any gear until she offered to pay him triple the going rate and left her credit card with him as security. She chose a para-sail with a quick-release harness because it offered the best control and she knew she would have to discard it quickly. "In case I land in the lake," she said. She tried to pick the darkest color possible, and finally had to settle for a blue sail with thin white stripes. She left the shop to get her camper van and easily loaded the gear into it because there were no poles to worry about. She drove off to the tram station, happily whistling the prelude to the Funeral March.

With everything she would need stuffed in her backpack, plus her para-sailing gear, Nazra took the tram to the top of *Tegelberg*. The view, of course, was stupendous. The whole of the Upper Bavarian plain was spread out before her and the fairy-tale castle seemed like no more than a spot of color below. There were three other glider buffs already preparing their gear for a mid-afternoon jaunt through the clear air.

Nazra joined in casual conversation with them as they got ready, asking about currents and updrafts, and then sat back in the shadows of some trees and made herself comfortable. She didn't plan to take off for a long while, yet. About an hour before sunset the conductor of the last tram to descend the mountain came up to her and urged her to go with him because it was going to get very cold, but she told him she had a sleeping bag and that she wanted to take off at first light. Finally, he shrugged and left her alone.

When everyone had gone down the mountain one way or another, she tuned in to Orlov, which was not a problem any more in spite of a persistent tug that tried to throw her off. She could ignore that easily now that she had already made contact. Orlov was still in the tower and she got a sense that he was reading or writing. She tried some remote viewing by mentally projecting an imaginary, flexible telescope right through one of the windows of the tower, and was rewarded with a sense of a table along a wall that was set for dinner for two. Probably a woman, she surmised.

What she intended to do was extremely risky, but then life was a risk, so what was the difference? She refused to dwell on what could go wrong, except to provide for contingency measures. Her basic plan was to glide as straight as possible for the tower, to land as gently as possible, to enter the tower as quickly as possible, preferably by the door but by a window if necessary, to dispatch Orlov as fast as possible with a bullet to the brain, and to escape as easily as possible by sliding down the tower on a rope and losing her pursuers in the woods. Naturally, a thousand things could go wrong, but demanding a guarantee for the future was like expecting a politician to keep all his promises. All you would end up with would be righteous anger, if you lived. Whatever would happen would happen, and she would deal with it no watter what form it took.

Nazra waited until she could sense that Orlov had gone to sleep. That odd grey-black smudge seemed to be in the room with him, but she got no sense of what it was and dismissed it as an anomaly. Even from her great height she could make out the tower that was lit by three spotlights. The night was moonless, the stars were bright, the air was almost still, with a scent of

284

evergreen forest. It was perfect. She donned a form-fitting, dark grey, micro-weave bodysuit and thin gripping gloves, tucked a .32 caliber pistol in her breastband, hooked a thirty-five meter ultra-thin and ultra-strong polyester line to a latch on her belt, and prepared the parasail for take-off. With the harness on and the sail ready, she stepped off the edge of the go-ramp and into space, trusting completely to nature and science and skill.

The pleasure of flying effortlessly above the world was almost orgasmic. What effort there was consisted of forcing herself to keep her attention on her objective. The familiar temptation to cast off the harness and soar like Peter Pan that all glide-fliers must deal with was automatically noted and suppressed as she spiralled downward toward the tower and Orlov. The wind was a little stronger up here than she had expected, so her flight took longer than she would have liked, but she would be at the ledge in moments. She noted that there was a dim light showing at the windows of the chamber. Perhaps a night light, because she knew that Orlov was asleep.

Nazra controlled the parasail like an expert, causing it to stall just as her feet touched the crenellated wall of the balcony. Releasing the harness and letting the canopy flutter down behind her like a dying bird, she stepped lightly onto the balcony itself and unhooked the line from her belt, dropping the loop that she had tied at one end over one of the merlons and tossing the the rest with its weighted end out beyond the lower balcony. Less than twenty seconds later she pulled out her pistol and tried the handle of the door to the tower chamber, noting with satisfaction that it wasn't locked because no one had imagined any need for it. Ready for anything, she opened the door and entered the room in a crouch.

As it turned out, she wasn't ready for anything. At the far end of the chamber she recognized Orlov, who was in the single bed and just emerging from a deep sleep. In almost the same instant she recognized the young man who was sitting at the table, reading a book by the light of a halogen table lamp. It was the Hawaiian! But how could that be? Was the damned boy indestructible? She was stunned into immobility for the briefest moment of time.

Incredibly, the boy recovered before she did. She was just

bringing her pistol to bear on him when he threw the book at her. The spine of the book hit the inside of her wrist, causing her to drop the gun. She leaped up to engage him with her hands, but he had grabbed the chair and held it in front of him like a lion-tamer as he called for help. Meanwhile, Orlov had slid down on the other side of the bed and was also screaming for help. A trapdoor on one side of the chamber was opening and an armed agent was already emerging. There were too many variables. Escape was the only viable option and she nearly cried with frustration. Damn the boy! She risked the time to say to the Hawaiian with all the venom she could muster, "You will die!" and she leaped backward out the door.

Keoki dropped the chair and rushed after her with the first agent right behind him. He looked over the wall and caught only a glimpse of her before she disappeared into the darkness. The agent didn't see anything, but he did notice the taut line looped around a merlon. He pulled out a pocket knife to cut it, but the line went slack before he got to it. A second agent was already using his radio to alert other agents stationed around the perimeter of the castle, but time passed and they didn't find anyone.

Nazra was gone.

Thirty

A Gift Of Bones

'Ano lani, 'ano honua
(A heavenly nature, an earthly nature)

Lani was still at the clinic in *Schwabing* when Keoki returned to Munich, only now he was able to get into a chair by himself and make his own way to the bathroom with the aid of a walker. He was using the device on a return trip to his bed when Keoki knocked and came into the room. When he saw the expression on Keoki's face he glared and said, "You are only as young as you feel, and I feel younger than you, in spite of how I might look."

"I didn't say anything," protested Keoki as he offered to help his grandfather.

Lani accepted the help into a chair. "No need. I can read minds, you know." He grunted as he dropped the last two inches onto the cushion.

Keoki laughed. "Okay, Gramps, would you like me to tell you what happened at the castle, or would you prefer to read my mind?"

The older man looked at him keenly. "Since you're hale and hearty and feisty, I assume it's good news, so go ahead and practice speaking, I hear it's good for you."

The younger man smiled and sat on the bed. "First, a gift." He handed Lani a plastic bag. Inside was a can of macadamia nuts. "Found them in a department store." Lani thanked him with pleasure and they shared a few nuts before Keoki went on.

"Things went well enough. I used the last few things you taught me. Made my *la'a kea* a dark grey color and told it to scramble my energy. I also told Orlov to keep thinking of me

287

and nothing else while I did a *kulike* on him, imagined myself to be him as well as I could, to try and draw Nazra to the center of the castle where we had set a trap for her. Before noon yesterday I had a really strong sense that she was in the area. I wanted to be in a place where I could see the people coming in, but the guy in charge thought that was too risky. So I spent most of the time in a room, nervous as hell, hoping she would come and hoping she wouldn't at the same time."

"She did come, though, didn't she?" asked Lani, afer sipping from a glass of water.

Keoki popped another nut in his mouth and chewed before answering. "I sensed her leaving the castle around noon and nothing else happened for the rest of the day, so I don't really know if those techniques helped or not. If they had any effect it was only temporary. Anyway, after sunset I started to get this really strong premonition that she was on her way back and that Orlov was in serious and immediate danger. They didn't pay any attention to me at first, but I put up such a fuss that they stuck me in with Orlov just to shut me up and even had dinner sent up for the two of us. Fortunately, Orlov was glad for the company and told me all about his boyhood on a farm before he went to bed."

The young man took another nut and chewed it while he got up and walked around the room. "I don't know what time it was, but it was late. Orlov was sleeping and I was reading a book about King Ludwig when the door burst open." Keoki stood still with a faraway gaze as he recalled the events in the tower. "There she was, all dressed in black, with a gun in her hand. It was like she just materialized out of thin air. She was ..." Keoki was about to say "beautiful," but he shook his head and changed it. He looked at Lani. "She was about to shoot Orlov when she noticed me and I guess that shocked her. I threw my book at her and luckily it knocked the gun out of her hand. Then I held the chair in front of me before she could jump me. Orlov and I were screaming our heads off for help and it's a good thing the place was wired for sound. A couple of agents started to come up and then she gave me real full-out stink eye and said that she would get me. Then she just disappeared out the door. I ran out after her, and I realize now that was a stupid thing to do, but she was

288

already over the side of the balcony, sliding down a rope she had already left there."

"So they didn't catch her?"

"Nope. They had people in the woods, but she got past them. No telling where she is now. I overheard that they are going to give Orlov and Mikalov new identities, like they do back home for witnesses. Anyway, I talked to Villier and Nichts a little while ago and we're out of the loop now. As soon as you decide to quit fooling around we can go home." Keoki was suddenly stunned at what he had just said. "Sorry, Gramps," he said with a stricken look. "I didn't mean that ..."

Lani chuckled. "No offense taken, Kanoa. It's the kind of thing a good friend would say."

They spent another half hour talking about how long Lani needed to stay there, and about travel arrangements back to Hawaii, and about how good some *ahi*, yellow fin tuna, black-eyed beans, and poi would taste, when there was a knock on the door, and this time no one entered right away. Lani said to come in and it was the young female BND agent who had been helping Keoki. She said that there was a courier from a message service at the front door, and he had a message that Keoki had to sign for. She didn't know know how he knew where Keoki was.

"Well I didn't tell anybody," said Keoki, upset. "For all the security around here you may as well put up a sign outside." The woman managed to look guilty and Keoki apologized, assuring her that it wasn't her fault. He went with her to the door and signed the pad handed to him by an uninterested bicyclist. He received the letter-sized brown envelope and the messenger took off before Keoki could even think of giving him a tip.

Back in Lani's room, alone with his grandfather, Keoki opened the envelope and took out a sheet of paper with a very short note written on it in a neat, feminine hand. "You got me into serious trouble with Nazra," it said, "so I gave her your mother's address. You also saved my life, so I'm telling you about it." That was all.

Keoki dropped the note on the floor and put his head in his hands. "Oh, God, what have I done?"

Lani bent over and retrieved the note and read it. "What does this mean?"

His grandson looked up, his eyes already red. "I'm sorry, Gramps. I bought a clock for Mom, and Brigid, I mean Marta, made me write down Mom's address because she was going to send it to her after she killed me and ..."

"This woman Marta gave your mother's address to Nazra?" Lani's voice was hard.

"I didn't know... I didn't mean..."

"Stop blubbering, Kanoa! We have to warn the family." There was a phone in the room and Lani was able to get an international operator almost immediately. Moments later the phone was ringing at the McCoy house in Kona. It rang eight times before someone picked it up.

"Aloha," said a woman's voice. It sounded like it was Hank's wife.

"Betty? This is Gramps. Let me speak to Lily."

"Oh, hi Gramps!. We've sure missed you. Lily isn't here. She went with some guy to pick up Keani."

"What guy?"

"I don't know. A *kanaka*," meaning a Hawaiian. "Gee, it sounds like you're in the next room."

"Right. Now listen, Betty, this is important. Tell me exactly what happened."

"Well, we were having coffee and talking about our food booth at the Boat Festival when a big *kanaka*, a Hawaiian guy, knocks on the door and Lily goes to talk to him and after a few minutes she comes back looking upset and says she has to go get Keani and that I should close things up when I finished my coffee and she grabs her purse and leaves. I was locking the door when I heard the phone ring and I came back to answer it."

"Tell me about the *kanaka*. Have you seen him before?"

"No, Gramps. He was just big, sort of like what Hank would call a 'moke.'" That was a local boy whose idea of a good time what to break somebody's arms. "But Lily went with him, so I figured he was okay. Is anything wrong?"

"I don't know, Betty." Lani thought quickly. "Tell Hank that I said to get in touch with Lee Chun right away and tell him that Lani needs a crew on standby and Keoki will be the *luna*, the boss. Got it?" If Nazra could get extra help, then so could he.

"Sure, Gramps. Lee Chun, a crew on standby, Keoki the

boss. Is there anything else?"

"No, Betty. *Mahalo*, thanks, and *aloha*. I'll be in touch." Lani hung up and turned to Keoki. "It's possible that your mother and sister have been taken by someone working for Nazra." Keoki groaned in despair. "Knock it off. We've got to do something. In reality, you have to do something because I'm no good for shit right now."

Keoki stopped his moaning mainly because he had never heard his grandfather cuss before. He finally gathered his wits enough to ask, "But what can I do?"

The older man heaved a big sigh. "You're going to stop her from hurting your mother, and maybe your sister."

"But ..."

"Enough with the buts! Do you want to protect your family or not?"

"Of course, but ..."

"Then shut up and listen." Lani was silent, then, forcing Keoki to wait for a response. He appeared to be having a hard time making a decision. "No time, so no choice," he mumbled to himself. To Keoki he said, "If you want to save the family you have to do exactly as I say. There's no time for questions and definitely no time for you to be squeamish. For once, will you do what you have to do without quibbling?"

This was not the patient and tolerant Gramps that he was used to. Keoki had to make a choice even more important than the one about following the path of the *kupua*. Up to this point Keoki had still been a boy playing dangerous games. Now he was at a *ni'o*, a sacred threshold, on the border between remaining a boy or becoming a man. He would have to give up the pretense of insecurity that had served so well for getting others to do things for him. He wasn't useless by any means, but he had avoided usefulness as much as he could. Everything he had done so far had been for himself. Was he even capable of devoting himself to to the welfare of others? Stupid question. He knew he was going to do it anyway. "Tell me what I have to do," he said, feeling as if he were about to dive off a *pali*, a cliff.

Lani took him at his word. "The very first thing is you'll have to kiss me."

Keoki looked startled, but he didn't say anything. He was

291

determined to follow through no matter what, even though it sounded weird.

His grandfather gave a quick smile. "Not really. There's an ancient ritual of passing on knowledge from a master to an apprentice, usually when the master is dying. It's called *hikianakopili*, very roughly translated as 'the power of one's success,' and it is passed on with the saliva."

Keoki wanted to say, But you're not dying, but he held his tongue.

"No, I'm not dying yet," said Lani as if he were reading Keoki's thoughts, "but neither can I do anything to help the family in the condition I'm in, so I might as well be dead. That means you have the responsibility. Now listen carefully. Here's what you have to do, now and when you get to Hawaii."

Twenty-four hours later Keoki was landing at the Honolulu airport in a 727. He had traveled first class and it was nice, but it wasn't like the time when he had returned from visiting relatives in Long Beach with his mother when he was eight. At that time Hawaii was treated like a very special destination, even for those in coach class. At the airport there had been a huge area of the lounge designed in Hawaiian style for passengers waiting for their flight to paradise. On board, all the flight attendants, who had been stewardesses then, wore Hawaiian-style dresses, and everyone had been served free *maitais*, even him. Without the alcohol, of course. And all the passengers had received *leis* when they landed. Then it was a major event. Now it was just an ordinary airplane trip, often leaving from one of the smaller gates with hardly any seats in the waiting area. Honolulu was merely one more destination on the monitor.

Hawaii was changing, as all things must. Even though many visitors still thought of Hawaii as a foreign country ("Back in the States..." they would say when talking of home), more and more mainlanders were moving to Hawaii to retire or to start a new life.

While many locals, a term used to describe either people born in Hawaii or those who had moved there first, thought that paradise was being ruined, the truth was that Hawaii had never been a paradise. It was a very beautiful place where most of the people were friendly and some were not. It might lose its charm as population and technology increased, but it would never lose its character, forged from a mingling of the spirit of the land with the spirit of a people whose essence was always present, even when they were invisible.

All of this was felt by Keoki more than it was thought about as he stored his bags in a locker at the terminal. It was mid-afternoon. That would allow him time to go into Waikiki, do what he had to do there, and get back in time for a flight to Kona. During the long trip from Germany he had slept as much as possible because he wasn't going to sleep again until this was over. There had still been time to think about what he was going to do, and to rehearse the chants that Gramps said would help him to absorb the *mana* of the stones.

Keoki also thought about the strange ritual by which he was supposed to have received his grandfather's spiritual legacy. He hadn't felt anything in particular during the transfer of saliva except for a slight revulsion. By the time he had been ready to leave, though, it was as if some kind of subtle change had taken place. Gramps had assured him that the transfer would not mean that his grandfather would lose any of his abilities, and that Keoki would not suddenly be a master. More than anything, Gramps said, it was a powerful symbol of a transfer of responsibility and of a greater readiness to learn the spiritual knowledge. Their final parting at the clinic had been like a farewell between friends. The relationship between grandfather and grandson had been one of a wise teacher and an immature student. It would never be the same again. Keoki still had a tremendous amount to learn, he knew, but that no longer seemed as scary as it had before.

Keoki took a taxi into Waikiki and tipped the driver in advance so he could be dropped off at the police station no matter how much traffic there was. On the way he mentally spread a *la'a kea* field around the stones to keep the area clear and divert people's attention from what he would be doing.

After he paid off the driver he stood at the intersection of the sidewalk and the path to the beach and gazed at the stones. Was there a glow around them, or was that his imagination? He decided to believe that the glow was really there. No one seemed to notice as a young man in shirt and jeans took off his shoes and socks and stepped onto the sand, and no eyes turned in his direction as he knelt beside the group of large lava rocks, placed his forehead and hands on one of them, and softly began to chant in Hawaiian.

"What are you doing here?" The harsh voice came from behind him, and for just a moment Keoki thought it was a policeman. Then he opened his eyes and found himself in a lush jungle. There was a strong smell of ginger flowers and a bird sang somewhere out of sight. Keoki turned around and all he saw was more lush jungle. "If you don't know what you are doing here, you don't belong here," said the harsh voice, again from behind him.

Keoki wanted to whirl around to face the voice, but somehow he knew that would be fruitless. Gramps had been right. This was the realm of *Kapaemahu*, The Invisible One. "I am named '*Okamea'ekanoa*, the son of *Kalehuaikanahele* (that was his mother's Hawaiian name), the daughter of *Ke'alapuniaokahiwalani*, descendant of *Wakea* and *Papa*, the First Couple." Keoki was glad that his family was not descended in a direct line from one of the noble families or he might have been there for hours reciting the whole geneology. As it was, Gramps had said that the short version would be acceptable, considering his lineage.

"That allows you to be here, but it does not tell me why you have come," said the voice, now moving around in front of the young man, but still coming from an unseen source.

"My family is in danger. I ask for the use of your *mana* to save them." *Kapaemahu* and the others were healers. Once he had gained permission to be in their realms such a request would not be refused.

"What is your *ho'okupu*, your offering?"

This was the tricky part. The offering was neither a payment nor a bribe. Depending on the context it could be considered as tribute, a tax, or a sign of honor and respect. Here it was the latter, but it had to be of such a nature that the honor and respect were not in doubt. And it went without saying that the more valuable the gift was, the more likely it was that the desired favor would be granted. "*Na iwi, ka ho'okupu*," said Keoki. "I offer my bones."

In traditional Hawaiian thought, the bones are where one's

mana, one's personal power, resides. The old Keoki would have been too frightened to make such an offer, because there was no way of knowing in advance whether it meant he would have to give up his life or whether he would be bound to serve as a healer whenever *Kapaemahu* called on him. Either way, he would be willingly putting his *mana*, virtually his destiny, into the hands of another. However, he had already decided that the lives of his mother and his sister were worth it, whatever happened to him in the future.

"*Ua papa'ale*, Agreed!" said the voice. And Keoki felt something enter him, something that changed him, not just his body, but his entire being. It felt so strange, and so wonderful, that he gasped, and found himself back on the sand by the stones at Kuhio Beach.

The process was much the same with the spirits of *Kahaloa*, *Kapuni*, and *Kinohi* though their realms were different, one being desert-like, the next on a high mountain, and the last under water. Keoki had wondered about the practicality of offering his bones to each one of them, but Gramps had said that things were different in *Po*, the spirit world, and that there would be no problem. At least, there would be no problem with them accepting his offer.

When it was over, Keoki returned his awareness to *Ao*, the outer world, and saw by his watch that less than a half hour had passed. He felt tremendous, even godlike, filled with incredible power. But Gramps had warned him of that danger. No matter how good he felt, he had to remember that he was still Keoki, not a god. The spiritual powers that he had on loan were limited by his ability to channel them and his good sense in using them. An unwise choice could make them just as dangerous to him as to anyone else. He must also remember that these powers came from healers, not from warriors.

He wiped the sand off his feet and put his shoes and socks back on. A panhandler asked him for money and he gave the man a dollar. A bus passed by spewing diesel fumes. An overweight lady with lobster-red, peeling skin waddled by licking a giant ice cream cone. A cute *wahine* in the back of a pick-up truck winked at him. He was back home again.

Thirty-one

Challenges

Ho'okahi no la'au a ka u'i
(Youth strikes a blow once and for all)

Many visitors to the Big Island of Hawaii who land by plane on the Kona side tell their friends that it is like landing on the moon, because the area around the airport is a mass of barren, black lava rock. For Keoki, however, the impression was one of coming home to the welcoming bosom of *Haumea*, ancient goddess of the Earth and mother of the volcano goddess, Pele. It wasn't a religious thing. Keoki considered himself to be a good Christian, though not a dedicated one. It was just that, for him, the Earth, the islands, and all the different aspects of Nature were living beings. His feelings toward *Haumea*, and even Pele, for that matter, were not those of a worshipper. Rather, he thought of them more like part of his family, sort of like aunts.

The flight from Honolulu was short and smooth; the skies were partly cloudy, like almost always. The top of *Hualalai* volcano was obscured by cloud cover, but the slopes leading down to the sprawling population center called Kailua-Kona that bordered the ocean on the western side of the island were sunny and clear, again like almost always. The Boeing 727 landed like a feather and taxied to the gate of the small terminal. The passengers, mostly visitors with some locals, gathered their belongings and exited by the front of the plane. It was a short, hot walk to the entrance of the terminal and a short wait for luggage at the carousel inside. Keoki found his bag and rolled it out to the loading area in front of the terminal.

A group of five men standing by a van were obviously there to meet him. Their eyes were fixed on him from the moment he

296

came outside. Two of them looked like Portuguese, one looked Filipino, one had Japanese blood, and the fifth was a tall, big Hawaiian. They all wore sandals, slacks and Aloha shirts, and they all looked very tough. He walked up to them and said, "*Aloha.*"

The men returned the greeting in a perfunctory way and the Hawaiian said, "Chun says you're da *luna*, the boss. You gonna prove it?"

It was said as if the man were simply curious, but it was still a challenge. In his normal state Keoki would have been too intimidated to follow it up, and the result would have been that they would have done what he asked without enthusiasm and without doing any more than was necessary to fulfill the obligation to their real boss. In the current situation that would have been disastrous for his family and for him. In his present state, carrying the spirits of the four ancient healers within him, he knew what was going on beneath the surface. He was being asked to demonstrate his right to be a chief.

In the days of pre-European contact the High Chiefs or kings had to go through a ritual to prove their right to rule when they landed on other islands in their domain. It is said that even Kamehameha the Great, who united all the islands into one kingdom, went through this ritual himself.

When the king landed his canoe on the shore of such an island he would find a row of spear-carrying warriors sent by the local chief. As soon as he was upright on the sand the warriors would start to throw their spears at him, with an intent to kill, and he was expected to successfully dodge the incoming missles. A really exceptional king, like Kamehameha, would snatch one of the first spears out of the air and use it to strike at the remaining spears, diverting their path away from him. If he made it through the assault without a scratch he would be acknowledged as the true king and received with honor.

Keoki knew that these men were not going to attack him, but he also knew that they wanted to see what kind of man he was before they committed themselves to his cause. He spoke to the other Hawaiian, trusting an inspiration that just came to him. "I will arm wrestle you."

The four non-Hawaiians chuckled and nudged each other,

297

but their leader simply looked at Keoki without expression and said, "*Imua!* Let's go!" Keoki was given the front passenger seat, the man with Japanese ancestry drove, and the rest climbed in back, with the big Hawaiian sitting behind Keoki where he would have the most room. So far no names had been offered and no one spoke during the short drive.

They drove to a small house in a quiet neighborhood a little way up the mountain and parked in a driveway filled with car parts at the farther end. The rusted hulk of an old pickup truck squatted on the dry lawn and a mango tree shaded the worn dirt path to the front door. The men trooped into the house, led by the big Hawaiian, and filed past barely furnished rooms to the back *lanai* where a heavy picnic table that looked like it belonged in a public park sat under a thatched overhang. The big Hawaiian took one bench of the table, facing the wild greenery of the small yard, and motioned for Keoki to take a place on the bench opposite him.

The Filipino man had stopped off in the kitchen and now set a six-pack of Bud on one end of the table. While he removed the cans from the plastic holder and distributed them one of the Portuguese men put a thin, folded towel in front of the two who were seated. In a nearly ritualistic way the six men drank the beer in silence. When the big Hawaiian was finished, which didn't take long, he took the folded towel that had been placed on his side of the table and adjusted its placement so that he could rest his elbow on it in what he felt was the most comfortable position. Keoki did the same, and their right arms bent forward to let their hands enclose each other in a gentle clasp.

Normal Keoki, had he even gone this far, would have been screaming about the waste of time when his family was in danger, but this Keoki was very aware that the ritual they were involved in was the fastest route to the help he needed. He and his opponent checked their grip for a few moments. The big Hawaiian nodded and the contest began in earnest.

It should have been over in seconds, of course. Keoki was not weak. He was healthy and perhaps a bit stronger than most men his age because of a workout system he used at home and the sports he played with his friends. On the other hand, which was a very large hand, his opponent had an arm which was just shy of the size of Keoki's leg and it did not seem to be made of fat. Outwardly, it looked like a contest between a sledgehammer and a stick. Still wearing a neutral expression, the big Hawaiian started to lay Keoki's arm flat on the table with all the expected resistance of turning a bottle on it's side. Keoki's arm did not budge.

It was not the power of the spirits that was holding Keoki's arm upright. They were healers and this was a challenge to Keoki's leadership only, so they were not accessible for such a ritual. Their very presence, or connection, to Keoki gave him more confidence, however, and his need opened him up to memories and abilities that he had rarely drawn upon in recent years.

As Keoki was preparing for the challenge he had extended his awareness into the *'aina*, the environment, and called upon the spirits of tree, rock, wind and sea to lend him their strength. To channel that strength he imagined his arm as a robotic construction of stainless steel and titanium wire, attached by a stainless steel rod to a gigantic gearbox sitting ten feet to his left that was powered by an atomic engine, capable of pulling twenty thousand tons with ease. A human arm of flesh and blood didn't stand a chance. When the big Hawaiian began his push it was not against Keoki's physical arm.

In his mind, Keoki was letting the atomic engine do the work, so he didn't have the sensation of using his own muscles to resist. It actually felt to him as if the rod was holding his arm in place. The big Hawaiian's eyes widened a little in surprise and he exerted more pressure. Keoki's imaginary engine had been at rest, so now he mentally flipped a switch and turned it on to full power.

All five of Chun's men would never forget that contest. They would talk about it for years, and even tell the story to their grandchildren more times than their grandchildren wanted to hear it. Without any apparent effort, Keoki slowly pushed the big Hawaiian's arm to his left. The big Hawaiian's muscles bunched, his jaws clenched, his eyes bulged, and sweat broke out on his forehead, but none of that helped. Like a tree falling in the forest to a woodsman's axe, his mighty arm collapsed onto the surface of the table.

Before anyone else could utter a word the big Hawaiian

withdrew his arm, massaged his shoulder, and said, "My name is Kimo, the Portugee brothers are Pete and Rico, Johnny brought the beer, and the guy with his mouth still open is Fuji. What do you want us to do?"

Keoki forced himself not to smile, and even the urge faded as he spoke. "My mother and sister have been kidnapped by a gang from Honolulu. There's a crazy woman who wants to kill them and me. I'll take care of the woman. I need you to take care of the gang."

"How many men in the gang and where are they?"

"I can find out in a few minutes. Do you have a phone I can use in private?"

Kimo glanced at Johnny and the Filipino handed Keoki a cell phone. "You can use the bedroom," he said. "Down the hall on the right."

Keoki took the phone and walked into the house. Once in the bedroom he set the phone down on an end table and sat on the double bed in a meditative position with his back against the wall. Okay, he said to himself. Let's see how good you guys really are. He closed his eyes, asked *Kahaloa* for help, and instantly felt his body filling up with a sensation of power.

He stepped easily out of his body and stood on a shimmering surface that some part of him knew was the floor of the bedroom. Around him he could see the framework of the house like a lattice of lights, with the walls appearing like very faint shadows. On what he knew was the *lanai* five ghostly figures seemed to dance restlessly without moving. He willed himself upward and in a moment he was hovering over a landscape of heart-rending beauty. In his physical body he knew that everything was alive, and in this body he could see that life, glowing and pulsing with ceaseless activity in every person, place and thing. He willed himself higher and the whole island lay below him like an emerald on a blue velvet cushion. From this position he could seen into hearts and minds and homes at will.

He didn't have to search for Nazra. There she was, a glowing black star high on the side of *Mauna Loa* on the south side of the island, some distance away from the little town of Volcano. Two bright stars were his mother and sister, alive at least. Nearby were four sparkling red stars, the hired toughs. Without needing

300

to think about it he was aware that a closer approach would alert Nazra, who might either move the two women or harm them. He willed himself back into his body and the power flowed out of him as he opened his eyes.

Immediately he called upon *Kinohi* He felt his body fill with a different kind of power, and with the power came a different kind of knowledge, a different way of thinking. In his normal state he knew what Gramps had told him about clairvoyance, the ability to project his consciousness to another location, or to follow the *aka* web to a chosen destination. Now, though, a completely new concept came to him. If he projected his energy toward Nazra she would be able to feel it, but he didn't have to do that. Now he knew—or assumed or believed or imagined—that everything was everywhere, and all he needed to do was to be aware of its presence. No need for energy or projection or any conception of distance at all.

The logical part of Keoki's mind was balking at the idea, so the thought came to him that it was like everything was both a television transmitter and a television receiver. To receive a particular program you only had to tune in to the right channel that was already being broadcast in wave signals that were all around you. You didn't have to call the station or send energy from your receiver to the source. You simply had to tune in. Along with this thought came a vague sense of amused tolerance of the kind a parent might have when oversimplifying the explanation of how a car works for a child.

With the quieting of Keoki's logical objections the power began to manifest. There on the bed in front of him, in perfect miniature, was a scene from the location on the mountain. There was a tent on a piece of cleared land that looked like part of a subdivision that had never been developed, a fairly common situation on the side of an active volcano where land was cheap and insurance was non-existent. Inside the tent, Lily and Keani were bound and gagged on two chairs that were fixed back to back. Nazra sat backwards on another chair, clad in a bodysuit similar to the one Marta had worn. Behind the tent, maybe fifty yards away, was a helicopter at rest in an open area just barely able to hold it. The pilot was sitting on a rock at some distance, smoking a cigarette. In front of the tent a dirt road led straight to the property, and lounging on the road about a hundred yards from the tent were the four toughs. It was clear that Nazra was expecting him to find her.

Keoki let more and more of the road come into view until he could see clearly how to reach the tent, then let the scene disappear and the power flow away. It had been ten minutes since he had entered the bedroom.

When he came back onto the *lanai* the five men stood up as he handed the cell phone back to Johnny and looked at Kimo. "The place we're going to is near the town of Volcano. It'll take too long to drive there, so we need a 'copter to get us up there and a van to meet us. Can you arrange that?"

"'*A'ole pilikia*, no problem." He nodded to Johnny, who started dialing the cell phone. "What are we up against?"

"Four men, all about as big as you. I didn't..." Keoki was about to say "I didn't see any guns" but he caught himself in time so he finished with "...get any word about guns, so I'm pretty sure they're not carrying. Not absolutely sure, though."

"You want us to break heads?"

"They are blocking the road to where my mother and sister are. I want you to do whatever is necessary for me to get past them." Kimo and the others nodded.

Kimo told Pete and Rico to get some gear and a minute later Johnny shut down the cell phone and said that the helicopter had been arranged and that it would take ten minutes to get to the heliport.

Fuji got the van ready, Pete and Rico dropped a heavy canvas bag into the back and the six of them drove to the helicopter field. On the way, Johnny used the cell phone to make arrangements for a van to come up from the town of *Kea'au* to meet them at a private golf course not far from Volcano where the helicopter would have to land.

The rotors of the helicopter, a seven-passenger Bell used for tourist rides, were spinning slowly when they arrived. The heavy bag was stowed in the rear and they all climbed aboard. Keoki sat in front with the pilot, who looked as if he had served in Vietnam. The pilot did mysterious things, from Keoki's point of view, and they were up and away.

During the flight down the coast and over the ridge of *Mauna*

Loa, across the coffee fields and drylands of *Ka'u*, the district of the Big Island that lay in the southwest corner, Keoki was busy developing an idea that Gramps had given him. Nazra was trying to set up a labyrinth, a situation that she could go into and follow the same path back out. So Keoki, using his knowledge of the structure of computer games, was busy setting up a maze in the guise of a labyrinth that could be launched into the psychic landscape that they both inhabited. If Nazra could be enticed to enter it she would go in thinking that she was returning by the same path, only she would end up somewhere else. It was a very curious exercise, though, because he had no idea of the form it would take in the outer world. The process involved a great deal of trust on his part, something that he was not ordinarily very good at.

By the time the helicopter landed by the golf course, the labyrinthine maze had been launched and Keoki was back in the outer world of present moment awareness. A blue, twelve-passenger van was waiting not far from where the 'copter had landed, and since the pilot wasn't supposed to land there he took off as soon as Keoki and the others had disembarked. Keoki rode shotgun again and gave the new driver directions on how to reach their destination.

A half hour later they were rolling along a dirt road that went uphill. They passed some weathered signs advertising "fee simple" (meaning full ownership) houselots and even a few lots that had been cleared to show prospective buyers how beautiful lumps of gray lava rock surrounded by gray-green trees could be. And then there was some color up ahead. Four large men in bright *Aloha* shirts stood across the road holding what looked at a distance like rather thick clubs. Just behind the men were a row of lava boulders intended to discourage anyone from trying to ram their way past the guardians. There was a flurry of activity in the van as the contents of the canvas bag were distributed, and the driver slowed to a stop a few yards in front of the barrier.

Kimo and his crew lazily got out of the van as the four guards lazily walked forward. Then all laziness vanished as the two groups played out their ritual combat. Keoki got out of the van and simply walked through the melee, certain that "his" men would keep the way clear for him. He was so concentrated on

303

his task that he only heard one scream and a loud grunt during his passage, although there were a lot more than that.

As Keoki reached the dirty yellow tent, Nazra stepped out to confront him. Keoki felt the same intense desire for her well up in him as he had experienced before, and he knew she felt a similar desire for him, but Keoki was able to keep his muscles relaxed and let the feelings be there without letting them interfere with his actions and intentions. Nazra seemed able to do the same, so Keoki waited until the woman spoke.

"You really do keep amazing me. I don't know why, but I expected you to come charging in here alone like a misguided hero. You've forced me to change my plans again, you naughty boy." Her tone was light, but her anger was evident. Now she appeared with short black hair cut in a bowl shape with bangs, black eyes, and white, untanned skin. She was very attractive, but too serious to be cute and too cute to be beautiful. Maybe this was how she really looked. And maybe not. Her black bodysuit was set off by a silver pendant, the Eye of Horus.

"I'm going inside to see my mother and sister," said Keoki, and he started forward toward the tent.

Nazra was clearly startled, and could do no more for the moment than step aside and say, "Be my guest." This was not the boy she had dealt with before. He hadn't said that he wanted to see them, and he hadn't asked permission. He knew they were there and he had simply stated his intent. Of course, he might have simply assumed they were inside, but it really sounded as if he knew. Yet, how could he have found out without her knowing about it? He was beginning to disturb her too much. Nazra removed a .38 automatic from a holster at the small of her back and entered the tent behind Keoki.

Keoki was reaching behind his mother's head to undo the gag when Nazra said, "No, leave the gags in place. You can undo the ropes that bind them to the chairs, though. But the gags and the cuffs have to stay on for the time being."

Turning around enough to see the gun, Keoki shrugged and undid the ropes. Then he lifted his mother and sister to their feet. Seeing that their eyes were filled with fear and confusion, he gave them each a hug and told them not to worry. Nazra laughed. "On the contrary," she said, "I think they should worry a lot. Go out the back of the tent, all three of you."

As they all stepped outside, the helicopter pilot stood up and asked what he was supposed to do. "Start the chopper," ordered Nazra. Then she turned to Keoki and shook her head slowly, almost sadly. "There's no way around it, George," she said, for the first time using his name that she had retrieved from the Interpol records. "You and I will have to have an epic battle. The Force is strong in you. Too bad we don't have any real laser swords. Oh, well. We'll just have to make do with wit and magic.

"I had picked a place where I was going to abandon you and your loved ones. The pilot said it was called a *kipuka*, and that the lava would probably overrun it in a couple of days at least. Now I've changed my mind. I'm going to have the pilot drop you and me onto the *kipuka* and fly around with your mother and sister, then come back and see who's left alive and pick that one up. If it's you, which I doubt, then he'll drop you off somewhere and you can all live happily ever after. If it's me, which I expect, then the only ones to live happily ever after will be the pilot and I, and I'm not so sure about him. You'll notice that I'm not asking your opinion about this. Into the chopper, now!"

When the three Hawaiians were in the back of the helicopter, Nazra spoke to the pilot. "Just to make things clear again, you are going to let that man and me down in the *kipuka* we talked about, fly around, and come back in a half hour. If you see me standing alone, you will pick me up and when we land I will call my contact and you will be allowed to live and enjoy your pay. If you see him standing alone," she gestured toward the cockpit, "you'll pick him up, land the three of them in a safe place, and you will call the contact. When the contact has verified that they are safe you'll be free and clear."

The pilot asked why he should bother to pick up the man if she wanted him dead.

"Because if he's better than me then he deserves to live more than I do. Besides," she said with a smile, "if neither he nor I get back safely then you are dead."

When they were in the air the pilot used the radio and learned that volcanic activity in the area had increased significantly in the past few hours. He gave this news to Nazra, who simply smiled again.

After passing over a substantial, steaming flow several miles wide, they arrived over a small area of green in a great sea of grey. Since Nazra and the pilot had last been here the *kipuka*, an oasis of greenery surrounded by lava, had been split by the flowing stream of molten rock. Now there were two patches of untouched forest, one not more than twenty feet long and fifteen feet wide, and the other roughly fifty feet long by the same measure wide. All around the larger patch of greenery the molten lava from the latest active phase of *Pu'u 'O'o*, the large vent that was erupting on the side of Kilauea Volcano, was oozing at a rate of about one mile an hour down the gentle slope of this part of the forest.

The lava was mostly in the form of *pahoehoe*, a pillowy, slow-motion series of waves fronted by a "surf line" of orange-yellow liquid rock with a probable temperature of 1650 degrees Farenheit. Behind that line the stone quickly became a semi-liquid expanse of slate-grey, still hot enough at 895 degrees in the faintly red spots to rapidly burn up anything organic. Where the lava stopped and solidified it generally turned darker and sometimes broke up into spiky chunks called *'a'a*, and in that state it could remain dangerously hot for days.

The *kipuka* itself was shaped like an island in a stream, and the reason that molten lava slid around such places was still not well understood because the configuration of the land did not seem to be a factor. This particular *kipuka* was composed of lumpy terrain from previous lava flows covered with a mix of *ohi'a* hardwood trees, softer *kukui* trees which burst quickly into flame when the the lava got too close, and various smaller shrubs and mosses. It was not dense enough for hiding and it was too rough for running. There was also no guarantee, given the current activity of the lava, that it would remain the same size for very long.

When the helicopter was hovering on one spot over the larger *kipuka* and the ladder was down, Nazra turned in her seat up front and pointed her gun at Keoki's mother, but spoke to Keoki. "This is going to be a very primitive encounter. Take off your clothes and climb down the ladder. This is the first and only time that we'll get to see what each other really looks like. Do it! Now!" She smiled with amusement to see Keoki's mother and sister avert their eyes as he undressed quickly.

While Keoki was descending the ladder she took off her own clothes, paying no attention to the covert glances of the pilot who was also trying to maintain his position in the super-heated air. She climbed into the back to access the ladder and paused in front of Keani. The girl still had her eyes averted, so Nazra took her by the chin and forced her head around. "Such a pretty thing," she said. She removed the gag and kissed the ut-terly shocked girl full on the lips. "Perhaps we can play together when I come back." Then she descended the rope ladder after Keoki.

It was very hot on the *kipuka*, but not intolerable. The ground was warm and waves of heat could be felt from the surrounding lava. There was a deep, background roar accompanied by a mul-titude of tiny chirps as the lava alternately hardened and cracked, and the cacophonous sounds of burning branches and leaves. A slightly sulphurous smell served as the base for the pungent odor of carbonizing wood. The naked man and woman facing each other ten feet apart in this setting made it truly seem like the scene of some Paleolithic drama. The helicopter hovering above, its sound barely heard, could easily have been some great preda-tor waiting to snatch up one of them as prey. It's spinning rotors sent up a cloud of ash that coated the sweating bodies of the two protagonists, causing them to look even more like savages.

Nazra waved the helicopter away and didn't move until it was out of sight. Then she removed her contacts and threw them away. Her multi-faceted, opalescent eyes glittered strongly, both from the lavalight and from within. Around her appeared a glow-ing aura and she looked every bit a creature of dark, seductive magic. She stretched her lithe, althletic body, smiling at Keoki's lustful gaze and the hardening of his manhood. She, too, wanted him with a terrible, ferocious desire, but to give in to that with this man would be a weakness, to her mind. Instead, she grace-fully bent down, picked up a fist-sized rock, and threw it straight and true at Keoki's head.

Meanwhile, Keoki was at a loss to understand what was going on. At first he had thought she was going to just leave him on the *kipuka*. He couldn't think of anything to do while she was holding the gun, so he had gone down the ladder without protest, evoking *Kapuni* to protect him from the lava. On the ground he had a vague idea of sending a telepathic message to bring a tour 'copter over to rescue him, the way Gramps had arranged for the taxi in Heidelberg. Then Nazra had come down the ladder, as naked as he was, and he had the wild notion that she wanted to play weird sex games like Marta had done. When Nazra had stretched and smiled at him he felt the lust rising in him like the lava in *Pu'u 'O'o*, but the healer spirits inside helped him to ignore the cravings of his body.

Now there was a rock heading right for him. Without thinking, he reached up and snatched it out of the air just before it struck his face. *Kapuni*, the healer with the power of psychokinesis, was actively helping him. Keoki understood, then, what Nazra had meant about an epic battle. This was not going to be a game. In spite of the strong connection between them she intended to kill him, and to do it in a way that would prove her physical, mental and psychic superiority. But if she needed to prove it, that meant she didn't quite believe it.

Keoki hefted the rock and threw it back at Nazra as hard as he could. *Kapuni* wasn't helping this time, however because it, or he, was a healer. Anything Keoki did to cause harm had to be done on his own, and *Kapuni* might even work against it while he was active. Nazra easily dodged the missle and laughed. She launched herself at him with her arms outstretched, their bodies made contact, and...

Keoki was swimming in dark, icy cold water, only he didn't think of himself as Keoki. His name was Tor, and he was going to rescue his beloved from the raiders. He swam as silently as possible, holding a bronze knife between his teeth. Ahead, he saw the raiders' sleek longboat anchored in a small cove, its red sail furled and hanging at an angle and its watch lights burning fore and aft. From his position in the water Tor could also see that a tent had been set up on the narrow strand. There was light inside it and he could barely make out some shadowy movement. A certain instinct urged him to make his way to the tent instead of the boat.

He reached the fine, sandy bottom of the shore and pulled himself very slowly out of the water. Flat on his stomach, he inched his way to the shadow of the treeline, and then followed that cover around until the tent was between him and the boat. Apparently thinking this a safe area, they had not posted a guard in the woods. He could hear sounds from the tent now, low moans and groans and whispers. The tent had been hastily put up and this side was only lying on the ground without any stakes to hold it. With extreme care he made his way to the edge of the tent, and ever so slowly lifted the cloth so he could see inside with his head resting on the sand.

The view was like a blow to the pit of his stomach. Inge was lying face down, only partly dressed, her arms folded and clenched to her sides and her eyes tightly closed. The man, the leader of the raiders, was lying half on top of her, pressing his face to her neck and caressing her legs and buttocks and shoulders as he made coaxing sounds in a language Tor didn't understand. The raider chief was partly facing the side of the tent where Tor lay, and if he hadn't been so intent on his prize he could easily have seen Tor spying on them.

Suddenly Inge opened her eyes and looked right at Tor. Her eyes grew very large, she bit her lower lip, and shook her head very slightly in a negative gesture. Then she made as if to roll onto her back and the man eased up so she could do so, looking somewhat surprised. Inge pulled down her upper garment, revealing her young breasts and the man said something that sounded like approval. Tor saw his beloved reach one hand down between the man's legs, put one hand behind the man's neck to pull him toward her, and wrap one leg around the man's hip as he eased over onto his side with his back toward Tor.

Tor almost cried aloud with despair. So that was the way of it! She had clearly told him not to interfere, and had emphasized the fact of her perfidious rejection by giving herself to her captor-turned-lover in Tor's plain sight. His world had been destroyed, the light of his life had gone out. Tor backed away noiselessly, lowered the tent cloth, and regained the woods. In a state of massive depression he wandered through the trees until he reached the shore and felt the black water touch his feet. He realizd he was still holding the knife and he threw it away. His life had been ripped apart and the pain was too much to bear. Out there, perhaps, in the waters of the deep, he would find peace for his soul. He moved into the water, not even feeling the cold.

Betrayed...betrayed...

Inge waited for the shudder and the cry that would end her unbearable torture. How she had prayed for Tor to rescue her, and now he had come! She had warned him not to act just yet, for the raider chief was a terribly powerful warrior. She had pretended to respond to the man's advances so that she could get him to present his broad back to Tor's sharp knife. How brave he looked with the blade in his teeth. But where was the blow? When would it come? As the minutes passed, and her body was brutally, thoroughly violated, she realized at last that the saving blow would never come. Tor had abandoned her. Out of cowardice? Never. Clearly he did not want a soiled woman, and soiled she surely was. Tor's love was narrow, selfish. He could not abide that she had even been touched by another, and so he had abandoned her to her fate without a further thought. Betrayed...betrayed...

There was a loud crackling noise like nearby thunder. Nazra and Keoki found themselves knocked apart as if by some explosive force that sent them flying in opposite directions. Keoki, lying on a pile of small, moss-covered rocks, felt as if his butt was bruised and there really were cuts on his arms. Nazra, lying in a similar position ten or twelve feet away, also looked banged up, but she recovered first. Her face became almost a caricature of intense rage and she screamed incoherently as she leaped to her feet with a rock in each hand and ran toward Keoki. The young man jumped up and dodged her first attack, but she was relentless in her pursuit.

Around the little island they ran, and jumped, and stumbled. Keoki was in a state of confusion. He didn't know what to do except to keep trying to escape, and it seemed like that was going to be a very short-term solution. Then the smaller *kipuka* caught his attention and he got a crazy idea. He had heard that some *kahunas*, masters, of old had been able to run across molten lava without getting burned. He didn't know how they did it, but the idea came to him to try it. However, he wasn't about to try the really molten stuff. First, however, he had to get some distance between himself and Nazra. *Kapaemahu*, I need you, he called silently as he ran and stumbled over the rough lava. Suddenly he heard Nazra gasp and he stopped. Turning around,

310

he saw Nazra with a shocked expression, looking right at him and around him as if he weren't even there. *So Gramps was right about this one, too. I'm invisible. Now was the moment.* With a sense of wild elation he made his way to the edge of the *kipuka.*

Without any experiential guidance he decided to become one with the rock, to shift into an attitude in which he and the rock would be of the same nature, of the same family, in perfect harmony. Nazra was following him with her eyes now, as if she were sensing his energy rather than his form, so he took off running across what looked to him like the most solid part of the lava flow that lay between him and the smaller kipuka. The stone substance under his feet felt only slightly warm as he touched it with his bare feet. In a few moments he was on the other side and turning around to look back.

Nazra had followed him to the edge of the larger *kipuka*, but then hesitated. She had watched Keoki, or at least his energy body, do the impossible run across rock that was heated to 600 degrees or more. She knew about firewalking. At least, she knew that, in theory, if you kept your attention on something cool or cold it was possible to walk across burning coals without getting burned. There were various explanations, but the phenomenon did exist. With her powers of concentration she should be able to do it as well or better than anyone else, and once on the smaller island she could make quick work of that traitor ... No, with that pest of a shaman who continually interfered with her plans, even if he was hard to see. Nazra composed herself, filled her mind with thoughts of Siberian snow and ice, and began to walk across the lava.

It was working fine until she was just over halfway across. At that moment the earth trembled and a large section of the semi-solid surface some forty feet long and ten feet wide collapsed into a swiftly flowing stream of bright yellow-orange, liquid rock about twenty feet down at the bottom of what was apparently an underground tunnel.

When molten lava runs strongly through a gully or crevice the exterior of the flow cools faster than the interior. As the exterior rock hardens the hotter interior keeps flowing and carves a path through its own cooler mass, forming what is called a lava tube. Sometimes new flows follow older tubes, and if the roof of the tube collapses from any number of reasons while lava is flowing within it, the opening is called a skylight. The temperature of the lava flowing within such a tube is usually 2200 degrees Farenheit.

Nazra was teetering on the edge of the gap. She saw Keoki fade into full physical view and step back onto the lava on his side of the flow and call to her. "Jump!" he cried. "I'll help you. I'll catch you." She didn't move. "Please!" he cried, with an arm outstretched. "I...I...I love you! I... I thought you had chosen the raider chief. I thought you were telling me to leave. I... I drowned myself in despair because I lost you."

The naked, ash-streaked woman stood completely still for several moments. She felt tears in her eyes and wiped them away angrily. She called out over the noise. "And I was giving you his back to stab. What a pitiful pair of lovers we make, you and I." She stood straight, with her arms down at her sides. Her body began to glow, and her eyes glowed even more brightly. "I love you, Tor. I will always love you, I suppose. It cannot work this time; we are far too different. As I am now I cannot, I will not, change for anyone. Perhaps there will be another time when we can try again." Then, with Keoki looking on in horror, she leaped up and outward, seeming to float for a long moment above the skylight before bending down and executing a perfectly graceful swan dive into the hellish gap and instantly disappearing into the molten stream.

Nazra was gone again. For good.

Epilogue

Ku'u ewe, ku'u piko, ku'u iwi, ku'u koko
(My umbilicus, my navel, my bones, my blood)

It was late afternoon in Hawaii, and although the tops of *Mauna Kea, Mauna Loa*, and *Hualalai* were covered with clouds, the whole western coast of the Big Island was clear and cloudless. The temperature was 72 degrees Farenheit, a light breeze counteracted the sun's heat, and the air in the area around Kailua-Kona was beginning to fill up with the fragrances of plumeria and *pikake*, jasmine. The ocean horizon was so clear there was a good chance that everyone who looked would get to see the green flash when the sun set.

In the large back yard of the McCoy house a *luau* was in full swing. Three open-sided tents had been set up, along with picnic tables, beach and lounge chairs, and a place for preparing and serving food and drink. The tent poles were decorated with palm leaves and ferns, and each table had a chunk of banana stalk with bright bougainvillea blossoms stuck in it. Cousin Hank was playing "Hula Moon" along with a friend on ukulele and Keani was dancing with three of her own friends. Some of the crowd of about a hundred neighbors, friends and family were watching and listening and some were not. There was space under the tents to do a lot of things, like stopping by a special table to express admiration for the unusual cuckoo clock which Keoki had brought back for his mother from Germany.

The main rush for food was over, but Lily was still serving chicken *laulau* — a mixture of chicken, fish, and young taro leaves wrapped in a package made of ti leaves and cooked by steaming — to everyone who hadn't had any yet, and Nani was forcing seconds and thirds of *kalua* pork — tender, shredded meat cooked for hours in an earth oven — on all those who came close enough

313

to grab. Betty was refilling the poi bowls and the dessert trays of white cake and *haupia*, a coconut pudding. Uncle Willy was away on a case, but he had called to give his blessings.

Under one tent Lani, wearing half a dozen flower *leis* around his neck, was in a lounge chair regaling a small crowd with humorous, quasi-fictional stories of all the trouble he got into while encountering the customs and habits of the Europeans. They particularly liked his story of how he spent a whole day in an elevator because he didn't realize that the second floor for an American was the first floor for a European.

Kimo, Johnny, Pete, Rico and Fuji were deeply involved in a chugalug-the-Bud contest with other locals. Johnny's head was bandaged and Rico had an arm in a cast, but aside from that, and a fair distribution of bruises, they looked okay.

Away from the tents, on a wooden bench under a blossoming flame tree, Keoki, also wearing lots of *leis*, was having a beer and snacking on the remains of a bowl of *poke*, spicy cubes of raw *ahi*, yellow-fin tuna, with Leilani Yamaguchi, a twenty-year-old girl who had just moved into the neighborhood, and he had just discovered that they were both fans of science fiction and fantasy.

Life on *Moku Nui*, the Big Island, was following its normal, laid-back course.

By the time Lani had recovered sufficiently to travel home from Germany the whole affair was over. Nichts was glad to see him go because his care was threatening the budget of the local station chief. In Lani's last meeting with Villier he had offered to bow out of the Interpol commitment, but someone in the hierarchy had decided that it was a good idea to have psychic investigators on the payroll, so he and Keoki were still officially employed by Section Four.

Kimo and his friends had had a good fight with the Honolulu gang until they heard and saw the helicopter take off. Then they all realized that there was no more point to the fighting, so both gangs went down to Hilo and spent half the night in a bar taking turns buying rounds of beer, after the various wounds and injuries had been taken care of.

Once Nazra's hired pilot had picked up Keoki, who had insisted that his clothes be lowered before he would climb the ladder, he and his mother and sister had been set down near enough to the Hawaii Volcano National Park Visitor Center that they could soon call for a ride with no problem. Shortly after Nazra had disappeared into the lava Keoki had felt the presence of all four healing spirits come to the foreground of his awareness at once. In a single voice that was not a voice they acknowledged him as a worthy family member and departed. As soon as their powers left him Keoki began to forget what they were. However, something from each of them had changed him forever.

Keoki eventually made a date with Leilani for the following Saturday night to go to a concert at the Blaisdell Center in Honolulu, and walked her back to the tent where Lani was still getting laughs from his audience. "Hey, Gramps," he said during a pause. "You know I hardly ever got to wear that suit. What am I supposed to do with it?"

Lani grinned. "Don"t throw it away just yet, Kanoa. I have a feeling you'll be needing it before too long."

Keoki laughed as if he didn't believe what he heard, and guided Leilani to where his own friends were sitting.

Lani gazed fondly at his departing grandson. What a great spirit that one is, he thought. Only one small thing gave him a tiny bit of bother. Once it had been a big thing, but he had worked it through and was at peace with himself about it. Still, it would probably be better for everyone if Kanoa never found out who the raider chief was.

He looked around at the gathering of so many good spirits, listened to the sounds of really expert partying, and sighed with deep contentment. *Maika'i no ke ola nei*, he said to himself, This is a good life.

Printed in the United States
763900001B